# VIRAL AIRWAVES

VIRAL AIRWAVES
Copyright © 2015-2016 by Claudie Arseneault.


Edited by Matt Larkin and Brenda Pierson.
Graphic Design by Gabrielle Arseneault.
Interior Designed by Lyssa Chiavari.
Interior Graphics by Vectorian and Macrovector.





claudiearseneault.com


ISBN: 978-1-5405-1963-4

# VIRAL AIRWAVES

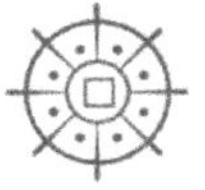

CLAUDIE ARSENEAULT

*Aux centaines de millers d'étudiants descendus dans les rues en 2012,*

*Vous avez marqué ma vie, mon imaginaire,*

*Voici un premier hommage.*

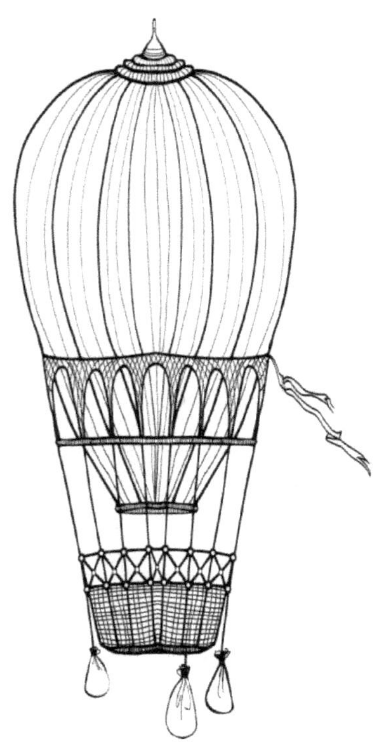

# CHAPTER
# ONE

 mourned his mother alone. He stood at her grave under drizzling rain or beating sun, commemorating the day the Threstle Plague had taken her life. Eight years had passed. Eight mornings. Today a rare storm prepared above his head and he could hardly concentrate on his mother. Today, Henry was mourning his town as much as he did her, and the new grief overpowered his thoughts.

The Plague hadn't killed Ferrea, however. The small town's life was entwined with the Annual Mount Kairn Races. The major sporting event used to bring hordes of tourists, providing Ferrea with its main source of revenue. Except the last two years hadn't been a big success and the small town's residents were dwindling, moving out to better, more secure lives. Only the grocer, his wife and the innkeeper were left, but how long would that last? After yet another afternoon hunched over the counter at Kinsi's grocery, listening to the National Radio Broadcast for news of the Races, Henry's hope was slimming. His mother was dead. His town was dying. All he had left was the two packs of instant noodles he'd just bought and the fresh cucumbers Tia had forced into his hands. Henry headed home, trying to forget the bleached gravestone he'd stared at all morning in favor of the fresh food he'd enjoy tonight.

He stopped as he reached the little ridge at Ferrea's outer limit. Down a slight slope and a curve was his house, with a dead and twisted tree as its only company. Once, it had stood proudly in the middle of colored tents, its backyard cleared for the balloon take-off, the oak green and flourishing. An empty husk remained behind. Alone.

Not today.

Henry squinted against the sun's glare to get a better view of the stranger at his door. The man was tall and pale of face, with white wind-blown hair whipping about, sometimes catching in his thin glasses. His shoulders were stooped from a long road.

A ghost in a dead town.

Henry wondered how many doors the newcomer had knocked on before he'd reached his. Or perhaps he'd gone straight to it? His home did house the Races' official tourist shop. His heart sped and he tightened his grip on the tote bag holding his dinner. What if this man had come to his door with the very news he'd expected from the radio?

Henry thanked the winds for the answer to his prayers, ran down the slope to his house, and hailed the stranger in as professional a voice as he could manage. "Hey, can I help you? Any tidings from the Annual Mount Kairn Races?"

"The Races? No, no, no. I'm not here for the race."

*I'm not here for the Races.* Those six words dashed Henry's hopes.

The stranger shrugged his bag off his shoulder and dropped it next to the door as Henry switched on the power. "I'm just a traveler. I need a place to stay. Seraphin Holt."

The man rolled his *r* a little, a hallmark of Regarians. Henry wondered what someone from the eastern province was doing so far from his home. Regarians weren't big travelers, usually. He was about to comment when his gaze met Seraphin's. His eyes were pale as a sunny summer sky, the pure blue only marred by a minuscule tinge of red in the background. He stared, transfixed. Albinism wasn't common and until the stranger cleared his throat, Henry forgot his manners. Then he noticed the hand offered for a shake and hurriedly took it, holding back a curse against his clumsiness.

"Schmitt! Henry Schmitt. There's an inn higher up the street, in the town proper."

Between the hostilities with Burgia, so close to the south, and the Races' absence, the owner hadn't been able to rent any rooms. Paul was a good friend and one of Ferrea's last residents. Henry didn't want to steal his customers.

"I know," Seraphin said. He did not pick up his pack.

"Paul doesn't charge much and he's a good cook."

"I don't doubt it. I'd rather sleep here, if possible."

Why would he avoid the local inn? This promised trouble. Henry had no desire to add to his list of problems.

"No. Go see Paul."

"I have my own food."

Henry hesitated. A single second. Long enough.

"I'll pay you," Seraphin added. "Sixty." He glanced around the room. "I'm aware of how little income Ferrea gets out of season. Don't pretend you don't need the money. All I ask is a bed to rest in tonight, and I'll be gone in the morning."

Henry glanced at the dinner awaiting him. A pile of cucumbers and two packs of instant noodles. Perhaps the winds *had* answered his prayers, just not the ones he'd thought.

"Only tonight?" he asked.

"I promise."

One night for sixty dollars? Too good a deal. Henry studied the stranger for signs of treachery. Seraphin bent forward, muscles wired tight, waiting for his answer. The bags under his eyes betrayed his fatigue. Perhaps he had good reasons to avoid the inn. Henry prayed that was it.

"You can have the bed, but I need to change the sheets."

"Thank you, I—that'll be perfect." Seraphin's shoulders sagged. He closed his eyes and leaned against the doorway. The sudden release of tension surprised Henry. Too much relief? What could it mean? Henry wiped his sweaty palms on his pants. Stay calm. It might not mean anything.

"You can come in," Henry said, his voice a bit thick.

Seraphin stepped inside the kitchen and sat onto one of the stools lining Henry's counter. The Regarian picked through his bag and brought dinner out while Henry fought against his mounting panic. Three seconds from decision to regret: a new record. The food Seraphin put on the table helped appease his misgivings. Two bottles of juice and a handful of bags decorated his counter. Henry's gaze moved from one choice to the next: dried fruits, beef jerky, nut bars, dried cookies, and a chunk of Burgian cheese. Nothing perishable.

"How long did you spend on the road?" he asked.

"Long."

Henry waited for details. Instead, Seraphin opened a nut bar and gestured toward the food. "Go ahead. It's the least I can do."

No need to tell him twice. Henry put his purchases on the ceramic surface, then brought a stool to the opposite side and grabbed a knife. The cucumbers would add freshness to their impromptu dinner. His stomach grumbled as he sat and cut the vegetable into slices. He hadn't eaten this well in weeks. The dried fruits went down first, followed by the jerky. As he chewed on the tough meat, Henry planned what would be next.

Ten minutes later, everything had found its way into Henry's stomach. Seraphin ate a few cucumber slices and nibbled on the same nut bar through the entire meal. His body remained turned toward the door and his gaze never left it. Henry's satisfaction at a healthy supper overrode his guilt about eating most of it. How many more would he get out of sixty dollars?

"If you don't mind, I'll sleep now," Seraphin said. "I walked all day."

Questions burned Henry's lips. What was the hurry? Why did he keep staring at the door? Seraphin would be gone by dawn, though, and his mother always said to mind your own business. No sense in prying. He slid off his stool.

"Right this way, sir."

A simple wooden door connected the kitchen to his bedroom. They left the empty cupboards and unplugged fridge behind and entered Henry's main living area. The bed remained undone and the sheets piled at its foot. Old shirts hid the wooden floor, topped by the occasional pair of boxers, and his pyjama pants hung on the desk chair. No one else came into this room anymore. Henry cleaned when no clear path remained between his door and the bed. Seraphin contemplated the mess with wide eyes.

"I'm sorry. Give me a moment," Henry said.

He bent over, swooping the clothes from the ground and gathering them into a large bundle. He dumped the entirety of it in his wardrobe before changing the bed's sheets.

"Paul's rooms are always clean."

Seraphin ignored the comment. He held the old picture of Henry's family that sat on the bedside table and studied the image. A ten-year-old Henry stood in front of a hot air balloon, wearing his father's pilot cap, while Lenz Schmitt wrapped his arms around the boy's shoulders. His mother had taken the picture. He could remember her laugh as the pilot cap was shoved upon Henry's head. Cheerful. Free of worries. No one had heard of the Threstle Plague yet. They'd thought she'd live long past Henry's fifteenth birthday.

"Is that your father?" Seraphin asked.

"Yes. The day of my first flight."

The stranger's gaze left the picture to study him. Henry squirmed under the scrutiny. Why did a family picture matter so much?

"Did the Plague take him?"

"It killed my mother," Henry said. "The loss drove him away."

"Oh. My apologies." He slammed the picture down, as if the deadly virus still contaminated it. Even almost a decade later, everyone was worried about the illness. Seraphin pressed his lips together. When he spoke again, he picked a different subject. "Hot air ballooning is not a common passion. Even back then, it was rather rare."

"Still the only thing we had in common."

Henry couldn't keep the bitterness out of his tone. When his father spoke of anything but balloons, he'd become a cold man. Sometimes Henry wondered if he would've mattered at all to him had he not shared this peculiar love. It didn't help that Lenz Schmitt's only message when he disappeared was a small note on the chest in which they stored the balloon: *Don't lose the envelope, Henry. Never give it up.* Like the great purple-and-gold fabric mattered more than him. No goodbye. No good luck. No apologies. Just a note.

Seraphin had reached for something under his long shirt, at his belt. When he spoke again, he adopted a solemn and warm tone. "I'm sure they watch over you."

"Doubt it." Why would a man who had abandoned him when he was fifteen spend his afterlife hovering above Henry and protecting him? Ancestors and family mattered to Regarians, however. Seraphin's wish did not surprise Henry. "Thanks for the sentiment, though."

Seraphin returned his attention to the picture, a frown on his bony face. Henry crossed the room, leaving his guest to the deep thoughts that marred his expression. When the Regarian woke from his lethargy, they wished each other a good night. As Henry closed the door, Seraphin put his glasses on the bedside table and removed his shirt.

Before the door closed entirely, Henry saw what he shouldn't have.

A gun.

An old-fashioned, flint-and-lock pistol, with a bright red string coiled around the handle. Seraphin's fingers had reached for it again, as they had a minute ago, under the shirt, and Seraphin traced the string. His *skeptar*, inherited from his own father. A token meant to carry his ancestors' spirit and protect them. Most Regarians incorporated the *skeptar* into trinkets—wristbands, amulets, decorated tools of their trade. Not Seraphin. He had a pistol.

Firearms could kill. And they were illegal.

Henry's heart thumped against his chest. He hoped Seraphin's prayers would cover the short click of the door as he closed it. All the questions repressed through dinner bounced around his head. Who had he allowed into his house? What was he running from? Did Seraphin intend to pay him, or shoot him down before he went on his merry way?

The evening replayed in his head as Henry made his way back to the ceramic counter. Every creak of the floor made his heart jump. Rain hammered on the windows and roof. His dusty house now smelled of humidity, and thunder rumbled in the distance. He ought to tell Kinsi. The grocer always knew what to do, even with situations involving a stranger and a pistol. Besides, Henry couldn't sleep here. Too dangerous. He strode to the door, put his coat on, and set his straw hat on his head.

His resolve faltered as he grabbed the doorknob. His tendency to overreact often got the better of him. Seraphin might have a special license for his weapon. The Regarian's story and secrets were none of his business. Could Henry brave the rain and sell him out while he slept? What if he was wrong about Seraphin? Come morning, Seraphin would no longer be his problem and he would have enough money to survive the month, at least.

Henry released the doorknob and wiped his sweaty palms. Wait and see. Always a good plan.

He undressed and went across the kitchen, through the open archway that led to his living room. Despite his speedy heartbeat, Henry lowered himself onto the old couch. The fabric was soft against his skin, smoothed by decades of use. Even in his teenage years, the sofa had smelled of dust and age. The reassurance that some things never changed eased his nerves. He remained motionless, listening to the soft rain and howling wind. The downpour would give a hand to the half-dead flowers lining Ferrea's main street. They needed water as much as the remaining residents needed tourists. If only the latter fell from the sky, too.

Henry dreamt of his mother, pockmarks covering part of her round, hollowed visage. She turned to him, her beautiful dark skin marred by the illness. He reached for her but she raised Seraphin's flint-and-lock pistol. Smiled. At the detonation he woke with a start.

The rain outside had stopped, and silence hung heavy in the house. He crawled out of the couch and snuck to the bedroom door. Closed. Henry exhaled. Outside, clouds obscured the stars. Long hours remained before dawn. Once again, he thought of warning Kinsi. Better not to wake him, though. He'd share the story Wednesday, on their weekly night at Paul's, when he'd buy the first round.

Unless Seraphin shot him before then.

The dark thought created a hole in his belly and his mouth watered. If he was to die, three in the morning seemed a good time to enjoy a final late night snack. Henry moved to the kitchen, grabbed his metal pot, and filled it with water. The pot clanked loudly. Subtlety had never been his strength. Seraphin didn't wake, however, and Henry soon sat alone at his counter with a bowl of instant noodles. He tried to eat slowly and appreciate every slurp, just in case, but nervousness overpowered his will and he shoveled the spoons in his mouth at high speed.

His gaze never left the bedroom's door. What kind of trouble would the stranger hiding there bring?

The answer crashed through the front door, gun in hand.

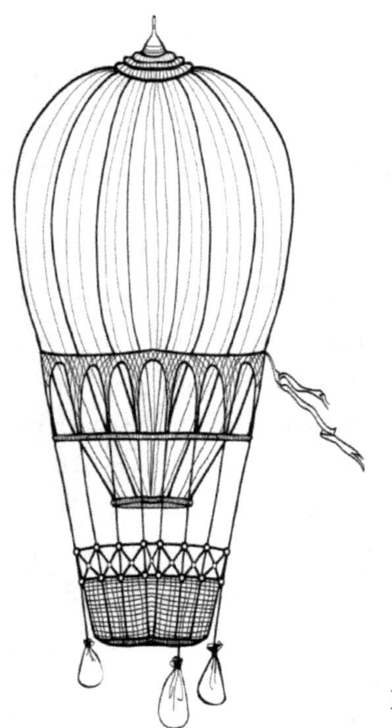

# CHAPTER TWO



Henry obeyed. Instant noodles hung from his mouth, dripping into the bowl. Powerful gusts swirled into the house. The door sagged sideways, broken by a kick. From where he sat, Henry had a great view of the gun pointed at him.

The deadly firearm rested in the stable hands of an army poster-boy. Tall and serious, with a square jaw and smooth chin, the man exuded confidence and competence. He strode into the kitchen, his rigid back displaying his clean beige uniform and the two officer's stripes on his shoulders. His gaze stopped on Henry.

"Where is he?"

There was no need to ask who 'he' was. A split-second glance at the bedroom door betrayed Henry's thoughts. The soldier walked past him without another word. When he kicked the door, wood splintered with a loud crack. Henry spewed his noodles out. The officer spun around to glare at him, but the gun remained trained on the Regarian inside the room. Henry raised his hands anyway, bumped the bowl. Splashed his last meal over the counter.

As he kept his hands mid-air, cold sweat running down his neck, his heart ready to explode, the soldier turned back to his initial target.

"You won't fit through that window," he said.

Henry leaned forward to see through the doorway. Seraphin stood bare-chested, hands on the windowsill, his glasses slightly askew as if put in a hurry. Moonlight lit his body. His ribs stood out against his skin and his white hair didn't hide the prominent collarbones. Not a ghost. A skeleton.

The two men stared at each other.

Wind cycled through the house: front door, kitchen, bedroom, window. Soup dripped upon Henry's clothes. His tongue stuck against his palate, thick from fear. He couldn't take his eyes from the two men: the commanding presence in the doorway, and the sickly shadow by the window.

And the gun. How he wished the gun didn't exist!

"Move into the kitchen," the officer said.

Seraphin made his way across the cluttered bedroom floor, one slow step at a time. Henry straightened and set his gaze on the dripping soup. In two hours Seraphin would have disappeared, leaving Henry with sixty dollars and all his questions unanswered. Henry would have preferred to satisfy his hunger over his curiosity.

Once Seraphin reached the kitchen, the Union officer cocked his gun. The click brought a solid ball in Henry's throat. He couldn't breathe. His hands were clammy. How could this man hold his weapon steady?

"Do you like it?" The soldier took two long strides and pressed the barrel against Seraphin's forehead. Unlike his hands, his voice shook. "How does it feel to be on the other end?"

"Don't play, Captain."

Seraphin's calm astonished Henry. Tension turned the Regarian's muscles rigid, but it was absent from his words and expression. His chin lifted, he stared at the captain with defiance. The officer scowled, took a deep breath. Readied himself.

"No!" Henry shouted.

He jumped to his feet, knocking over the stool with a crash. Both men glared at him. Henry wished he could disappear, but he assembled the shattered pieces of his courage.

"You can't. My house... Don't—"

"Mind your own business."

An order from the commanding officer. Henry swallowed hard. He didn't have the guts to add more. Seraphin forced a smile onto his bone-thin face.

"Close your eyes, Henry. It'll be easier."

Sound advice. One he was incapable of following. His eyes locked onto the trigger finger and his feet remained cemented to the floor. He didn't want to see this. Or hear it. Or smell it, either! Yet he couldn't move. The universe had refocused on the pair in his kitchen and their gravity held him in place.

"Last words?"

"The same as your brother's," Seraphin said. "At least look into my eyes when you shoot."

"Did you?"

"Yes. Can you?"

No answer. The wind, whipping Seraphin's hair. The salty smell of soup. The trickle down Henry's pants. The house, silent, waited. The captain's hand shook.

"I... No."

It was but a whisper. He lowered the gun, closed his eyes.

Seraphin barreled into the officer and grabbed the firearm. They crashed to the ground with grunts and hisses of pain. Seraphin's glasses dropped from his nose, sliding away. The soldier, bigger and stronger, rolled on top right away but Seraphin, agile beyond expectation, melted from under him. Henry watched the dizzying fight for the gun. He ought to help, but *who?*

Neither. Don't get involved in others' business, his father always said. If it didn't apply now, when would it? Time to do what he should've done when he saw Seraphin's pistol: go to Kinsi. Henry started around the counter. He made it to the broken door before a great detonation pierced his ears. Horrible images formed in his mind. Bloodied flesh scattered on the floor, a dark red pool. Nauseated, he turned.

A new hole decorated the wooden planks. No blood. No corpse.

Seraphin stood over the captain, gun in hand. The officer remained still, propped up by his elbow. Their breaths came in short gasps. The gunshot's echoes bounced around Henry's head. He stepped outside.

"Stay."

The coldness of the Regarian's voice surprised Henry. He obeyed, shifted back inside, shivering from the night's drafts.

"You missed," the captain said.

"I didn't." A disquieting smile played upon Seraphin's lips. "You're not your brother. Stand up, Vermen. We're leaving."

The soldier's bushy eyebrows connected into a deep frown. Henry willed him to obey. Vermen lumbered to his feet and dusted off his outfit. Calm. Almost serene. How could he wrestle his emotions under control so fast? Henry still wanted to run and scream and eat a dozen bowls of noodles.

"Henry?" Seraphin asked, his voice soft again.

"Y-yes?"

"Do you have strong rope?"

"The best. For the balloon."

"Perfect." Seraphin waited, tilted his head to the side. "Go get it."

Henry gave Seraphin a pleading look. *Don't get me involved.* The captain watched him.

"Without rope I can't leave with him." The Regarian cocked the gun to stress his point.

"I'll go, I'll go!"

Henry raced past them, through the living room and into the oldest section of the house. As he opened the connecting door, a breeze lifted the film of dust. He coughed on it but hurried between the small shelves that cluttered the space. Figurines of old racers stared at him. President Jacob Kurtmann's frown made him stop, clean its tiny head, and apologise. Three-time winner, accomplished doctor, President of the Union—Kurtmann deserved better than that. Then he recalled the two dangerous men in his kitchen, and moved on.

Past the shop was his back store—an empty room devoid of windows, with a large trapdoor hidden under heavy boxes. Everything related to the hot air balloon waited there: envelope, basket, burner, and ropes. Henry cleared the space, fumbled for his key, and removed the lock.

The stairs creaked the same as his weekly visit, but this time they gave him shivers. He flipped the lights on and held his breath as the neon flickered to life. The chest rested in the middle of the room, his father's memo on top. *Don't lose the envelope, Henry. Never give it up.* He'd almost set the note on fire the first time he'd read it.

For once, he did not come to ask silent questions to a bit of paper. Henry walked past the chest to the spare spools of rope and heaved one onto his shoulder. He climbed out of the basement without a look back at the locked trunk. Better not to linger. Seraphin's finger might get twitchy.

Neither man had moved. Had they talked? Breathed? Henry dared not ask. He handed the cordage to the Regarian.

"You tie him," Seraphin said. "Then get my pack, my shirt and my glasses."

None of the weary warmth from their earlier dinner remained in his voice. He'd become cold, ruthless and efficient. Henry obeyed the orders, afraid to hesitate. The officer's outfit was rumpled and torn at the shoulder, no longer fit for promotional posters. He muttered an apology. Vermen stayed as silent as Kurtmann's statuette. Would he remember Henry? Blacklist him? Would his fellow soldiers come to save him sooner or later? This mess wasn't his fault. He had no choice. They couldn't call this complicity in the capture of a Union soldier, could they?

"Search for my wallet in the front pouch," Seraphin said. Henry's fingers trembled as he unzipped the bag. He found a plain black wallet right away. "Good. Take your sixty dollars and put it back."

"What?"

"Take it!"

Henry watched the gun's barrel shake and did not argue. He grabbed the bills, slapped them on the ceramic counter, and stored the wallet. He backed away from the pack as though it were on fire. Why pay him? Staying alive was enough for him. Now he'd become a real accomplice.

Seraphin slung his pack over his shoulders and seized the ropes at Vermen's wrists. The soldier stumbled after him. He kept his shoulders squared, but no energy lingered in his steps. Defeated—like Henry's father after the Plague took his mother. Strange, how certain expressions did not change from one man to another.

"There's another door in the living room," Henry muttered.

The Regarian did not grant him an answer, but he tugged the captain in the opposite direction. Henry stayed rooted in the kitchen and watched both men disappear through the connecting archway. Grayish rays lit the clouds on the horizon. The air felt lighter, devoid of humidity or electric tension. No one had died. Sixty dollars awaited him on the counter.

The backdoor slammed shut on the strangest evening of his life.

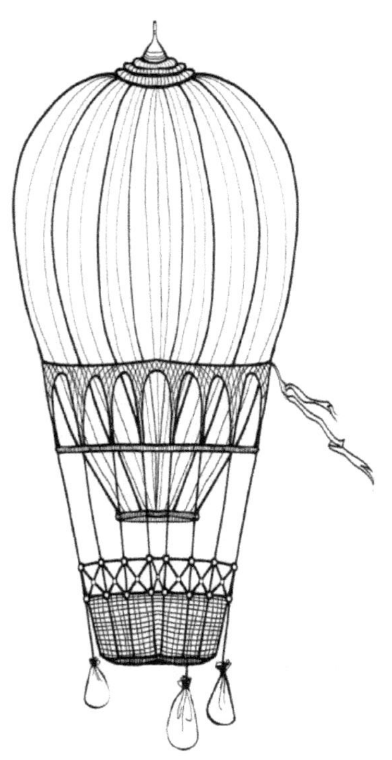

# CHAPTER THREE


before his feet? Nine hours had trickled by since the White Renegade had walked him out at gunpoint and led him into the forest. Captain Hans Vermen fought for every step. His concentration eluded him. Not enough food. Not enough sleep. Conditions worse than the army's forced marches. His enemy right behind, watching his every move. He would not stumble. He could not fall.

Branches snagged on his ruined uniform. Vermen brushed them aside. Behind him, Seraphin stumbled. Twigs cracked. The Regarian caught himself against a trunk with a grunt. Exhaustion had apparently caught up with both of them. If Hans gathered his strength, perhaps he could escape. He had to wait, bide his time, and the next time Holt tripped...

The roar of a waterfall welcomed them into a small clearing. How had he missed the powerful sound before? Vermen slowed his pace, stopped. The bright light reflected by the flowing water dazzled him and he raised both tied hands to protect his eyes. A deep pond occupied the majority of the area, its surface upset by the great waterfall. Mount Kairn's cliff side loomed over them.

Seraphin pressed the gun against his back. Was that it? Had they come all this way for him to die in the restless water?

"Move," the Renegade said.

Vermen glanced at either side. No clear path pierced the forest on Mount Kairn's slopes. He took a hesitant step to the left. Only the cliff lay on the right.

"No. The other side."

The strain in his voice put a small balm on the captain's heart. Seraphin feared him, despite the rope holding him, the firearm at his back and, most of all, despite his earlier failure to shoot him. Had Vermen managed to scare him? It didn't quite qualify as vengeance, but he'd take it. He obeyed the order, a meager smile on his face. Soon enough, they stood in front of the stone wall. The drizzle refreshed him.

"What now?" he asked. "Into the solid rock?"

"Turn forty-five degrees to the left. Take a step forward."

Vermen hesitated but complied. The uneven stone brushed against his right shoulder. Water crashed down a few meters ahead of him.

"Another."

"Don't play games. Shoot now and be done with it." Vermen closed his eyes and straightened his shoulders. Better to die with honor than demean himself further.

"Just take that step!"

The tone's urgency surprised him. Seraphin's cold calm from the previous night had disappeared, eroded by the endless trek. Did Vermen want to test his patience? The Renegade had no qualms with murder. He'd proven that years ago. Vermen moved forward. Understood right away what Seraphin had led him to.

A stairway in the mountainside. Impossible to see unless you were upon it, and masked from the airships by the great waterfall. The perfect entrance to a secret hideout.

The gun pointed at his back left him no time to admire the craftsmanship. He started up, careful not to slip on the wet stairs. His tied hands upset his balance and more than once, Vermen was forced to lean against the stone wall to avoid falling. He pushed his cramped muscles into one last effort and reached the entrance to a network of caves. Seven feet tall at its highest point, it had a squarish and irregular shape, with a small narrow ledge in front.

Amazing. The White Renegade had led him straight to his rebels' headquarters, without even a blindfold. What an idiotic decision.

Round lights lined the stone tunnel's walls, linked together by electric cables. Vermen squinted and noted three branching corridors, two of which had their own string of lamps. How big was this complex? Seraphin arrived behind him and heaved a sigh of relief.

"Don't stop now."

The rebel leader stood half a foot behind him, pistol at the ready. The ledge they stood on offered so little space that a push backward would send Holt tumbling down the steep stairs to a likely death, giving the captain time to run. If the Regarian hadn't shot him first. The barrel waited less than an inch from his back. Even with the exhaustion, he doubted Seraphin would miss. He gritted his teeth and advanced into the rebel hideout.

They didn't need to go far. Seraphin walked him to the first intersection then spotted one of his men. He hailed the tall man and the rebel whirled around. He strode to them without hesitation, every step the same length, with a distinct rhythm that marked him as a soldier. Vermen studied him as he approached, off-put by the familiarity of the dark blond hair, deep-set eyes, and beakish nose. The captain tried to work through his fatigue and remember where they'd met.

Seraphin stepped forward and handed the firearm to him, his bony shoulders slumped. "Guard him. I'll send Andeal to you. He'll know where to put him."

"Yes sir."

The quick military answer bothered Vermen. Murderers and outlaws did not deserve the deference one gave to army officers. Holt was a lowly criminal and should not be addressed with respect.

"Don't kill him," the Regarian added as he headed down the passageway.

The rebel clacked his tongue in disappointment as his leader vanished around a bend. He trained the gun on Vermen but kept a safe distance between them.

"I imagine he'll want the honor. I can understand. Your family's been a plague on his life."

The captain tensed at the reference to his brother. He withheld a reply, still raking his brain for memories of this man. He pictured him with the Union soldiers' beige uniform instead of his marine shirt, then cropped his hair even closer. His mind completed the picture with a rich decor, an untouched glass of champagne, and the buzzing of a chattering crowd. A cocktail. They'd shaken hands at a military cocktail, with ranking officers and influential figures of all spheres.

"We've met." Vermen leaned against the wall. He remembered him now. Stern Cypher. "You dogged General Clarin at a cocktail. You were his little pet, his new protégé. He'd had you promoted all the way up just so he could keep you close. The sex must've been fantastic."

Stern's jaw clenched and his knuckles whitened as he tightened his grip on the gun's handle. Apart from glaring at him, however, he did not retaliate. Not physically.

"Jealous?" Stern asked. "You shouldn't be. Most soldiers I've met used to gossip about the precious time Lieutenant Lungvist and you spent together."

David Lungvist was his best man. Quick of wits, loyal, determined. Not the best shooter but an incredible tactician. He'd be hunting for Vermen now. He would find him.

"Lungvist earned every promotion he ever had."

"But I didn't, is that it?" asked Stern.

"You betrayed your fellow soldiers."

A thin smile stretched the rebel's lips. Vermen wanted to pounce on him and wipe the expression off his face. He'd be dead before he reached him, however.

"My fellow soldiers," Stern repeated with a sneer. "You're so proud of your army, aren't you? Glad to belong to such a group of fine men. I used to be like that, too. What better way to honor my country? Then one day I served under a general who trapped half a village in its tavern and slaughtered them. The following morning, my best friend walked into the encampment with his family's old gun to avenge them, ready to die in the process. I thought, there you go, the bad apple is gone. I stayed a soldier. I climbed the ranks. I found more and more of these bad apples. The truth is, the further up you go, the more there are. The real soldiers are here, scraping by, not drinking champagne with the worst war criminals."

"You make hiding and thieving into such a noble endeavor. I can only commend your bravery."

In one swift movement, Stern flipped his hold on the pistol and smashed the cross into Vermen's face. Pain burst in his jaw and sparks flew before his eyes. He held himself against the wall, his legs threatening to give in, and spat bloodied saliva on the ground. If his head didn't spin from the combined ache and exhaustion, he could've used the opportunity to jump the ex-soldier. He clutched the side of his face and they glared at each other. Stern broke away first.

"I cheered when I heard the gunshot that killed your brother. I will again when your turn comes."

"That's not a very nice thing to say, Stern."

The new voice took them both by surprise. Vermen spun on his heels to face the newcomer and froze, his eyes widening. Blue skin. What kind of freak had blue skin? Vermen slid away, keeping his back to the rock wall. The easy smile on the blue man's face vanished, replaced by a pained expression. It sufficed to stop Vermen. He was a captain of the Union army. He would not be scared by an aberrant skin color.

"Why would I be nice to him?" Stern asked.

He received a shrug as an answer. "You shouldn't need a reason. But it's okay, you don't need to stay anymore. I'll take care of him."

"Seraphin asked me to guard him."

"Until I arrived, yes. I've made arrangements for his cell."

This must be the Andeal mentioned earlier, then. He put his hands on the rope tying Vermen's wrists and gave a slight pull, signaling they should go. The captain squirmed at the proximity but started after Andeal anyway.

Stern followed. "He's dangerous."

"I can handle him."

He heard Stern's derisive snort despite the roaring waterfall. Andeal's grip on the ropes tightened, his shoulders tensed, and he walked faster. *Hit him*, Vermen thought. *Turn around and hit him*. Wouldn't that be the most perfect escape? The freak fighting with his deserter colleague, giving him a chance to reach for the gun and get away. Too bad Andeal did not seem to be the violent type.

"Go flaunt your superior military training elsewhere," he retorted. "Trust me, I can knock out a man about to fall over from exhaustion."

"This isn't any man. Or did Seraphin forget to warn you?"

Despite the precarious position he was in, Vermen was beginning to enjoy himself. Stern's fear flattered him. Had all of Holt's rebels grown terrified of him over the last years? He had shoved quite a few of them in prison.

Andeal slowed and turned around, giving Vermen another cursory glance as he answered Stern. "He said we had a prisoner and to be wary."

"A prisoner." Again, that mocking snort. It was enough to trigger any man's hatred. "Andeal, may I introduce you to Captain Hans Vermen?"

Andeal's eyes widened and his mouth opened into an almost perfect circle. He'd stopped moving and his gaze went from the stripes on Vermen's shoulders to the captain's face, then to Stern. The astonished expression lasted about two seconds, then the blue man gave a noncommittal shrug.

"Still just a man." He grabbed Vermen's hand and gave it a false shake.

"A pleasure."

He started off again, tugging a surprised Vermen along. How could he be calmer than the trained soldier? Did he have some sort of hidden trick, something only blue people could do? No. That was nonsense. They weren't in some kind of fairytale, and monsters didn't exist.

After a few steps, Vermen noticed Stern hadn't followed this time. The ex-soldier remained behind, the gun still in hand. The white lights sharpened his annoyed frown into a cold and hard expression. The captain offered him a large smile before turning away.

As Stern disappeared around a bend, so did the remainder of Vermen's energy. His shoulders slumped, his feet began dragging on the ground with every step. He might've been able to overpower Andeal—the blue man had no weapon—but his willpower barely kept him standing. He focused on putting one foot before the other, tried to remember the path they chose for later. A fuzziness encroached on his mind, however, and he couldn't distinguish between one irregular tunnel and the next. Before long he'd lost track of time and when Andeal stopped in front of a door, he almost bumped into him.

"Sorry."

Vermen regretted the reflex apology right away. What was he doing? He should punch the freak rebel, not apologize to him. He had to get a hold of himself and keep his wits about him until he was alone. He concentrated on the little room Andeal had just shown him into. It begged one strange question: was he a prisoner or a guest?

His living quarters looked nothing like a cell—he'd slept in worse places as a soldier. Two layers of sheets rested on the hard bed, with an additional blanket folded upon them. Soft to the touch, inviting. An old wooden desk adorned the corner, accompanied by a mismatched plastic chair. The modern white spherical lamp clashed with the ensemble and spread a cold light in the space. None of the furniture fit together. The rebels must have pieced together the room's decoration, one element at a time.

Then Andeal untied his wrists. Vermen squirmed at the blue fingers' touch but refused to protest. He quelled his disgust at the strange skin and kept his calm. What were they thinking? He could attack his captor now. Not exactly what he called 'being wary'. Vermen stepped back, then shook his hands to ease the blood flow.

"Is this a game?" he asked.

"I have better things to do. Why did Seraphin bring you here?"

"Ask him."

"I will." Andeal shuffled backward and wiped his fingers on his pants. "Have you slept recently?"

What did sleeping have to do with this conversation? Vermen crossed his arms and worked through the exhaustion to bring up his best smug smile. No, he hadn't slept in days. The blue man didn't need to know that. Andeal leaned on the doorway, unfazed by his silence.

"Have you eaten recently?"

Vermen stretched and cracked his knuckles, determined to keep his distance, but the question unnerved him. Why did he care? Why did Andeal study him with that reluctant, almost worried expression? Had the rebels never learned how to treat an enemy?

"Okay, I get it. You won't talk." He rubbed his temples. "You may think silence is your friend but, trust me, you'll regret it soon."

Andeal left and, after he closed the door, Vermen heard chains and a lock. The cozy room and lack of manacles did not change his situation. He was a prisoner here, at the rebels' mercy. At Seraphin's mercy. He had to get out before the Renegade came to his senses and executed him.

That, however, required rest. Vermen strode to the bed and collapsed. He could plan his escape another day.

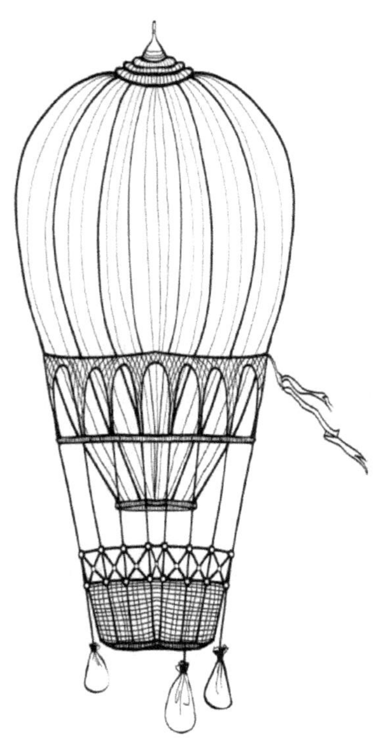

# CHAPTER FOUR

 consequences of Vermen's capture sunk in Henry's mind. Missing Union officers did not go unnoticed. The last time Kinsi visited his daughter in Reverence, he'd brought back rumors of citizens disappearing—militants for peace and other dissidents. Henry never protested or caused trouble. He didn't deserve to be taken away. But if they traced the disappearance to his house? He could be next. Captain Vermen must have had friends.

He started by cleaning his kitchen. He threw the spilled noodles away with a pinch to the heart, then wiped the soup clean from the floor. He lifted a fallen stool and set it so the foot hid the bullet hole. Perfect. The place looked the same as before. Except for the door.

Henry ignored this slight problem and picked up Seraphin's money from his counter. Where to put the bills? Under the mattress? He moved to the bedroom, slammed the window shut, then gathered the remainder of his clothes from the floor. He then reached under the bed to make sure nothing was left. His fingers closed around a cold and smooth cylinder. He swallowed hard, fear swirling in his stomach, and ran his hand down the barrel, along the trigger and to the cross. The coarse string pricked his fingertips.

The pistol.

Henry flattened himself against the floor. The holster laid a few inches away. How could Seraphin forget his *skeptar*? Did it fall when he'd tried to flee? It was a family heirloom, a religious symbol, and a weapon. Seraphin's only link to his ancestors was too important to leave behind. He had no right to dump it on Henry like that.

Henry threw it on the undone bed, moved to the kitchen and set water to boil. His stomach heaved left and right but food would settle it. In a half hour, Henry had cooked the second pack of instant noodles, devoured it, and cleaned the pot. The salty meal calmed his mind. He could hide the pistol somewhere far from the house. That would work.

Another surprise waited for him in the bedroom. The old picture decorating his side table had vanished. Did Seraphin take it? Henry searched the surroundings again, found nothing. It had to be him, but why? Another mystery—one he didn't have time for.

He wrapped the *skeptar* in a tissue bag, held the package at arm's length, and walked out of his house. Vermen's electric pick-up waited for him outside.

"This mess wasn't worth sixty bucks," he told the vehicle. He strode to the door, pulled it open. No keys, of course. "A thousand dollars wouldn't be worth it."

Henry dumped the pistol inside, set his shoulders against the back, and started pushing. Clouds lingered in the sky but the sun pierced through. Within a few minutes, sweat rolled down his back and drenched his shirt. It took hours before he reached the tall grasses near the forest. Mount Kairn hid half the sun, and the shade cooled his overheated body.

The pick-up's dark army color blended with the forest behind. Almost.

It wouldn't matter. Henry headed back home, his feet dragging on the ground. What did he expect? A Union captain had disappeared. They would track him down, notice the broken door, and discover the military vehicle. Try as he might, Henry would be blamed. Arrested. Executed. All he could do was sit at his counter and wait.

He did. They never came.

The following evening, Henry collapsed onto one of Paul's wooden chairs in front of Kinsi. Only the three of them occupied the inn's common room. The empty tables waited for customers that had disappeared through the years. He remembered the buzz of conversations drowning the music and smoke from multiple pipes hiding the ceiling. Today the National Radio filled the silence and only Paul lit his cigarette.

Henry's life:slow, ordinary, dreadful.

A welcome change from the previous days.

He tried to relax and concentrate, but couldn't. Since Seraphin had left, he'd been living in a weird daze, unable to focus on the present. Kinsi had been scrutinizing him ever since Henry had offered to pay for the first round.

"Where did you get the money?" insisted the grocer.

"I helped a stranger out," he said. "He must be filthy rich. He gave me enough to live for a month."

Kinsi answered with a doubtful stare. Henry's lying skills hadn't improved in the last day. There were other ways to avoid a topic, however. Like forcing another one onto the table.

"Anything on the radio?"

"The usual. Dead soldiers in Burgia, student unrest in Altaer, and nothing on the Race."

"It's early in the season."

"It's not," Kinsi said.

Silence stretched between them. Henry recalled the surge of hope from yesterday, when he'd first noticed Seraphin at his door. News from the Races at last! Ferrea was saved. They would have waves of tourists, Paul's inn would fill up within the week, and the smattering of residents left in his small town could hang on another year. He'd rushed down the slope, headlong into crushing disappointment.

"There will be no Annual Mount Kairn Race this year," he said.

The grocer blinked, then smiled. Relaxed. Why didn't he react more? Didn't it scare him?

"Ready to admit it, I see."

"You knew?"

His foster father laughed, took a long draw from his ale. "You should've, too. We've both lived on the outcomes from the Races for almost a decade. Preparations should've started three months ago. When you didn't receive a single shipment of trinkets for your father's shop I figured they'd canceled. Are you so surprised? Attendance was at its lowest last year. This is the result."

He could've told him outright. Instead Kinsi had let him stew and worry and hope. He'd listened to the dull radio every single day, like it was possible, like they might hear something important from it! Henry repressed his flare of temper. Kinsi would have a solution. He would know how to solve this problem.

"What do we do?" Henry asked.

"We leave."

No. They couldn't abandon Ferrea. They belonged here. For years, they had breathed life into the squat houses. Without their presence, the town lost its heart and expired. Henry couldn't imagine living anywhere else.

"Never," he said.

"I can count Ferrea's inhabitants on my left hand. We're ghosts, roaming a dead village's streets. There's a life elsewhere, full of opportunities. We can't stay, Henry. The world moved on without Ferrea. There is nothing left."

Henry fought against the words as each of them smashed his heart to pieces. Anger built under his earlier relief, spinning his head. He couldn't accept this. Kinsi had it all wrong.

"Ferrea is all I have left."

"It's not. We're here for you."

"Yes, it is." Henry gritted his teeth together. "It's not much and it's crumbling, its empty houses like the pus-filled sores on those infected by the Plague—like my mom's before her last breath—but it's all I have left. And your solution is what? Run away and let it die? Father did that once and you called him a coward for it. You're no better."

The grocer set his tankard down, edged forward, and put both palms flat on the wooden table. His lips formed a thin line, his eyebrows connected—Kinsi's stop-being-stupid expression. Henry shuffled in his seat.

"I remember the fifteen-year-old boy buying his first instant noodles with a smattering of coins because his father had run off, taking away the money stashed in their safe. Your father fled from his grief and responsibilities. I'm accepting mine and protecting my family. We're broke. It's over. But you can come with us to Reverence. We'll house you as long as you need, or want."

Henry struggled to find a retort. He didn't want to give up on Ferrea, not yet.

"What about Paul?"

The innkeeper turned in their direction at his name. He hadn't missed a word of the conversation.

"I have a friend in Agrinon who needs help starting a pub. I used my savings to buy a small house by the waterside, with a nice boat and all."

They all had a plan. Henry's world slipped through his fingers and his friends, the last of Ferrea's residents, helped it along. It left a bitter taste on his tongue and Kinsi's pleading expression worsened his anger. How could he do this? Henry refused to even imagine life elsewhere. Only the radio filled the silence, the announcer's voice droning on, dead as Ferrea.

"...well-known for leading a band of criminals suspected of theft and terrorism. This man is also accused of murder. He is five-foot-ten, weighs 135 pounds and hails from Regaria. He can be distinguished by his long white hair, extremely white skin, and pale blue eyes, tinged with red. The authorities called him extremely dangerous. They demand you do not approach him but contact them if sighted."

Henry stared at the radio. How many Regarian with albinism ran around fleeing the police? One. Only one. And for murder charges. Didn't they talk of Vermen's brother? Merciful winds, what if Seraphin's *skeptar* was the murder weapon?

"I have to go."

He jumped to his feet. His heart drummed in his chest and panic blurred his thoughts. A criminal under his roof. He'd covered the tracks. What had he been thinking? Kinsi stood after him.

"Henry, wait!"

He didn't. Henry crossed the pub without looking back. He shoved the front door open, ignored a second call from Kinsi and walked down the street, head bent. He'd shared a meal with Seraphin, helped him capture a Union captain, got rid of the illegal weapon. They could charge him with complicity now. Or worse! Henry didn't want to think about 'worse'.

His belly grumbled so loudly he thought another storm prepared itself. Dark clouds covered half the sky and hid the moon. Didn't one stormy night suffice? At least the air was lighter than the previous days. If the weather stayed like this, the night might become his last pleasant one as a free man. Not a thought he wanted to linger on. Henry tore his gaze from the clouds as he reached the slope's top.

Once again, a man stood in his doorway. Nothing white about this one, however.

The stranger wore a heavy leather coat, with similar gloves and high boots. The hood from a dark sweater concealed his features. It couldn't be Seraphin. He was too small and his posture too relaxed. Not a Union soldier either. What kind of man showed up at your doorstep, all in black and hiding their features?

Hitmen. Assassins. Seraphin's lot.

Henry backtracked and dashed for the long herbs of the field. He flattened himself on the ground and hoped the man at the door hadn't noticed him. He crawled farther along the hill and peeked up. The killer hadn't moved. Henry was safe. For now.

He could run away. Escape Seraphin's hired gun and warn the local authorities. The closest police station was in Colhurt—an entire day's walk. His belly rumbled as a protest. Too long a trek to go without food and he couldn't get help from Kinsi or Paul. If he talked to them, they'd become targets too. No one would solve this problem for him.

Henry had one tool, though: Seraphin's pistol.

He crawled through the long grass. His hands and knees sank in the muddy ground and in a matter of minutes his white shirt turned brown. He progressed at a snail's pace and described a long circle around his house. The rustling of green blades accompanied his movements, his heart hammered like thunder and an earthy scent saturated his nose. His head spun. As he passed through the fields around his home, his hands began to itch and turned red and puffy under the cake of dirt. What a mess. He should've turned Seraphin away.

At last, the electric car's shape appeared through the jungle. Henry lumbered to his feet, flung the door open and grabbed the tote bag. His hands shook as he took the firearm out. The pistol burned his sweaty and itchy hands. He could kill a man now—the one at his door. Perhaps the day's walk to Colhurt was a better option after all. Then what? Live on the run? Away from Ferrea? No.

He crept down the road, his fingers clutching the cross. The squish of mud under his soles rang loudly in his ear. Every blade brushing against his forearms made him jump. He made his way back toward his small house, crouched and ready, his puffed fingers barely fitting next to the trigger.

As he neared the road and his door, the moon peeked between the clouds and shed its white light on the scene. The hitman raised his head and the hood fell off.

Smooth blue skin.

As it registered, Henry wondered what kind of monster he was and a thousand horrible stories popped into his mind, coalescing into terrified surprise. He closed his eyes and pulled the trigger. The shot blasted into the night. The man crashed to the ground as wood splintered with a loud crack. Henry coughed on the cloud of gunpowder.

"Holy Lady! Don't shoot again. Please don't."

Henry dared to look. The stranger lay on the ground, protecting his head with one hand and holding his arm with the other. Although his gloves hid the hand's skin, there could be no mistake about his face. Blue as the Kairn River. He hadn't dreamt it. Henry stepped out of the grass, dazed.

"Are you all right?" he asked.

"You just shot me!"

"You're blue!"

"I..." He rubbed his forehead and nose with a gloved hand then struggled to his feet. A sad smile materialized on his round face. "Am I? Sometimes I forget."

They stood in an uncomfortable silence. A batch of straw-yellow hair topped the stranger's head and sweat rolled down his cheeks. Long leather coats weren't meant for summer. His blue eyes stood out, matching the skin's color. Henry followed their gaze as it fell upon the pistol.

"Is that Seraphin's?" he asked. "Bone handle, red string...it is! How could he forget his *skeptar*?"

"Ask him."

"Already did, kind of. He won't tell me anything about his face-off with

Captain Vermen. I don't need to know, apparently." The blue man lifted his right hand from his arm. In the dim light, the blood on his gloves shone black.

"Did I actually hit?" Henry couldn't tell if that would make him proud or terrified.

"A splinter grazed my arm. More scared than hurt, though. You hit the door." He pointed at the hole in the broken wood. "I'm glad you can't aim. Can we go inside and talk? I swear I'm not here to hurt you, or I wouldn't have stood on your doorstep for hours!"

Everything about this was so incongruous. A friend of Seraphin clad in suspicious black clothes had waited for him and now he assured him all he wanted was a talk. A talk! Yet something about his genuine smile washed away Henry's earlier terror—or perhaps his life had just passed some sort of weirdness threshold and he no longer cared.

"Sure. Why not? It's not like I just shot you."

His new companion possessed a good sense of humor. He laughed and gestured for Henry to lead the way through the broken door. They sat at the counter, where he'd shared a meal with Seraphin. The man's pistol rested between them. Nothing abnormal there either.

"I'm Andeal," the blue man said. "It's a pleasure to finally meet you."

Finally? It didn't make any sense. The evening's frustration and stress kicked in. He cut the chase short. "What do you want?"

Andeal reached into the enormous pocket of his coat and brought a framed picture out. Henry, with his dad and the balloon. The picture shook in his hands and he couldn't keep his voice from trembling as he spoke. "Seraphin gave it to me. You said this was your dad, and he flew the balloon?"

"Yes."

Could this get any stranger? Stolen pictures, unexpected topics and Andeal's unexplainable excitement.

"Lenz Schmitt, right?"

Andeal held the picture at arm's length, inches away from Henry's face. Annoyed, Henry shoved it away. Why did it matter?

"Yeah."

Andeal slammed the frame down and brought Henry into a tight but brief embrace. It was finished the moment it started, leaving Henry dazed. Relief showed through every muscle of Andeal's body. He pulled his gloves off then ran a hand through his hair. His palms were a paler blue than the rest of his skin. Andeal seemed to be struggling for words.

"This is fabulous. I've been looking for you."

Henry studied the picture and pushed it away as his stomach twisted. Eight years, and for the first time, someone had information on Lenz Schmitt. He'd given up a long time ago. Did he want to hear it now? To get involved with Andeal and his eager grin?

"No. I'm done with all of this. Seraphin, the captain, my father...I don't want to hear any of it."

"Not...anything?"

Andeal's smile vanished as he tried to swallow the words. Henry avoided his incredulous stare, walked around the counter and reached for the cucumbers' bag. His sausage-fingers let one of the vegetables slip twice but Henry fished for it again. His hunger grew as this conversation progressed, along with his frustration. He wanted that cucumber.

"None of it." Was it so hard to understand? Henry grabbed a knife, set the cucumber on the counter, and sliced through it. "He disappeared from my life eight years ago and never gave any news. I spent years opening the mailbox every morning hoping I'd see his handwriting. Thousands of tourists filed past my house for the Races, and I watched them. Maybe one would walk up to me and share a few kind words from him. Maybe they'd tell me he'd come back, that he didn't mean to abandon me. But no!" He cut faster and faster, his cheeks flushed. "He entrusted me with the balloon and let me deal with the questions and the grief. He cared more about that stupid envelope than he ever did about me. Do you know how hard it is to wipe your father out of your life even when you know he's out there?"

"Yes."

Henry froze. He hadn't expected an answer to his rhetorical question. Even less an affirmative one.

"So does Lenz," Andeal said. "He talked about you all the time. He never forgot you."

"Then he should've returned earlier!" Henry gave one big slice into the cucumber then slammed the knife down. He pushed the slices onto a small plate. His head buzzed. He didn't want to hear any of it, it was too hard. A change of subject was in order. "It's too late. Tell me about you instead."

"If I do, you'll learn information the Union intends to keep silent. Are you sure you want to get involved deeper in this?"

Henry bit into a cucumber slice, as though its freshness could clear his mind. He glanced at his broken door. How long before the Union found him? What would they do to him?

"You're afraid. We can protect you," Andeal said. "We could make you disappear until everything calms down. Seraphin's been off the grid for six years now and they haven't caught him."

"What do you call that night then? That captain came one finger itch away from putting a bullet in his forehead."

Andeal smirked. He'd baited him into commenting on the evening and Henry fell for it. Time to wipe that smug expression off his face.

"Perhaps he should've. It'd be one less murderer on this earth and I wouldn't have a freaky blue man knocking at my door with ghost stories of a father who couldn't be bothered to send a single message to his only son. Just the one! Saying he was okay and he did love him despite dumping him the morning after his mother died!"

The smile did vanish, replaced by a glare. Andeal's angry expression brought Henry no satisfaction.

"You have no idea what you're talking about. Did it ever cross your tiny brain that if Lenz didn't send word, it might be because he *couldn't*? That maybe something bad had happened and he was going through living hell with said freaky blue man? That sending mail when you're in a minuscule cell isn't exactly a possibility? But the best part is that he did write a message and get it out." Andeal drew an old rag from his coat's pocket and slapped it on the counter. Then he slid off his stool and cast Henry one sorely disappointed look. "Here it is. Who would have thought that when I'd finally find Lenz Schmitt's son, I'd discover a man too afraid of his own shadow to even hear his father's last words?"

A hundred different retorts jostled in Henry's mind but they all vanished when Andeal finished his rant. He put down the cucumber slice he was about to eat.

"Last words?"

"He's dead, Henry. Shot down by Union soldiers."

Shot.

Every bit of information Andeal let slip about his father made it sound as though he was part of something complicated and scary—as though he'd been more than a grief-ridden shopkeeper who'd run away. Part of him wanted to ask about it, to know what Andeal meant by 'living hell' and how his father had wound up in a cell. What if there was more to this story? Maybe he'd done it *for* Henry, or for his mom, and there was a way to explain everything. But how could anything justify disappearing without a single word? With nothing but that enraging note? No. Henry didn't owe it to his father to get involved. He refused to stir that hornet's nest. The last few days had filled his adventure quota for years.

"I'm sorry to hear that. I'll add a symbolic grave next to my mother's, that way he will have visited it at least once."

Andeal's expression morphed into one of disgust. He put his gloves back on with angry, jerky movements.

"Your father was a hero. It kills me to see his son is a spineless coward."

Henry tapped on the counter with his index finger. Guilt had worked up a large lump in his throat. He was being a horrible son, but then again, Lenz Schmitt had never been a great father either. He had abandoned him. This, Henry repeated to himself, was a fitting end to their relationship. So why did his eyes always return to the rag?

As Andeal pulled his hood back up, the squeal of tires traveled down the slope from Ferrea. Henry's stomach clenched. He had expected that sound for two days and knew right away what it was.

"Union soldiers." Andeal grabbed his forearm. "Please come with me. Giving me this message is almost the last thing your father did. I protected it and I can protect you, too."

Henry tore his gaze from his windows and the sound of impending doom. "And leave Ferrea?"

"You can stay and tell them what you know and pray they believe you're innocent, if you prefer." A tight fear was growing in Andeal's voice, as though the very idea scared him. "I wouldn't. When they cuffed me I vanished from existence for two horrible years. I'm not waiting around for it to happen again."

Vanishing didn't sound like any fun to Henry. Even less than leaving Ferrea.

"Okay. Okay."

He said the second 'okay' more forcefully, to give himself the courage to move. While Andeal shoved the pistol, the rag with his father's message, and his family portrait in a sack, Henry hurried to get a change of clothes. He grabbed whatever he could, threw it inside on top of everything else, then muttered a third "Okay". They slipped through the back door as tires screeched to a halt in front of Henry's house.

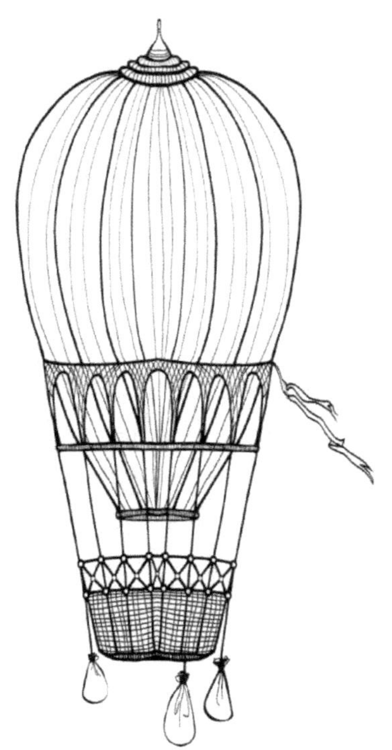

# CHAPTER FIVE

 the rough trunk of a birch tree and slid to the ground. The past hours had brought the discovery of new muscles in his legs. His soles burned and his mouth had turned drier than Ferrea's streets after a month of harsh sun. Every new step increased his hatred of walking. Too much of it packed in a single day. He refused to go on.

"Tired?" Andeal stood over him. His breath was a little short, but he showed no other signs of fatigue. He smirked as Henry fought to calm his panicking heart.

"You said we didn't have far to go!"

Once they were certain there was no pursuit, Andeal had let him sleep as best as he could on the hard ground. They had set off again in the morning, Henry grumbling while his strange companion walked with a new skip to his steps. He had assured Henry it wasn't a long walk.

"Indeed. We're already halfway there," Andeal said.

"Only halfway?"

Henry groaned. He would not stand and continue now. How could Andeal not tire? Did he train for hours every day? This hike through the forest was torture. Henry had to delay their next departure. Even if it meant breaking the avoid-all-serious-topics truce he'd established with Andeal since they'd fled. Henry picked the only thing he could think of that did not concern his father.

"How can you be friends with Seraphin? They accused him of murder on the radio. Vermen said the same, too."

"I don't approve of what he did and Seraphin knows it." Andeal let his pack slide to the ground. A good sign. "Family and ancestors are everything to Regarians, however. I understand why he'd go after the man who exterminated his."

Henry had no desire to know the story. The hatred between the two men had shaken his household once and that was more than enough. Learning more might help him avoid sinking in deeper into this mess, however.

"I told you about what happened in my house," he said. "Won't you trade that for their tale?"

"No. I tricked you into giving me that information. Besides, you were there to witness. I didn't know Seraphin when he shot Vermen's brother. It's not my place to talk about it."

"At least I know he shot him," Henry muttered. "Anything else interesting you'd care to share?"

"I'd tell you how I met your father, but you don't want to know."

Henry ignored the reproachful tone and raked his brain for another topic to keep them busy. One look at Andeal offered an obvious idea.

"Why are you blue?" he asked.

Instead of answering, Andeal shuffled from one foot to the other. More than once, he opened his mouth to begin a sentence, only to close it a second later. Henry waited. He had all day.

"When I was a student at the Altaer University, Union soldiers arrested me for participating in a large protest that turned violent. They never released me." He paused, ran a hand through his blond hair. "Instead they brought us—that's how I met Maniel, my wife, and your father—to some kind of laboratory and experimented on us. Among other things, they put silver flakes in everything I drank. Maniel is convinced that's how my skin turned blue."

Fight as he might against it, Henry could not dismiss the information about Lenz. "So my father's skin..."

"No. Just me."

They fell into an uneasy silence. Andeal wrung his hands together and Henry felt bad for pushing the topic. The haunted expression on his companion's face said more than words could. He ought to distract him.

"Do you have water?"

"Always."

Andeal rummaged through his pack, brought a large bottle out, and threw it his way. Henry caught it, pulled the stopper out and drank. The water refreshed his parched mouth. He savored the moment and forgot his hurting feet.

"If you want a break, you could just say so."

"I'd sleep here and never move again if you let me."

"Ten minutes, then?" Andeal asked.

Henry agreed and stretched his legs forward. Tree trunks turned out to be more comfortable than expected. He closed his eyes and let himself relax. They'd walked south for hours, into the thick forest and straight toward Mount Kairn. Andeal avoided the road but never once stopped to decide which path to follow. They snaked between the trees, following a trail only his guide could see.

No matter how often he asked, Andeal kept mute about their final destination. No village decorated the slopes of Mount Kairn. Nothing but trees and the murderous trail used every year in the Race. Where was the man leading him?

"Ready to start again?" Andeal asked.

"So soon?"

His companion laughed and sprang to his feet. "I'm afraid so. Come on, we've got to be there before sunset."

Henry grumbled but struggled to his feet nonetheless. His aches returned with the first step but he kept going. Andeal had promised a comfortable bed and a warm supper. He'd endure four more hours of torture for it. He had little choice: returning to Ferrea implied the same effort but in the other direction.

They advanced into the thickest area of the forest. Pine trees closed around him. Their branches reached for his face and clawed at his shirt while the sprawling roots hidden by the thick undergrowth threatened to trip him. Henry struggled with every step and swatted at the mosquitoes that buzzed around his head.

Pine needles obscured the sun's ray, but Andeal's shape remained visible in the dim light. He moved with ease, unbothered by insects or plants.

Henry worked hard to keep the pace. His guide stopped when he fell too far behind. The road's increasing difficulty pushed Henry's mind into escaping the suffocating trees by recreating his father's mysterious life.

Lenz Schmitt had loved the open skies and entrusted his faith to the changing winds. How had he fared locked up in a cell? How long had he spent there? Henry tried to find comfort in the idea that, without the imprisonment, he would have given his son more than radio silence. Perhaps he'd even have returned home. The message might say. The thought gave him hope and when the ground began a steady upward slope, Henry attacked it with renewed strength. The space between the trees increased and their progress sped. Andeal led him to a stream bouncing its way downhill and followed it up. A quick look through the foliage confirmed Henry's suspicions. They headed straight for Mount Kairn's peak.

What could it mean? They had nowhere to live there. As he raked his head for an answer, the stream's steady run turned into a low rumble. Henry identified the landmark right away: the Delgian's Fall. They'd gone around the mountain and now traveled along its southern flank. With a good vantage point they'd be able to peer into Burgian territory and follow the Delgian's course—a splendid view Henry rarely enjoyed. The majestic waterfall inspired many artists but it was too far from his house. He'd admired it once, from the basket of his father's balloon.

Never by foot. Never from so close.

Amazement gripped his heart as he emerged from the forest. A monster of water roared in front of him. The strong current tumbled down the cliff and crashed into a great white mist. The setting sun cast a red light on the scene. Henry stopped walking, stopped breathing. He couldn't tear his gaze away.

"Home sweet home," Andeal said.

"You're blue, not a fish. Nobody lives on Mount Kairn."

"True enough. About twenty of us live *inside* it."

Andeal patted Henry's back and strolled closer to the large pool at the waterfall's foot. He followed its edge to the cliff's face as Henry remained rooted, grounded by awe. Only when his guide called did he move with a start. He joined Andeal in front of a strange dent in the rock, invisible from farther away. It led into an imperceptible crevice and a set of carved stairs.

"Hurry up," Andeal said. "We might be late for dinner."

Best incentive ever. Henry ignored his companion's warning about slippery rock and climbed the steps two by two, hands on the stone wall to keep from stumbling. His empty belly ushered him into a newer, stranger life.

Despite Andeal's words, Henry didn't believe anyone lived under Mount Kairn until he reached the entrance and saw the string of white globes that lit the way. They followed a corridor and plunged deep into the mountain. A simple guide into the heart of a strange man's home. Henry glanced back at Andeal. His father's friend was beaming at him, like a child barely containing his thrill. The enthusiasm he'd restrained ever since their fight put Henry ill at ease. Why was he so happy to have him? If Andeal expected great things out of him he would be, once again, sorely disappointed.

"Great lights," Henry said, desperate to break the silence. "You said something about dinner?"

"I did! Right this way." Andeal motioned down the corridor and took the lead. "My wife will be waiting for us."

As they followed the string of lights, Andeal explained how solar panels stolen from the rooftops of an abandoned house were hidden on the mountaintop and now powered the rebels' entire network. Henry tried to follow the details of their setup but the circuit was far too complicated for him. He was too exhausted and hungry to bother anyway.

"How did you learn all that?" he asked to interrupt the lesson. "On a good day I can barely change a light bulb!"

Andeal laughed. "I used to study electrical engineering in Altaer. We're here."

Henry went through an arched passage and into a far larger cavern. Enormous stalactites hung from the high ceiling, occasionally connecting to equally big stalagmites. Henry stretched his arms out as they walked past one to compare the width, drawing a chuckle from his guide. The stalagmite's base was without a doubt larger than the span of his arms.

In the cavern, Andeal's lamps climbed higher, hanging between the rocky growths and shedding their pale lights on several tables. A handful of men and women sat at these, chatting while they gathered empty plates. Henry's stomach tightened. Had they missed dinner? He could still smell cooked fish and garlic so it couldn't have been long ago. Just as he turned to ask, Andeal waved at someone, grabbed Henry's wrist, and pulled him along.

They headed toward a smaller table, set apart from the others by a somewhat less-imposing stalagmite that created a deep alcove and offered some privacy. A tall woman leaned against the rock formation, her dark eyes following their progress through the dining area. Her natural hair hung loose on her shoulders, thick and frizzy, and she waited with her arms crossed. The sky-blue robes contrasted with her dark skin.

"We're home, sweetheart," Andeal said.

"You're late."

The corners of her lips curved upward, as though she was trying to suppress a full smile. When Andeal's shoulders slumped, she laughed, and her deep voice echoed off the walls. Henry found himself smiling, too. There was something reliable and welcoming about her. His house had been ransacked by soldiers, his peaceful life might be gone forever, but her laughter made him feel better. Safer.

"I'll forgive you this time," she teased. "You brought back an honored guest, after all."

"Honored?" Henry didn't like the sound of that. What could his father have done to deserve this much respect? The man couldn't even control his grief enough to stay with his son! "I'm here because I didn't have a choice."

Her thin eyebrows arched at his answer. "Did my husband capture you? I'm good with rescues from evil monsters, if you're in need."

There was an edge to her voice when she said 'monster'. Henry thought of the blue skin, of how terrified he had been at first. Better not tell her he'd shot Andeal. He lowered his gaze, his cheeks flushing with shame.

"It's all right, Maniel," Andeal said. Henry couldn't help but feel this was also addressed to him. "Union soldiers arrived. We fled before they could spot us."

There was a tense silence and Henry glanced up, confused by it. Maniel studied her husband with such intensity Henry felt compelled to look away. Yet Andeal held on, his gaze unflinching.

"Are you certain they didn't see you?" Maniel asked, her voice subdued.

"Yes."

"And you left no tracks? They can't—"

"We're fine." Andeal put a hand on her arm and squeezed. "We're safe. They're not coming for us."

She closed her eyes, took a deep breath, nodded. "That was close." Her gaze turned to Henry and her smile returned. Her anxiety from a moment ago had vanished. "But I imagine if Andeal hadn't gone, they would have you now. It's good to know we could save Lenz's son. We owed him as much."

"Did you, by chance, owe him dinner?"

All this talk about horrible danger and owing his father unsettled his stomach. He had been promised a meal and the smell of fish still tickled his nostrils. While his reply confused Maniel, Andeal chuckled.

"We've been walking all day and I did say there'd be a meal," he explained. "To be honest, neither of us had much to eat since morning. There was no time for provisions at Henry's home."

"Well, aren't you lucky I thought to keep some safe? You two sit down while I go get it. You've done enough walking for the day."

They had done enough for a lifetime as far as Henry was concerned, so he collapsed into a chair with a huge sigh of relief. Andeal first caught his wife by the waist, stopping her as she tried to walk away.

"Nuh-uh," he said with a playful smile.

"Already desperate for more? You've barely been gone more than a day."

Despite her protest, Maniel was smiling and did nothing to escape his grasp.

"Too long." He pulled her a little closer. Henry felt like an intruder. "Besides," Andeal added, "I'm doing it for you. If you wait until I eat, I'll have garlic breath."

She laughed, but not for long. Andeal linked his hands behind her back while she settled one on his shoulder. Her loose hair slid forward and obscured part of her face as she bent to kiss him. Henry couldn't help but smile as they remained locked together. In a way, he envied the ease of their relationship and the obvious attraction between the two. It had never been that simple for him, that clear-cut. Tia had told him she was the same, that she'd never experienced sexual desire or attraction, and that seemed a good enough way to describe it to Henry. Andeal and Maniel made him wonder what it was like, though. And they made him glad that whatever would have happened to Andeal if they'd been caught hadn't come to pass. Maniel pulled away and pushed her hair back.

"You'll have to wait for more," she whispered. "I think we've made our guest wait long enough for his due."

Andeal allowed her to go with a reluctant pout. Henry watched her disappear with an excited smile. As heartwarming as their little reunion was, he could not remember being this hungry.

By the time dinner was over, a dull ache had settled in Henry's muscles and stiffened them. He'd let Maniel and Andeal hold most of the conversation, chipping in when asked direct questions or when the topic drifted too close to his father. He didn't want to think about him. Andeal had said Lenz Schmitt talked about him all the time, but that brought no joy to Henry. The man had still left. Henry had needed him more than ever but he'd vanished. Time had patched the grief but whenever the couple mentioned his father with fondness, Henry felt the cover tear away and the hurt return.

He wasn't ready for the message. He needed time to think, to rest, to let all of this sink in. Henry's world was unbalanced and he knew better than to take another step without first regaining his footing. Then, perhaps—if he felt like it—he could deal with his father's last words.

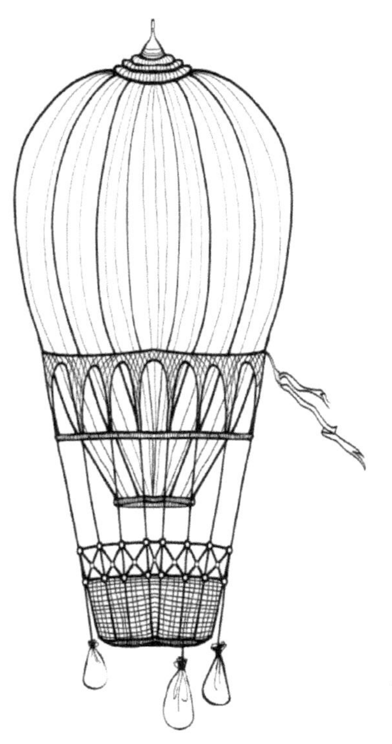

# CHAPTER SIX

*Henry's room in the rebels'* headquarters was a small, irregular cave with a thin bed, a single light, and a tiny wooden desk out of a classroom. The mattress was hard, but to his sore legs and back it was paradise. It took most of the first day for him to work up the courage to crawl out of bed. He moved to his pack, in which he had a change of clothes, and sat on the stone floor to rummage through it.

His fingers brushed against the solid frame of his family picture. He hesitated a moment, then took it out of the bag, set it on the desk, and detailed his father's expression. The man on this picture was free of worries. He smiled, eager to take off for the only flight he'd ever share with his son. That had been the best of their relationship. The only part that seemed to matter to Lenz Schmitt, really. Anger twisted Henry's stomach and he slammed the frame down, hiding the picture.

He reached into his bag again and this time his hand fell on a rough hilt. Henry froze as he recognised the string wrapped around it. Seraphin's *skeptar*. Perhaps he should make that today's mission: return the pistol and reward himself with a nice meal. Good plan, except for the walking element.

Henry was on his way within a few minutes, groaning with every step. He had to stop for directions once but as he approached the rebel leader's quarters, angry shouts guided him to a handcrafted wooden door. He stood engrossed on one side and eavesdropped as Andeal and Seraphin fought. The clash of their voices rattled his bones.

"How many paper trails will you require as proof, Andeal?" Fatigue and anger made Seraphin's voice taut, like it was about to break. "We've gone into every office owned by the Clarin twins we could find. We hid our goals well enough when we sabotaged their newspaper outlet last year, but it won't last. This chase is ridiculous. We already have what we need."

"Don't say it," warned Andeal.

There was a slight pause. Henry clung to the *skeptar*. He didn't know what Seraphin wasn't supposed to say, but he prayed the rebel leader wouldn't.

"You're living proof of what he did—of what he can do. The paper trail is useless, dangerous."

Andeal's sharp intake of breath told Henry this was exactly it. He leaned even closer to the door. Bad time to give the pistol back to its owner. Henry imagined himself barging in, their animosity all redirected toward him, the gut-crushing unease. He should leave. He didn't move.

"I'm not spending my life as the freak show we brandish as proof."

"Well I'm not spending mine as bait!" Seraphin's voice had flared but when he spoke again, it was so low Henry had to take another step closer to hear. "He had that barrel pressed to my forehead, Andeal. I thought I was dead."

In the following silence, Henry tried to convince himself not to eavesdrop any longer. He failed.

"The bait tactics are over anyway." Was that a hint of resentment in Andeal's tone? Henry wished he could see his expression! "No one but Captain Hans Vermen had that kind of obsession with you and he's here to stay."

"Are you mad at me? I didn't have a choice." Henry recalled the click of the gun as Seraphin had demanded rope from him. There had been so little emotion in his voice, it gave Henry shivers even today. "Would you rather I'd shot him?"

"No! I'm glad you brought him instead. It's just..."

"Look, I know you hate the idea, but we've been sitting ducks for too long. Sooner or later they'll find us, Andeal. We can't win this game of hide and seek."

"We'll have to." His anger had returned. Andeal had never been this defensive, not even about Henry's father. "This isn't a problem you solve by walking up to those responsible and putting a bullet through their brains."

Henry's breath caught in his throat. Wasn't that what the captain accused Seraphin of? He didn't need to be inside to feel the tension in the room. Andeal could not have picked a worse moment to add Henry's name to the conversation.

"I think Henry might help us. Lenz always seemed to know more than he told us. His son might have something."

*Him?* It took all of Henry's willpower not to burst through the door and deny all possible involvement in their mess. He knew nothing and he sure as heck didn't want to. Seraphin scoffed at the idea. At least someone else thought this was ridiculous.

"Schmitt is a soft cry baby. One threatening question from the authorities and he'll give us all away."

Henry's heart thundered and he stepped back, afraid they'd hear it. He didn't relish the thought of keeping Seraphin's *skeptar*, but it would be a thousand times better than to step in now. He turned around, intent on leaving before he heard the entire conversation about him.

"They would've had that chance had I not intervened," Andeal replied as Henry slipped farther away. "Give me one more month, Seraphin. If we have nothing good by then, I'll play your defaced monster to trap Clarin."

Andeal's voice grew louder, then the doorknob turned with a squeak. Henry spun back to face Seraphin's quarters. He didn't want them to think he was leaving and had heard everything. Andeal stopped in the entrance, his blue skin growing paler as he caught sight of their visitor. He licked his lips then crossed his arms.

"What are you doing here?"

Henry raised the *skeptar* and fumbled for words. Sweat made his palms slippery and he feared he'd drop the precious pistol. He shouldn't have stayed. Andeal understood the message despite Henry's inability to form a proper sentence and a weak smile drifted onto his face, gone as quickly as it'd come.

"You heard all that, didn't you?" he asked.

Henry's shoulders slumped and he lowered his arms. "I'm sorry, I—"

"No need to apologise." Andeal walked up to him. "Don't think you're not welcomed here. You are."

Henry swallowed hard. Andeal patted his shoulder and continued on his way with false serenity. He imbued every step with forced ease but even Henry could see through the lie. Awkward.

Seraphin cleared his throat from the doorway. Henry whirled around, startled. Had the rebel leader thinned or was it the light? His cheekbones seemed even more prominent now, yet the Regarian had shed all his fragility from first night. The cold gaze studied him, confident and unreadable.

"I'm here to bring your pistol back!"

Henry blurted the words and showed the *skeptar*. Stress shortened his breath and flushed his cheeks.

"Come in," Seraphin said as he stepped aside.

Henry rushed into the small bedroom. Inside was a single bed, a stylish glass desk covered in papers, and a scrapped wheeled chair. Rips in the padding were taped and the bed's sheets had been sewn and patched multiple times. The room's only luxury was a bright red rug in the middle.

"That's your room?" He'd expected more from a so-called rebel leader. Even his tiny room had neater furniture.

"It's all I need."

Seraphin leaned on his desk, hands on his thighs, a grim look on his face. When Henry drummed his fingers on the pistol's hilt, the Regarian cleared his throat and gave a pointed look at the firearm, causing his glasses to slide down his thin nose.

"Oh! Sorry."

Henry stepped forward, extended the *skeptar* and its holster, and tried to keep his hands steady as Seraphin took them. He tied the holster around his waist then wrapped his slender fingers around the pistol one by one, each whiter than the bone hilt. He lifted the weapon and caressed the red string. His lips curved into a smile and, eyes closed, he whispered a few words. A private conversation with his ancestors. Henry did not catch the words, for which he was thankful—intruding once today had been enough. He took a careful step backward.

"I thought you'd throw it away," Seraphin said. "Firearms are illegal."

Henry avoided the Regarian's gaze. "I did. I hid it in the soldier's car and pushed them away. Took me all day. A hot, sweaty day."

Seraphin studied him, serious and solemn. He wanted the rest of the story, which Henry was reluctant to give. No need to worsen the rebel leader's opinion of him. He shuffled on his feet.

"Why go back, then?" Seraphin asked.

Curse it, how could he evade direct questions? He'd never learned to lie or dodge. "I...I mistook Andeal for an assassin. Someone you'd sent after me. So I crawled back there to get the pistol and defend myself."

A smile cracked Seraphin's cold expression. The Regarian struggled to keep his calm.

"Don't laugh! I'd just heard you were accused of murder and Andeal was clad from head to toe in black! I was terrified, okay?"

Seraphin's mirth vanished at the mention of accusations against him. Henry cursed his tongue. Why did he always say the wrong thing? He tugged on his pants and readied for the inevitable storm. A dangerous glow lit in Seraphin's eyes.

"Don't believe all you hear on the radio."

"But it was true, wasn't it?"

His own aggressiveness surprised Henry. Seraphin's fingers clenched around the *skeptar's* hilt, but Henry refused to withdraw his words. What the announcer had said matched the Union captain's story. Pushing for the truth behind the little face-off at his house seemed the least of things. Without it, he'd still be living a tranquil life at his house in Ferrea. He'd have spent a peaceful night commemorating his mother's memory instead of chasing after his elusive father.

Seraphin returned the *skeptar* to its holster and his expression softened. "Don't let who I am influence your judgment of the others. They're good people."

No denial. No guilt. Henry tried to read something in the tired traits—a hint of regret, or even pride! Nothing. A shiver ran down his spine. How could anyone give murder so little care? It had to be a façade. Henry clasped his hands behind his back and cleared his throat. Perhaps Seraphin shared his unease, because he changed the subject.

"I thank you for my *skeptar*. Was there anything else you wanted?"

Sure. He wanted to hear the story behind Seraphin and Vermen. He wanted to know why anyone would treat his father like a hero and why he'd vanished. And maybe read that message. He wanted to know more about these hidden tunnels and stop feeling like a lost child. Yet he also wanted to run away before he became more involved, to return to Kinsi and apologise. Most of all he wanted to rewind time and rediscover the sweet tranquility of Ferrea while the town still lived.

His courage faltered before he asked any of this. Instead of the vital questions, he asked:

"Where's the kitchen?"

It drew a sympathetic smile from Seraphin. The Regarian gestured for Henry to follow. "You'll get used to the twisting tunnels."

Henry hoped he wouldn't stay long enough for that.

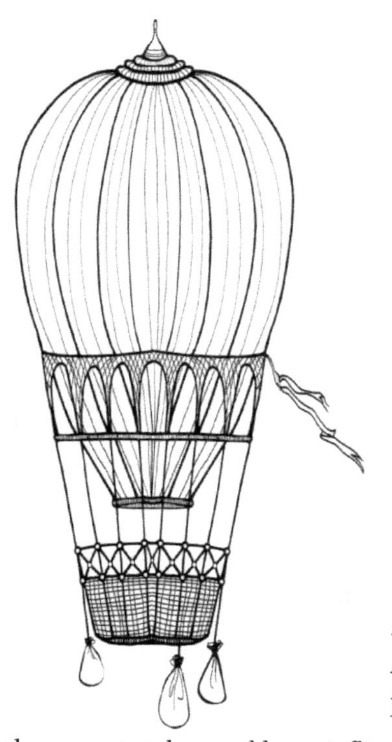

# CHAPTER SEVEN

 Andeal obtained his first reaction from Hans Vermen. He had decided from the very start he would not inflict on their prisoner what he had lived through. Every day he brought the captain his meal, and while the man ate, Andeal chatted. He talked about his parents and his time in Altaer, studying electrical engineering like his mom. He talked about Maniel, about the weather outside, or the most recent news on the National Radio. Anything. Vermen occasionally rewarded him with a nod or a snarky comment. He never engaged the discussion. After ten, thirty, sometimes sixty minutes, Andeal picked up the empty plate and left. Their forced guest might as well have been a statue.

Today Vermen gulped down his meal as though he hadn't eaten in days. He set the bowl down and laid back on his mattress. Andeal frowned but finished his account of the weather outside. Experience had taught him that when one lost track of time, sanity soon followed. He refused to keep a prisoner in conditions that'd risk driving him insane.

"Leave me alone," Vermen said the moment he fell silent. "I never asked for company."

"No need to ask to receive."

"What if I want to be rid of it?"

Andeal chuckled despite the captain's seriousness. "I cannot imagine why you'd want such a thing." Truth was, he could. A misguided sense of duty or a complete ignorance of what imprisonment was. Both, most likely. "If you're tired of my talking, you should consider participating in the conversations more."

Vermen didn't rise to the bait. He stared at him, lips sealed, until Andeal had enough. With an exasperated sigh, he rose, snatched the bowl, and made for the exit. Stupid stubborn captain. He'd erected a wall around himself and refused to let it down, not even for his own sake. Perhaps rotting in his cell for days would make him change his mind.

The bed creaked. A strong hand grabbed Andeal's shirt and jerked him. As the dish slipped from his grasp and crashed to the floor, Vermen stepped aside, pulled him back, and slammed him against the wall. The shock sent waves of pain up Andeal's spine and light flashed before his eyes. The captain's warm fingers wrapped in a tight grip around his throat. Well...at least he no longer squirmed at the thought of touching him?

"I've had enough of your game," Vermen said. "What do you expect? You think coming here and chatting will turn me into a traitor? I have vowed my life to protect and serve Ferrys. President Kurtmann put it—and all the United countries—back on their feet after the Plague. I am proud to defend the Union, like my brother before me, and I will not break my oath."

"No?" Andeal wriggled against the wall. His heart hammered against his chest. He could tell him the truth, that he was trying to make Vermen's stay bearable. But that wasn't all, and he'd at last made a dent in the fortress. He intended to push it. "Tell me, proud defender, why don't you kill me now and escape? Why did you leave your troops to go running after Seraphin?"

Vermen's grip faltered and Andeal gulped the welcome air. His shirt stuck to his arms and back from sweat. Perhaps provoking him wasn't the best idea. The man's eyes narrowed. He pressed his body closer.

"I asked permission. I am charged by General Clarin to hunt your lot down."

"I investigated. They called you a deserter." Anger flashed in the captain's eyes and he shoved him hard into the wall. Andeal gritted his teeth against the throbbing in his back but continued. "You disobeyed and risked your entire military career to kill Seraphin, yet you never shot him. What now? What is next for Captain Hans Vermen?"

His question went unanswered. Vermen let go, spun on his heels, and returned to the bed. A new mask hid his feelings. Andeal rubbed his neck. His words had hit a nerve. All he needed was to go just a bit further. He cleared his throat, hoping the captain would turn around and look at him. No such luck.

"If you had answers for this question, you would've tried to escape."

Andeal bent and picked up the dropped bowl. The leftover sauce had spilled into a lovely white pool. Vermen could clean with whatever he wanted if it bothered him. For now, Andeal left his unwilling guest to his thoughts.

It occurred to him this spat might fortify his resolve and hatred for the rebels. Andeal hoped this dangerous game would be worth it.

The message taunted him.

Henry had flattened the rag on his empty school desk, next to the face-down family picture. At this distance Henry could see brown scribbles in the familiar cursive of his father's handwriting but not read them. He wasn't sure he wanted to, either.

Henry had avoided reading it in his first few days. It could wait: he wouldn't leave until he was certain the soldiers were no longer in Ferrea. Instead he had rested his still-sore muscles and visited the dining area. The network of tunnels still confused him, but he had learned the path to the large cavern by heart. There always seemed to be a handful of rebels there— more at any given time than Ferrea's entire population. The population of four. If Paul, Kinsi and Tia hadn't left yet. The thought had dampened Henry's mood on his first visit. He'd sat alone at a table and watched as rebels played a game in which they threw tiny sacks of sand at a wooden board with holes of different sizes. The larger the hole, the fewer points it was worth. Cheers and taunts echoed off the stalactites with every throw.

After a while one of the rebels invited him to play. He had the angular nose and dark traits typical of Burgians, and an easy smile to go with them. The latter might've been inviting if not for his bright red hair. Henry had never left Ferrea in his life but even he knew that was how Burgians marked those they exiled for petty crimes. He'd refused. They had laughed and teased him for his obvious fear. The Burgian—his name was Joshua— repeated his offer on the second day, then the third, until Henry gave in and proved to them what a terrible shot he was.

Through all of this something nagged at his mind, however. Sometimes the rebels would discuss their operations. They would argue over which suppliers to see next, or how long it'd take Seraphin to finally execute Captain Vermen and whether or not they'd find the evidence they were looking for. Although mention of the cold execution sent a shiver down Henry's spine, it was the rare talk of evidence that bothered him. True, the rebels seemed more concerned by food supplies—which he approved of—and vengeance—which made him uncomfortable. But wasn't the paper trail their ultimate goal? He couldn't get Andeal's words out of his head. He had thought Henry might know something. He was wrong, but what if that something was in the message?

What if the very words sitting on his desk right now contained an answer to the rebels' problems?

Henry didn't know what to expect anymore. The man Andeal and Maniel spoke of was not the father he'd known. Would these words come from Lenz Schmitt the hero or Lenz Schmitt the deserter? Or better yet, would they be from the father? Henry briefly reached for the rag, then pulled back his trembling hand. Panic quickened his breath and drilled a hole in his stomach. Better not to hope for the father.

He cast a glance at the tiny, stifling room. Was it growing narrower? No. That was him. Henry forced himself to take deep breaths. He trailed his gaze along the contour of his desk, switching from inhaling to exhaling as he passed a corner. It worked better with rectangles such as doors, like Tia had taught him, but with time the void in his belly diminished. He continued until his hands no longer shook.

He could read this message. He had to. Eight years of false hopes and riddles were enough.

Before he took the plunge, he closed his eyes and offered a prayer to the winds. Let it be personal and meaningful. Let it justify the departure and mend his wounds. Let it answer his questions.

A strange calm settled over Henry Schmitt. His eyes fluttered open and he let his gaze find the first of his father's words.

*"Henry, if you have this I must be dead. I'm sorry I never came back. Now listen, you better have kept that balloon safe. Inside it a double pocket is sewn. You'll find a recording there, and important papers. Get the word out. This cannot be silenced.*

*Lenz."*

You'd better have kept that balloon safe. Henry reread the sentence, again and again, anger speeding his heart. *Keep the balloon's envelope safe.* Words scribbled on a memo, left in the dead of night as Lenz vanished from his life. And now, words written in blood on a scrap of cloth, crashing into him with more strength than the waterfall outside.

With a cry of rage, Henry threw the bloody message across his room and slammed his fist on the desk. What did he care about the balloon? He wanted *love*, not another ghost-given mission! He shouldn't have read it. Lenz had never cared about him.

He rose and his chair crashed to the ground. Fresh air. He needed fresh air, to help him think. He stumbled across the room. The cavern's walls closed upon him but he escaped through the door. As he exited, Henry smacked into Andeal.

"Henry! I was just coming to...what's wrong?"

"You were right. About the information." Henry's voice was rough. He strode back to the torn cloth on the ground, picked it up, and shoved it into Andeal's hand. "Here. Take it. Read it. In fact, why don't you follow his orders and accomplish his will? He'd love it, I'm sure!"

"Henry..." The engineer did not look down or close his fingers around the rag. His blue eyes were filled with worry.

"No, it's fine, really. I'm only good at eating noodles and being a coward. You can be his son. I'm tired of it."

Henry pushed past him to the exit, even though he had no idea where to go. Anything was better than here. Andeal called after him but Henry refused to slow. What a great idea he'd had! Lenz Schmitt had sacrificed himself for Andeal and Maniel, so why didn't these two finish his dirty work? They were capable, courageous, willing. Perfect candidates.

And while they spread the word about whatever was in that balloon, he could build the tranquil life he deserved.

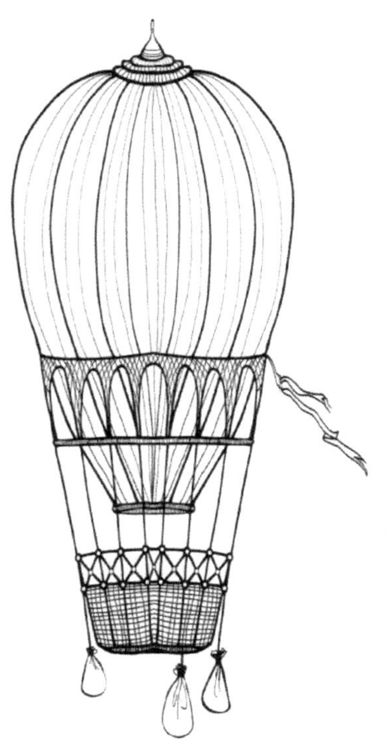

# CHAPTER EIGHT

 still hadn't attempted an escape. Was Andeal right? Did it prove he could not decide where to go, or who he was? Nonsense. He was Captain Hans Vermen, proud defender of his country...and a deserter? He rubbed his arm, as though he could remove an invisible layer of dirt. Andeal must be lying. They had said no such things. Lungvist would've told them it was impossible, he would not desert. If he returned now, would they give him a chance to explain? He'd gathered more information on the rebels by following Seraphin than anybody in years. It had to count for something. If he could escape, they would crush the ragtag band and end this ridiculous threat. If he could escape.

Andeal had implied it wouldn't be so hard. And the longer he waited, the less suspicious they'd become. He could stay, observe, gather information.

Stall.

He had their location. What else did he really need?

Vermen straightened up and slid off his tiny mattress. He could not remain here another minute. He had a rebellion to squash and a reputation to retrieve. The captain stretched his muscles and approached the door. He reached for the handle but as his fingers closed around the wood, the chain outside rattled. Vermen's heart jumped and he backpedalled as the door opened.

Andeal's wife stood in the opening with his meal. Although he had never met her, half of his blue companion's chatter was about his oh-so-wonderful wife and he had no trouble identifying Maniel. Her dark skin had no hint of blue in it. Nothing strange in her dark hair's long braid either. She wore a dark orange robe, black leggings, and knee-high boots. He could not find a single unnatural thing about her. Somehow, he had expected her to be just as weird as Andeal. Vermen averted his eyes, ashamed of his ridiculous assumption.

She stared at him until he stepped further back, then set the plate on his desk. Did not say a word as she turned back to the door. Vermen's heart pumped faster. No. She couldn't leave him like that. He hadn't had any news in the last...three days? He wasn't even certain of that anymore. He closed the distance between them and grabbed her forearm.

"Wait!"

She turned around in slow, uncaring movement. Her high cheeks and thin smile formed a perfect mask of disdain.

"Yes?"

"Where's Andeal?" His voice shook. He cursed himself and wrestled control over it. "Did something happen?"

"No, nothing." Maniel lowered her gaze to his hand and he let go. She brushed her arm off before crossing them. "Except for the part where you bruised his entire back and left clear strangle marks on his neck. He will not return if I can help it."

Vermen's stomach tightened but he refused to let it show. He lifted his chin in defiance. It was for the best, really. Until now he hadn't realised how much he relied on Andeal to keep track of time and entertain himself. He needed to find another way, to depend only on himself. Maniel continued with a resolute calm that clashed with Andeal's mirth.

"If it were up to me, you would be in a small and cold cave. Alone."

"Well, we don't always get what we want."

"I haven't tried yet, captain. Do you wish me to?"

Their gazes locked and he held her stare. Did he want to be transferred to another room and forgotten? Without Andeal's timely visits, his thoughts whirled down the same spiral every day. He would think of his brother, of all they'd shared. He'd remember his abrupt death and the swirling anger when he'd learned the perpetrator had escaped. All these years he'd dogged Holt, coining the term "White Renegade", unraveling their plots, capturing rebels, trying to worm his way up to him. He'd had him, at last. Always, he came back to that last confrontation with the Regarian. To his failing courage, his inability to avenge his brother. A flush crept up his cheeks and he lowered his eyes.

"I don't know."

He regretted the admission the moment it escaped his lips. It shouldn't matter where he was held. He'd escape, return to the Union army, and give them the hideout's location. What difference would Andeal's visits make? When the troops arrived, he'd be caught with the rest of the bandits. Better not to get too attached. Vermen's fingers played with the fabric of his pants but he tried not to show his discomfort. Maniel tilted her head to the side.

"Interesting. Too bad we don't always get what we want."

She gave him a sweet smile and waved as she left. Vermen stood, speechless, as the door closed and the clanking chain was put back in place.

Andeal sat at his large angled desk, studying the blueprints before him for the hundredth time. A single mistake would mean a crashing death for the first rebels to use his machine and no matter how often he verified his math, terrible nightmares haunted him. What if the helium didn't suffice? What if the propeller was too heavy? What if Lenz Schmitt's idea was unworkable?

He had to admit, however, that he would not catch any flaws today. He spent more time staring at the smooth cavern wall than at the numbers. His mind was elsewhere, with the strange prisoner he'd wanted Maniel to meet. She had to see for herself how different he was from what they'd imagined. Andeal wondered what could take her so long, why she had not returned an hour ago, as expected. Could they really have talked that long?

Heavy strides from the corridor warned him of her return. She slapped her feet on the ground with too much zeal. Not a good sign in his experience. Andeal leaned in his rotating chair and turned toward the bedroom's door.

Maniel flung it open as she entered and smashed it closed even harder. He set his pencil down and rose from the desk.

"He is the most arrogant, prideful jerk I have ever met—and I spend my days around Stern! How you can stay hours in there is beyond me."

Andeal strode across the room and wrapped his arms around his wife.

Her immense frustration could mean but one thing. "So you talked with him."

"I—" She pushed him back. "Curse you, Andeal. Yes, I talked with him and I didn't like it."

"Do tell. You said you'd put the food down and leave."

Maniel's eyes narrowed. She knew him, knew what he wanted to hear.

"I tried, but he held me back. He grabbed my wrist and asked about you."

"I knew it!" His heart soared. He'd worried about how Vermen would react to their last fight—that if Andeal pushed too hard, the captain would push back and his allegiance to the army would grow deeper. "I told you, Maniel. He's not a brainwashed idiot."

"He looks every bit like one." She moved to the desk's chair but did not sit, staring at his blueprints instead. "But he's not. Which means he's more dangerous than you think, not that he's a friend."

"He could be. He must be."

Her hand tightened around the armchair and she turned around, rage lighting her dark eyes. "Must be?"

"Yes." Andeal wiped his palms on his pants. At first it had only been his instincts talking but now he had a practical reason. Lenz Schmitt's message was clear: there was a recording sewn into the balloon envelope. It had to be about Galen Clarin, which meant they might at last leave Mount Kairn to expose the horrible scientist. "We might be on our way soon. Would you leave him behind, locked up?"

Maniel's jaw tightened and she closed the gap between them in one deliberate stride. Andeal's heart squeezed tight. With Maniel, you knew you'd crossed a line when she contained her fury into a calm, unwavering anger.

"We are not talking about a generic soldier. This is Captain Hans Vermen. Is there a single season since we've known Seraphin when we haven't heard his name? When we haven't learned the danger of underestimating him? He short-circuited half of our operations, can be blamed for all of our deaths. Must I name them, Andeal?" Her face came inches from his and she looked down. Her slender finger tapped his chest with every name she gave. "Erika. Desmond. Andeal. Jus—"

"Stop!" He grabbed her hand and lowered it. His voice shook. "I know them as well as you do. But they knew the risks, and if Hans wasn't behind our losses, someone else would be. Maniel, we're talking about imprisoning someone for an indefinite amount of time. Is that what you want? Have you forgotten?"

Maniel stepped back with a sharp intake of breath. She looked like she'd been slapped and Andeal regretted his words. Of course she hadn't forgotten. He reached for her shoulder, softly, and his voice fell to a whisper.

"I refuse to inflict that on *anyone*. Not even Hans Vermen."

"He'll betray you. Don't fool yourself, Andeal. He is a Union officer and your kindness won't change that. When given the choice, he will abandon you."

"He didn't shoot Seraphin. That has to count for something."

She studied him in silence, worry battling anger in her gaze. Try as he might, it was hard to dismiss Maniel's assessment. Was she right? Would his trust in Vermen be disregarded on the first occasion? Could he risk the entire rebel encampment because of the persistent voice in his head, telling him he was worth the risk?

"I'll be careful," he said.

A bitter smile curled her thin lips. "You never are."

Andeal chuckled and smiled back. "True. Once we retrieve the envelope, though, things might start moving faster. I don't want a prisoner while we go after the Clarins."

"You can't decide if he's trustworthy by yourself. We'll cross that bridge when we get to it. With Seraphin." Maniel had added just a bit of weight to her tone as she mentioned their Regarian friend. She knew they'd fought. They probably would again. Andeal ground his teeth together and let her go on.

"Any news from Henry?"

This time his shoulders slumped. He moved to their two-seater and let himself fall into the cushion with a sigh. "He wants to leave. I tried holding him back but nothing I say will change his mind."

Maniel settled next to him and slid her fingers in his. "You can't force him, Andeal."

"But it's so wrong!" He pulled his wife closer, then started playing with the leather band on his ring finger. "He's bitter, I get it, but Lenz is his father and Henry being a part of our fight was his last wish. If I had any news from *my* parents, I'd be overjoyed!"

"They didn't leave you." Maniel was running a hand back and forth through his hair. He let the feeling of her slender fingers brushing against his scalp calm him and closed his eyes to focus on them and her voice. "Nothing excuses abandoning Henry the way Lenz did. He has a right to be angry."

"So what do we do?"

"Let him go." He tensed at her words and she chuckled. She must have expected this reaction and went on with barely a pause. "Before he leaves, however...I think he ought to know more. Even if he never forgives him, he should learn what kind of man his father really was. You should show him Lenz Schmitt's legacy."

Andeal's eyes flew open. She could only mean one thing by that. He turned to face her, a childish grin stretching his lips.

"The Lenz Balloon?"

Her soft laugh was music to his ears. "Of course, the Lenz Balloon. If you hadn't been so obsessed with that captain, you would've shown him ages ago."

A pang of guilt mitigated Andeal's enthusiasm. She was right, he'd spent a lot of time with Hans. In a way, the gruff captain was easier to deal with.

"He'll love it," Andeal said. "He has to."

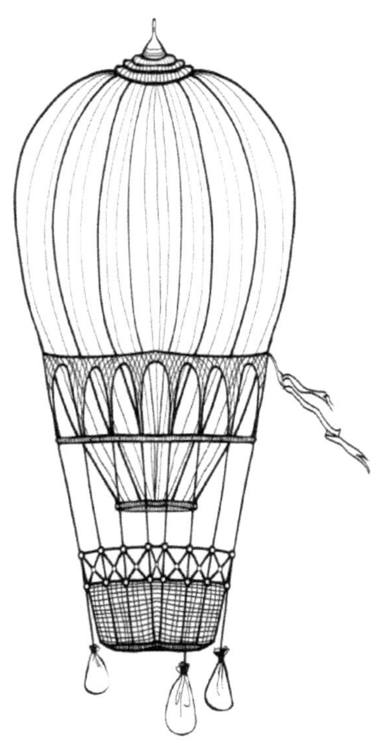

# CHAPTER NINE

 cards, desperate to find a brilliant solution and trump Joshua's great move. He tapped on the table with his fingers to vent his building frustration. What could he do without any faces? He was beaten. Again. Perhaps if he tried a hundredth time, he'd finally beat Joshua! Not today, though. He dropped his cards on the table and raised his hands in defeat.

"Okay, you win! I give up."

Joshua chuckled and gathered the spread cards. "So soon?"

Henry crossed his arms. If the redheaded Burgian wanted to be cheeky, fine, but he'd have no help storing the deck. The other rebels cast them sidelong glances and shook their heads. None of them played with Joshua anymore. They'd learned with time that they couldn't beat the man and preferred games of skill to a game of cards. That was why the sandbag game was so popular. At least they stood a chance there.

Losing didn't bother Henry, though. He was used to it. Paul and Kinsi had the upper hand in most of their Wednesday night games. Henry played for the company and when it came to talking, Joshua was hard to beat too. He'd been strangely serious and silent today, however.

"Something on your mind?" Henry asked. "By now, you should be all over your genius strategy."

"I heard you were leaving us."

"Oh." Henry squirmed on his wooden stool. "Yeah. There's nothing for me here."

He'd decided to leave while crouched in the rebels' kitchens, munching on a bowl of noodles he'd miraculously found behind a pile of rice bags and cans. He'd return to Ferrea, gather what little the army had left, and head for Reverence. The hike terrified him but he still had most of Seraphin's sixty bucks and once he reached a bigger town, he might manage to hitch a ride to the capital. He'd figure it out. Anything was better than staying in these underground tunnels. Nothing moved here. No leaves danced in the wind's caress, no animals scurried away at your passage, no birds plagued your morning sleep with their songs. Only the occasional snippets of conversation and the flickering of the large electric lights brought a semblance of life to this place.

"You'll be missed, y'know." Joshua tapped the deck of cards on the table to align them into a neat pile. "I hadn't played that game in ages. The others avoid it all the time."

"I noticed. You should've let them win every now and then."

"No way!" His eyebrows shot up and he wiggled his finger at him. "A win's worth nothing if you didn't earn it for yourself. The Lady Luck watches over all, but it's up to you to work with what she gives."

Henry shrugged. The Burgian goddess lacked an eye for fairness, if you asked him. She'd given it all to a few men and left the others to struggle. Joshua didn't seem to mind, even though his red hair proved he'd seen his share of troubles. He wondered what the man had done to be branded by his kin. Not to mention why he'd never shaved or hidden the clear mark of disgrace. Henry rubbed the bridge of his nose. How had he wound up hiding under Mount Kairn with criminals?

"Can't you be convinced to stay?" Joshua asked. "We need all the men we can get."

It warmed his heart to know others wanted him here, but he shook his head. "I'm not a hero. Or a rebel or whatever you want to call it. I wanted to hear my father's last words and as it happens they weren't really addressed to his son. It's safe home now, so I'm leaving."

"You think I'm a hero?" His mirth started as a low chuckle but the more he considered the thought, the harder Joshua laughed. Henry bided his time until Joshua wiped the tears from his eyes and became serious once more. "Look around you, Henry. Most of us are petty criminals, men and women down on their luck. We sought shelter and something to eat. But we shared our stories with others, and Andeal told us what the Clarin brothers had done to him, what they might've done for the Union and we thought 'man, there's something wrong with this.' Some are used to lying, thieving, risking, but most had never held a firearm in their life. We didn't stay because we had the skill set. No one's a hero. Why should you be?"

"I don't want to be a part of this. I can't lie, risks scare me, and if the winds are willing, I'll never hold another pistol in my life. Peace and quiet are all I'm asking for. I won't have them here."

Joshua snorted. The words peace and quiet had brought a slight sneer to his expression. He stored his deck of cards. "Fine then. Go back to the ignorant flock. Wait, see, do nothing."

His sudden contempt surprised Henry. Joshua might not understand, but the flock was exactly his goal. He clenched his teeth and ignored the insult.

"I will."

"When?"

Henry opened his mouth to answer but realised he had none to give. He thought a lot of leaving but had yet to make a decision about the date. In truth, he'd yet to do anything about it. Joshua must've guessed because his smile returned.

"Looks like I have a few games left with you."

Not wanting to confirm or deny his deduction, Henry changed the topic. "You never told me *your* story. How did you get branded? Cheated at cards?"

"I stuck it where I shouldn't have." He leaned back, his hands behind his head. "Love, my friend, will get you in trouble faster than anything else."

"Love isn't a crime among Burgian tribes. Neither is sex, as far as I know."

"Oh, it all depends what kind of sex and with whom. My people were not keen on man-on-man action, even less so when it came to the chief's son." An amused smile drifted across Joshua's lips, as though his entire exile was a joke. "It's all good, though. Seraphin more than made up for the trouble."

His tone implied a lot more than shelter, food, and friends. Joshua seemed about to add to the story when his gaze caught something behind Henry and followed it. He leaned forward and whispered. "I think I'm not the only one who'd rather see you stay."

Henry spun on his chair. Andeal had just entered the mess hall and made a beeline for him. Would he ever let it go? Every day since he'd read the bloodied letter, Andeal sought him out and tried to change his mind. He seemed in a great mood this time and arrived with a confident smile. Henry cut to the chase.

"I said no. I leave tomorrow."

Joshua's eyebrows shot up. Andeal frowned but if he was surprised, he didn't let it show.

"Good thing I found you, then! There's one last thing I have to show you."

His cheerful tone rattled Henry's nerves. Someone needed to learn what 'no' meant. He remained firmly seated. "What if I'd rather play another game with Joshua?"

A mistake. Joshua stood, raising both of his hands, then stepped back. "Sorry mate. I was on my way to the kitchens. A hero's got to eat, y'know."

He winked at Henry, who held back a curse. His friend's quick departure left him alone with Andeal, with no excuses not to follow the engineer. Joshua's desire to see him stay must be strong if the hardcore player was willing to skip a game like this. Henry sighed.

"You could show me a warehouse full of instant noodles and I'd still be leaving."

"And I'll help you with the planning if you want. I'm not here to hold you back, not anymore. I just have this pet project I want to share with you before you go. I think you'll love it!"

His enthusiasm intrigued Henry. Although suspicious of Andeal's sudden acceptance, he rose and agreed to go with him. After all, he could always leave if this week's routine started once more. Andeal led him out of the mess hall, but to Henry's surprise, he did not head to his room. The engineer took tunnels Henry had not explored before, and when asked what their final destination was, he responded with a mysterious smile. They climbed inside the mountain and his curiosity grew as they gained in height. Why were they going up? A familiar flutter in his stomach reminded him of the excitement when the Annual Race's goodies arrived at the shop. Opening the crates was like receiving a gift. Half the fun came from the built-up anticipation and guessing, and Henry had cherished the ritual for as long as he remembered. Even before the Plague, Lenz had allowed him to look into the boxes first.

Henry pushed the thought away. Better not to think of his father now; it'd ruin his mood. Besides, Andeal had reached a large opening, behind which the electric lights seemed dimmer. He hurried to catch up.

Henry stopped as he caught sight of the cavern behind Andeal. The ceiling extended high above their heads to a neck-breaking height and the lamps lined along the wide, irregular walls did not suffice to reveal its details. Shadows hid the relief, leaving Henry standing under a dark void. He tore his gaze away. The breathtaking dimensions of the room could not retain his interest for long.

Not with the strangest hot air balloon basket he'd ever seen standing in the middle.

Although Henry Schmitt recognised it for what it was, several major changes disturbed him. It hung in the middle of the room on a construction scaffold, set in a long wooden ramp that headed straight into a sideways tunnel. Wheels under the basket allowed it to roll along the small slope if pushed, its direction controlled by the linear construction. Worst of all, however, was the large plastic propeller under it. The flat blades ran the length of the basket and while the sight was impressive, their usefulness was doubtful. The added weight would only complicate the flight.

"You can't take off with a propeller," he said.

"It's not for take-off, silly. It's for direction."

Without waiting for an answer, Andeal grabbed his wrist and dragged him into the room. A few rebels worked on the railing, near the tunnel entrance. Their voices bounced off the cavern walls, distorted in the echo. Like ghosts in an empty space. Henry shivered and tried to ignore the disturbing sound. He focused his energy on the decrepit table next to the basket.

Complicated plans had been taped to the musty surface. Although Henry made out the balloon's general scheme right away, he took some time to disentangle the mess of lines and notes. Andeal had drawn the propeller on the side here and when Henry studied its support, he realized it was connected to a lever inside the basket. He lifted his head but could not see. Without a word he left the plans, climbed upon a small stool, then heaved himself into the balloon.

The large lever inside was built from the same material as the propeller. Henry tapped it; it rang hollow. Good. Less added weight. He grabbed it and pulled. The large blades underneath creaked, but he lacked the strength to move them with one hand. When Henry put both arms to work, however, they shifted, heading for the side of the balloon. The scaffold soon interrupted their movement. At his feet lay a small battery and flexible green solar tissue. More than enough to power the propeller. How often had his father complained the wind direction stopped him from flying around Mount Kairn? Henry couldn't help but smile.

"It was his idea, you know," Andeal said from the ground. "I did the math and the plans, but he imagined it."

"I'm not surprised." His smile vanished and he ran his hand along the inside. He'd always loved the stringy texture and strange relief. Nobody flew balloons anymore. They demanded gas and it'd almost all been wiped out in the Last Drop War. His father had used the last of his stock to fly him, just once. Then the Threstle Plague arrived and all air traffic was shut down except for the army's war zeppelins.

"Why a balloon? You can't fly it. You have no gas and no envelope!"

"We stole gas years ago. We wanted to finance our activities with it but never found a safe buyer. Those cans brought us the first of the Union's attention. Then Stern deserted and brought us some of General Omar Clarin's confidential correspondence and they set Vermen after us."

"Great, so you can take off if you find an envelope." Henry ignored all the information about their illegal activities. "You'll still be spotted and reported within the hour."

"Doubtful." Andeal strode to the stool and climbed into the balloon with practiced ease. "Gas is a luxury these days. You've got to have a few thousand to waste to acquire any and the rare hot air balloon that takes off is to satisfy a man's longing for an old-fashioned pleasure flight. Would you see a balloon and think it's controlled by an underground group of outlaws? Or is it much more likely someone earning twenty times your salary is enjoying himself up there? I guarantee you that until the Union learns we built this and demand it to be reported, no one will think twice about us."

He might be right, but it seemed a dangerous gamble to Henry. Propeller or not, hot air balloons were slow and easy targets. If they sent zeppelins after the rebels, they would not stand a chance. Not his problem. The rebels could take all the risks they wanted, he would not be there to suffer from it.

"I don't want to know what you plan to do with this." He gave a slight kick to the inside, then set his hands on the railing and passed one leg over it.

"We'd have been happy to have you fly us across Union territory if you weren't leaving tomorrow. I guess I'll have to, then."

Henry stopped. After his first flight, he'd begged his father to teach him. Somehow, he promised, he'd make a job out of it. Fly for those with money or in zeppelins. He couldn't imagine staying grounded all his life after that day. Until his mother fell ill, aircrafts had been his only obsession. Time, poverty, and loss had crushed it.

But he could fly, if he stayed. Pilot for the first time.

Then what? Be branded a criminal for a few hours in the sky? End his life in a spectacular crash after a Union zeppelin shot them down? Absurd. Henry pushed himself off the railing and landed on the ground. From the basket, Andeal waited for his reaction.

"You can't cross that big a distance in a balloon. You'll use up an entire container of gas in a few hours."

Despite his best efforts, his voice shook as he spoke. Henry clenched his teeth and took a step back.

"This one can fly weeks without landing, if need be. Take a look at the plans. There's—"

"I don't care," Henry interrupted. "Good luck with it."

He hurried away from the scaffold. Better to put some distance between himself and the basket now before he did something unreasonable. He could not fly. Too dangerous. Too beautiful. He ought to forget everything about this balloon, the rebels, and his father. It hurt more than it helped. Leaving tomorrow was his best decision since...he couldn't remember since when. The last week had been a succession of mistakes.

Andeal landed with a soft thump and hurried after him. He ran in front of Henry and walked backward, keeping his pace. "I said something wrong."

"You promised you wouldn't try to change my mind again. Couldn't help yourself anyway?" They'd nearly reached the tunnel. Henry sped up. Andeal stepped in his way and blocked the exit.

"That wasn't the point. I swear. Lenz would've loved for you to fly this balloon, but I won't press the issue. I just thought you'd want to know the Lenz Balloon existed. You told me that was all you had in common."

Andeal was right about the shared passion and it only made Henry angrier. "Move."

Andeal didn't budge. "There's something I need to ask of you. A favor."

"I leave tomorrow!"

"But you won't look into the envelope."

"No!" They'd had this discussion already. Next Andeal would speak of his father's last wish, of how important he'd been to Lenz. Anything to convince him. Henry pushed Andeal aside with surprising strength and strode down the corridor. The engineer winced as he hit the tunnel wall but dogged after him.

"Can we have it?" he asked.

Henry slowed and turned around, confused. "What?"

"Lenz's old balloon envelope. Could we use it? It'd save us months of work and risky missions to find the right fabric. And it'd be an honor."

Passion burnt bright in Andeal's eyes. He'd finish his pet project and fly it, no matter what. A hot air balloon conceived from Henry's father's plans. Henry's breath caught in the back of his throat. Andeal carried Lenz Schmitt's last desires better than him. A strong bond had formed while they endured the labs together and it surpassed what little connection Henry felt for his father today. He studied the blue-skinned engineer, then stared at his feet. Andeal was more apt to this task than Henry could ever be.

"It's yours. Do what you will with it and the recording sewn inside. Lenz would be proud, I'm sure."

He hurried away before this conversation could further deepen the growing void in his belly. All the questions, doubts, and disappointments—his father's ghost was eating at his tranquil happiness. He had to leave now before the last of it was gone.

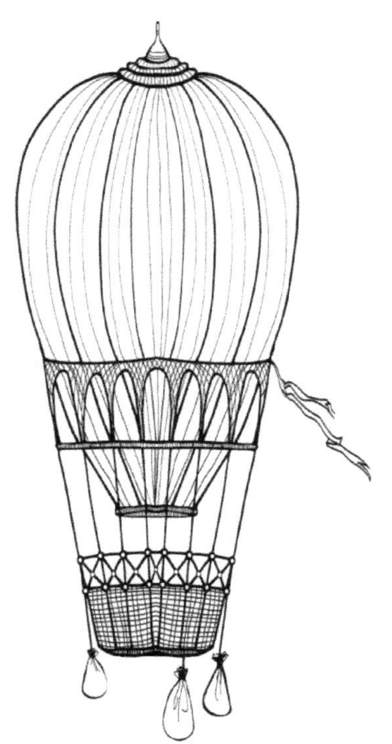

# CHAPTER TEN

*Three sharp knocks at his* door startled Henry Schmitt. He stopped packing what little he had to stare at the old wood. Probably Andeal again, here to annoy him. Henry didn't want yet another reenactment of their dispute. If he stayed silent, perhaps the engineer would go away?

"Henry, I know you're here. Please open."

Maniel's voice surprised him. He hadn't expected her to come and try to talk him out of this decision. She'd always seemed more understanding. Henry hesitated, decided to stay still and silent anyway. After a few seconds she called through again.

"Andeal said you were leaving tomorrow."

"I am," he said at last. "Nothing you tell me will change that."

"That's fine, Henry. I just scolded my husband for trying." He could hear the mirth in her tone, the barely-repressed laughter. It brought a slight smile to Henry's lips. She might've been lying, but he was inclined to trust her—more than he did Andeal now. If Maniel had something to tell him, she would be straightforward about it. "Nevertheless, I'm not going away. Don't turn this into a siege."

Henry couldn't suppress his chuckle. He had no food supplies packed away yet and couldn't withstand a siege. "I surrender!" he called before he opened the door. "What *do* you want?"

Maniel stood in the corridor with a small basket on her arm. Her hair was contained in one long braid and she smiled. "Since this is your last night with us, I wanted to offer you a supper at the summit."

"Only racers go to the summit." No one was allowed to hike Mount Kairn. Henry remembered a time when Ferrys' government posted guards at the trail's start to ensure the respect of this long-standing tradition. Broken barriers now stood in the way but they wouldn't stop anyone serious.

"There are no more racers, right? I thought you'd enjoy the fresh air."

"Yes! Yes I would!"

"Before, however...I also think you should hear how your father died and why he matters to us."

Henry tensed. He wanted to refuse now but his desperate need for a cool breeze crushed his reluctance to discuss Lenz Schitt. Besides, he had a feeling Maniel would be respectful about this—that she wouldn't use the story as a tool to guilt him.

"All right. I guess."

"Great. We'll just need to select our dinner first, then."

Maniel led him to the kitchens, where they stuffed her basket with dried beef, fresh fruits, a small bottle of Burgian wine, and a few extras. She remained silent as they set out. The path followed an upward slope and she turned at intersections without the slightest hesitation. Her strides were long, determined. Henry soon lost track of the route and relied on her sense of direction. She brought him to a small room with makeshift wooden stairs leading up to a high ledge. The wooden steps had a smooth crease from years of passage, yet another proof of the rebels' long occupation of these networks.

After the ladder came the longest tunnel of all. It climbed in a steep and straight line. The electric balls became sparse and Henry advanced in half-light more often than not. His lungs soon burned and his soles complained once more. Maniel, in perfect shape still, waited for him at another intersection. Strands of hair drifted by themselves, casting wavering shadows.

Wind. Wind caught in her black braid.

Henry sprinted the remaining distance until he reached the corner and the breeze hit him. The sweet cool air invaded his lungs and refreshed his burdened brain. The bliss from that single draft surpassed that of a pack of instant noodles after days of famine. He let the sensation sink in, eyes closed, arms stretched out. He'd found paradise.

"You're not even out yet," Maniel whispered. She grabbed his hand and pulled him along. "Wait until powerful gusts of wind buffet you. It's intense."

A few minutes later they reached the exit. The tunnel ended near an abrupt cliff, a dozen feet away from the roaring waterfall. Henry flattened himself against the rock wall, afraid to tumble to a crushing death. The large lake near the hideout's entrance seemed tiny from here.

Maniel climbed a narrow set of stairs at their right, deft as a mountain goat. Spray from the waterfall turned the stone steps into a slick trap. Henry built his courage and steadied his feet before he followed. He kept his gaze straight ahead, at the gray clouds above, refusing to glance down. His heart thumped hard in his chest and he saw no need to worsen it. They reached a large platform that remained, by Henry's standards, too small and close to the edge to his liking. His companion did not have such qualms: she walked to the edge and sat down, her legs dangling above the empty air. He searched for a secure, flat rock and settled down.

"We come here when we need to feel alive," Maniel said. "On rare occasions we've even jumped into the water below."

Henry gulped and closed his eyes. "You should be dead."

"Don't worry, the pond is deep."

No body of water was deep enough for a jump of that height. Why would anyone risk their lives for a few seconds of thrill? Henry rummaged through Maniel's basket and placed the dinner on his stone. Apple, cheese, bread, beef, wine—where to start? As he considered his options, sitting high at the top of Mount Kairn with powerful gusts snapping at his loose shirt, Henry relaxed.

Maniel stretched, grabbed an apple, then popped his bubble of calm with a single sentence.

"I'm sorry the message didn't have what you wanted. You would've deserved it."

It felt like a stone had landed at the bottom of Henry's stomach. He forced himself to meet Maniel's gaze. She understood. The soft sympathy in her tone and the tinge of sadness in her smile was all he needed to know.

"When he vanished all he left was a note about his precious balloon envelope," Henry said. "Same as his dying message. I don't think he ever cared about anything else. Especially not me."

"Oh...Henry." She put a hand on his forearm. "Whatever is on that recording, he wanted to entrust it to you. Not Andeal or me. You."

Henry snatched the dry beef and munched on it as he considered her words. She might be right but the very thought angered him. Lenz Schmitt had vanished one day to let him deal with grief and brutal poverty. He couldn't crash into his life again eight years later, drive him into his mess and expect Henry to be eager to dive in.

"Andeal called me an ingrate and a coward but..." He frowned. How to say it? "I like my life simple and safe. Since Captain Vermen broke down my door, it's been neither. I want all of this to be over."

"Tomorrow it will be." Maniel took a deep breath and turned away, looking into the empty space above the waterfall. "Please leave knowing who Lenz was in the end."

Henry rubbed his eyes with shaky hands. He might as well. He had agreed to this story, coming here, and it seemed to matter so much to Maniel. He could listen for her.

"All right. Tell your story."

Maniel rose from her dangling seat and resettled on the rock, closer to him. Her calm and seriousness appeased him. She would dispel this particular mystery without pressuring him into staying.

"It was cloudy and gray when we escaped, too." Maniel started in a slow voice. As she spoke, she opened the Burgian wine and poured him a glass. "We hadn't seen the sun in two years and it hid from us. Your father never had the chance to see it shine again."

Henry brought the glass to his lips. He'd wiped his father out of his life a few years ago, but the reminder of his death still made his heart sink. It was no longer a probable reality. It was there, right in his face, and he had to get used to it a second time.

"The labs are on the western shores of Mikken, in a grounded and disrepaired airship, perched near a cliff. They are isolated and well-guarded. We shouldn't have escaped. Malnutrition, constant testing, illness, and hopelessness weakened us. Only Andeal thought we'd ever make it out alive. He always believes in such impossible things..."

Maniel paused to compose herself and steady her voice. Henry kept eating in slow, distracted movements.

"One day an explosion rocked the laboratories. We never learned what caused it, but when it happened a scientist was in our cell, to force-feed Andeal the silvered water and give me antibiotics. His armed guard stumbled. Lenz crashed into him and stole the weapon while I overtook the tester. It all happened so fast. Suddenly we were running away, our bare feet slapping against the metallic floor. I don't think we ever discussed a plan. We just...acted. I remember little of the flight. My heart pumping. The doors and corridors filing past, all the same, so endless. Lenz's deep voice, urging us on. The sliver of hope, threatening to burst through my chest."

Henry stopped eating, hanging on her every word. Maniel's voice faded, and only the waterfall's roar remained. She bit on her apple, lost in her thoughts for a moment. Henry resisted the urge to press her on.

"They rang the alarm as we reached the exit. There were so many men, Henry, and they were all armed. They ordered us to stop, to stand down, but once you've felt that first draft of freedom...you realize you'd rather die. Your brain is on fire, you don't think. Not anymore. Because all your instincts are telling you there's a life out there, past the electric fences or in the water a hundred feet below. We ran for the cliff."

The wind freed long strands of her frizzy hair and blew them about. Maniel stared at the plunging waterfall with a haunted expression. Dread constricted Henry's heart. He squeezed his pants' fabric to keep his hands steady.

"Lenz...He didn't follow. He pressed that rag into Andeal's hands and told us to find you. He might've thought he was already too sick. I remember the sprint to the cliff. The longest hundred meters I ever crossed. Andeal held my hand, pulled me along—forced me along. Twigs dug into my heels but I never slowed. When I looked back your father was running across the field, to the gates. He had the guard's gun. He barreled straight at them and fired, again and again, until they forgot us and focused on him. They shot him down as we reached the edge and jumped. Tears streaked Andeal's cheeks. I must have been crying, too." Tears filled her eyes and she wiped them away. Her voice remained steady and she met Henry's troubled gaze. "Without his sacrifice we would all be dead."

Henry's skull buzzed, the noise covering the deep rumble of water. Maniel's story was incredible. Lenz Schmitt had been a cold man, a distant paternal figure with whom he'd shared very little. A love for hot air balloons and his mother, at most. He was not a man who gave his life for friends, sprinting toward death. But one did not fake the intensity of Maniel's sorrow. It had to be true.

"Maniel..." The shake in his voice scared him. He shivered in the wind. "Why did he leave me? Did he ever...did he ever say?"

She crossed her legs and stared at the gray sky. A childish part of Henry wanted her to lean over and hug him, but she stayed put. "He often said the Union had to be taken down, no matter the cost. Toward the end of the tests, he became sick. He would cough a lot and I found a buboe near his neck. It seemed to terrify him more than any other test they'd done before. That's when he wrote the message. He's doing it again, he'd said, but he never told us what. I'm sorry, Henry."

By now the bitter disappointment was a familiar friend. Henry heaved a sigh, finished his glass of wine, and rose to his feet.

"I'm glad he saved you," he said. "You're a better person than he ever was." He would be glad to put this last week behind him. When Maniel pushed herself up, he raised a hand to stall her answer. "Thanks for the last meal. And the story."

Henry headed for the slippery stairs leading into Mount Kairn, but his last words didn't quite seem enough. Tomorrow he would be gone, leaving them with all the problems his father had tried to thrust upon him. Henry turned and gave one long look at Maniel, standing on the mountain's summit, her long braid snapping in the wind. She was strong. She would manage. But still...

"My father believed the winds guide one's path in life. I hope they stay by your side and keep you on the right one."

As he returned to Mount Kairn's engulfing darkness, he heard Maniel's 'thanks', thick with emotion.

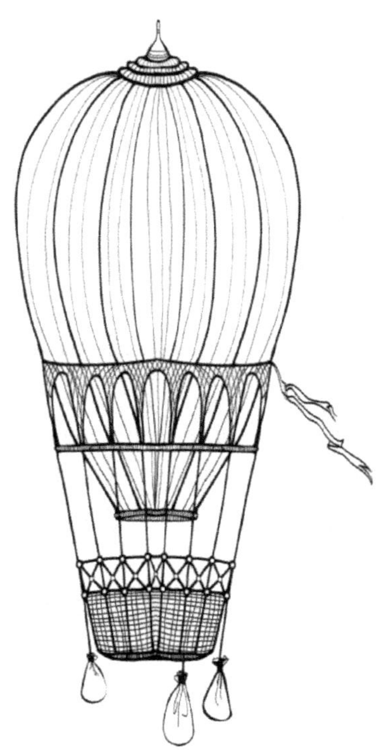

# CHAPTER ELEVEN

*Vermen wrenched control* over the wild beating of his heart one long breath at a time. He turned the room's wooden chair upside down, strained his muscles, and broke one of its legs. The resounding crack shook his bones. He now held a wooden stick, almost two feet long. A weapon for his escape.

Andeal's visit earlier had been the last straw. The engineer had come in, all smiles as usual, but he couldn't stay to chat. He gave Vermen his meal—the size of which got smaller with every passing day—and a warning. Tomorrow the rebels had a meeting to decide his fate. Vermen's head spun. Who had the final word, he'd asked.

Seraphin did.

Leaving the captain with two options: wait for his death sentence or escape tonight and bring the Union's wrath down on these criminals. An easy choice.

Vermen called upon his training and focused his thoughts on the here and now. It ought to be nighttime now. He needed to remain alert, at the height of his physical prowess. The rebels might not be numerous but alone and unarmed, he wouldn't last long. His discipline would see him through.

He approached the makeshift wooden door and gave it one powerful kick. The planks cracked and splintered but held together. Vermen hit them again and they gave in. The door hung, half-unhinged, parts of it scattered through the corridor. The captain stepped out and glanced to each side. No one. The chain he heard every time someone entered lay on the ground, loose and useless. It had never been tied. What games were they playing with him? Did they *want* him to escape or did they think he would never even try? Whichever it was, they had made a mistake.

He wasted no more time on questions and stalked down the tunnel. Only a vague memory of the exit route remained. He could trace his path halfway back to the entrance, and hope something would jog his memory before then. Otherwise...a quick glance at the generic corridor gave him little hope. He should've paid better attention.

Improvised club in hand, Captain Vermen hurried through the rebel compound. The electric balls guided him through the maze, past multiple doors similar to his. His crouched figure cast a long shadow. Voices reached him as a distant echo but he couldn't estimate where they came from or how far away their owners were. At least the constant roar of the waterfall buried his footsteps.

He reached a T-intersection and made a left turn. He'd barely advanced before a voice traveled down the length of his tunnel, loud and clear for once.

"Sure thing, let me get another deck!"

Vermen held his breath. It wasn't addressed to him, but the speaker headed his way. He backtracked to a crossroad and flattened himself against the wall, out of sight. The man whistled a careless summer hymn. Excellent. It made his progress easier to track. The captain tightened his grip on the club. Waited.

Ten steps away. He leaned forward, ready to spring.

So close. Five steps. No, one now.

Vermen spun around the corner and swung his club. The rebel's eyes widened and he raised his black hands. Too slow. The chair leg smacked against his temple, knocked him right out. A deck of cards slipped from his hands and scattered. They traced a strange pattern around his inert form. The captain knelt and pushed away the rebel's long reddish hair to check his pulse. Still alive. Perfect strike. He flipped the man onto his back to allow more breathing room.

A knife sheathe at his belt drew his gaze. Vermen's pulse quickened as he slid the blade out and tested the edge. It nicked his finger. Good quality. His situation kept improving.

Satisfied, Vermen continued on his previous path. He snuck through the winding tunnels, choosing his path on instinct and memory, careful not to go up or down. His cell and the exit were on the same level, that much he was certain of. He roamed for half an hour, perhaps more, dodging rebels to avoid leaving a trail of bodies. Although it didn't feel like he walked in circles, he knew it shouldn't have taken so long.

Then he felt a draft from a side corridor. Vermen stared at the slight downward slope with suspicion. The waterfall's rumble came clearer and louder, too. Had he been too exhausted to notice the rise at his arrival? Two days without sleep or food *could* do that to a man, just as ten days of imprisonment taught him the difference between fresh air and the recycled atmosphere of caves. This had to be it.

He forced himself not to sprint. Stay in control. Stay alert. Until the water's constant rumble turned into the forest's peaceful silence, he had not escaped. The tunnel curved. At the end, electric balls gave way to the night's sky. The exit. His head felt light from the rush of blood.

Then he heard running steps from behind. A voice hailed him. Vermen tightened his sweaty grip on the redhead's knife but kept moving at the same pace, ears perked up, until his unwary opponent was upon him.

Captain Vermen stopped and bent his knees. He reached over his shoulder and grabbed the rebel's outstretched arm. As he pulled and swung the man around, spinning on his heels to give his movement more strength, he registered the hand's blue skin. Andeal crashed into the wall to his left. The impact threw an electric light off its hook and it shattered on the ground. His friend grunted and his legs gave in, but the soldier allowed him no time to recover. He grabbed the front of his shirt and brought the knife to his throat. Andeal froze, panting.

"Whoa, knife." He stretched out his palms, well in view.

"A gift from that redhead I smashed across the head."

Andeal's expression went from surprised to horrified in a blink. "Joshua? Is he…"

"No. I checked."

"Oh, thank the Lady." He wiped his brow and cast a bothered glance down. "You don't need this, Hans. I came to warn you."

Vermen did not lower his knife. All his muscles waited, taut, ready to react at an instant's notice. "Warn me?"

"Don't go out there. Our best snipers are in position with orders to shoot. Stay, please."

The captain's stomach clenched. It had been too easy. How would he get past the rebels' bullets with nothing but a small knife? Unless...

"Do they have orders to shoot if a hostage is involved?"

"Why do you—oh." Andeal's smile vanished and his shoulders slumped. "Should've thought of that."

An uneasy silence stretched between them. Shock had stolen Andeal's voice and energy. He stared ahead, absent, perhaps absorbing the sudden reversal. Why must *he* be the hostage? Vermen cared little for the others, but the engineer had made his stay bearable. Perhaps he'd convince his superiors to be lenient. He withdrew the blade, pulled Andeal closer to the exit and bent toward the opening. He searched the surrounding rocks for human shapes but could not spot the shooters. Was it all a bluff? He leaned farther out and prayed they did not have a clean shot on him yet. The flat grounds between the exit and the small stairs were empty of shooters and so were, as far as he could see, the surrounding rocky slopes. The rebel snipers had either mastered camouflage, positioned themselves above the exit or did not exist. He had to risk it. With Andeal.

"You and I have a trip to the closest regiment scheduled," he whispered.

He examined the distance to cross one last time and established a mental path. The straight line was too dangerous. Better to keep his back protected by the larger rocks and describe a half-circle. As he focused on the next step, he stopped paying attention to his prisoner. His grip loosened.

Andeal wrenched out of the hold, sprung at Vermen, and reached for the knife. Instincts kicked the captain into immediate reaction: he spun on his heels and slashed in front of him. A warning strike, to force the engineer to retreat. Andeal did not jump back. He accepted the deep cut across his chest, grabbed the captain's hand as it passed close to his face, and sank his teeth deep into the flesh. Vermen cried out and dropped the weapon. Pain burned his hand and clogged his mind. Andeal crashed into him and they fell to the ground.

Warm blood poured from Andeal's chest wound as the two men rolled over the ground, crushing shards of broken glass from the shattered lamp, wrestling for control. Andeal's strength astonished him and Vermen struggled to dominate the fight. His gaze fell upon the knife, to his right. He stretched his wounded hand, desperate for an advantage. Andeal smashed the fingers and a new wave of pain coursed through the captain's arm. Before he could react, the engineer sat across him, the blade at his throat.

Andeal's breath came in raspy gasps. Blood blackened his loose gray shirt, all the way down to his pants. The cut ran from under his right armpit to his left shoulder. Despite the constant loss of blood, his grip on Vermen's shoulder showed no sign of weakness. His jaw remained set, his eyes wide from...panic? His voice trembled as he spoke.

"I'm not—not going back. Not to the labs. You think you know *anything* about imprisonment? You're fed, you're given the time of day, the weather, news from outside. You're not tested on. You can't...you can't even imagine what it's like." Terror danced in Andeal's eyes. Vermen knew fear, had once led men convinced they'd die into battle. The intense despair he'd glimpsed for a moment disquieted him. Andeal forced his breathing to slow and his emotions receded. He removed himself from Vermen and straightened up. "Stand."

The captain obeyed, shaken. He held his bitten hand close, gritting his teeth against the pain. Andeal had sure sunk his teeth deep.

"You have a choice now." Cold anger replaced the quiver in his voice. "Either you walk out there alone and die, or you follow me back to your cell and I'll vouch for your sorry skin."

Vermen frowned and glanced at the exit. What did he prefer? Die now in an attempt to be free or wait for Seraphin's inevitable condemnation? Andeal held the knife at ready. His arm shook and blood loss turned his skin to a pale and sickly blue. How long had he been held prisoner? Tested on? In the brief instant he'd held Vermen down, Andeal had opened a window to a different part of him. Gone was the optimism, the undeserved trust—all replaced by terrible memories. And Vermen had threatened to bring it all back.

He turned to Andeal and stepped away from the exit. "I don't understand. Why would you even vouch for me?"

"It's called decency," he said with a hint of his usual good humor. "It's the little thing that showed up out of nowhere and stopped you from shooting Seraphin at point blank."

By that logic, if Seraphin had shot another at point blank, did it mean he had none? Vermen held the thought back but it brought a smile to his lips. He took another difficult step away from the exit.

"Very well. I'll take my chances with your decency."

Andeal sighed, lowered the knife. Vermen noted the growing signs of weakness: the man's shoulders hunched from exhaustion, his breathing became ragged, and he glanced at his cut all the time, biting his lower lip. In addition to his bloodied shirt, a red line now travelled halfway down his pants. The fabric absorbed most of it for now, but Vermen wondered how much he'd lost already. When Andeal signaled for him to follow, he watched his companion's weary steps.

They made it to the first intersection before Andeal stopped and put his hand on the wall for support. A pained expression contorted his visage and his breathing was slow and shallow. He wiped a new film of sweat from his brow, tried to smile, but his paleness alarmed Captain Vermen.

"You've lost too much blood. Don't you guys have a medic?"

"Yes. Somewhat." Andeal leaned on the wall and touched his wound. "Maniel has...she has a bit of training. Was nearly finished with nursing when they took us. Perhaps we could make a little detour?"

"Maniel. Of course."

Andeal laughed at his bitterness, then flinched from the pain inflicted by the movement. He groaned, pushed himself off the wall, took a hesitant step—like he had to fight to even drag his foot forward. Vermen grabbed his arm to support him. His uniform, already creased, torn, and dirtied, now had a bloodstain bound to grow. Part of him protested: if Andeal could not follow him, he could escape again. There had to be other exits, or he could use the unlighted tunnels and lose the rebels for a while. His oaths to the Union and its army demanded he leave the engineer behind and flee.

Yet when the strain became too much for Andeal, when the blood loss seemed to beat his resolve and he collapsed, Vermen caught him. He lifted his friend and carried him without a word, without hesitation. He fought against dreams of freedom, of the sun on his skin and the wind through his hair. After all, he *was* free now. It was his decision to save Andeal's life. There would be time for regrets once the rebels shoved him back into a cell.

The captain marched through the tunnels, taking turns at random until he heard voices again. The echo made them impossible to track but he did his best. Unintelligible sentences became audible words. Maniel's voice.

"Calm down. We'll find him. If he'd left, we would know."

Vermen stared down the tunnel. Three makeshift doors lined the walls, along with the usual white lights. He hurried down the path to find which room Andeal's wife was in, tracking the sound of her voice.

"This place is a maze for the uninitiated. He won't find you and barrel into—"

Hans stopped at the right door and kicked it. It flew open without breaking, and Vermen hurried in.

A bit larger than his cell, this cave had a smaller alcove at the back, hidden behind a curtain. It also contained a double bed, an angled desk covered in large sheets of paper and a tiny nook at ground level that resembled a fireplace. The two-seater and small library added to the impression of a cozy living room. On a small table near the curtain rested an open first aid kit. As he entered, Maniel was pulling on the curtain.

She wasn't his main concern.

Seraphin Holt leaned on the angled desk, his pistol aimed at him. Vermen's cheeks flushed as anger and shame tightened his throat. Something in the man's piercing blue scrutiny squeezed his insides, even with the glasses half-hiding it. It reminded him of the stress when high-ranking officers inspected them—an intense fear of critique mixed with the thrilling hope of potential compliments. No, worse. It reminded him of impulses when other men attracted him. Except this was Seraphin Holt, the White Renegade, his brother's murderer, and these feelings were all wrong. He tore his gaze away. Maniel was staring at her wounded husband.

"Andeal..."

Three long strides brought her across the room, to his side, and she bent to touch the wound and the burning forehead before caressing his jaw line. She lifted her head and planted her eyes on Vermen's. The captain took an unwilling step back at her intensity.

"You did this," she said.

"I—yes."

"Put him on the bed. Now." She pointed and he reacted without questions. As Vermen set Andeal down, she grabbed her tools, knelt next to the bed, and rummaged through the first aid kit for the appropriate bandage. "Seraph, I'll need boiling water."

He scowled and lowered his pistol. "But—"

"No buts! He brought him here, he's not going to kill him. Your hesitation might. Go!"

The Renegade's jaw dropped but he holstered his weapon and hurried out of the room. He paid Vermen a warning glare and the captain smiled back. Maniel gave him no time to celebrate the small victory.

"Help me remove his shirt. Why didn't you do this earlier? No, never mind, I don't want to know why, or what happened. I might kill you."

Vermen froze. Maniel could've intimidated an entire army if she'd wanted, and for a moment he didn't know how to handle it. She whirled around at his non-reaction, furious, and his discipline kicked in. In these matters she was his superior. A scary, make-a-mistake-and-you're-dead superior, but one nonetheless. He grabbed the bottom of Andeal's shirt and, despite the pain throbbing in his hand at every movement, he helped her.

They worked together to disinfect, sew, and bandage the large cut. Seraphin brought the water, stared at Vermen's back as they worked for a while, then left without a word. Maniel's technique, despite her unfinished training, was efficient and methodical. She knew her business and seemed to obliterate all thoughts of *who* she was treating, concentrating on what. Not once did she hesitate, even when Andeal regained some consciousness and moaned from the pain. Trained nurses on a battlefield couldn't have done better.

By the time they were done, blood soaked half her sleeves and the mattress below Andeal. A large bandage wrapped his torso, his breathing had stabilized, and his fever diminished. Maniel sat back on the ground with a deep sigh. Eyes closed, she undid her destroyed braid and ran a hand through the curly hair before retying it into a simple ponytail. The simple movements seemed to comfort her. Vermen remained standing, shifting his weight from one foot to the other. The silence hung heavy, threatening to choke him. He had to say something.

"I'm sorry. I didn't mean to..."

She looked up at him, then struggled to her feet. "A week ago I told him he couldn't trust you. I don't know if this proves me right or wrong."

Vermen had no answer for her. What did tonight prove? He'd put Andeal's life before his chance at escape—his sole opportunity to fulfill his oath and uproot the rebels. Did this make him a traitor? A coward? Would he do it again? Vermen couldn't tell. His burgeoning friendship with the engineer was a professional mistake but he could no longer deny it. Somehow, he'd have to find a way around it.

"Give me your hand."

Absorbed in his thoughts, Vermen hadn't noticed Maniel approaching with a bandage. Bite marks lined the back of his hand, deep and red, but they no longer bled. He allowed Andeal's wife to look at them anyway, and before long she'd treated them and gave him some painkillers. Vermen clenched his fingers. The movement remained difficult but soon it wouldn't hurt so much.

"Thank you," he said, at which Maniel only shrugged.

She grabbed a book from the library, dragged the two-seater sofa closer to the bed, and collapsed onto it. She flipped through the pages to find her marker but as she read, her gaze flitted between the words and her husband. Vermen clasped his hands behind his back. She ignored him and he was tempted to walk out. Instead, he cleared his throat.

"He'll be okay now, won't he?"

"Yes." She lowered the book. "Get the desk chair and sit. Enjoy the rare hours out of your cell. Between Andeal's cut and Joshua's head wound, I doubt your conditions will get any better."

Vermen's stomach tightened at the thought. He accepted her offer and brought a seat close to the bed. Maniel dove back into her reading, not the least bit concerned about his presence, so he leaned into the chair's back and closed his eyes. The night's events played in his head as he tried to make sense out of them but, no matter how hard he tried, he could not reconcile his mission and duties with his current actions. Questions spun in his head until he fell into a fitful sleep.

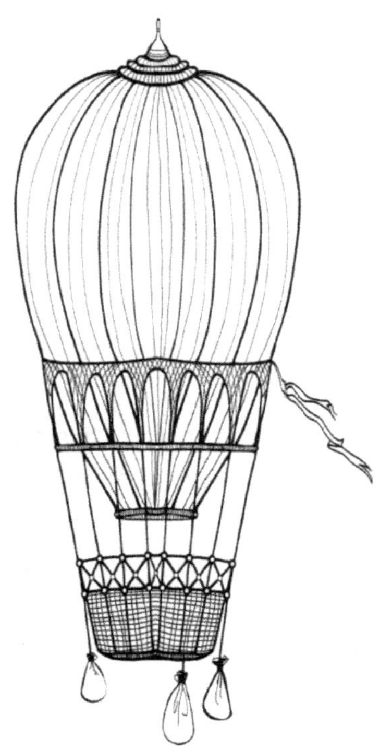

# CHAPTER TWELVE

 chest and a wracking headache welcomed Andeal back to the world. The familiar cave ceiling danced before his eyes then came into focus. His mind needed more time to regain full functionality but as he grasped for shreds of concentration, his memories returned. After he'd shown Henry the balloon, he'd decided to test his trust in Vermen and tell the captain his escape window was growing narrow. He expected him to stay in his cell.

Events had proved him wrong.

The evening blurred in his feverish brain—all but one moment: the crushing panic that took over when Vermen spoke of dragging him to the army. Of delivering him to the labs. His world had collapsed, taking with it any regards for his safety. Better dead than a lab rat. He'd nearly had his wish fulfilled.

"Andeal? You awake yet?"

Sharp pain burst in his head at the familiar voice. Andeal turned his neck with a groan. At first he saw a humanoid blur but his eyes readjusted to the new focus and Joshua's visage became clearer. Red hair framed bright eyes, a long beakish nose, and a mocking smile. A purplish bump now marred his temple's dark skin.

"Somewhat," Andeal muttered. "How are you?"

"Fine and dandy! I have a horrible headache that'll last through the week, but who cares? I'll live."

Andeal forced a smile to his lips. It seemed the terrible pain had not killed his friend's bitter sarcasm—proof he was indeed fine.

Strength trickled back into his muscles and Andeal pushed himself on an elbow. The floor tipped for a dizzying moment, then stabilized. A glance at his clock on the wall told him he'd slept through the night, morning, and part of the afternoon. His heart sped and his mind cleared.

"What happened? Where's Vermen?"

"In his cell." Joshua smacked his lips and stood. He moved to the living room table, on which a cold meal waited, and brought it back as he spoke. "I don't know what you did to him, but while the good captain didn't mind smashing my skull in, he couldn't leave you bleeding out on the ground. He carried you here. Maniel even allowed him to stay the night. Seraphin was...let's say 'not pleased'. Here, eat."

This time, Andeal's smile came of its own. He'd have a huge scar to remember the evening, but at least it hadn't been pointless. No one could brand Vermen as an uncompromising enemy now. Andeal rubbed his wounded torso, thoughtful. The captain didn't qualify as an ally either—yesterday was too close a call for that. He had to be more wary.

First, though, he should hold his end of the bargain and defend him at the meeting. There'd be no one to be careful around if they decided to execute him.

"I hope Seraph will calm down before the meeting," Andeal said as he straightened up, sat cross-legged in his bed, and accepted the plate of food. Rice and beans. No meat. Their stock must've run low again. He took small bites, forcing himself to eat despite feeling like his heart blocked his throat and threatened to come out anytime. Joshua linked his fingers together then raised his gaze at the ceiling.

"They might've already started the council," he said.

Andeal dropped the spoon and swallowed hard. His Burgian friend would not look at him. "What do you mean, they already started? They can't have. Not without me."

Joshua gave him a dismissive shrug. "Maniel protested at first but Seraphin insisted. They left me to watch over you."

"No..."

Panic built from Andeal's guts and up his throat. It pushed his fever away and returned strength to his muscles. The engineer threw his blankets away before sliding off the bed. His head spun and black stains obscured his vision. He waited for them to fade away before taking his first hesitant step. Joshua stood and half-supported, half-restrained him.

"You're in no state to fly to your captain's rescue. Sit down and eat."

"I can talk. I can walk. I'm fit to go." He grabbed Joshua's fingers and removed them one by one. "I have to."

Joshua gave him a long and silent look—an odd, serious expression for him. His redheaded friend spent more time joking and gambling than making important decisions and thinking through consequences. He was a boon to the rebels' morale but not their chief planner.

"The Lady must love that man. He doesn't deserve a champion like you."

He stepped back, hands raised in defeat. Andeal hurried out of the room, stumbling through the first steps, and Joshua called after him as he crossed the door.

"I'll eat your breakfast though!"

It brought a smile to Andeal's lips but he didn't stop to reply. He strode down the corridors, a hand on the wall for support. The tunnels seemed narrower than usual, as though they'd close in on him. Every step sapped his strength. The pain from his wound grew as he advanced, numbing his other senses. It left behind nothing but his anger. Seraphin knew he'd defend Hans but instead of waiting to hear him, he forced an early meeting. The blatant attempt to circumvent set his mind ablaze. These were his friends, his wife! He'd trusted them but it seemed Vermen's unilateral execution was more important. Andeal's outrage carried him through the network.

When he reached the meeting room, he felt woozy. His temporary vitality had vanished. He waited, his back to the wall, for his mind to clear once more and his balance to return. The voices inside felt distant but he knew he should hear every word. Settled against the wall, Andeal couldn't help but giggle. What mess was he about to create?

He took a deep breath, wiped the sweat from his forehead, and entered the room.

Everyone hushed as he stepped into view. He walked to the wooden table around which Maniel, Seraphin, and Stern sat and grabbed the back of a chair for support. Stern glared at him from his left, tall and serious while Seraphin leaned back, his lips a thin line. Maniel moved to stand but Andeal stopped her with a raised hand.

"No, please, go on," he said. "I'd love to hear what decisions you'd make without me."

The silence endured after his intervention. Stern tapped his finger on the table, Seraphin cracked his knuckles. Heat rose to Andeal's cheeks as they confirmed his doubts: they didn't dare repeat what they'd said in front of him. He stood and set both hands on the table—as much for the support as for the impression. He captured Seraphin's gaze and held the red-tinged eyes.

"This is disgusting."

"Andeal..."

He ignored Maniel. Her agreement to this farce hurt him more than anyone else's. Seraphin hadn't twitched. He'd removed his glasses and waited for the onslaught.

"Did you throw your decency to the winds, Seraphin? This man spared your life and saved mine. He's not a sick horse to execute but here you are, ready to condemn him. How is that fair? He doesn't stand a chance without anyone to defend him." Andeal's breath was shaky and his fever fueled his anger. "You're scared of what I have to say. Scared that I'm right, that he's not his brother, that he knows what justice and honor mean. That he could be an ally. How can you fight a corrupt government and its suspicious ascent to power then cheat on a simple meeting? This is..."

A bout of dizziness forced him to stop. The table pitched and he stared at his blue hands until the world stabilized. Seraphin had maintained a straight face through his tirade. When he spoke, however, his voice turned cold and sharp.

"Are you done now?" he asked. "Sit down."

Andeal plopped into the creaking chair, knowing his legs wouldn't support him any longer. His Regarian friend leaned forward and continued.

"We let you rest because executing Captain Hans Vermen was already out of the question. Maniel made it clear from the start she wouldn't come unless we respected your wishes. Perhaps you should spend less time at his side before you forget who your friends are."

"I..." Andeal rubbed his face. Shame replaced his outrage and a headache built under his skull. "I'm sorry. I shouldn't have said..." He wrestled control over his voice and lifted his chin. He'd made a huge mistake but now was not the time to flatten and give up. Andeal shoved his growing guilt in a corner of his brain. "I got carried away. I apologize. What, then, were you discussing?"

"Not much." Stern didn't have Seraphin's calm and his anger showed through his gritted teeth. "We lack a better solution. We can't free him but we can't feed him forever. There's barely enough for us to eat."

Maniel set her hand on his forearm. "You should return to our room. You're still running a fever and I can tell you're dizzy and weak. We can do this alone."

"No. I can stay." Screw his headache, his temperature, his shaky hands. He knew Vermen the best here and could help find a solution. He'd started thinking about this days ago. "In fact, I think I have your answer."

Seraphin's gaze went to Maniel. Did Andeal need permission from his wife to speak now? He squashed his rising anger—his hurried deductions had caused enough damage for the day. She sighed and withdrew her hand. Her exasperated frown told him he was in for a scolding tonight. Nothing irritated Maniel like someone disobeying her medical advice. Andeal gave her his best apologetic smile then gathered his thoughts into a coherent string.

"Two things pushed Hans Vermen to try an escape. First he thought his life was threatened. Second, he's inactive. He roams his cell in circles, doing nothing but the occasional push-ups, and it's driving him crazy. Tell him there'll be no execution, take him out of his cell, and make him work."

Dubious stares welcomed his suggestion. Beads of sweat formed on Andeal's brow but he resisted the temptation to wipe them. He wished he'd seen Hans before this meeting. He had no idea if the captain would agree to help them. The poor man might be preparing for death even now.

Stern voiced his protests first.

"When there's a spy in your midst, you don't show him your secrets. One of our enemies just tried to escape and you want him to roam free in the tunnels?"

"He's not our enemy." Andeal's gaze flitted to Seraphin, who shifted in his chair. Its loud creak filled the uncomfortable silence. "He's Seraphin's. He fought the rebels to get to him, not us."

"I am not responsible for his actions. He caused these men's deaths, not I." Seraphin set his palm on the table, a habit that usually hid their shaking. "He made himself *our* enemy. The others will never accept working at his side. Letting him loose is not only a risk for our security. It's a risk for his and mine."

Seraphin was poised on his chair, as if ready to bolt. The unnatural whiteness of his knuckles and the widening of his eyes betrayed him. A plea. Don't let it happen again. Seraphin's fear of Vermen reminded Andeal of his own—of the labs, the white coats, the minuscule cells, the tests.

"He won't hurt you," Andeal whispered.

"You can't know that."

No. He only hoped for it. Vermen was devoted and restless. If they could capitalize on his energy...Andeal's guts told him that after last night's events, the captain would not betray him. No proof confirmed his instincts, however.

"We should chain him," Maniel said. "Remember those long shackles we stole from Reverence's police station, two years ago? With those at his feet, he could walk but not run. He could work but any attempt to escape would be easy to thwart."

Andeal restrained his sudden urge to kiss his wife. What a brilliant compromise! Once Vermen was out, he could meet other rebels, get to know not just him, but everyone. With time, perhaps, he might forget the tattered uniform he clung to. A smile birthed on his lips as he considered the future but Stern's severe expression killed it.

"How wonderful a target he'll be, then! Do you have any idea how many of us would love to smash his nose? How many are eagerly awaiting this council, hoping that we *will* shoot him? This will cause problems."

"We're all civilized folks," Andeal said. "I'm sure they'll find the discipline to hold their punches."

"Discipline!" Stern sneered. "They aren't soldiers."

Andeal's hand curled into a fist. Always, Stern lorded his military background over them. The rebels might be a potluck of outlaws, idealists, and homeless people, but they'd proven their determination and strength through the years.

"It doesn't make them savage brutes. Proof: I'm not a soldier and I'm not punching you."

Anger flashed across Stern's face and he stood, rattling his chair on the ground. Before he could say anything, Seraphin snapped.

"Enough!"

Their leader glared at both of them in turn, then motioned for Stern to sit. The soldier obeyed, biting back his retort, but his gaze never left Andeal as Seraphin spoke.

"Captain Vermen will have his hands free. He can defend himself, as Joshua can attest to. I am inclined to try Maniel's suggestion." Every word seemed to cost him and he enunciated them with care. Although he'd chased the fear from his eyes, his jaw and neck remained tense. "This, however, assumes our good officer will accept."

"He will."

"He can't," Stern countered. "Not anymore."

The finality in his tone took everyone aback. A lump formed in Andeal's stomach. Stern refused to meet Seraphin's gaze, a clear sign he'd gone against orders—and when it came to Vermen, there was but one clear order: don't kill him. The Regarian's tautness did not vanish.

"What do you mean?" he asked Stern.

The man's discomfort was obvious, but he kept his shoulders squared. He took a deep breath in and stared at Andeal as he answered. "Most rebels have not forgotten those killed by Hans Vermen. They wanted justice."

"No..."

"Where?"

Stern ignored Seraphin's question and gritted his teeth together. Andeal's urge to stride around the table and break his nose grew with every passing second. Before he could give in to the desire, Seraphin slammed his palms on the table.

"Dammit Stern, tell me where!"

"No!" This time Stern met his leader's gaze. "I'm doing the right thing. You know it is, you just don't have the courage to do it."

"The right thing was to shoot Klaus Vermen. And when the time came for it, I got my father's gun, strode into his tent, looked into his eyes and pressed the trigger. But Hans is a different man. If you believed for one second this was right, you wouldn't be here, at this table. You'd be there and you'd at least have the guts to watch him die. Now, where are they?"

"The-the summit."

"Good. To your room, soldier. I'll want a word after."

He spun on his heels and hurried out of the room. Andeal cast a dark look at Stern and scrambled after him. He managed two steps before his vision blackened and a strong hand caught his wrist, holding him up.

"Don't you dare follow him. You have an appointment with your bed." Maniel guided him toward the exit. "You'll have to trust him, this time. You're in no state to help."

Heat burned Andeal's cheeks as they proceeded through the corridor. He hadn't given them a chance to defend themselves and prove him wrong, earlier. Perhaps he never should've left that bed. In a single rant, he'd damaged his two most important relationships for the sake of a man he barely knew—a man who might be dead already, thanks to Stern. Andeal wiped the sweat from his forehead. With every step he took, he leaned a little more on his wife. By the time they reached their room, his burning fever put an indistinct haze over the rest of the world.

Maniel was right on one thing: he was in no state to help.

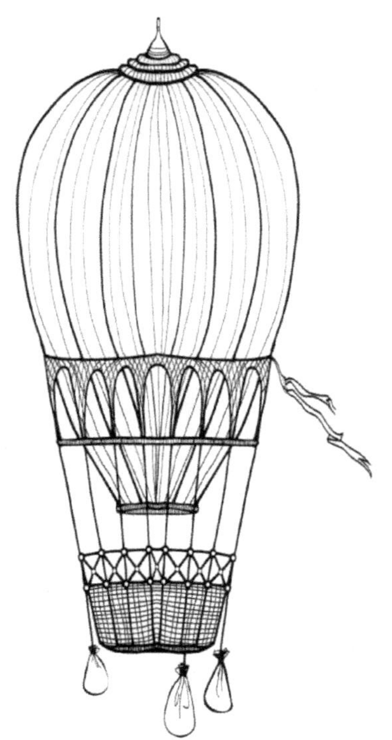



*The day after his night* watching over Andeal, the rebels gave Vermen a new definition of a rude awakening. They broke through the damaged door, thrust a bag over his head before he could even straighten up, then shoved him to the ground. Confused, his heart pumping, he tried to push himself back up but a boot stomped his right hand, straight on the bite mark. He retracted it with a cry of pain, bringing a smattering of chuckles from his assailant. They grabbed his wrists, tied them behind his back, and lifted him to his feet. Vermen took a moment to regain his balance, his breath short, his head already hot in the bag.

"I'm going to go ahead and guess Andeal's not aware of this," he said.

"Aye. Somebody wounded him so bad, we couldn't wake him."

Vermen gritted his teeth. This couldn't end well for him. He'd known this might happen when he'd caught Andeal's bloodied body, had accepted the risk, but the prospect of dying so soon formed a lump in his throat. He hadn't even talked with Andeal one last time. They pressed a gun—a shotgun, from the feel of the barrel—to his back.

"Move."

Another rebel pulled him along, out of the cell. He wouldn't die in his room, then. That explained the bag over his head. As they marched him through the corridors, it occurred to Vermen this wasn't how he'd expected it to go. The rebels' treatment of him had been ridiculously considerate since he'd been dragged in by Seraphin. They'd granted him a comfortable cell and he'd had a companion to chat with every day—not that he'd made the most of the conversations—and he was well fed, at almost regular hours. Maniel had even let him stay out of his cell for the night. He'd thought...This should be Holt leading him to the block. Not a random rebel he'd never met. The Regarian was a cold-blooded murderer but not a coward.

"I'm guessing Seraphin's not aware of this either."

This time, an awkward silence followed his statement. He imagined them, glancing at each other, ill at ease. Vermen snickered.

"What a cute band of lawless killers. You can't even wait for your leader's approval."

A baton crashed against his back, knocking him down. He fell forward and landed on his face. Vermen struggled not to scream despite the pain running up his spine and tried to slow his breathing. The bag gave him the impression he was slowly choking.

"Shut up," they warned as they heaved him up and pushed forward.

Vermen obeyed, more because he had nothing to add than because he cared about what they wanted. They led him through the tunnels going up the mountain, the slope steeper with every minute. The waterfall's background roar covered the sound of their footsteps, but Vermen thought he counted five rebels. The air in his tiny bag grew hot and stuffy. Sweat drenched his forehead as they progressed, and soon he couldn't breathe properly. He swallowed, tried to calm his quickening heart. He'd suffocate in this bag long before they reached their destination.

A sudden draft of fresh air blew the thought away, piercing through the tissue's mesh. Three steps later, strong gusts of wind blew from his left, pushing against his body. He could feel the sun's warmth on his clothes and hands. They'd left the caverns. He'd die outside, somewhere on Mount Kairn's slope. Better than buried under tons of rock.

The rebels led him up a tiny staircase then pushed him along uneven rocks. Wind buffeted him. He kept placing his foot where there was no flat surface and fell twice, each time bringing a string of chuckles. His elbows and knees hurt from the successive impacts but he clenched his jaw and held his protests in. Any kind of insult or plea would amuse them further. Instead he straightened himself back up, ignoring their jests at his expense.

"Look at him, so dignified. Stern would've had a blast."

"He's way cuter with that bag over his head."

"Think he'll fall again? You know what they say: third time's the charm."

He did not stumble a third time. He reached a large flat rock and stopped. The five rebels had a short whispered argument on whether or not they should remove the bag. Stern's name came up more than once in the discussion. From what he overheard, at least one of them insisted he should stay standing, his head free. Judging from his voice, he was younger. He couldn't convince the others.

Hans felt their return by the way their bodies blocked the wind. With the sunlight he could make out general shapes moving through the bag. They surrounded him. Not a good sign. You did not surround a man you were about to shoot, not from this close—you'd get your clothes bloodied. The one in front of him spoke.

"Do you remember Erika?"

Of course he remembered her. Curly brown hair, quick wits, multiple charges of thievery already registered against her. He'd caught her two years ago, sent her to prison. He turned his body to answer the voice. Before he could pronounce a single word, however, a bat crashed against his side. He flinched and jumped away. They pushed him back to the middle of the circle.

"And Justin. You remember Justin?"

The hit came from the front this time, crushing the air out of his lungs before he could recall this one. He'd say it was the young blond from Mikken they'd killed in a shootout, when they'd caught the rebels in Serenity. That boy *was* dead, at least, not just imprisoned. Vermen swallowed hard. Were they going to name every rebel he'd put in jail and call it murder? How long did they intend to keep this up? Perhaps he could speed it up for them.

"You're missing Desmond and Lei," he said.

This time he expected the blow. Something heavy and metallic smashed against his hip, then the first bat smacked his knees. Vermen collapsed on the cold stone, shock and pain taking the legs from under him. Blood and saliva mixed in his mouth. He wanted to spit but it'd catch in the bag's tissue. The captain rolled over, trying to ease his breathing despite the throbbing in his side. The ringing in his ear and the roaring waterfall buried the insults they threw at him. He did feel the boots connecting with his legs, then thighs, however, and as pain wracked his muscles Vermen fought to keep still, to keep silent. He refused to give them the pleasure of hearing him scream. He'd die here. They would beat him like a dog and shoot him out of his misery when he was bloodied and battered. What dignity he could retain by taking the blows in silence, he would. He was a captain of the Union army. He did not plead with criminals for mercy.

"Enough," a young voice said, the same who'd wanted to remove the bag. "Finish this."

This one didn't approve. Vermen could almost like him for that. Almost.

As they lifted him back to his feet he tried to turn in the boy's direction, to get a glimpse through the bag. His head spun, his knees gave out, and he almost fell again. They caught him, made him kneel then pressed the shotgun against the back of his skull and pushed his head down. Too bad he'd never know who he should thank for the small reprieve. Vermen's throat clamped down, his innards churned. At least he was outside. He tried to picture the landscape below.

"Captain Hans Vermen, for your crimes against the rebels, we sentence you to death."

Klaus would've mocked their solemn declaration. He'd had no patience for fakes and despised ceremonies. Vermen shut his eyes. It was better to die his brother's way. No warning, no ridiculous announcement. Just a man with a gun and the guts to hold your gaze as he pulled the trigger. Vermen took a deep breath. Sharp pain stabbed his side at the movement and he winced. The cold metal against his neck shifted ever so slightly.

A gunshot rang. A dozen feet behind them. Not in his head.

"Step back now!"

Seraphin's voice whipped the cool air. They all obeyed at once, dropping their weapons. Vermen started breathing again, a huge uncontrolled gulp. His heart hammered against his chest. He dared not move. What if Holt had decided this was a great idea but it should be him holding the gun? It'd still be better than these cowards.

"What were you thinking? We do not execute prisoners, no matter who the prisoner is. And if it was to happen, ever, it would be my responsibility and I can guarantee he would not be kneeling on the ground, beaten. Now get inside. All of you."

"But Seraphin—"

"I said go!"

The depth of his anger surprised Vermen. Why did it tick him off so much? Had he not dreamed of doing this very thing? He'd threatened to shoot him in front of the noodle boy and the captain doubted he'd have hesitated. Vermen waited as they shuffled away, ill at ease with the thought Seraphin Holt had just ordered his men *not* to shoot him. This was backward. It should've been Andeal interrupting. Then maybe everything would've made sense.

Once his men were gone Seraphin skipped across the rocks to reach the small platform. Vermen could hear the light steps and swallowed hard as he knelt by his side. He didn't dare to move. What if it somehow changed Holt's mind? When the Regarian loosened the bag and removed it, the captain lowered his head, averting his eyes from the sunlight and from the pale, piercing gaze. He should say something, but he could not bring himself to thank him. This was the White Renegade. The man who'd shot his brother.

"Your men have no discipline."

Seraphin answered with a derisive snort, picked up the shotgun then helped Vermen back to his feet. Vermen struggled to stay upright despite the strain in his left knee, the hands tied behind his back, and the sharp pain in his side. Seraphin kept a hand on the captain's shoulder to help him, and Vermen felt a distinct twinge of disappointment when the other man removed it. That was not a feeling Hans would ever allow to blossom.

For a long moment, the Regarian studied him in silence, a hand shielding his eyes from the sun. Vermen looked wherever else he could. Not far from his feet, several streams connected into a larger one and the Delgian's Fall plummeted off Mount Kairn. The summit. They'd brought him to the summit. The land sprawling before him formed a breathtaking vista, nearly enough to take his mind off the relentless scrutiny.

"Why didn't you do it?"

Seraphin's voice broke the charm. Emotion thickened his Regarian accent. Vermen did not need to ask what 'it' was. He forced himself to look back at Holt. Wind buffeted his long white hair about. Vermen's gaze lingered on the Regarian's wiry body, magnetized by it. Seraphin's jaw line was taut and his fingers were clenched around his *skeptar*. He had no other weapon on him and Vermen realized belatedly that the gunshot interrupting his execution had come from the very weapon that had completed his brother's. Acrid bile burnt his stomach.

"Decency, a friend said." Vermen straightened, ignoring his muscles' protests at the movement. "One day justice will catch up to you and you'll pay for your crime. It won't be by my hands. There are laws. I know my place."

"That's cute."

Vermen scowled at the mocking tone. It brought a thin smile to the Regarian's lips.

"No, really, I admire your faith in our corrupt system. It speaks volumes of your degree of brainwashing. Andeal must be wrong about you."

"How is he?"

The question burst out before he could control his worried tone. Seraphin let another awkward silence slide by, walked around Vermen and untied his hands. Then he deigned to answer.

"Feverish and paranoid. Yet somehow he got to his feet earlier, stumbled all the way to our meeting room, and made a desperate and useless plea for your safety."

"I don't think useless is the right word." Vermen gave a pointed look at the shotgun slung on Seraphin's shoulder.

"I never intended to kill you."

Another silence. The waterfall's constant rumble filled the holes in their conversation. Vermen tried to enjoy the sun on his skin. Impossible. Not with Seraphin staring at him, detailing him, measuring him. Not when part of Hans hoped he liked what he saw.. The captain squared his shoulders as much as his wounds would allow. He did not want to appear as vulnerable as he felt.

"Why not?" he asked.

Holt had no answer ready for him. His slender fingers brushed against the *skeptar's* hilt as he reflected on the question. There was something captivating about his thoughtful expression, as though it broadcasted his every emotion clearly—confusion, anger, relief, hesitation. It shouldn't be so easy to read, and Hans found himself wishing he could understand every single one.

"Where to start?" Seraphin said. "I have no need. I owe you for Andeal's life. More than that, however...You're not your brother. You didn't kill my family. Yes, you are responsible for the deaths of fellow rebels but they are not part of my ancestry. I am not beholden to avenging them."

"That's some stupid Regarian logic."

"Congratulations, then. You owe your life to some stupid Regarian logic."

An amused smile played on Seraphin's features. Vermen felt an unspoken challenge to continue this banter. He refused to give the Renegade that pleasure.

"What now?" he asked.

"Andeal thinks you'll work for me."

"Never. I'm not one of your outlaws."

"You're *an* outlaw."

Vermen clenched his jaw. He'd defied orders to go after Seraphin and they'd labeled him a deserter. They were wrong. He hadn't betrayed his oath to serve and protect. He only needed time to sort himself out and escape. Before the captain could deny the accusation, however, Seraphin brushed it aside with a dismissive wave of his hand.

"In truth, you'd be working for Andeal. Moving crates about, doing manual tasks."

"I don't want to contribute to whatever this is."

Seraphin shrugged. "Suit yourself. It's the only way you'll get out of that cell, however."

That struck a nerve. Vermen hated the cramped little cave. Andeal's visits might help make it bearable but there was only so much he could do. The daily exercise kept his body in shape but the immobility grated on his mind. He licked his lips, considered the option. It would only be a temporary deal. He could discover more about the rebels, learn to navigate their headquarters, and find a way to escape that did not involve taking Andeal with him. Seraphin tilted his head to the side, studying him, perhaps trying to gauge his reaction.

"Andeal's on a short mission. When he returns, he'll want an answer. Now come."

Seraphin signaled for him to follow and headed back into the mountain. Vermen took a first hesitant step, found a way to shift his weight as he walked to diminish some of the strain, then followed the Regarian.

As the stuffy underground air enclosed Vermen once more, weighing on him, the captain knew then that when his friend returned, he would accept.

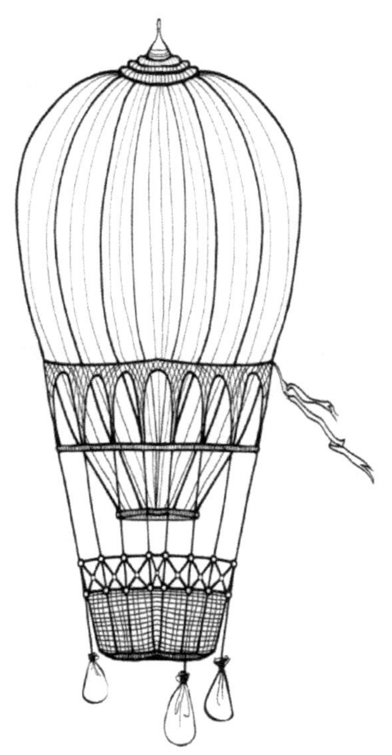

# CHAPTER FOURTEEN

*Henry opened another pack* of instant noodles and threw them into the boiling water. His heart pinched a little. Kinsi might be gone, but eating the grocery stocks without paying felt like thieving anyway. Days of pilfering the edible goods had not diminished the guilt, yet he had to feed himself and there was nothing else left in Ferrea. He could always pay his friend once he saw him.

He had left the rebels' hideout the morning after his supper at the summit. He'd trekked all the way back to Ferrea and with every step away from Mount Kairn, his heart lifted. Free at last, he'd told himself. A pleasant breeze drifted through the leaves, caressing his skin. He no longer had to live underground. He could go home and build a life for himself. A tranquil, law-abiding life. Far from his father's expectations.

Henry had reached his hometown at sunset and strolled down the main street. His house squatted at the bottom of the hill, motionless and peaceful. Had anything changed while he was gone? It had felt like the village awaited his return, fixed in time. He'd smiled and hurried to his door.

His broken door. It hung, destroyed by Captain Vermen, exactly how he'd left it. The kitchen, however, hadn't been left untouched. Henry had stared at the open cupboards and thrown drawers, the stools scattered on the floor among the kitchen wares. The army had stormed his house, looking for its officer. Henry had taken a step back and torn his gaze away—not daring to enter and discover the full extent of the disaster. Besides, nothing remained there for him. Nothing but a message from his father he did not want to hear.

He'd moved on, climbing the hill's slope at a determined space. The empty town welcomed him. Every rooftop was black, devoid of the soft green hue emanating from working organic solar panels. Even Paul's inn no longer produced any electricity. A quick investigation revealed the last three survivors had deserted Ferrea. Only Henry remained behind. He hid in Kinsi's grocery, reluctant to abandon the quaint streets he'd always walked. Ten days had passed since his return. It had turned out far more difficult to give up on the village than it'd been to quit the rebels. Tia's garden was in full bloom, he had supplies for a month, and he could relax in Ferrea's quiet emptiness. Why would he leave?

Henry turned off the stove and poured his instant noodles into a large bowl. He walked out to sit on the tiny stairs in front of Kinsi's, ready to enjoy the last sunrays as he ate his dinner. Another peaceful evening, away from Andeal's insistence and the oppressing weight of rocks above his head.

His butt cheeks had barely touched the stairs when the low rumble of an engine and voices traveled up the street to him. They came from the south, from his house and the large camping grounds. Henry put down his bowl and stood. He recognized the voices, knew what they were doing. Andeal had finally come for his father's balloon envelope.

He should leave the rebels alone. Stay away, hidden in his perfect bubble. Yet Henry's steps led him straight to Ferrea's edge and the small road heading to his home. He set one foot in front of another, his body acting without his mind's consent, until he stood at the top of the hill. A military truck waited before his door, pieces of vegetation stuck in its wheels and windows. Vermen's car, Henry guessed. They must've found it on their way. No one kept watch outside.

Henry sat down, setting his palms flat against the dusty road to keep his hands from shaking. He wished he'd brought the noodles with him now. Inside, a blue-skinned man unearthed his father's last message. A man with the strength and will to do what was necessary. Andeal and Maniel were the best choice for this. They'd had Lenz's trust and love. So why did it feel so wrong to be staying on top of this hill? Where was all his rightful anger at being used? He imagined Andeal removing the note demanding Henry care for the balloon's envelope and opening the trunk. He couldn't wrap his mind around the sight. That chest had remained locked for years. How many hours had Henry spent, staring at the mysterious message—the only one left by his father—wondering what was so special about the envelope? Now Andeal would find out. Not Henry.

He pushed himself off the ground and dusted off his pants. At first he trudged down the hill, but his strides soon lengthened until his feet hit the ground at full speed. He ran to his house, skidding to a stop at his doorstep. His sweaty shirt stuck to his back and his breath had turned into short gasps. He hesitated before entering. A warm bowl of noodles waited for him at Kinsi's. What he'd find inside his home remained unknown. Another risk.

Another mistake, most likely.

He crossed the threshold anyway, walked straight past the counter and to the shop section of the house. He almost slammed into Joshua, leaning against the closest shelf, whistling to himself as he touched an ugly bruise on his forehead. The man grabbed him just in time to avoid a full collision. His surprise quickly shifted to a large grin.

"Hey, mate! What are you doing here?"

Henry hushed him right away. His friend's voice rang through the rows of old tourist gifts and made him wince.

"I don't know."

He left a confused Joshua behind and moved to the back store. The boxes had been pushed aside and the trapdoor lay open. Light surged from the basement. Henry set his foot on the first step and was greeted by their familiar creak. A sound that used to be a prelude to hours of silent questions, staring at a tiny bit of paper. Why the envelope? What had his father been up to? Perhaps today, the creaking would prelude answers to those very questions.

He should run away from them. Turn around and return to his noodles. Leaving the rebels had given him such relief, so why was he here now? Common sense had abandoned him. He needed to know, though. He thought about the Lenz Balloon, about his father's sacrifice, about how the man behind these things was so different than the one he'd known. He needed his answers. Henry walked down the stairs.

Andeal sat in the middle of the basement floor, in front of the unopened chest. Relief flooded Henry. He let out a breath he hadn't noticed he was holding and leaned a moment on the wall. He'd arrived in time, Andeal hadn't read anything. Henry cleared his throat, as loud as he could.

The engineer jumped and turned.

"Henry?"

"I'd like to do this. Alone."

"Of course!"

Andeal scrambled to his feet, then winced at the sudden movement. Henry made a mental note to ask about their injuries while the overjoyed engineer stopped to give his forearm a solemn squeeze. Henry waited for his steps to disappear upstairs before approaching the ancient chest. He caressed the worn wood. The flaked blue and gold paint came off at his touch. Regarians passed symbolic tokens from one generation to the next. His family had kept this chest and his father had stored his most precious belongings in it. And in the envelope, he'd apparently hidden his deepest secret. Henry's hands trembled as he clicked the simple lock and lifted the lid.

A waft of musty air choked him. Dust had gathered inside for a decade and Henry took a step back, coughing. During all those years watching over the balloon, he hadn't dared open the chest. Now he grabbed the envelope and extracted it without ceremony. He spread the smooth fabric, covering as much surface as he could. The balloon was too large for his tiny basement.

Henry crawled over the envelope on his knees and ran his hands over it. His boots left specks of dirt behind but he continued his tactile search. Stains could be cleaned later. Even so, it seemed wrong to smear the beautiful gold and purple envelope he should be caring for. He was so out of place here, crouched on this balloon, pursuing Lenz Schmitt's intrigues. Yet somewhere in this sea of fabric was the recording and his last chance at answers.

His fingers brushed against abnormal sewing lines. Henry stopped everything—moving, breathing, thinking. That was it. That had to be it.

His heart sped as he traced the small pouch. Henry wiped his sweaty hands and retrieved a pocketknife. He slid the blade under the threads and cut them with caution, careful not to tear the fabric. A glassy disc slid out of the pocket, wrapped in folded papers and protected by an old plastic bag. His name was written on it. The handwriting was the same as his note, the same as Andeal's bloodied message. Henry took a deep breath and started with the crumpled sheets. The first was an official letter, written with a typewriter. Signed by Galen Clarin, but not sent to his father. This looked like important correspondence. How had Lenz Schmitt acquired it? Henry browsed through the papers. All letters from either Galen Clarin or his brother, General Omar Clarin. Big people from the big circle. The kind of communications you don't find sewn in a balloon's envelope, hidden in a basement. Henry set them aside. None of this was addressed to him.

Maybe the disc was.

He picked it up, sprinted upstairs, rushed past Andeal and Joshua and stopped in front of his old radio player. He slammed the disc into the reader and turned it on. Static replaced the heavy silence. His two friends appeared in the doorway just as the first words pierced through.

It was a man, but not his father. The voice was smooth and delicate. Educated.

*"I dare to believe our time has come,"* he said. *"None of the speakers have the slightest idea of how to stop this Plague, the poor confused idiots. All they could conclude is that they dealt with a supervirus! A five-year old would've deduced as much. I have not heard an ounce of optimism about slowing the Plague, let alone curing it. Have you, Omar?"*

*"No. No optimism."*

The second voice was deep and brutal. Henry shivered at the light tone they used. They must be discussing the Threstle Plague, yet they treated it as they would a fundraising cocktail.

"And don't you think it'd be cruel to let these hopeless folks wallow and worry? How many have died already from my masterwork?"

"Thousands. The Plague is out of Ferrys. It swept over Mikken to the north and is going east, into Regaria."

"Excellent. The crisis grows and our good citizens despair. It is high time to give them heroes, and restore our name to its former glory."

The sound of running water cut the conversation. Henry heard shallow breathing over it. Was that his father? He closed his eyes and tried to picture him, hiding, shaky hands holding a recorder. He doubted the two men knew they had an audience.

"We need a third party, however. They need a hero whose job it is to save lives. Yours is to crush them, and I create artificial versions of life. But I have found just the man, a certain Jacob Kurtmann. He's a doctor on the front line against the Plague. His wife perished from it and now he treats patients without care for his own safety. I asked our newspapers and radio to pick up his story, to frame him as a kind, grieving husband. Imagine what it'd be if we gave him the cure."

"They'll love him."

"Exactly. I'll contact Doctor Kurtmann with news of a possible antivirus against the Threstle Plague. Offer all men under your command to help spread the cure and suggest he requests the entirety of Ferrys' army. Together we can give our young surgeon all he needs to save his country—and others—from a terrible devastation. He'll be a hero. And with a little push from the media, we'll have a brand new president within a few years. We might even be able to unite everyone under his benevolent guidance!"

The soft-spoken man laughed and his footsteps became louder, then turned into static. Henry's eyes snapped open. When he slammed the stop button on his radio, the buzzing in his skull replaced the heavy silence. The Threstle Plague had reaped thousands of lives across the continent. It had taken his mom. He'd grieved and told himself there was nothing to do, that sickness was a force of nature that struck without distinctions. But this wasn't nature. This was a man's work. Galen Clarin's work.

His father had known.

Bile rushed up Henry's throat and he stumbled back, to plop onto his large sofa. Grief hadn't driven Lenz Schmitt out of his home. Vengeance had. Jacob Kurtmann had been elected president shortly after his miraculous work to spread the antivirus against the Threstle Plague. Three countries had united under his banner. And the Clarin twins, acclaimed for their role in these events, were never far from the president. A perfect ploy. A sick one.

If a man had to leave his teenage son behind to put the story out, could he be blamed?

Henry dug his fingers into the cushy sofa. His gaze went to the back door and he traced its frame, forcing his breathing to slow down before he risked a glance at Joshua and Andeal. The engineer stared at the radio, open-mouthed, wordless. His gambler friend played with his precious deck of cards, ripping the corners and tapping his foot on the ground. Henry doubted Joshua noticed either action. He swallowed hard.

"I'll fly." No reaction from Andeal. "Your weird balloon. I'll fly it."

Andeal's horrified expression morphed into surprise as Henry's words sunk in. Then Henry himself realised what he'd just said. Panic rose from the bottom of his stomach and stuck at the back of his throat. Had he just promised to pilot an illegal hot air balloon? Launch into the sky like he actually knew how to fly? Did he propose to openly defy the Union?

"So you'll come back with us?" Andeal asked.

Henry forced himself to nod. When Union airships shot him down, would he remember this as the moment he'd decided to throw his life away? Or, perhaps, as the one he'd stopped being a helpless bystander to his own life? He'd watched his mother die, had done nothing as funds ran out and the Annual Mount Kairn Race got canceled, had stood by as Vermen and Seraphin pointed a gun at each other. He never *did* anything about it because, really, what could a coward like him do about these things? But perhaps Joshua was right. It wasn't about transforming into unbeatable heroes. It was about trying with what little you had going for you.

And he, at the very least, could fly a hot air balloon.

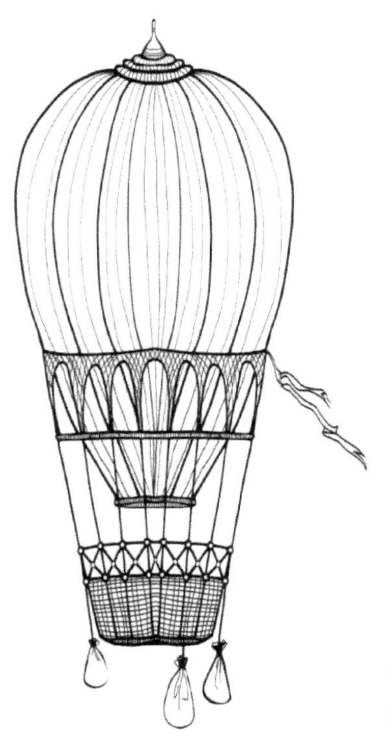

# CHAPTER FIFTEEN

*Once Galen Clarin's voice* died out and the recording clicked, nothing but silence filled the private dining booth. As soon as they had returned from Henry's house, Andeal had borrowed the recording from him, grabbed a bottle of wine, and forced Seraphin and Maniel to dine with him. His legs still hurt from the long trek but this couldn't wait. They needed to hear it now. After all these years hunting for proof of Galen's schemes, all the risks they'd taken to bring his conspiracy to light, they finally had the proof they'd been looking for.

It had taken all of Andeal's willpower to wait until they had finished eating. He poured one last glass of wine as Galen's smooth voice summarized his plan to his twin brother. Neither of his companions said a word. They both understood the significance of what they were hearing. Maniel squeezed Andeal's hand tight while Seraphin stared at the disc reader for several minutes after it was finished.

"We have it on tape."

Seraphin's hushed voice broke the tense silence. He sounded like he needed to convince himself.

"We have it on tape," Andeal repeated. "This is it."

Seraphin removed the disc from the reader and set it back in its protective case. His fingers wrapped around his glass of wine and he lifted it, but before he could bring it to his lips, a small chuckle shook his shoulder. A wide smile lit his face. Andeal couldn't remember when he'd last seen such a relaxed expression on Seraphin. His old friend lifted the glass toward the center of the table.

"Remind me never to doubt you again, Andeal." His pale blue eyes shone behind the thin glasses. "You asked for one month, and here we are, with the most beautiful and concise proof of Galen's guilt we could ever hope for."

They clinked their glasses together, raised them, and drank.

"I told you."

Despite his bluster, Andeal had to admit he hadn't been so sure of himself. He had needed something to placate Seraphin when he had told him he believed Lenz might have known something and passed it on to Henry. Sure, Lenz often spoke as though he was more involved than he let on but Andeal had nothing solid to base his guess on. He'd followed his guts and he had been right. Andeal turned to his old friend and met his gaze.

"We can move to the next step now," he said, "and I'll serve as extra confirmation if you need me to."

Seraphin set the wine back on the table, his mirth replaced by a more serious expression. "Everything will help, but don't...don't think about it for tonight."

Easier said than done. Andeal couldn't wait to be out from under Mount Kairn. He had done all he could to make the mountain's network of caves into a home, but in the end the tunnels were just that: tunnels. It didn't matter how many lights he lined upon the walls. This wasn't where he'd wanted to live. Not after the labs. He longed for the sun coming through a window, or a warm breeze as he sat on a balcony in summer. Just a normal house to live in with Maniel, and raise a family in. The time to leave couldn't arrive fast enough.

And yet, it couldn't wait long enough either.

As the conversation moved to where they would gather supplies for all the rebels and how they might split their small group to cover as much ground as possible, Andeal wondered what it'd be like outside. Memories from his short travels with Maniel after they had escaped the labs flooded back. He had been called a monster by strangers catching sight of him. They had been run out of smaller towns on multiple occasions and the two of them had been forced to scrape by with stolen money, what little they knew they could eat from the woods and the very rare generous stranger. Maniel would enter towns on her own to avoid bringing attention to their presence.

The labs had turned him into a caged animal. Traveling through Ferrys made him feel like a wild beast, always roaming at the edge of civilization. He had grown restless and bitter, angry that they had escaped only to be pushed out from society. Only Maniel's patient love kept him from striding into the National Radio Tower and demanding that Galen Clarin face him. She had convinced him to bide his time and be careful, had found these tunnels in the mountain. He would've gotten himself captured or killed a long time ago without her.

Once they left Mount Kairn, he would have to face strangers again. He wasn't alone, however. If there was one thing he had learned, it was that with Maniel at his side, he could get through anything.

Maniel put her hand on his leg, under the table, and Andeal realised he'd stopped paying attention to the conversation. He shook his head a little, pushing the dark thoughts away. He had friends now. It would be better. Andeal smiled at Maniel. "I'm sorry. What did I miss?"

"Seraphin thinks we'll be ready in a month," she said.

"That's great!" He forced cheerfulness into his tone, trying to assuage their obvious worry. Both Seraphin and Maniel were staring at him, their smiles a little bit stiff. His wife wasn't buying it, but she said nothing. Andeal finished his wine. "The sooner, the better."

"I agree," Maniel said. She leaned forward and what had been left of her smile vanished. "Something has been bothering me about this recording."

Andeal frowned at the shift in her mood and exchanged a glance with Seraphin. Had they missed something important? As the three of them had built the rebels' network, Maniel had always been the one to point out key details and keep them from running into important problems. They waited for her to explain. She pinched her lips and a haunted look crept into her eyes.

"Do you remember when Galen poisoned Lenz? How Lenz would repeat 'he's doing it again' over and over but never explain what?" She grabbed the edge of the table, took a deep breath. "Andeal, what if Galen Clarin was testing another Threstle Plague on us? Lenz died and you were sick. I think the silver in your water saved you—it *is* antibiotic. And they gave me unknown meds which could have protected me altogether from it. But if that's true...What if he could unleash a second pandemic whenever he wanted?"

Andeal's heart skipped several beats and his fingertips grew cold. Another Threstle Plague. Everything shutting down again, the stench of death in every street, moans and weeping drifting out of windows. Victims dying within days, feverish and demented. Andeal shuddered as memories of Lenz' illness mixed with the years of the Threstle Plague. How many would die this time?

"He wouldn't…" He would. Andeal closed his eyes, took a deep breath. "He must never get the chance."

"He won't." Seraphin had straightened in his chair. All the determination and certainty in the world filled his tone. Pale hands swept the air in a grand gesture as the Regarian continued. "We are the White Renegade's rebels, are we not? We have escaped authorities for years, pilfered gas containers from them, infiltrated General Omar Clarin's close circles and stolen vital information, captured our most bitter pursuer, and acquired an explicit recording of Galen Clarin's scheme. Five years ago there was only the three of us. We knew something had to be done, but we'd never have guessed how far we would get. This *is* it. We will go out there and spread the word." Seraphin smiled at Andeal, and the red streaks in his eyes seemed brighter than usual. "The Clarin twins will never know what hit them."

It took more than a week for Andeal to stride into Vermen's cell, a pair of shackles slung over his shoulder. He was humming to himself, a satisfied smile upon his features, and threw an enthusiastic "good morning" at him.

The contrast with their last meeting was so abrupt that for some time, Vermen could not form a coherent response.

"You don't act like someone I almost killed."

Their gazes met. Andeal's unfaltering smile did not reach his eyes.

"I prefer to act like someone you saved," he answered after some time.

"Why?"

Andeal had never explained why he put so much effort into Vermen—why he visited all the time despite Vermen's categorical refusal to participate in the conversations, cared enough to bring meals at regular hours, share the weather and latest news, relate half of his life in an endless monolog. Vermen had thought he'd caught a glimpse of the answer when Andeal had overpowered him, and now he wanted the whole answer. Andeal lifted himself onto the desk and sat, his legs dangling over the edge.

"You could have let me die and fled. When you slashed me, I knew I might not survive the wound and I didn't care. It would have been better than the labs. But you chose to stay. I'm glad you did."

"But why do you care? Your friends seemed pretty intent on killing me when they paid a visit."

"Don't mock them." Andeal brought his legs up and crossed them, his tone hardening. "You captured and executed good men and women. They were passionate, determined. They had plans for the future. We lived with them every day and they became a second family. You of all people know how it is to seek revenge for the death of a family member."

Vermen's anger flared at the comparison. He clenched his fists and took a step forward, but pain shot through his muscles and forced him to calm down. The bruises from his recent beating still throbbed and kept him mostly inactive.

"It's not the same."

"No, you're right." If Andeal was the least bit intimidated, it didn't show. "Your brother had a presidential sanction to commit atrocities. We don't even have permission to live."

The captain's muscles tightened. Another word and he'd spring on Andeal. His brother had not been a monster—these were lies built to sully his name and justify Seraphin's actions. Vermen would hear none of it.

"They were criminals. With a criminal record."

"You think that diminishes their loss? You took loved ones away."

Vermen struggled for an answer, a way to deny Andeal's words. It had been his duty to dismantle Seraphin's group, to capture the rebels and put them behind bars. He'd acted within the parameters of his mission, respecting General Clarin's orders—until he quit to go after Seraphin on his own, at least. He would not apologise for those deaths. He did not regret his actions.

"So why stop them? Why interrupt their well-deserved vengeance?"

"Do I look like I care for this bloodshed? It doesn't solve anything and it goes on and on!" He set the shackles on the desk and jumped down. "I don't want it here, in my home. But you...you didn't shoot Seraphin."

Andeal made it sound like a compliment. He'd lacked the courage to go through with his plan and avenge his brother, yet somehow that made him better than others. Vermen averted his eyes. His cheeks burnt from the rising shame.

"And that's why you're helping? Because I broke your little cycle of angry revenge?"

He described a circle with his index with a sneer. He shouldn't have started this conversation. All of it was ridiculous.

"Yes. And no." Andeal crossed his arms and waited for Vermen to look at him before he continued. "When I was locked up I wanted nothing more than a chance to get out, walk around, do something. Even if it meant more tests, more examinations, more pain and sickness. It reminded me I was alive. There was a world out there. Sometimes I'd even get lucky and glimpse the sky, and those fleeting moments kept me sane. I will never put another human being through the same."

"Who did it to you? The labs, the blue, the prison..." The question had hung at the back of his mind since his first day in the rebels' headquarters. Not that he could've asked—it'd imply an interest in who these people were. Trying to deny he cared for Andeal now would be ridiculous, however.

His friend allowed his gaze to rest on Vermen. He was choosing his words with care—not a habit in Andeal's case.

"This is dangerous information to give you."

"Rebel secret?" Vermen couldn't keep the mockery out of his voice. As far as hiding precious information went, Holt's group had done a very bad job so far.

"State secret. I meant dangerous to *you*, not to us." An amused smile flickered on his expression. "It wouldn't do a lot of good to Galen Clarin's reputation for it to be known he tested several highly dangerous bacterial strains and vaccines on people. He had a hard enough time erasing his contributions to the engineered bacteria that ate everyone's oil supply."

Vermen blinked. Galen Clarin was the Union's most famous and controversial genetic engineer. He'd designed a vaccine against the Threstle Plague when everyone thought the virus would exterminate them, then handed it over to President Kurtmann, a young doctor at the time. Those two, with the second Clarin twin—General Omar—pretty much led the country today. They were the Union's spine.

"How can you be sure of this?" His voice shook. Andeal could be bluffing, trying to shake his convictions.

"Because he came to check on the progress of his pet project on a regular basis. He seemed particularly fascinated by the growing rash Lenz showed toward the end, and the nausea his foul-tasting water gave me."

Vermen gritted his teeth and averted his gaze. If he hadn't seen the utter terror in Andeal's gaze at the mere mention of a capture, he'd call him a liar. The Clarin family had been a major force of Ferrysian politics—and the Union's, once the countries fused—for decades now. Galen had grown from a teenage science prodigy into a fine man devoting his intellect to the country. How could he also be that horrible person testing on unwilling human subjects?

"That's…"

Andeal raised a hand to stop him. "He managed to leave no accessible paper trail, but we'll get him."

"Get him?"

The question left his lips before he could hold it back. It drew an eager smile from Andeal. His engineer friend leaned forward.

"This is what the rebels are about, Hans. Years ago, Stern brought us information that indicated Galen was—"

"Stop. Right now."

Captain Vermen's anger flared as Andeal tried to push their ridiculous agenda. He could believe Andeal's story; he'd witnessed its effects firsthand. That did not mean he wanted to hear the fantasized conspiracy of evil from a group hell-bent on putting a bullet through his skull.

"I don't give a rat's ass about the rest of your band of criminals. They tried to kill me last week. You're a decent man and it's a shame they've used your personal experience to cram your head with those crazy stories, but just because I didn't let you die doesn't mean I want to share in your collective delusion!"

His tirade seemed to take Andeal aback, and for a moment, the engineer stared at him in slight confusion. Vermen held the blue gaze without flinching. Andeal's lips thinned into a determined line. He grabbed the shackles and threw them at the captain. They crashed to the ground and slid to his feet.

"No one crammed *my* head, Captain. Do you think Seraphin started this alone? I'm the one who asked him to build the rebels and help me bring Galen to justice." He pointed at the shackles. "Put them on. I'll show you the work."

As Andeal left the room, Vermen realised he'd never agreed to help. He considered staying inside, imagined the endless weeks of maddening boredom, sighed, then picked up the chains and clamped the shackles around his ankles.

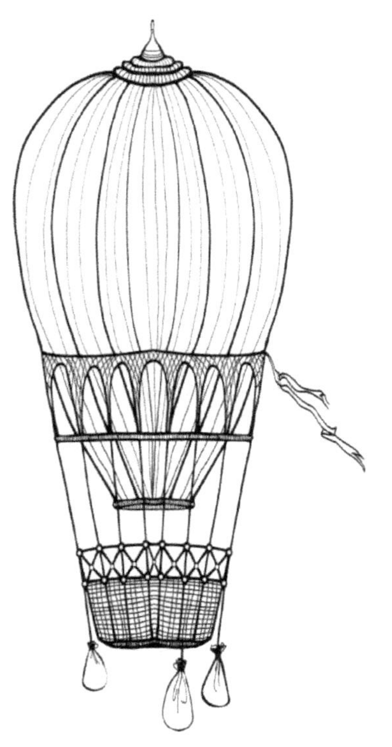

# CHAPTER SIXTEEN

*Henry melded into the* crowd of ordinary folks and walked to the pub's wooden counter. He slid onto a high chair and signaled the barman over. The smoky pub's atmosphere was both strange and familiar. It reminded him of Paul's inn at the height of tourist season, when complete strangers competed at the dart boards or shared stories of their homes around a dark ale. Back when they held the Annual Race yearly. Back when Ferrea was alive.

The men gathered in Galway's pub knew each other, however. Fishermen assembled here after a long day's work to compare haul and discuss business. Whenever someone entered, he was greeted by at least two comrades and could sit with them at the green-dyed tables. Henry expected to be asked to leave any moment now. He was an outsider intruding on their evening's leisure.

Once, he'd have felt close to these men and their hard, daily labour. Normal lives with normal worries. The fishermen didn't concern themselves with evil conspiracies. They spoke of fish, weather, and trade, feared winter and loved their wives. Henry remembered how it felt to wonder when the next meal would be, but the question felt trivial now. Far from his world.

No, that wasn't right. It was him who'd stepped away from a normal life, not the other way around. Henry grabbed his pint and downed half of it in one shot. He wished he could forget what he'd learned and chat with these sailors, like he was one of them. A normal man, not a rebel.

Perhaps coming to Galway wasn't such a great idea. He'd needed to prove he could walk in his father's footsteps, but he'd been a nervous wreck all day. During the drive north he'd harassed Joshua with questions—about their task, about the village, about anything he could think of—until his friend's patience ran out and he told him to shut it. The two rebels riding in the seats behind heaved sighs of relief. Henry wrung his hands but remained silent the rest of the way to the reputed fishing village.

Although little more than a few dozen houses cluttered around an asphaltroad, Galway was known throughout the Union for its smoked fish. Stern's cousin held a prolific business on the shore of Lake Callenhal and, every few months, he gave the rebels a shipment of dried landlocked salmon, walleye, and rainbow trout. The merchant proved to be a gentleman—far more agreeable than Stern, who seemed intent on living up to his name.

By the time they'd paid for and packed hundreds of dried fish, the sun had set the western horizon ablaze. As the light diminished the solar panels decorating the roofs began glowing green. In large cities it sufficed to light the streets, but villages like Galway complemented the nightly hue with normal white globes. As they lit up one by one, Henry recognised the lights used by the rebels in their underground network. How many had they stolen through the years to brighten their tunnels?

"I suggest we don't drive at night," Joshua had said. "We're remarkable enough during the day. I see no point in bringing extra attention to the vehicle."

Both of the rebels with them sneered. The lanky one with short blond hair—Bran, or something like that—shook his head. "I know where that's going."

"Forget the pub, Joshua," said the other, a flat-nosed woman from Mikken who'd never even introduced herself. "You saw all those stares we received."

"Indeed I did! It's why I need to hit the pub. Where else could I apologise to everyone at once?"

"Like you intend to apologise," the woman answered. "I'm not getting involved in this."

Joshua's eternal smile held strong as he turned to Bran, who shook his head right away and even took a step back. This time the corners of the Burgian's mouth did fall a little. His gaze went to Henry.

"You're coming with me, right?"

Henry stuttered and glanced at the two other rebels. They mouthed 'no', perhaps hoping Joshua would abandon the idea if he remained alone. Good ale was almost non-existent at the headquarters, however, and he missed his Wednesday nights with Paul and Kinsi.

"Of course. Someone's got to watch your back."

"Great. Go ahead and save a seat for me. I'll help them pack everything in the car."

Scouting out the pub: a task he had been glad to accept. Yet as Henry finished his first pint, he wondered how many he'd have time to drink before Joshua deigned to show up. Every few minutes, his gaze trailed back to the door. Had something happened? The others had been worried enough not to come. What if his friend never made it to the door? Henry tapped on his empty mug with increasing speed as he grew more and more nervous.

"Waiting for someone, stranger?"

A broad-shouldered man plopped into the seat next to him, a large smile stamped on his face. Despite the locals' warm dispositions, distrust slithered up Henry's spine. Or perhaps because of it. None of the fishermen had even greeted him since he entered, and the villagers they met in the streets gave them more suspicious glares than smiles.

"I am."

"Wouldn't happen to be a red-haired Burgian thief, would it?"

Henry stiffened and his fingers clenched around the mug. "He's not a thief."

"So you are waiting for him."

The satisfied tone sent his heart tumbling to his toes. Once again, he'd talked too much. The underlying threat now clear in this fisherman's tone did nothing to reassure him. Henry released his mug, ready to dash out and find Joshua. A powerful hand crashed onto his shoulder and forced him back in the chair.

"Don't panic. We're all waiting for him." He gestured at two of his friends, who took places on either side of the entrance. "You see, last time your troop visited town, your friend emptied our pockets. Cheated respectable men out of their money. All we want is to take back our due."

Henry gulped, hard. These men had played cards with Joshua and lost. No surprise there. His friend had made an art out of bluff and strategy. He also had a dangerous love of showmanship. It seemed Galway's locals had a different kind of game in mind for tonight.

The front door swooshed open as Joshua stepped in, all smiles. The grip tightened on Henry's shoulder and immobilized him as two thugs moved in. Joshua's eyes widened in surprise as they grabbed one arm each and dragged him out. He chuckled and did not resist.

"Whoa there, gentlemen! I didn't know you were that eager to see me again. Maybe if you unhand me, we can talk?"

His voice trailed off as the door slammed shut behind them. A couple of locals snickered but no one stood up to protest. Who would defend a red-haired Burgian? The bright dye marked him as a criminal and served as a warning to all. Most exiles preferred to shave, since keeping the red hair was interpreted as pride in one's crime. The two inches of brown at the root of Joshua's hairproved he'd never cut his. Henry turned to his guardian.

"W-what will you do to him?"

"They won't kill him. Sit and relax, and you'll be safe."

In short, act like they aren't beating him up, and it won't happen to you. Henry closed his eyes and took a deep breath. He couldn't save Joshua alone. They were tall men, determined and muscled. He was all bones and skin, with a bit of a gut. Months of a strict instant noodles diet had vaporised what strength he'd had left and the labor around Andeal's balloon had just begun to build it back. If he stayed behind, he'd be in better shape to pick his friend up after. Abandon Joshua to help him later. A coward's decision.

"All right..." He shrugged off the fisherman's hand. The local brute set it down on the counter instead. Henry gestured at the bartender. "A glass of the strongest stuff you've got."

His heart hammered in his chest. In a nearby alley, two men kicked and punched at a fellow rebel, a friend. He flinched as he imagined the pain in his chest, the cracked ribs, or the blood running down his nose. And Joshua, who might take it all with an unshakable smile. Alcohol would be essential to survive the evening.

He grabbed the shot with a shaky hand. Come on. Deep breaths. He could do this.

Henry Schmitt downed the clear liquid in a single shot and slammed the glass down hard on his watcher's left hand. The strong alcohol brought tears to his eyes and made his head spin, but he seized his empty mug. The fisherman's pained exclamation turned into a howl when Henry smashed the tankard into his face.

Henry stumbled away, dazed. Had he just done that? Euphoria rushed to his head and he grinned. The fisherman was twice his size, but right now he held his cheek and clutched the counter, dazed. Others rose in the pub and Henry understood he could not stand still and celebrate his victory. He dashed for the exit before the locals fell upon him.

The fresh air calmed his fired-up brain and forced him to slow. He couldn't just rush ahead. Step one: find Joshua. Step two: create a plan.

The meaty sound of fists hitting a body, followed by grunts of pain, made the first step easy. They were in the alley right next to the pub. Henry snuck in their direction, one careful step at a time. The two thugs taunted Joshua, over and over. How could his friend remain silent at their bad jests? Henry's anger rose at every insult. His jaws hurt from clenching it shut so hard. He made his way around the building and squatted behind a large trash bin. His hiding spot offered him a disgusting view of the scene.

One of the men held Joshua from behind while the other punched. The green glow from the roofs gave a sickly hue to his friend's skin. He hung limp in his assailant's arms, too drained to defend himself. Perhaps that explained why he formed no rebuttals to their insults. Hard to retort with a few missing teeth and your mouth filled with blood.

"My turn?" the one holding Joshua asked.

"Sure."

They dumped him on the ground and he fell with a grunt of pain. He had time to roll over and wipe the blood from his mouth before the punching thug gave him one last kick. Henry bit his curled fist in empathetic pain. He ought to jump into the fray and fight. Quick, before the man he'd attacked in the tavern came to help.

He remained rooted to his spot. Paralyzed. Terrified.

One of the two thugs gasped and backpedalled across the alley like Joshua had burnt him. He set his back to the wall and pointed at the prone rebel.

"Gun!"

The other local had more courage than his companion; he bent over Joshua without the slightest hint of fear. He reached inside the coat and removed a small black firearm. Henry bit his lips to keep from cursing. The calmer thug spat on Joshua.

"Illegal firearms. Congratulations, you upgraded from scoundrel to criminal," he said. "Let's get him to the station. A night in a damp cell would do him a lot of good."

His companion tentatively reached for Joshua's arm and helped lift him. Henry crouched forward. He had to act. Except now, they held a gun. And all he had was his shaky fists. He should've ordered more than one shot. Or eaten a pot full of noodles.

Before he could jump out of hiding, his earlier guard stumbled into the alley, wild-eyed. Blood trickled down his cheek and he moved with a strange, almost drunken stagger. He waved for his two friends to stop.

"Did the other one come out? I can't find him!"

"No sign of him. This one has a gun."

A short silence followed. They all tensed. Afraid. Asking themselves who were these strange men they'd attacked. What had they gotten themselves into? Henry remembered a surreal evening, as he'd stood on Ferrea's hill and stared at the black-clad stranger at his door. He'd panicked, mistaken Andeal for an assassin. The three fishermen bathed in green light, with an armed red-headed Burgian at their feet and another, vanished man, had every reason to do the same.

Joshua's body shook as he chuckled. He struggled to raise his head and Henry barely made out his smile in the feeble light. His mirth added to their terror. His friend coughed—a deep, throat-rattling sound that sent a shiver running up everyone's spine.

"Gone to warn the others. You think your local police can hold up against a dozen well-trained guerrilla snipers?"

Henry almost bolted out to call the bluff. He wanted to reassure these men, tell them they were safe, that he wasn't a dangerous criminal. He didn't. They released Joshua, who collapsed in the dirt again. The one who'd spat earlier took a hesitant step forward.

"Just...just don't come back."

They exchanged another swift glance and hightailed out of the alley, Joshua's gun in hand. Henry waited for their footsteps to disappear before he rushed out of his hideout. His friend struggled to his knees, but the effort triggered a loud coughing fit. He spat blood on the ground and wiped his mouth. Henry hurried to his side and held him up. Line of pains distorted his smug smirk.

"And they wonder why they kept losing. Such an easy bluff."

Henry stifled a chuckle and heaved him up. "C'mon, let's get you to the car. We've caused enough havoc for one night."

His friend groaned and took a sharp breath in. His voice fell into a whisper. "Henry...did they keep my gun?"

"Yes."

Joshua let out a soft curse. "Seraphin will kill me."

Seraphin slammed his palms on the council table. His chalky skin had turned to an angry red as he glared at them, heaved a sigh, and started pacing again. Long, furious strides. The same he'd had five minutes ago. Or fifteen, when Joshua had to explain the source of his wounds. Their short encounter with the Galway locals had put the rebel leader in a foul mood. Every time he seemed about to speak Henry gritted his teeth for impact, but Seraphin passed his frustration on the table and never formed a coherent sentence.

Henry couldn't help shifting from one foot to another, but Joshua waited for the diatribe with an enviable cool. He played with his deck of cards and watched Seraphin pace with little more than a passing concern. Even two days after the attack, he couldn't open his left eye completely and half his face was a big wounded mess. Judging from what Henry had seen as they drove back to Mount Kairn, his chest probably had its own constellations of bluish marks by now.

His calm was a bluff, too. The first thing he'd worried about in Galway was Seraphin's reaction. It mattered, for all the detached glances he threw around the room.

The rebel leader spun on his heels and plunged his gaze into Joshua's. He took a deep noisy breath, and with it Seraphin's anger seemed to rescind. It burned bright behind his red-tinged eyes but he when spoke, his tone was level. Dangerous.

"Do you realise how endangered everyone is now? You already have a warrant on your head. They arrested Stern's cousin and are 'questioning' him. If they're bright enough, they'll trace the gun back to Clara, and interrogate her too. Any regular suppliers you met with could become a suspect. Who knows what they'll say? How much they've deduced with time? By the Ancestors, you knew the Union's men are on alert for us but you couldn't help yourself! In a single night, you destroyed years of trust and precautions. And for what—a night of gambling? A couple of extra coins and a drink? What were you thinking?"

Joshua kept his eyes on the ground through the rant. He took a deep breath, as if working up the courage to meet Seraphin's gaze as he stepped forward to answer.

"I'm sorry Seraph. I—"

"Sorry won't fix your mess."

"I was trying to fix it!" Joshua raised his chin. "When we arrived in town nobody would greet us. They glared or looked elsewhere, and I knew it was because of those games. So I insisted on going to the tavern. I wanted to give them back some coin and apologise before they barred us from the village entirely."

"And lo and behold, they did so anyway. Worse, they flagged us. Great work." Seraphin rubbed his eyes under the glasses. His shoulders slumped and he sank into his chair. "Your recklessness will be the death of us."

No answers. A silence so thick Henry thought he'd choke on it.

"What now?"

Henry's voice came out as a high-pitched squeal, and a smile flitted to Seraphin's lips.

"Neither of you is allowed out for a month. Minimum. We must keep a low profile and delay all plans to spread your father's recording. Reaching out to our network would be too risky. I don't know how long it will take for everything to calm down. Sometimes they forget in a week. Sometimes a year." Seraphin took a deep breath. "At least they don't have Captain Vermen listing my sins like a religious psalm. They'll move on quicker."

"And Stern's cousin?"

"The only thing we could've done for him was to warn him in advance. You left without speaking to him. With luck he'll have heard about the fight before the Union knocked on his door. I doubt it, though."

Henry's heart squeezed until it felt smaller than a raisin. Why hadn't he thought of that? He'd run out of Galway, too worried about a pursuit to think straight. Whatever happened to the good merchant was his fault now. His stupidity had destroyed a man's life. Henry's stomach revolted at the thought and he worked hard to keep his breakfast down.

"Can't we do anything else?"

"No."

"But he's one of yours! We can't abandon him."

Both Seraphin and Joshua shook their heads. Henry's hands balled up at his sides. This was unfair. How could they give up without a fight? Without a hint of guilt? Had years of experience washed their regrets away?

"In our world, Henry, a single mistake will cost someone his life. William's life is in his own hands. Pray he denies any knowledge of us and covered his tracks enough to avoid the worst."

"Pray."

Henry spat the word out. He'd prayed for many things in the last decade but never received an answer. Were they to stand by and watch, then? Hadn't he done enough of that in his life?

Seraphin made no further comments on the subject. He stared above their shoulders, lost in thought, his brow furrowed with concerns. Running through scenarios and options, maybe. Henry shifted his weight from one foot to the other, then his stomach emitted a low grumble. The rebel leader startled and Joshua cracked a smile.

"Sorry," Henry muttered.

"No, it's okay." Seraphin's voice dragged as he spoke. Exhaustion stretched his visage downward and made him look older. "Joshua, dismissed."

Joshua scowled but did not argue. He hurried out of the room and Henry turned to follow, glad to escape the stifling atmosphere.

"Not you, Henry. I'd like to talk."

He froze. Of course. His first expedition with the rebels turned into a bloody mess. What would they do with him now? Throw him out? Perhaps Seraphin wouldn't allow him to fly the hot air balloon. He should've listened to Bran. Forced his friend not to go to the pub. Where was his paranoia when he'd needed it? He'd failed at his first simple task. Not very heroic. The door clicked behind Joshua. Henry waited for his condemnation.

"I wanted to thank you."

"What?" Henry's ears rang. He must've misheard.

"For sticking with Joshua."

"But I—"

"You saved him." Seraphin leaned back with a tired smile. "Joshua could not have escaped without your help. Once, four years ago, Vermen uncovered one of our operations. They captured old Trent and forced him to admit his crimes. I saw him at the execution. He had fresh burns and scars from torture. Caught with a gun, Joshua would never have a chance to claim innocence. They would hurt him until he spilled all he knew. I can never thank you enough for sparing him that fate."

Henry's stomach loosened as Seraphin erased his disaster with praises. He straightened and tried to stay dignified, but his cheeks burnt with pride. Like a child complimented by his parents—ironic, as Seraphin could not be more than two years his elder.

"You really think I was useful?"

"Between your recording and this latest rescue? You are essential. I regret my early doubts."

A party started in Henry's mind, with confetti, trumpets, and a large cake. He puffed his chest, forgot about Stern's cousin and the major setbacks their mess had caused. For once, he had succeeded at something, anything.

"I...well, thank you. Sir. I try. Now can I...?"

He pointed at the door, knowing Andeal waited close by, perhaps worried to death. Seraphin laughed and nodded.

Henry strode out of the council room with one destination in mind: the kitchens. The imaginary cake had set his stomach rumbling again.

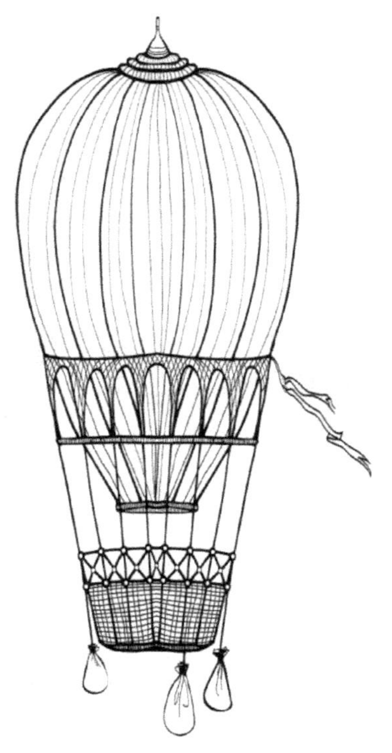

# CHAPTER SEVENTEEN

*Every morning since their* fight, Andeal had come to Captain Vermen's cell, unlocked it—they had added a real chain now—and led the officer to a large hangar. The stony walls shot up into the darkness, giving him the impression the cavern could be hundreds of feet tall. Was half of Mount Kairn hollow? Every time he stepped inside, he looked up and wondered at the hugeness of it. What could've created a space so big?

The days left him ample time for suppositions—too much time. He had to pick up the supply crates brought into the rebels' headquarters and carry them where they belonged. All day, he moved through the corridors, his mind wandering, the hours dragging by. Andeal had installed colored strings to help guide him to key destinations, but before long Vermen could find a few by himself.

While he struggled with the heavy loads, the rebels worked on the strangest thing. A shabby wooden railing entered the hangar from one of the side tunnels and stopped at the center, where they'd built a custom launch platform—at least, he assumed the balloon basket sitting in the middle of it was meant to fly. He didn't ask. Andeal might think he wanted to hear their crazy story again. They'd barely said anything to each other since then. Vermen wished they did. The days grew heavy on him, redundant, but he had no idea how to bring down this new wall between them.

Today he had a bunch of barrels to roll down to the kitchen. Not enough to fill the hours until dinner, so Vermen took his time carrying the first through the corridors. He no longer needed a guide for this one: almost half of what the rebels snuck into their hideout was food. When he arrived at the door he sighed. This always turned out to be the worst part. Depending on who was inside, he'd get anything from angry glares to insults, changing his name from Vermen to 'vermin'. Once he'd found Schmitt, and the noodle guy had managed a terrified greeting before babbling on about how he was so terribly sorry for what had happened and he hadn't known about the rebels at the time and he'd heard he'd saved Andeal's life and was really glad for it. He would've gone on—for hours, perhaps—but Vermen stopped him with a quick 'Shut it, I don't care' and moved on. It was a small lie: he preferred Schmitt's frantic groveling to the other rebels' hostility.

He wasn't lucky enough to encounter Schmitt today. When he pushed open the door, he discovered Stern staring at him. The ex-soldier stopped cleaning the dishes and sneered.

"Look at that. My favorite slave."

"Look at that. My favorite traitor." Vermen pushed the barrel inside and set it against a wall. "Is that your punishment: dish duty?"

The glare he received was answer enough for Vermen. A grin split the captain's face. The last few days had been rough on his morale and he would not refuse a little fun at Stern's expense.

"On a scale of one to ten," Vermen said, "how disappointed are you Seraphin stopped your little execution?"

"Ten." The answer came, immediate and uncompromising. "They took their sweet time."

"Don't blame them. They're just undisciplined thugs who couldn't resist beating up a man who can't defend himself. That's what you get for allying with criminals."

Bitter laughter escaped Stern's lips. He straightened and crossed his arms, looking down on Vermen. It might've been menacing, had he not been wearing an apron.

"I don't care what Seraphin and Andeal say. Those fellow rebels you killed? They deserve to be avenged."

"You people need to check your information network again. The only rebel I killed was that kid during the shootout in Serenity. The others I sent to prison."

All of them had been criminals of one sort or the other, registered in the Union's databank. Whether or not they'd worked for Holt, prison was all that had awaited them. They could blame him all they wanted for that. He wouldn't apologise for doing his job and bringing outlaws to justice.

"Oh, yes. Prison. Where they all had those strange accidents."

Vermen's heart skipped a beat. He pushed a barrel in to let the implications sink in, then asked. "Accidents?"

"Deadly accidents, of course. All the rebels you put behind bars seemed to mysteriously die within the year."

A chill ran up Vermen's spine as the news sunk in. They couldn't all be dead. The only rebel he'd ever sought to shoot down was Seraphin. The others could do their time in prison as far as he was concerned.

But he wasn't the only one concerned, was he?

Vermen recalled Andeal's story, Galen's secret labs, the idea the rebels had something on him that could bring the scientist down. If they held such precious information, would Galen hesitate to wipe them out? Would a man capable of experimenting on other humans shy away from murder? But the genetic engineer had no influence in prisons. His twin brother, however, held sway over the Union's entire military machine. He could reach into other parts of the law and order corps. Could General Omar Clarin also be involved in this?

"I have nothing to do with this." His denial came out in a husky voice. His mind sped through the possibilities now. General Clarin hadn't ordered the manhunt on the White Renegade until Stern deserted him—bringing vital information to the rebels, according to Andeal. His sudden interest had pleased Vermen. He'd been allowed to chase Seraphin and hadn't paid attention to what happened to those he captured along the way. They weren't his problem. In fact, once behind bars, they shouldn't have been anyone's problem. Prison sufficed...unless you meant to silence someone for good. Vermen swallowed hard. They'd used him. *If* this was true, they'd used him. "I'm not part of the accidents. All I wanted was Seraphin."

"Yet you ruined lives. Good folks who'd struggled on their own until we helped them. You saw a criminal file and ignored the people and stories behind them. And so you sent beautiful human beings to their deaths, all because you wanted Seraphin.

"I *needed* Seraphin," he corrected, and even him could hear the hollow in his voice.

Before Stern could form a snide retort, Vermen strode out of the room. He set his back against the wall, using the cold stone as an anchor. He had been grieving, and angry, and they'd abused it to wipe their tracks. Somehow, that felt even worse than killing his brother, even more insulting.

Vermen did not bring the remaining barrels inside, leaving them right at the door instead. He'd meant to mock Stern but in the end, he had a hard time telling who'd had the last laugh.

Captain Vermen reached the cut end of his red string and stopped. He set his crate down and crouched to examine the brightly colored rope. The guides installed to help him navigate the lighted network had been the target of frequent pranks by other rebels since he had started working for them.

No matter how often the engineer asked for him to be left alone, however, the rebels found a new trick to pull. They were all too happy to have a distraction—something to vent their frustrations on.

Except this time, Vermen had no intention of wandering around, helpless and lost. He pushed his crate against the side of the tunnel and picked up the cut string. He backtracked toward the balloon's hall, rolling the string as he went and leaving the cargo behind. Not a minute passed before he heard a small group scramble after him. Predictable. His chains rattled on the stone as he turned to face them.

They didn't look like much. Four undisciplined time wasters. Had any of them been there on the summit, ready to execute him? A tall woman, well over six feet and with a hawkish nose, stepped forward. Her cargo pants and baggy shirt couldn't hide the famished thinness. A cursory glance at the others revealed they were in no better shape. They'd fed him without problems in the last days. Why not them?

"You're supposed to deliver the box. What are you doing?"

"Do it yourself." He raised his hand to show the string. "My task is to bring this box where the string leads. It brought me here. Job done."

Vermen spun on his heels before they could reply. He stalked down the corridor, expecting their footsteps to echo behind him. Instead there was the grating of wood against stone and hushed arguments. Would they really transport that crate? Too easy. Unease crept up the captain's spine as he made his way back.

From the doorway he scanned the large cavern for Andeal. The engineer stood at the end of the wooden railing, gesticulating as he explained a task to another. Seven men worked today. Vermen had never seen more than ten at once and though faces changed every now and then, he doubted there were more than twenty-five rebels living in Mount Kairn. A tiny community.

The captain finished rolling his string before he crossed the room. Conversations died as he passed the workers and restarted the moment he was out of earshot. Weeks had upgraded their insults into a momentary silence. Considering a handful of them had tried to kill him, Vermen didn't complain.

Andeal gave him a slight welcome sign and finished his explanations. Had he also thinned? Though he looked nowhere near as sickly as Cargo Pants Girl, Vermen could tell he'd shed a few pounds.

"Your friends cut the rope again." Vermen dumped the red string in Andeal's hand. "I dropped the box there and told them to finish the job."

His friend blinked. "Did they?"

"Yes."

"Excellent! You're done then."

Andeal's usual smile had lost its sincerity. He rubbed his eyes and walked toward his worktable. Instead of returning to his room, Vermen followed.

"Done? I've barely worked at all! I'll bet it's not even past noon."

"I know the time, Hans!" Andeal snapped. "There is no more work for you. There will not be for another month, at the very least."

Vermen bit back his retort. His friend's shoulders were rigid as a metal bar and large bags decorated his eyes. Last week he'd supervised the troops with a skip to his steps and an easy confidence. Now Andeal gave all the signs of a man near breaking point.

"You look defeated."

Andeal gathered the plans on his table and rolled them up. He cut the red string with a small knife and tied the papers together with it, then let his fingers trail on the soft fabric.

"So did those idiots who cut the string," Vermen continued. "Exhausted and famished."

"Your work's done." A tired smile. Andeal didn't bother hiding his problems. He headed toward the exit. "You should return to your room."

Vermen grabbed his forearm and stopped him. Seven heads lifted from their tasks and turned to them. A few hands reached for tools they could turn into weapons. The captain released his friend and leaned in.

"What's going on?"

"Why would I say? You made such a fuss about *not* being a rebel last time."

And it was out at last. Weeks had passed since they'd fought, but Andeal's attitude had changed since. He avoided any sensitive topics, kept his conversations with Vermen short and to the point, and fell back on generic statements whenever the captain asked for more details. The moment Vermen had allowed himself to be more engaged with him, Andeal had pulled back.

"So that's it. If you can't convert me to your little cause, I'm not worth your time? Where are all your big speeches about prisoners now?"

"No, Hans..." Andeal raised a hand to calm him. His shoulders slumped. "I haven't *had* a lot of time these last days. I wish I could've sat with you for hours to chat again, but we were stepping up our game. You made it painfully clear it wasn't an available topic and I couldn't afford to talk about anything else."

Vermen scanned the balloon's cavern. The curious rebels had returned to their work, although they risked a glance their way every now and then. The captain strode down the tunnel with Andeal.

"*Couldn't. Were* stepping up." He repeated the past-tense verbs, hoping Andeal would explain what had changed.

"Yes."

Andeal's jaws remained clamped. He pretended to study the white globes as they walked toward the living quarters, the engineer always half a step ahead, guiding Vermen. His silence unnerved him. Andeal *always* conversed, no matter his mood.

"You worry me."

"Good." The light deepened the bags under his eyes. Had he slept recently? "We're going dark. No contact with the network for a month, if not more, which means no food. The one provider we dared to call upon refused to sell anything. In two to three weeks, we'll run out."

"Oh." That explained everyone's distress. Had they tried to hide it from him by feeding him full rations? That was ridiculous. "It's just a few months, no?"

"It might be *just* a few months for you, but I've been stuck in this forsaken mountain for six years now. With Henry's help we had everything we needed. I wanted out." Andeal slapped the wall with his rolled-up plan and huffed. "How long before I can stop hiding like some sort of monster? Before my name isn't on a death list? I want to choose a nice spot to settle down with Maniel and raise a family. I want to find a job and work like everybody else and I want to tell my parents I'm alive too. I just want to live, damn it. I'm not asking for much!"

Vermen reached out to squeeze his friend's shoulder but withdrew his hand before he touched him. He shuffled on his feet, cleared his throat. He'd always thought Andeal was happy with the mountain, that somehow he'd acclimated to this living place. He was the one who'd built the light system and disguised solar panels up top, after all, and he called Mount Kairn a home every now and then. It seemed the heavy stone over their heads dragged his morale down as much as it did anyone's.

Andeal ran a shaky hand through his matted hair. "You'll find your way, won't you? I need sleep."

He spun on his heels and backtracked up the corridor—the opposite direction from his bedroom. Vermen watched him disappear and rubbed his forearm, uneasy. He'd never been good with comforting others, and always ended up standing there with nothing but an urge to help.

"We'll figure it out," he said, though he knew that in order to give Andeal what he wanted, Hans might have to give up a lot of his own life.

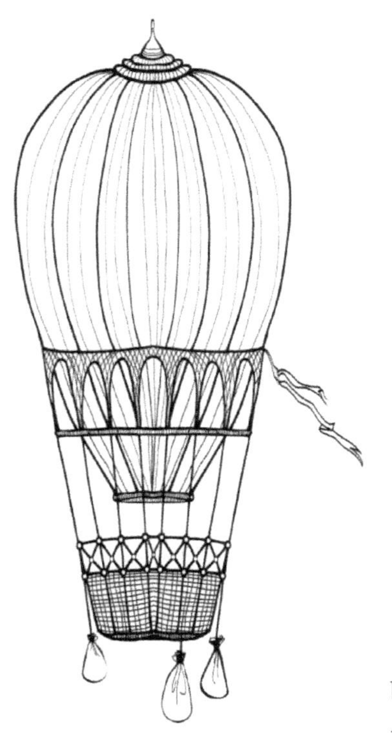

# CHAPTER EIGHTEEN

 bright globe and examined the shaky railing. Lack of wood had prevented the rebels from solidifying the structure. In the first week, Andeal's pet project had stalled. No materials, no work. But the engineer had poured hours over his plans and redesigned the slide leading the balloon's basket to its lift-off ramp so it'd 'use wood in a more efficient way and remain as solid as before'. The return of regular work was welcomed by everyone. When they hammered planks together, they forgot their empty stomachs.

Examining the result, however, Hans Vermen doubted Andeal's estimations were right. Fatigue must've inserted mistakes in his work. The railing would never hold. A good thing they tested it now, before they truly needed to take off.

He searched for signs of doubts in the rebel next in line: his favorite red head. Except he'd shaved the bright red rastas and a tiny brown stubble began to grow back. The Burgian kept rubbing his temple where Vermen struck him—one of many scars he now sported. His left arm hung limp at his side, either broken or badly damaged. He had been part of the failed supply run weeks ago, that had so upset Andeal. Joshua seemed in a strange daze, like he could barely bring himself to care about this test.

Quite the opposite from the man on his other side.

Henry Schmitt would never voice a doubt about this enterprise. He clutched his bright light with a wide grin, staring up the tunnel at where the basket would come from. Of everyone held prisoner under Mount Kairn, Schmitt had adapted the best to their recent problems. Skipping meals seemed to suit him fine.

A refreshing breeze wafted through the tunnel and their lights swayed. Twenty something rebels had lined up next to the railing, spread on both side of the wooden structure. He'd been placed in the middle of everyone at Seraphin's express demand but Vermen didn't complain—at least they hadn't stuck him in his cell. Vermen tapped his foot on the ground and the nervous habit clanked his chains on the floor. Accusatory looks turned his way. What was Andeal waiting for?

The engineer's warning call echoed down the hall, followed by excited whispers. The railing shivered; they must be pushing the basket. Wheels creaked as they carried the apparatus forward. Everyone held their breath. Vermen's heart sped and he extended his arm, spreading his lamp's light further.

The vibrations turned into a worrisome rumble. *Tac-tac-tac*, the basket's wheels clipped nails in their wild slide down. Vermen gritted his teeth as the rattling bounced around the walls and rang his ears. In the swaying lights, he'd swear the mountain itself shuddered and rumbled. Henry Schmitt took a sharp breath as the contraption appeared.

It sped past them, shaking Vermen's bones and creating a draft of air that drew a squeal of glee from Schmitt. The captain snorted. Once you saw a man frozen in terror, noodles hanging from his mouth, it became hard to take him seriously. It did not help that Schmitt ran after the basket like a child. Perhaps he worried it'd crash through the barriers erected at the end of the track.

Andeal sprinted on the other side in a useless attempt to keep up. He bumped into the still Burgian on his way, waking him from his torpor. All the rebels followed and Vermen found his strides leading him toward the cliff's edge. Fear lit their gazes. The basket rushed too fast. Everyone would be needed to reel it in.

As the captain reached the tunnel's end, the heavy contraption crashed into the end barrier. It had been built to keep the basket from flying off the cliff and crashing into the mountain side. Andeal cringed at the snapping sound of breaking planks and skidded to a stop. One long nerve-wracking creak followed. Everybody froze. Would the blockade hold? Or would their only basket go through it and tumble down Mount Kairn's steep cliff?

Vermen didn't wait to find out. He strode across the launch platform, strong gusts whipping his chains around. He grabbed the basket with both hands and hung all his weight to hold it back, pulling it back down the slight, upward launching slope. Before long a lithe form jumped in to help. Hans glanced aside, ready to mock the lightweight trying to contribute. His gaze met Seraphin's and he bit his tongue, a dizzying wave of heat spinning his head. Holt's proximity upset him. Hans tried to ignore it. Soon others brought assistance and they pulled it back.

When the basket rested safely on the railing, everyone heaved a sigh of relief. Vermen crouched and rubbed his ankles, where the chain scraped through his pants.

"Speed is good," Andeal said. "It'll carry us further away from the cliff."

Henry crept closer to the edge and risked a glance down. Andeal's comment pulled a nervous chuckle from the future pilot. Seraphin clapped his hands to catch their attention.

"All right, everyone inside. We're a shining spot on the mountain side right now."

They gathered in the great cavern but their minds remained on the breathtaking trial run. Smiles decorated the emaciated visages for the first time in weeks and pride straightened their back. Vermen leaned on the wall, in the background. Holt had found a crate to climb upon. Every day made him more skeletal.

"There's a surprise for you in the mess hall. Food's been scarce but tonight we all deserve a bit of celebration. Besides, it's not like we'll need to drink a lot to feel it on our empty stomachs, is it?"

The rebels laughed and converged on the exit. Vermen briefly watched the flow and shook his head. Let them party. He had work to do. He found the closest spools of rope and slung them over his shoulder, then grabbed a toolbox. He'd need all night to dismantle the barricade and camouflage the exposed railing.

The thundering echo of twenty-something walkers died as he prepared to leave to cavern room. It had muffled another conversation, which now carried through clearly and Vermen stopped in his tracks. They might be whispering, but Andeal's and Seraphin's words were audible by all.

"Let them clean up. You've worked non-stop for weeks. You deserve that drink more than anyone else."

Seraphin's concerned tone unsettled Vermen. This man could hold another's gaze and blow his brain out. He was supposed to be all ruthless efficiency, not a kind man insisting his friend rest. It reminded him too much of the Seraphin atop Mount Kairn's summit, the one who'd saved his life.

"Not yet," Andeal said. "I need to inspect the railing and note the weaknesses for tomorrow. Besides, that basket is almost as tall as I am. Three won't be too many to drag it back up."

Three? Vermen glanced around and spotted Henry Schmitt. The man waited near the railing, his own toolbox in hand. Great. A babbling fool was exactly what he needed to make his night better.

"All right," Seraphin said. "Don't take too long. I miss trouncing you at the bags' game despite my horrific eyesight."

The tease brought defiant laughter out of Andeal. "Oh, I'll beat you one day, you'll see. Give me an hour and take a drink or ten while you wait."

"What, and improve my aim?" Seraphin clapped Andeal's back as he started out of the large cavern. "Can't wait to see by how many points you'll lose tonight!"

The Regarian's steps smacked on the stone floor as he followed the rest of his troops out. When Andeal approached them and clapped his hands, Vermen forced a neutral expression to his face and tried not to seem bothered by the friendly exchange.

"Let's go," Andeal said. "We have work to do."

Lots of it. They traveled down to the launch platform. Vermen set his toolbox down and handed one of the ropes to Andeal. He tied one end to the basket's upper-right corner while the engineer looped the other spool to the upper-left corner. They advanced on each side of the railing until the ropes were taut.

"Schmitt," Vermen called. "You push."

"Yes sir!"

Vermen didn't bother to hide his smile. Noodle Man was the only rebel who treated him like an officer and the captain enjoyed striking fear with a few well-placed commands. The undignified shackles at his feet did not suck away all his prestige and authority.

They pulled and Henry pushed, up the slope. The wheels creaked and refused to roll smoothly, adding friction to the basket's weight. Despite their combined strength, the task proved harder than the training Vermen had gone—or put trainees—through. He strained his muscles, ground his teeth against the building pain in his arms, and legs and forced his breath to come in regular bursts. Beads of sweat rolled down his face and into his thick beard. He could no longer feel the cool night's air beyond his burning skin.

But he wasn't alone. Henry panted so hard it covered all other sounds, except when he stumbled. Andeal's blue skin had turned almost purple. His blond hair stuck to his forehead and sweat drenched his short-sleeved shirt.

Ten meters left. Ten meters of laborious slope before they finished. Vermen gave a final pull, taxing his muscles to their limit. All three added their energy and their joint efforts brought the basket over the ridge, to the flat ground where it rolled with ease. Andeal sat down and rubbed his hands while Schmitt fell to his knees. Vermen paced around the cavern to still his breath. The ropes had dug red marks in his palms and he massaged them.

"My head's swimming so much I can barely see straight," Andeal said.

"If I go now, no amount of alcohol will save me from public humiliation."

"I don't think the party will die anytime soon," Henry answered between two short gasps. He rolled on his back and stared at the ceiling. "I don't even have the energy to go back to the launch site."

Vermen stretched his arms up and smirked at them. The army's rough training sessions had their benefits and he'd been careful to keep his physical shape intact. Andeal wouldn't mock his daily exercises now.

"You two take a breather. I'll scrap the blockade. The basket did half my job anyway."

Neither of them protested. Andeal raised a fatigued hand to wave him good luck. Vermen picked a small and protected lantern to light his way. His eyes wandered across the railing's shabby frame. How had these men built such a solid construction? Not just the rebels. Him, too. The captain frowned and gave a little push to the wooden plank. It creaked and held. He'd helped with the redesign, same as everyone. He repressed the rising pride and quickened his pace.

The sweet breeze calmed his thoughts as he arrived at his destination. His heart throbbed as he glanced up, but the low clouds blocked the stars. Another time, if he could convince Andeal to accompany him. The captain was reluctant to ask for this favor. The more bridges he built with the rebels, the more confused he became.

He picked up a crowbar and hammer, eager to work and forget. After dragging the balloon's basket all the way up, disassembling the blockade was a child's game. Vermen worked in short bursts, taking a few planks down at a time and throwing them upon a pile. He allowed himself small breaks to stretch his muscles and enjoy the cool night. No need to push his strength to the limits. He was in no hurry to return to the mountain's still air and bleak tunnels. Even less his cell.

By the time he threw the last broken slab upon the junk pile, he contemplated climbing down the cliff to escape. His chained legs and the almost vertical drop forced him to discard the idea. He flattened himself at the cliff's edge and stared down. The mountainside disappeared in the darkness.

"Scary, isn't it?"

Schmitt's voice startled him. Vermen pushed himself up.

"Terrifying. I judged you for a coward on our first meeting, but I was wrong. Launching off takes a specific form of suicidal courage."

"No, coward was about right."

The answer took him by surprise. Not that he doubted its truth, but few men would admit to a lack of courage. Saying it out loud was a form of audacity in itself. Henry picked up the lantern and approached to examine the launch rails. His face remained red from the earlier effort.

"Why fly it, then?" Vermen asked. "You don't seem the type to throw your life away, pathetic though it is."

Schmitt's expression darkened. He stopped his inspection to lean on the structure and reached inside his pocket, removing an old dirtied cloth from it and handing it over. Vermen squinted at it, made out scribbled words, but the dim light prevented any reading.

"My father wasn't that type either. Not until he overheard the Clarin twins say they'd created the Plague to grab power. Not until he understood they were doing it again. Changes your perspective of what qualifies as reasonable risk."

Vermen staggered a step back. In a single casual sentence, Henry Schmitt had thrown to his face what Andeal had spent the last weeks trying to show him. The enormity of the accusation registered.

"Lies," he called it. "Laughable lies."

"He recorded them. That message you hold is the last thing my father wrote before dying. It told me where to find the disc." Henry pushed himself away from the railing and stomped to the pile of planks. "Gathering proof is all the rebels did in—"

"Shut up."

He'd heard a soft whirring in the sky, far above them. He scanned the clouds.

"No, you listen—"

Vermen sprung forward and clamped a hand over Schmitt's mouth. He dragged the astonished man back to the tunnel before he released him.

"Not a word. And douse that lamp!"

It took all the commanding strength he could muster to turn his whisper into an urgent order. Schmitt cowered and did as told, wide-eyed. He switched off the light and froze in place. Vermen's heart thundered and he could hear Noodle Man's panicked breathing. It took all his will to focus on the sounds outside.

The engine's buzzing and the soft hum of a zeppelin's electric system were unmistakable. And whoever said *zeppelins* always meant *Union army*. Vermen swallowed hard, gave Henry's rag back, and stalked to the tunnel's entrance. He risked a peek up.

Where there was nothing but clouds an hour ago, he could now distinguish the shape of a large and flat warship. It flew lower than standard and lingered above Mount Kairn. The captain allowed his eyes to adjust. His gaze went to the telltale containers on the front and aft of the ship and he backpedaled inside.

Bomber blimps did not hover above targets by coincidence.

"Run!"

Schmitt remained rooted to the spot and Vermen held back a curse. What wouldn't he give for disciplined soldiers now?

"Get your ass moving Schmitt! In twenty minutes, tops, they'll drop all the holy explosives they have on board and if that balloon isn't ready to launch before then, it never will. GO."

This time Henry spun on his heels and sprinted. Vermen did his best to follow but every time he lengthened his strides, the chains went taut and impeded him. He stumbled more than ran, scraping his hands on the rocks and railing as he caught himself and pushed onward. Each step caused the shackles to bite into his skin and pain flared up his legs. Warm blood trickled from his ankles. By the time he reached the balloon's grand cavern, it had soaked his socks.

Henry and Andeal had packed the propane tanks in the basket and now heaved the one crate of emergency provisions left untouched. When Vermen emerged in a cacophony of rattling chains, Andeal whirled about and threw a small metal object his way.

A key. The captain caught it midair and knelt. His hands shook as he inserted it in the lock. He could barely breathe through the lump in his throat. The shackles opened with a soft clink.

"Go warn the others!" Andeal called.

Vermen dashed off without wasting a second. His ankles throbbed but nothing hindered his movement now. Adrenaline carried him down the network of caves. Tomorrow he'd have bloody messes instead of feet, but tonight he could not stop. They counted on him.

As the thought struck, he slowed his pace. If he alerted no one, these caverns would collapse on the heart of Holt's band. He could scramble for an exit and leave his fellow soldiers do their work. Then all this nonsense would be over. No more wild conspiracy theories. No more Seraphin.

He ought to ditch them. He was a proud captain of the Union Army. He'd vowed to defend President Kurtmann, to avenge his brother. His task was to take out the White Renegade's group, not save them. A special permission granted by General Omar Clarin. He'd never asked why. He should have.

A wild cheer traveled up the corridor and filled his ears. Vermen refused to be used to silence these men and women. He refused to let Andeal die trapped in the mountain. His heart hammering, he whispered an apology to his brother and sped up again.

And how easy it was! His strides had none of the heavy fatality burdening him as he brought a dying Andeal to his wife. In choosing the rebels—even only one of them—over his duty, Vermen had set himself on a path he could not counter. His sprint lined up with a reality he'd denied for weeks: he had already betrayed his vows. He could not return to the Union's army.

Instead he burst into the ongoing rebel party and killed the mood. Half of them jumped to their feet and reached for possible weapons—anything from pistols to mugs and forks. They froze when he remained in the doorway, hands on his knees, out of breath. His lungs burned and pain scrambled his thoughts. He focused and formed a coherent sentence.

"There's a bomber blimp over the mountain."

An alarmed whisper ran through the rebels. Holt glanced at his troops and tilted his head to the side.

"You're alone. And unchained."

Vermen gritted his teeth and straightened. "Andeal and Henry are preparing the balloon for take-off. He gave me the key."

Dozens of little conversations started at once. The men argued with one another, disputing his claims or pushing for an evacuation. They remained seated and wasted the precious time he'd bought them in useless debates. Idiots. How had they survived this long?

"Seraphin!"

Maniel's voice buried all others. Seraphin met her gaze. He seemed uncertain, fragile—accessible and human.

"Evacuate."

Holt licked his lips. He studied Vermen, as if he could read the truth from his stance. The captain swallowed hard. He detested the cold scrutiny—like Seraphin picked his insides apart to better understand how he worked. Hans didn't want him to understand, but a part of him wished Seraphin would trust him, that he wouldn't need to understand to believe in him and his word. And that desire, small though it was, scared him. It implied a certain intimacy he shouldn't be wishing for.

When at last Seraphin broke the stare and climbed on his seat to capture the rebels' attention, Vermen exhaled.

"End of the party, everyone. Form the evacuation groups. Joshua, Tanya, Ennio, get what supplies we have left and report to your respective leaders."

The rebels scrambled to their feet, some emptying their glasses first. They moved with surprising discipline, regrouping around three of theirs. Those named dashed out of mess hall to get the supplies. These men might not be soldiers, but they had obviously rehearsed their escape multiple times.

"Captain!" Seraphin sprung out of his chair and crossed the room with a newfound assurance. The rebel leader was in control. "Return to the balloon. You'll take off with Henry. I want Andeal and Maniel to stay together."

"Yes sir."

Before he could regret the instinctive deference he'd just given Seraphin, the first explosion rocked the ground with a deafening boom. A few plates slid and crashed to the ground. Rebels screamed and their hurried steps broke into sprints. Vermen propped himself against the wall and sought Maniel. She stood straight and calm in the burgeoning chaos, giving concise directions to the panicking rebels. When she noticed him, she nodded at the tunnel. *Hurry up.*

The captain pushed himself off the wall and dashed away. As he ran up the corridor, punishing his ankles once more, the second bomb exploded and the electricity fizzled out.

Vermen let his fingers trail on the cool stone wall as he progressed in the dark. He slowed his pace and stalked along. Blood coursed through his body and made him light-headed. His brother's towering shadow scolded him. *Don't participate in their escape. Betray them. Let them die and avenge me.* The captain took a deep breath and pressed forward.

Three consecutive bombs blasted the hideout and slammed Vermen to the ground. The shock expelled air from his lungs and stole his remaining breath. A low rumble followed. Under his stinging palms, the corridor began to shake. Dirt and tiny rocks fell on his head. How long would the tunnel hold?

Vermen scrambled to his feet and ran. He took three long strides before the first deafening crack. Large stones detached themselves from the ceiling and crashed ahead of him. A shard clipped his cheeks and he flung his arms up to protect his eyes. He stumbled back and a fourth explosion threw him on his ass. Vermen retreated, on all fours, as the tunnel ahead collapsed. He curled against the wall and waited for the chaos to still.

Dust stung his eyes and dried his throat. He crawled forward, coughing every few feet, until his fingers touched cool stones. He groped around the boulder but his hands only found more rock, so the captain stood and climbed the crumbled pile. He pushed off gravel and pebbles, fumbling for a way through. He grabbed a stone and removed it, but more immediately fell on his hands. He scraped and pushed at the top of the pile but the mount would not budge. The tunnel was sealed.

Vermen rubbed his face and felt grit and blood. He wiped it off with his shirt and stumbled down the pile, his stomach clenching. He could no longer reach Andeal. His only option was to follow the rebels and trust his long-time enemies.

Hans did not bother with a wall-guide this time. He forced his faltering steps to lead him back to the mess hall.

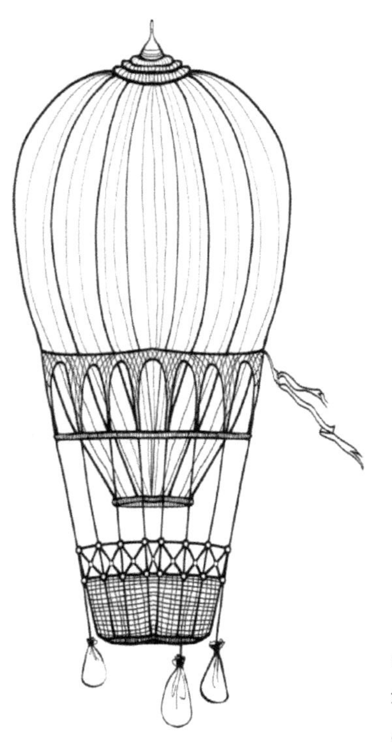

# CHAPTER NINETEEN


rope to its corner of the balloon basket and pulled on the envelope. He dragged the heavy fabric up and threw it over the balloon's burner, centering it as much as he could before he gathered the remaining fabric at his feet. The basket turned into a gold and purple cocoon, protected from the outside world, with Henry kneeling at its center. He spread his palms against the bottom to stop the shaking which had slowed him throughout lift-off preparations. He needed his hands steady for the launch, could not afford to panic as the entire balloon leapt off the railing.

This is it, he thought. First flight. First test.

If only he could munch on uncooked instant noodles. That'd ease his stomach and stress.

He pushed himself up and peeked from under the tent-envelope. How long had Andeal been gone? He'd run off to get the recording and papers. Captain Vermen had warned them: twenty minutes tops before the bombs. How many had they wasted now? He glanced upward, half-expecting the ceiling to crumble without warning, then back at the entrance. No Andeal yet.

Henry wiped the sweat from his face and climbed down the basket. Only one step left to preparations. He tried not to think of what came *after*, of the long drop and desperate maneuver to lift-off and the very real possibility of a crushing death. No, better not to linger on that. They would be just fine.

He hurried across the room, collected the empty helium pocket and folded the thick plastic. Without this pouch at the top of their balloon, they'd waste a whole tank of gas to fly a hour. Andeal argued helium could keep them aloft an entire week on the same amount of fuel. Henry plodded to the basket with his precious load. He stretched his arms and dumped his cargo inside, flattening the envelope under it with a *woomph*.

The first bomb hit as he clambered up the ladder and the impact shook the railing. Henry clung to his perch, eyes snapped shut, his clammy palms threatening to slip and let go. He wasn't high, no more than two feet above ground, but the thought of falling terrified him—as if letting go meant never reaching the balloon again.

"Henry!"

He dared to open his eyes. Andeal ran the distance to the balloon and scaled the railing, not bothering with the ladder. He'd rolled the papers and stuck them in his belt.

"Is everything ready?" he asked.

"Almost. Tie the helium pocket."

He mustered his courage and climbed the rest of the way. Together they unfolded the pocket then slipped under the envelope with it. They set it atop the burner, then fastened it to each corner of the basket. Henry plugged the helium pump in, started the machine. What a strange sandwich they'd built: the envelope on top, the helium pocket under it, then the burner, them, and finally the basket. A dozen ropes hung from it, pooling at the bottom for now, color-coded to identify their function. As the gas filled its pouch, it began to lift, taking the envelope with it. Their sandwich-tent rose.

"Did you get the provisions?" Andeal asked.

"Yes."

"The extra rope?"

"Yes."

"All five tanks of propane?"

"Of course!" Henry dragged the helium pocket down before it floated too far up. The tunnel down wasn't all that high and they didn't want to scrape the top while rushing along the railing. "I know my job. Remove those brakes! We need to launch."

His snapping tone took Andeal by surprise. The engineer lifted his eyebrows but reached over the basket's edge to the brakes' lever. Once he pulled it, nothing would hold them in place. His gaze was on the corridor where Vermen had disappeared. Henry put a hand on his shoulder.

"We can't wait for him."

"I know. It's just..." Andeal shook his head, turned to Henry. "Are you ready?"

"As ready as I'll ever be."

Andeal laughed and pushed the lever.

The basket lurched forward and Henry clung to the pump. The tiny wheels creaked and the railing trembled under their weight. They gained momentum and his teeth clattered as they sped through the tunnel. The wind caught in the envelope. Andeal scrambled to grab the line and keep their sandwich from flying off. Why hadn't they thought of something to hold the fabric until they'd reached the launch ramp? They should've known. Henry's heartbeat shifted into frantic mode. They improvised too much, hadn't predicted everything. Most likely result: their homemade balloon flattened on the mountainside with their crushed bodies inside.

The helium pocket finished inflating as they careened out of the tunnel. Henry slammed his heel on the pump's stop button just as the basket reached the launch slope. The sudden shift in angle made him lose his balance and land on his ass. The pouch of light gas slipped out of his fingers, floated up, caught in the envelope. They lifted. Andeal released all rope lines and whispered a prayer as the sandwich rose far above their head. Henry scrambled up and grabbed the burner's lever.

Their gaze met. *This is it.* Either they flew, or they died.

The wheels left the railing.

Andeal reached over the side and released them. For an instant they floated through the dark night sky. Wind flapped at their deflated envelope and the bomber blimp's whirring engine filled the silence. The basket's upward curve stopped and they began to fall.

Andeal snatched a line and pushed it as far as he could from the basket, enlarging the opening. Air rushed into it and inflated the envelope with a great snap. Henry prayed the reinforced sewing lines would hold and pressed both burner levers. Flames sprung to life and a wave of heat washed over the basket's occupants. The fire reached far into the envelope, a two-meter high brazier. Andeal flipped the propeller on to give them what little extra lift they could. But would it be enough? Gravity pulled them to the ground with alarming speed. Henry squeezed his eyes shut. They'd never get enough upward momentum in time.

Three bombs exploded across Mount Kairn's side, flashes of light and sound. It rattled Henry's bones, but he felt detached from it. The cavern could shudder and collapse now—he was out. In the sky. Plummeting to his death.

"I think we're slowing," Andeal said. "Henry, it's working!"

Henry risked a glance and regretted it. In the last few seconds they'd crossed half the distance to the mountainside. But Andeal was right. They'd lost speed. The propeller's spinning blades under the basket were a blur and the air above shimmered with heat. Hot air wrapped around the helium pocket and pushed the envelope upward, fighting gravity's pull. If he survived, Henry promised himself two potfuls of delicious noodles.

Then his eyes caught the cloud of dust and stones that rolled down the cliff—rocks torn away by the bombs. A growing rumble buried the blimp's engine and crushed his meager hope. Their fall brought them straight into the landslide's path. Henry cursed and pushed hard on the burner's switches, well aware it'd change nothing. Everything that could slow their fall was already used at max capacity. The boulders tumbling down would catch in their envelope and rip it to shreds, then crush the basket and everyone inside.

Bitter disappointment swirled at the bottom of his stomach. Dead. He would have no noodles, no flight, no chance to honor his mother's memory. He would perish on this mountainside, the recording with him.

Andeal sprung into action. He set one foot on the provision crate, the other on the basket's edge. One blue hand clamped on a purple rope—the helium pocket ones—and the other on the burner's metal support. He leapt out of the balloon and pulled the rope down, outward, forcing the helium pocket to slide to the side, away from Mount Kairn. The entire envelope shifted with it. Andeal set his feet firmly against the basket's side, his knuckles whitened as he held tight. The propellers' deadly blade spun inches under his friend's soles. He pulled harder. Henry's legs threatened to give under him. He swallowed hard, wished he could help, but if he let go of the levers, they lost the flames, their only real source of lift.

Instead he stood frozen as their balloon angled out of the landslide's path, slowly at first. As their fall slowed to a crawl then stopped, however, the horizontal shift became more important. They floated still for a seemingly endless moment, leaning to the side, then the aircraft rose. A stifled sob escaped Henry's lips. The tumbling rocks swooped under them, smaller stones clipping the propeller and bouncing away. Andeal released the helium pouch, climbed back into the basket and collapsed on the floor. Their vertical lift returned to maximum and they gained in speed.

Flying. They were flying!

Andeal remained on the ground, shaking with hysterical laughter as their balloon ascended. Henry fought to urge to cheer loud and high, to tell the whole world he now roamed the sky. They'd brushed with death, survived a suicidal take-off. People needed to know of their exploit.

Then they passed their launch ramp. A thick cloud of dust emerged from the tunnel and large boulders had destroyed the wooden railing. He squinted to see through. Demolished planks remained scattered across the stone ledge, but the original structure was unidentifiable. The bombs had ruined weeks of hard work.

He released the burner's levers and closed the propane valve, his blustering enthusiasm doused by the scene. The bomber blimp hovered above Mount Kairn, tiny lights lining its form. That aircraft was hundreds of feet long, far more imposing than their measly balloon. Henry held his breath. They'd never hear him above the engines, but he refused to take chances. Andeal's fit of laughter died and he rose in silence.

Four consecutive explosions lit the sky and thundered through the empty air. The force blew away entire sections of Mount Kairn, sending huge rocks flying, tumbling down. Henry wondered how much would be left. Would the Races' trail remain? He could no longer hear the roaring waterfall, couldn't distinguish anything but destruction in the darkness. He scanned the landscape, his heart beating fast, but they entered the lowest layer of clouds and everything disappeared.

Andeal slumped to the ground and held his head. Henry had a sudden urge to hit himself. How selfish could he be? While he thought of dead races and aesthetics, his friend's world collapsed on itself. Gone was his only refuge for the past years, gone were—perhaps—his wife and friends. Henry sat beside him and patted his shoulder, awkward.

"They'll be fine. The captain will have warned them in time."

He wasn't sure he believed it himself.

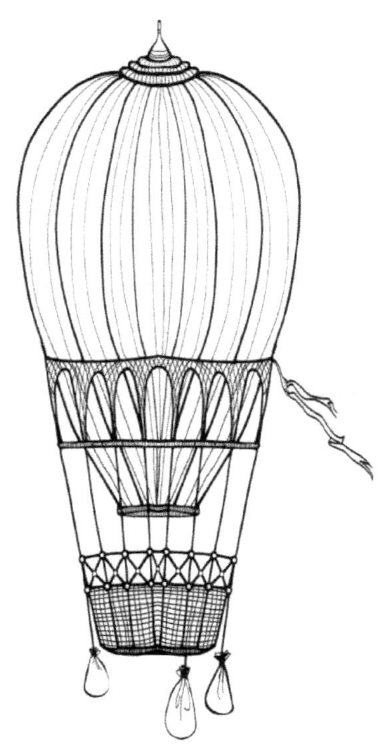

# CHAPTER TWENTY


three rebels were left in the mess hall.
Maniel paced from one table to another,
her thick ponytail bouncing behind her, frizzy hair escaping the hair band.
The two others—a teenager with a tuft of brown hair and the Burgian he'd
wacked on the head during his escape attempt—sat on a long bench and
whispered together. A single lamp provided illumination, bathing them in
pale white light. Sometimes Maniel melded into the shadows, only to
reappear a few seconds later. He noticed the rubble behind her and guessed
part of the ceiling looming in the darkness had collapsed. More bombs would
come. They had no time to waste. Vermen mustered his courage with a long
deep breath and started across the room, his ankles burning with every step.
As he got closer, he called out to the three rebels.

Maniel stopped mid-step then hurried to the lamp. She grabbed the handle and crossed the hall with urgent strides, plunging her two companions into darkness. When she got closer, she lifted the lamp. Worried surprise flitted across her expression before she schooled it into a mask of calm.

"What happened, Captain?"

Vermen shook his head. He remembered the first time he'd accompanied an officer to tell a young woman that war had made her a widow—how he could barely breathe because of the lump in his throat, let alone talk. He had let his superior handle everything. He couldn't pass this task along today. Vermen wiped the grime from his face and tried to push the words past his knotted throat. A coughing fit overtook him and he bent forward, unable to speak. He'd inhaled so much dust he expected it to cake the inside of his lungs.

Maniel took his arm and led him to the table. She forced him to sit next to the others. As soon as his weight no longer rested on his feet, the pain in his ankles alleviated. Vermen heaved a sigh, surprised at his own intense relief. He gathered his thoughts once more.

"The tunnel collapsed before I could reach him."

Next to him, the Burgian snickered. "Convenient."

Vermen slammed his fist on the table. He did not have the patience for petty accusations. "I almost died under a ton of rock. If you don't believe me, you can go check for yourself."

"No." Maniel interrupted their argument with a snapping, stop-being-children tone. "We're leaving. Joshua, get Andeal's bag for Hans, will you?"

Joshua slid along the wooden bench until he reached a large backpack then pushed it toward Vermen. The captain swallowed hard, uneasy at the thought of taking Andeal's place. He pulled himself together, grabbed the pack, and waited. He wanted to delay the moment he had to stand as much as possible. Maniel explained their general heading—down in the network of caves under Mount Kairn—in a soft but calm voice. While her long nose cast a deep shadow across her face, obscuring part of her expression, she showed no signs of grief in what he could see. Vermen recalled how well she had handled herself when he had arrived with a bloodied and dying Andeal in his arms. Maniel dealt with pressure better than many fellow soldiers he'd known.

"I tried," he said. "I swear."

"I know." A distant rumbling interrupted Maniel—another collapsed cave. She frowned and held her hand out to help him up. "Will your feet be all right?"

"They will as long as I need them."

"Let's move, then. I'll tend to them once we're safe."

She motioned for everyone to follow and they fell into a line behind her. They advanced into a tunnel going ever downward, sometimes in a slow slope, sometimes in abrupt drops they had to climb. The distant echo of bombs followed them as they made their way deeper into the bowels of Mount Kairn, a reminder that the Union's army—his army—wasn't far behind.

By the time Maniel called for a pause, a cold film of sweat covered Vermen's forehead. He shivered despite the exercise and had trouble keeping his focus on anything but the light ahead. At the edge of his vision, shadows flickered, sometimes forming the familiar shape of his brother. Vermen ignored the hallucination and concentrated on the next step. Every time he set his foot down, a jolt of pain rushed up his leg. He was glad to stop, even for a moment.

They had followed a river for some time now—Vermen had no idea how long they'd been walking—and Maniel stood in front of a branching tunnel, with a smaller stream at the bottom, plunging into the river. They could cross it with ease, the current was not strong. Why didn't they?

Maniel crouched and snuck into the side tunnel, knees and neck bent to avoid touching the low ceiling, the lamp held high to avoid contact with water. Joshua followed, then it was his turn. Vermen gritted his teeth as he lowered his foot in the water. The last hours had turned everything below his tibia into a fleshy mess of pain. The water soaked his pants up to the knees and focused the diffused throbbing into sharp agony. Vermen gasped but forced himself to move forward, cringing with every step. He hoped they didn't have long to go. He felt like a rat scuttling in the darkness, undignified and desperate.

He stubbed his toes on a large rock. An excruciating flare zapped up his leg and he lost balance, crashing into Joshua and bringing them both down in the stream. Water filled his ears and blocked all sounds for a moment, then strong hands pulled him out. He sat, spitting and panting, water dripping from his hair and beard. The Burgian had already jumped to his feet with a string of curses while Maniel studied the captain with a worried frown.

"We're almost there."

"I can limp along."

He ought to try harder to impress the rebels with his endurance, but he didn't have the strength for such games. Maniel motioned for the teenager to get closer. He hesitated—was he scared?—then offered Vermen a hand.

"Captain, this is Jan. He'll help you."

"Hum...Hello."

As Jan whispered his greeting, Vermen recognized the young, dissenting voice from the rebels' improvised execution. "You were on that summit."

Even in the dim light, the captain noticed the deep flush on the teenager's cheeks. Jan avoided his gaze but managed a small guilty nod.

"Thank you for trying to get the bag removed." Vermen grabbed the still-extended hand and accepted the lift up. He flinched as his weight returned in full to his ankles but Jan slid under his shoulder right away. He tried to enjoy the guilty confusion on his helper's angled face but even half-carried along, the remainder of the trek required all his concentration.

They emerged into a larger, L-shaped cave. The stream's blubbering source was in front of their entrance, in the shorter part of the L. The rest of the cave stretched around a bend on the left, dry and dark. Vermen angled toward the corner, leaned on the wall and slid down. He heaved a sigh of relief and watched as the rebels headed to the end of the L-shape and removed certain rocks, revealing a cache. They retrieved a large box from it and begun spreading the equipment within on the ground—food, batteries, bedrolls and dry clothes.

Joshua snatched one and took off his soaked shirt right away. Vermen's eyes widened as he noticed the many darkened bruises on his chest and shoulders. They had to be a few weeks old, and he wondered when the Burgian had taken such a beating. Vermen ought to look away, to give him what little privacy this cave would offer. He didn't. His gaze lingered until Joshua grabbed another dry shirt and flung it his way.

"You looked jealous."

Flustered, the captain grabbed the piece of cloth and averted his eyes, unbuttoning his drenched shirt to change. Maniel joined him with a first aid kit.

"Can I ask what the plan is?" Vermen asked.

"Wait for the danger to pass, go back to our headquarters to see what we can salvage then head to Reverence." She knelt by his side. "Let's see what I can do for you."

She pulled his wet pants up and began cleaning the wounds, causing him to hiss in pain. There were bright bloody lines were the shackles had dug into his flesh and the skin was raw. Maniel worked with impressive discipline. She had to be worried about Andeal, but she had yet to waver in her assigned role as leader and nurse of this group. He wondered how long her resolve would last. She squeezed the bandages tight and a pained exclamation escaped his lips.

"Don't tell me you've never had worse," she said.

"I broke my leg once when I was seven. Fell down a tree. My brother had to carry me."

"*The* brother?"

Maniel's voice softened. He answered with a curt nod, but added nothing. The last thing he wanted was to talk about Klaus with rebels. Maniel must have understood his silence. She avoided the topic and continued with a teasing tone.

"Not that much of a grizzled soldier, then, are you?"

Vermen sketched a smile and rested his head on the stone wall. It felt like weeks since he'd woken up and helped the rebels put the finishing touches to their balloon's launch rail, yet it couldn't be much more than a day. In a single day, he had thrown his life-long allegiance to the Union away and saved Seraphin's rebels. Not just one man. All of them.

And yet, despite his pained ankles and uncertain future, Hans Vermen had rarely felt so good about himself.

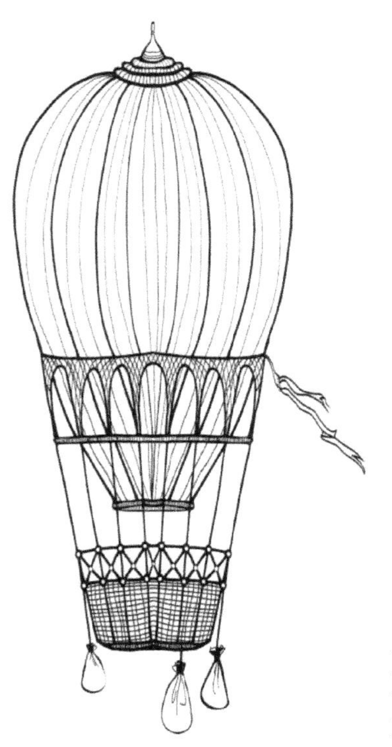

# CHAPTER TWENTY-ONE

As soon as he woke up, Henry rose and massaged his stiff neck. He stretched himself, causing his back to pop, then glanced around. The clouds had lifted during the night and a warm sun caressed the balloon. Wind carried them northeast and Mount Kairn was just a tiny rise on the horizon now. He checked their altitude, surprised they still seemed so high. A little under twenty thousand feet. The balloon's air had cooled through the night, but the helium pouch sufficed to keep them far above ground. They wouldn't need to burn any gas today: the warmth would do most of the lifting.

Andeal slept on the other side of the basket, half-sitting against the basket's side. Henry stepped over his legs to open the storage, then withdrew two solar panels and their cables, along with a pack of delicious noodles. A shame they couldn't afford the extra weight of water to cook them. He shut the lid with care and hurried to his corner of the basket, under the burners. Andeal grunted but didn't wake. Good. He deserved the rest, after last night's frenzy.

Henry set aside his meal for the moment and focused on the solar panels. They were almost the length of the balloon's basket and the rebels had welded two large hooks behind. The photosynthetic material was thankfully rather light and he had no problem lifting the panels to hang them outside, one side each, where they'd catch the sun. He then plugged both into the propeller's battery. Bright weather like today's would keep their propeller running but if they ran out of power, only the winds would guide their direction.

Not that he knew where they meant to go. He ought to ask Andeal.

Henry pushed the thought away, for later. He wanted to enjoy the morning. He took the pack of noodles and smashed it against the basket, crushing the thick brick into smaller chunks before he opened the sack. As he leaned on the railing, he brought the first bite to his lips.

The noodles crunched under his teeth, perfectly salted. His stomach rumbled—not a protest, for once—and Henry crammed more in his mouth. He'd missed the pleasure of biting into a flavored hunk. And today he could savor it thousands of feet above the air, in a special balloon designed by his father. The Lenz Balloon. That's how they would call the model, if ballooning ever became common again. For now, however, they were the only ones roaming the sky. He wondered if there was anyone on the ground to see it.

A thick forest stretched below them and from above the trees looked like broccoli. A river frolicked out of the woods, snaking through the countryside. Henry followed its path as far as he could. What a splendid vista. He plunged his fingers into his noodle bag, munched his breakfast and took a deep breath. When had he last savored such a delightful morning?

"You ate without me?"

Andeal's teasing question surprised Henry. He hadn't heard his friend wake or stand but the engineer leaned against the basket's side with a wide grin. Henry faked horror.

"I would never."

He brought the bag to his lips and poured all that was left in his mouth. It pulled short-lived laughter from Andeal but his friend soon sighed, ran a hand through his disheveled hair, and crossed his arms. He cast a look at the landscape.

"Where are we?"

"Drifting high in the sky, in a corner of paradise."

Andeal scowled. "Not what I meant. *Where?*"

"Northeast. We flew northeast." He kept his voice low. Andeal's raised voice had carried through the sky. "I didn't touch the direction. It's not like I'd know where to go."

"Reverence."

"What?"

That was the last location Henry had expected. Andeal wanted him to fly straight to the capital. Henry searched for a sign of amusement in his expression. His friend had to be joking. They'd barely escaped the bomber blimp, their home was destroyed, and they had no idea if their little flight would go unnoticed. And Andeal wanted to go where union forces would be the thickest? Great plan. Yet his friend showed no sign of jesting. Henry rubbed the back of his neck.

"Why Reverence, of all places?"

"I don't see another option." Andeal leaned back and closed his eyes. He looked so…sad. An unnatural expression for him. "We can't stay near Mt. Kairn with the balloon, not for now. When Joshua got attacked, however, Seraphin sought me out. He thought this might happen and told me the contact in Reverence was a good friend. We could wait for them there. He thinks she won't refuse us. No matter the danger or…or that I'm blue."

Andeal wrung his hands together. Henry searched for something to say—wise words to reassure his friend and bring his smile back—but his mind remained blank. Instead he walked to him and squeezed his shoulder. Andeal shrugged it off.

"I know a way in," he said, "but once we're in the city, how do I sneak around? I'm impossible to miss."

"We'll go at night. You almost look Burgian in the dark. We've got days of flight before we arrive. Don't overthink it. Eat instead. It always works for me."

He motioned at the chest under his friend and his comment drew a smile. Andeal obeyed and rummaged through the chest, selecting his breakfast: enticing strips of beef jerky.

While his friend ate, Henry returned to work and checked the bright blue flag tied to a cable. It fluttered in a constant northern wind that pushed them at a slow and peaceful pace. Combining the breeze with the propeller's strength would be easy. Since he could not put the spinning blades anywhere else than under the basket or on one side, he grabbed the direction rope and pulled. The balloon slowly turned around, bringing the blades west. Perfect. Henry plopped down in the bottom of the basket, wondering how precise he could be. He'd never flown for real, let alone combined two unequal strengths to guide his aircraft. What choice did he have, though? He would have to become a pro, and fast. He checked the battery's level, smiled at the growing green bar, and leaned back against the sides. The only sound so far above ground came from the whirring propeller, soft and reassuring.

He should feel terrible about those thoughts. The bomber blimp had blown Andeal's world to smithereens. Everyone might be dead, buried under a defaced Mount Kairn. The Races' trail must have vanished among rockslides and new craters. But he couldn't stress or panic here. The balloon soothed him. Calmed his otherwise unstable nerves.

It seemed to have the opposite effect on Andeal. His friend played with his breakfast, his gaze lost into the clear sky. He put the food down without finishing, stood to glance at the ground, sat again. And all through this routine, he kept running a hand in his hair or staring at his palms. Nervous.

"Andeal?"

Andeal turned and held his breath. Fear looked almost as unnatural as sadness had on him.

"She'll be okay."

Andeal's gaze dove into his, perhaps searching for a sign of falseness. But Henry trusted Maniel to endure any hardships. She had this calm strength he envied, and if anyone could keep her head straight while bombs fell upon it, it was her. Andeal smiled, his breathing eased. He leaned on the rail and stared out at the beautiful scene below their feet.

Neither of them would admit she might be dead. What would be the point? There would be no changing the balloon's slow course. Whether or not anyone else had survived Mount Kairn's bombing, they would go to Reverence.

The winds only knew what they could do from there.

A loud splash downstream startled Captain Vermen and he jumped to his feet. The sudden movement of air blew their four-story card castle to the ground, drawing a curse from Joshua and a disappointed 'aw' from Maniel and Jan. Vermen hushed them. No paper castle would save them from a union squad. While the two rebels turned to Maniel for orders, Vermen stalked past the cave's bend. He picked up a hand-sized rock on his way and flattened himself next to the entrance, against the wall. Holding his breath, he listened to the approaching intruders.

One to three men. Hard to tell with all the water.

Vermen looked at Maniel, lifted one finger, then three. She nodded and raised a pistol. The captain's eyes widened in surprise. No one had told him the rebels hid a firearm here. He resisted the urge to cross the cavern and grab it, to feel the cool handle under his fingers. The last time he'd held a pistol, he'd pointed it at Seraphin's forehead. Ages ago, it seemed. He was no longer the captain who had held that gun. Now he was a man with a rock.

The splashing steps grew louder. Almost there. Tension sped Vermen's heartbeat and forced him to steady his breath. He watched for Maniel's reaction; stationed at the corner, she would see the enemy before him. Vermen wished their bodies didn't cast long shadows on the ground. Whoever approached would've noticed the light, though, and dimming it would attract attention. He readied himself and hoped for the best.

"Maniel?"

Seraphin's uncertain question carried out of the tunnel and a collective sigh of relief escaped them. Vermen dropped his rock and pushed himself off the wall. Joshua knelt and begun gathering his cards. Maniel lowered her pistol.

"We're here."

The Regarian emerged from the long cavern and stepped out of the stream. He held his boots in his hands and his skeletal feet caught Vermen's attention. Seraphin's skin seemed stretched upon bones, with minimal muscles under it and no fat at all. Had everyone thinned so much? He ran a finger along his cheek and glanced at his bony wrists. Rations were scarce. He doubted any of them looked healthy.

"You scared us," Maniel said. "What news?"

Seraphin detailed Vermen from head to toe, letting a tense silence linger, then turned to Maniel. "Everyone reached their hideouts safe. Except, it seems, Andeal."

"The tunnel collapsed before I could reach him."

"A bad surprise for all of us."

Joshua snickered at Seraphin's answer. The captain gritted his teeth and lifted his chin. He had just saved their collective ass. He would not let them shame him because he had not arrived at the balloon's hangar in time.

"Yes, including me."

Vermen's retort brought an amused laugh from Seraphin, but his mirth did not last. He turned to Maniel. "Soldiers are roaming these caves. Stay hidden for now. We'll regroup in three days." He paused, licked his lips. That strange vulnerable expression resurfaced again and Vermen found himself staring. Drawn in by the concerned, friendly side of Seraphin, the one he'd always refused to consider might exist. "I didn't hear anything about a hot air balloon. They don't know Andeal and Henry took off."

Neither do we, Vermen thought. No one pointed it out. No one wanted to underscore the very real possibility of their deaths. When the silence stretched on, with no other response from Maniel than a distant nod, Vermen cleared his throat.

"What's next?" he asked. "Once we regroup, what do we do?"

The question warranted him a second suspicious examination from Seraphin. The rebel leader tilted his head to the side.

"We?"

Vermen gritted his teeth. He was not a rebel. He did not want him thinking that either. "Well, I'm stuck with you for a while, am I not?"

"I guess you are." Seraphin's amused tone grated on Vermen's nerves but he kept silent as the Regarian continued. "Andeal will be en route to Reverence. We'll join him before we figure out anything else. With a detour through Elmsfield to resupply."

"Elmsfield?" Joshua lifted his head and stopped gathering his deck. His sudden interest made everyone else smile.

"Yes, Elmsfield. Mayor Riley will not refuse to help us."

"Of course not."

Joshua returned to his task with renewed enthusiasm, his grin even wider than usual. There had to be a girl behind his reaction. Vermen scowled. This was no time to think of silly romance. They were stuck underground with little food, Andeal might well be dead and their hideout had been blasted to dust. He ought to get his priorities straight.

Seraphin's gaze trailed on the remainder of Joshua's deck, still spread on the cavern's floor. "Everybody's either stressed or bored to death yet here you are, playing card games. I should've thought of that and put you on my team."

"Building card castles, actually," Joshua corrected before adding with a confident wink. "You should always keep me on your team, Seraph."

"Well, I'm not going back until I've helped you rebuild what I destroyed."

He strode to Joshua and crouched near him. For a moment, no one else moved. Vermen stared at the Regarian, a strange tightness in his throat. He wasn't going to sit for hours building something with Holt. No way. He stayed away for the first minutes but as the castle took shape once more and Vermen's boredom increased, he gave in and joined the ridiculous endeavor. Every now and then his gaze trailed back to the White Renegade and always, he found pale blue eyes staring back from behind his glasses.

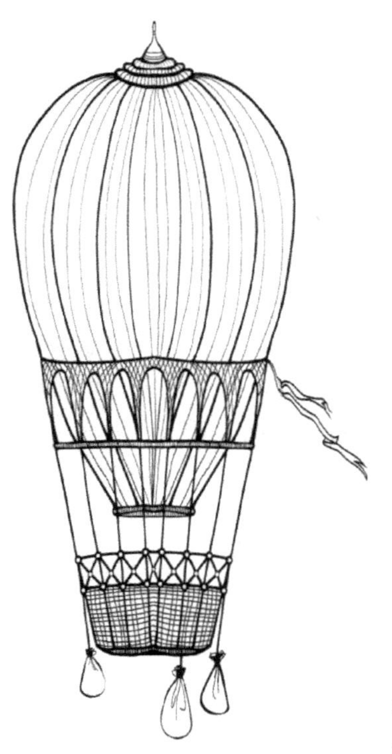

<h1 style="text-align:center">CHAPTER TWENTY-TWO</h1>

*Henry faced the catacombs'* entrance and wished he could return to the Lenz Balloon.

They'd landed in a thick forest five hours out of Reverence and hid the aircraft in the bushes to the best of their ability. The fake greenery seemed obvious as he walked away. Unmistakable. Of course someone had to hike by it first, which would involve serious bad luck. Perhaps that's why he was so fearful. Chance had never favoured him.

They needed to enter the city, though, and Andeal's way in provided plenty of other things to worry about. He wanted to creep through the catacombs.

Reverence hugged a large mountainside and its rocky ground had never offered a lot of cemetery space. When the Threstle Plague spread through the city, the few lots available vanished and a new solution had to be found—

something to keep the rotting corpses from piling in the streets and infecting others. Thousands were buried in the mountain's bowels, thrown into common pits and sealed. Tunnels still existed, with openings both in the city and around the mountain. As Henry stared into their chosen entrance, he wondered if there was a single cave network the rebels had not heard about.

Henry swallowed hard. He didn't want to leave the sun's fading warmth to thread through the rotting corpses of the Threstle Plague's victims. He turned to Andeal with a pleading look.

"Perhaps we could paint your skin?"

"No. We've had this discussion. We'll be fine. Seraphin used the entrance before."

Andeal raised his mechanical torchlight and spun the crank until a white beam lit their way. All of Henry's willpower went into the first step and he almost never took the second. Cool underground air and darkness enclosed them as they advanced. Soon they relied on the torchlight to see.

The first hundreds meter consisted of a natural cave. After months spent in smooth round tunnels, this mountain's tall ovoid-shaped passages disturbed Henry. He stretched his hands but couldn't reach the ceiling, yet the way was so narrow he couldn't walk besides Andeal. Disturbing as they might be, the egg tunnels remained better than catacombs. Henry started to hope he'd escape the dreadful sights as they progressed deeper inside—until the beam of light stopped upon a rotten wooden door. The handle creaked as Andeal turned it. He pushed and the wood grated on the floor, stirring a cloud of dust. When it settled enough for the beam to pierce through, Henry gasped.

Hundreds of skull lined the wall and the shifting light created angry glares into the empty sockets. Henry huddled closer to Andeal as they crept forward. He covered his mouth with his shirt, afraid to catch the Threstle Plague despite his vaccine. The skeletons' accusing gazes followed their every step. He tried not to breathe too loud, not to slap his soles on the stones. The catacombs reeked of decomposition and blackened bits of flesh sometimes hung to the bones. Death imposed its silence here. Henry's gaze trailed on the ground but bones littered the way forward. He could not escape the dead.

The Plague had devoured their lives.

Henry reached for his vest's pocket and the tiny disc within. Galen Clarin had killed those buried under Reverence—thousands of nameless souls sacrificed in a bid for power. These bodies had been piled into the recesses without regards for their dignity or religion. The pandemic had turned most into hysterics. Nothing had mattered but the need to contain the plague.

The Clarin twins had counted on it. Henry forced himself to look at the skulls and ribcages. These were the people who had paid for the twins' ambitions. He traced a clean jaw with his finger. Had this been a man or a woman? How many siblings had they left behind? Did they also rest here, somewhere in the piles of unidentified bones? When his mother had died, Kinsi and Tia had helped Henry bury her. None of these people had received a proper funeral.

No one would give it to them. No one could.

No one except him.

A peaceful resolve overcame him, washing his fears away, erasing his doubts. The catacombs no longer scared him, as though these dead souls had given him their blessing. As his gaze drifted from one skull to another, his father's words came back to him, written in bloodied letters on a rag.

*This cannot be silenced.*

He was right. Henry didn't know how yet, but he intended to start an unstoppable signal.

The tunnels' exit offered a splendid view of Reverence's layout. The capital's streets snaked between the rooftops and down the mountain, dark lines amid the soft green glow of the roof solar panels. Black lightless smears on the landscape indicated buildings devoid of electricity. Half the houses near them were little more than shacks in disrepair and gave no radiance but the dark spots became rarer as the city progressed away from the catacombs and toward the outer rim, where rich skyscrapers lined up into an almost perfect half-circle. Henry's breath caught in his throat as he tried to imagine all the people crammed into such a tight space. Reverence must be thousands of times bigger than Ferrea.

Andeal didn't pause at the sight. He clicked his torchlight off and took the stairway down the deserted ledge they stood upon. Henry hurried after him, breathless. His feet hurt from the day's long walk but he didn't protest. He knew his friend wouldn't rest until they'd reached their contact.

At the bottom of the stairs, Andeal motioned him forward.

"Go ahead. I'll shadow you."

The tightness in his voice convinced Henry to accept the lead. He traveled through the asphalted streets and Andeal followed, alert for strangers who might take note of their presence. In the catacombs he'd felt watched by ghosts, but here he'd swear the living waited for a chance to call union troops on them. The green glow that bathed the streets gave Andeal's skin a sickening hue. Anyone who more than glanced at him would realise his partial Burgian ancestry wasn't the source of his darker skin.

They couldn't linger, but it'd help if they knew their way around the city. None of the roads described a straight line or fit a pattern. They wound down the mountain like ski slopes, criss-crossing each other, and soon Henry could not tell north from south, let alone find a specific neighborhood in this maze of possibilities. Left or right? Should they go through that park or move forward? Continue downward or climb back to the unlit alleys?

As Henry began to despair, his friend pointed at a disused bus stop. The glass display on the side exhibited an enlarged map of their area, with a smaller version of the whole city. They traced the lines on the plan, searching for their streets. Henry's heart sped. If they took too long, somebody would notice them for sure.

"There! Sparkler Street."

It turned out to be a main avenue, further west of their position. Andeal smiled and his shoulders eased. In a quarter hour they would be safe.

"Let's go," he said. "Time to test her loyalty."

Henry agreed and started off once more. This would be his second interaction with a rebel outside of Mount Kairn. He wondered what had happened to Stern's cousin. Would their presence here bring the same fate to Reverence's contact? What if Seraphin was wrong and she turned them away? Or worse, sold them out? He pushed the questions away and tried to summon the resolve he'd felt in the catacombs. Thousands had died from the Threstle Plague, including his mother. He owed it to them to take such risks. Knocking on a stranger's door was just the first of many dangerous steps.

Andeal's already speedy heartbeat quickened even more as he spotted their destination, a three-story house squeezed between two bulkier buildings. Time had washed away all color from the brick facade and smoothened its lines. The long windows created dark voids in the front—all except one on the second floor, with a tiny light on. Their contact was still awake. She'd also pepped up her house's appearance by painting the front door a bright green which caught the rooftops' glow and seemed to multiply it. Standing in front of it gave Andeal the impression somebody shone a spotlight on him.

He touched his cheek and shrunk away. Whoever this contact was, she was in for a big surprise. How could Seraphin be so certain of her loyalty? People said many things, but when danger came…

Henry knocked three times, then wiped his hands on his pants. Andeal sucked his breath in. His stomach churned. This was worse than welcoming newbies at the headquarters. Perhaps even worse than waiting on Henry's doorstep. He wished Maniel was by his side. He felt alone. Vulnerable.

The lights downstairs were flipped on. Endless seconds passed. Someone rushed down the stairs inside. Andeal's throat tightened as the door swung open.

He squinted against the glare as light spilled in the street and made out the dark shape of a tall woman. Henry froze. Why didn't he say anything? Greet her, apologize for the hour. *Something.*

She spoke first.

"Good evening, mister stranger."

Andeal's heart leapt. That voice. The familiar bouncy playfulness and welcoming warmth that used to greet him whenever he came home from class. How long had it been since he last heard it? Eight years? Suddenly Seraphin's faith in their contact made perfect sense.

"Hi. Hey. I'm Henry, I—"

Andeal pushed his friend aside to get a better view. There was no mistaking the dark green hair cascading down her shoulders or the slightly prominent teeth in her wide grin. Treysh might be wearing pajama pants and a flouncy blouse instead of her usual flashy attire but here she was, miles away from Altaer and the university where they'd lived together. How? His mind refused to believe what his eyes told him.

"Treysh?"

His voice broke as he pronounced her name. What if his blue skin repulsed her? They'd shared a flat before his capture, when he was still somewhat a fat, chubby pale brown nerd. The long hours he'd spent holding her head above the toilet while she purged her excess of alcohol did not ensure Treysh would welcome him.

"Andeal!" She closed the distance between them in a single stride and drew him into a tight embrace. She touched his skin without the slightest hesitation. A soft warmth spread through his stomach and though his heart beat hard, it was no longer from stress. She didn't care.

"You haven't changed at all!" she declared as they pulled apart.

A choked laugh escaped from his lips. "You did. You look more mature."

"Don't be fooled, it's all smokes." She made a dramatic gesture with a poof sound. "Come inside. You two look exhausted!"

Andeal hadn't felt so alive since they'd launched out of Mount Kairn and he followed with pleasure. Henry fell behind, muttering something about dinner. The poor man must be dying for a real meal.

On a peg inside hung Treysh's favourite outfit: a long trench coat dyed in a deep red and a large-brimmed hat of the same color, with a new fluffy white feather. Years had worn the leather and paled the rich color, but it'd still stand out of any crowd. His old friend had always loved to clash with her surroundings. Next to her, his blue skin might even look normal.

She led them into a cozy living room, no bigger than Andeal's cavern chambers. A low sofa occupied most of the space and faced a fire hearth. Large bookshelves covered the walls, filled with adventure novels. He recognized some titles from their time together and the familiarity put him at ease. Elements of the decor here—the books, the large fireworks poster on the wall, the finger puppets of famous chemists—had been part of his home years ago, when the world seemed normal and safe. Sitting in the middle of them, Andeal allowed himself to relax.

Treysh grabbed a chair in the dining room and dragged it over. She spun it around and sat in reverse, her forearms set on the chair's back. That, too, brought old memories back.

"How's Maniel?"

Treysh's question brought him back to the brutal reality. He met his friend's brown gaze, surprised.

"How do you know about her?"

"Oh, come on, Andeal! Don't you think I've kept tabs on you all these years?" She had her mischievous grin—exactly like when she'd stolen chemicals from her school's lab or came back with ninety-percent-pure ethanol for drinks. "Been working with Seraphin and taking news for some time now."

"He never told *me* about you." He couldn't keep the anger out of his tone. Why had his friend not told him? Then he realised that if Treysh knew, if Seraphin had tracked down friends from his old life, he might have done the same with his family. "Do my parents know? About me. About…"

His voice trailed but he lifted his hands and stared at the bluish skin. Inside his palms it was paler, almost its original slightly-tanned skin. How horrified they would be.

"Sorry, no." She leaned back with an apologetic smile. "We thought about it, but Seraphin thinks the Union might spy on your parents in case you return."

Bitter bile welled in his stomach. Every year when his birthday came, he thought about seeking his parents out. Altaer was miles away, on the eastern shores of Regaria, and he never had the courage to cross the country. Not alone, with his blue skin. He'd tried to convince Maniel to follow, once. She'd had a girlfriend in Altaer—a fairly serious relationship—and she might want to send word to her family. But they both agreed that if they were caught, they would be dragged straight to Galen's labs. Nothing was worth that risk.

"All right. Not yet. Once this is all over, though..."

Andeal ran a hand through his short hair and took a deep breath. How long would that take? The rebels were scattered or destroyed. How were they supposed to bring it to an end and give him back his life? Treysh put her hand on his knee.

"You never told me how Maniel was," she said.

"Because I don't know." Every word pained him. "We were separated when they attacked Mount Kairn."

"So it's just the two of you?"

"And the balloon," added Henry.

"Wow." She leaned forward and a fire burned in her eyes. Andeal recognized the passion their old tricks prompted but time had added a layer of seriousness to it. She knew this was no freshman joke. "Will you tell me what happened? Since the first bombs fell a week ago, the National Radio has been spilling out ridiculous lies three times a day. Can you believe they recorded that dreadful announcer and just replay the same text over and over?"

"I can." Henry turned as red as Treysh's trench coat and wrung his hands together. "It's just...I used to listen to it all the time. They always put news on repeat."

She glanced at her clock—a hexagon with lines jutting out of each corner, probably meant to be a benzene molecule. How typical. Like everything else about her, Treysh's obsession with chemistry exceeded normal boundaries.

"It'll be on soon if you want to hear it," she said.

"Yeah, I'd love that," Andeal said. "But do you have something to eat? We didn't have much on the road."

Henry's pleading eyes told Andeal he'd been holding the question back since forever. Treysh jumped to her feet.

"Of course! I make a terrible host. Let me start that radio and I'll fix you a late dinner while you listen. I sure don't need to hear it all over again!"

Treysh flipped the radio on. Her receiver had a smooth wooden arc and flowery motif etched around the speakers. Although the pattern was delicate and lovely, it clashed with Treysh's science decor and eccentric tastes.

"Where did you get that?"

"A boring ex."

Treysh grinned and scurried to the kitchens before Andeal could press her with questions. The announcer's dragging voice filled the room, words flowing out with a metronome's regularity.

*"As thousands of citizens mourn the destruction of Mount Kairn's top,*

*the Union soldiers continue to search for the White Renegade's rebels, who have claimed this attack on one of the nation's most powerful icons. Traces of the chemical substances used to produce the bombs were found and the authorities fear there might be more to come. We recommend that all citizens stay on high alert and report suspicious activities as quickly as possible."*

Andeal's fingers clenched on his pants. The Union had snuck in during night and ruined his home and life, and now they blamed the rebels for it. Such a simple lie, but why would anyone doubt it? This week's newspaper probably told the same story.

"Was it always like this?" Henry asked. "It all sounded so real, but..."

"Almost always," Andeal said. "The Clarin family built their empire on communications. They own the newspapers and the National Radio."

Henry's expression turned into a mix of guilt and frustration. He must be reviewing all the big news he'd heard, questioning it. There were few other sources of information available and the world seemed to shift once you learned not to trust the radio. The radio's neutrality—reinforced by its announcers' drone voice—was taken for granted. Like the belief policemen would always protect the innocent. Then you were arrested, imprisoned, and snuck into a lab to be tested on, without warning or explanation, and all you could do was follow, thinking every step of the way that it had to be a dream, because these things did not happen in the real world. The handcuffs, the gruff officer, the unidentified van, the long interrogations—all scenes from a bad action flick. It had to be fake.

It remained surreal, even today, but he had his blue skin as an indelible mark of his passage in the labs.

"Andeal?"

Treysh held a warmed platter of curry. The spicy scent tickled his nose and made him salivate. He grabbed it and stuffed the first bite right in. His throat burned, and his eyes watered but a meal had never tasted so good. Gone were the minuscule meals of beef jerky, raisins and instant noodles. This was fresh, fiery, flavorful. He devoured his plate in minutes. At his side Henry was already chugging a whole bottle of water to help the food down. Once their plates were clean, Treysh sat back in front of them.

"Put that on the floor, I'll clean later." She brought her legs up and crossed them. "So what really happened?"

"They came in the middle of the night with a bomber blimp. Vermen..."

"Vermen?" She repeated the name with the inflection of someone who'd heard it before.

"Yes. That Vermen. We'll have time for that story later. He heard the blimp and warned everyone. Henry and I took off in the hot air balloon. The others must've followed the original plan and gone underground. *If* they weren't crushed under tons of rock."

"Oh." The news smothered her good mood. "I'm sorry, Andeal."

"They're fine," Henry said forcefully.

"It's okay." It wasn't. Strong claws squeezed his heart whenever he thought of it. He didn't want to imagine living on without Maniel. Not while there was hope. Andeal's shoulders sagged and he leaned back into the sofa. "We have to carry on. If only for them."

By the time Treysh showed them their rooms, pink light climbed into the sky. Henry had spent half the night sleeping on the couch while Andeal relived old tales from university with the weird girl. At first he'd listened, fascinated to discover their mischievous streak and propensity to get into trouble. As one night-time expedition followed the other, however, all the stories melded into one in Henry's brain. For a time he stared at Treysh, watched her laugh or cringe, studied the crazy green hair. But even that lost interest. The long hours of walking caught up to him, his eyelids shut by themselves and he woke with the dawn, when Andeal decided to catch some sleep.

His friend shone brighter than the rising sun. Treysh had breathed a new life into him—his old one. Henry wondered if one day he'd be allowed his back, too. As he climbed the steps to his room, he missed Kinsi more than ever. Andeal had promised to return to his parents once "all this" was over. Henry had no idea what "all this" would turn out to be, but one thing was sure: once it was done, he'd seek the grocer and enjoy another tranquil beer with him.

And then, maybe, they could find a way to bring back the Races to Ferrea.

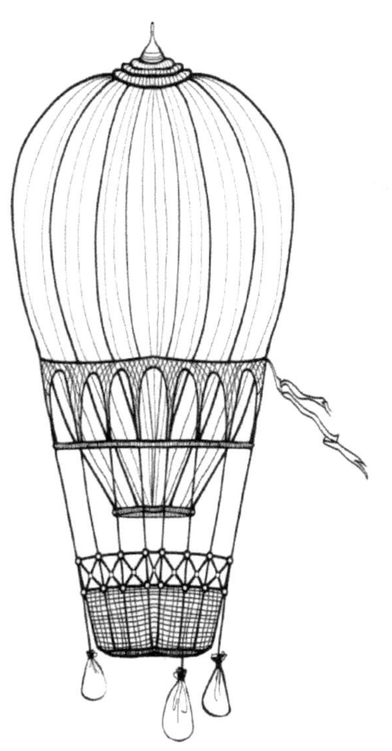

# CHAPTER TWENTY-THREE

*Cards castle quickly grew* boring and were abandoned after a high tower crashed at their feet. Joshua wasted no time finding a new source of entertainment and had begun teaching magic tricks and other sleight-of-hand techniques to Jan. Vermen watched at first. The Burgian's skill impressed him and brought its share of questions. Was Joshua skilled at card games or did he cheat his way to victory? How often had he slipped an extra ace from his sleeve as they played, early in their confinement? No, not possible. Not unless he had another deck hidden. Although watching him make cards and coins vanish with ridiculous ease, Vermen didn't put it past the sly man. The dim light—toned down to save its remaining power—amplified the routine into true magic.

An act, of course, and one that soon did little to amuse the captain. He slid away from the group, turning the L-shaped cave's corner and striding over the budding stream. The stone walls formed a comfortable alcove next to the source. Since Seraphin had left again, he'd taken to sitting there, in the dark, eyes closed or set on the entrance. Sometimes he slept, although he had a hard time telling dreams from memories. Whenever he settled in this spot—his spot—his mind wandered to a past long gone, in which he still had a brother.

It always started with the same souvenir. He played outside with Klaus' new toy, a radio-controlled model of a copter. The sun shone bright and hot, wind danced with the summer leaves. A perfect day to climb the hill and fly the machine above its steep side. He'd promised to be careful with it. Even as a boy, Klaus' anger had terrified him. Later it'd strike fear in soldiers, allies and enemies both.

When the copter clipped a tree and plummeted down the cliff, Hans had sprinted down with it. How enormous it'd seemed, at eight, to break his brother's toy. He'd stumbled, of course, and tumbled down the cliff, tucked in a tight ball for most of the ride. Not a wise thing to do. Years later he remembered the pain as he'd lain at the bottom, every bit of his body throbbing. When he'd arrived, bloodied by numerous cuts and scratches, covered in dirt and half his clothes torn, the broken copter had mattered little to anyone. Although Klaus wouldn't lend him another toy. Out of fear he'd go and kill himself, he said.

His back to the cool cavern walls, Vermen relived the memory every time, along with other important milestones in his life. Always, his brother was there, looking over his shoulder, teaching him, praising him. Teasing and pushing, sometimes. Hans Vermen basked in the remembered fraternity and solid companionship between them, but the path of his youth had only one deadly end. It was another perfect morning, without a cloud in the sky, and his commanding officer had asked to speak with him. The man had his formal uniform, with every medal and honor pinned on. When he had offered Vermen a seat with a grave tone, Hans—still a young soldier—had understood. He'd refused.

Before he heard the fateful announcement again, Vermen plunged his naked feet in the bursting stream. Icy water stung at his still-raw ankles and anchored him to the present. Once, these scenes fueled his anger and drove him after Holt. Today they brought another kind of sorrow: the quiet, grieving one that leeched life away. He didn't want to slide into depressed inaction.

"You look like you've seen a ghost."

Seraphin's voice startled Vermen and he scrambled to his feet. How had he not heard him splash up the stream to their hideout? The Regarian stood right beside him, his hair cut to shoulder length. Vermen glared at him with a sudden urge to wipe away his amused smile.

"He wouldn't be a ghost if you hadn't shot him."

The mirth vanished from Seraphin's expression and he climbed out of the water. Vermen stiffened and prepared for some sort of mockery. Instead Seraphin put his hand on Hans' shoulder and squeezed it briefly. It didn't feel like an apology. More like a silent acknowledgement that Vermen hurt, and he understood that. The captain's anger at Seraphin vanished, replaced by newfound respect.

The other rebels had stopped their magic games and gathered around. Instead Seraphin addressed the group:

"We're ready to move out. Stern's group already joined up with mine. You're the last."

Maniel turned to the others with a smile. "Pack up. It's time to surface at last."

She didn't need to say it twice. Joshua set to work with a gleeful exclamation, shoving everything he could into their packs without regards for order. Vermen scowled at his random packing. He was about to head over and teach him how to split rations and survival equipment between everyone even in a rush when Seraphin's hand landed on his shoulder and held him back.

"Not you," Seraphin said. "We need to have a word."

Vermen very much disagreed. He did not want a private talk with Seraphin. Whenever the rebel leader was around, Vermen could not help but watch him. He'd grown nervous about what he would say or do, as though Holt's opinion mattered. It shouldn't. Yet after saving this rag-tag band of criminals, he found himself yearning for some respect. Or maybe gratitude. Either of them would be a nice change of pace from his usual snark. Vermen would rather cling to the tiny shoulder squeeze than ruin the moment with a talk that'd inevitably remind him of why he couldn't get along with the Renegade.

"Now?" Vermen asked.

"Yeah. We can always catch up to them after."

Seraphin could. If he ditched Vermen in the network of caves, however, the captain would never find his way. He studied the Regarian for a long moment, unable to contain his suspicions, but if Seraphin wanted him dead he would've let his men shoot him at the top of Mount Kairn.

"Let's get this over with."

Vermen jumped down the stream and followed the rebel leader into the tunnel. They followed it until they reached the river, then Seraphin lead him some distance away, perhaps to make sure Maniel and the others wouldn't show up in the middle of their discussion. Vermen wiped his sweaty palms on his pants. Part of him wished the long, awkward silence would go away. The other preferred not to know what the following conversation would contain.

Seraphin stopped and turned around. Their dim flickering light emphasized the thinness of his traits, making his hollowed cheeks even more angular. His white hair and eyelashes seemed to absorb the light and have a glow of their own. Vermen stared, entranced by the strange effect, until Seraphin cleared his throat.

"Is there a problem?"

A deep flush rose to Vermen's cheeks. He stammered, ashamed, and struggled for a plausible justification.

"No—no. I just...you cut your hair."

"Congratulations, Captain. You have reached a new level of perceptiveness." Seraphin ran a hand through it with an amused smile. Before Vermen could form a proper retort, he explained. "It'll be easier to hide."

"Glad you didn't do that while *I* was tracking you. You wouldn't believe the number of witnesses that reported 'flowing white hair'. I guess you reached a new level of intelligence."

This drew a laugh from Seraphin. The rebel leader did not seem insulted in the slightest. "Did it never occur to you that while I trekked across the country, easy to track but always a step ahead, other rebels operated in the field, unseen? Long white hair makes a fantastic lure when your enemy is obsessed."

Shame formed a lump in Vermen's throat. He recalled sitting in his office one evening, flipping through several witness accounts, his boots on the desk. He read the important parts to Lungvist, his most trusted lieutenant and the best brains the army had to offer. After a while Lungvist had suggested exactly that. He'd leaned on the wall and voiced it as a supposition, asking Vermen to consider the White Renegade's sightings might be a distraction. Vermen wouldn't listen. Distraction or not, he wanted to catch Seraphin and would not be diverted from his path.

"My lieutenant knew. I didn't care. I wanted *you*, Seraphin. Anything else was extra."

Their gazes locked for a long time. A lot had changed since he had held his gun to Seraphin's forehead, unable to pull the trigger. The power balance shifted and, worse of all, Vermen had no idea how to qualify the new dynamic. The part wanting to know Seraphin battled with the part that had spent so long loathing him. He hated this uncertainty.

"What about now?" Seraphin asked, echoing Vermen's thoughts.

The captain lowered his gaze. He'd done his best not to think about the rebels and his role in their survival. Joshua's antics had distracted him for a while, but his mind soon drifted back to his confused future. He turned Schmitt's declaration in his head, over and over. The other rebels had reasons to lie about the Threstle Plague. It gave them an excuse for their criminal actions, a well-intentioned pretext to sow chaos. But Schmitt? One glance at him was enough to tell he was a coward who'd rather plump his ass in a sofa with a bowl of noodles and listen to the National Radio, safe and peaceful, than to live like a rat in a hole, putting his life on the line for a fabricated conspiracy. Something had convinced him to abandon his security and join the fray—and that, more than anything Andeal could say, bothered him. Noodle Man's participation in this mess gave disturbing weight to the rebels' story.

"I can't go back." He raised his head again, with a slight frown. "Stern told me what happened to the rebels I sent to prison. I might be next."

"Then you can either hide on your own or continue helping us."

Continue. Vermen closed his eyes as he considered the choice of word. Was Seraphin trying to tell him something? What did he want? Hans studied him, worried there was a trap here, a subtext he was missing. The rebel leader seemed...hopeful?

Before he could answer—before he even parted his lips—a powerful explosion rocked the cavern. Vermen stumbled backward and put his hands against the wall as dust fell from the ceiling. Bombs again, deeper in the mountain. Seraphin swore and covered his head, taking a step toward him.

"They're close," he said. "In our hideout."

The army didn't want to take the chance of rebels returning to their headquarters, it seemed. Vermen wondered how much dynamite they'd used. 'A lot' would be his guess. The confirmation came with two quick-paced explosions, forcing them into a crouch. The captain straightened back as soon as he could, his heart hammering against his chest. Blood pulsed against his temples, almost loud enough to cover the rumble of a collapse. It wasn't just the hideout that was collapsing. They were destroying the entire mountain.

"We can't stay—"

The fourth bomb exploded, stronger and closer than any of the others. He heard a loud ripping sound overhead and looked up to find a large crack in the ceiling. Vermen's breath caught in his throat, his feet remained cemented to the ground. Time seemed to slow as he watched a heavy boulder detach itself above him.

Another weight smashed into him before the boulder could crush his head—a lithe pale form, pushing him to the ground. Dust swirled as part of the weakened ceiling gave way, stone crashing all around. Vermen snapped his eyes shut and held his breath. The roar of the collapsing cave filled his ears. All he could feel was Seraphin's warmth against his and man's hair tickling his cheek.

Neither of them moved as the rumbling died and dust settled. Seraphin clung to his clothes, panting hard, his eyes wide from fear and his mouth quirked in a grimace. His glasses had fallen off. Vermen still held his breath. Seraphin had saved him. Hans had never been this aware of the cold stone against his back, of the warm body against his, gripping his clothes and panting. Of another man's lips inches away.

Hans stretched his neck and kissed him.

It lasted a second. A soft, intense second in which he forgot everything else.

Then Vermen's mind caught up to his body and he shoved Seraphin off him. The Regarian landed with a pained cry while Vermen scrambled away. The captain glared at Seraphin, breathless, bitterness riling up as he berated himself for being so stupid. You didn't do these things with your brother's murderer. You just didn't.

Seraphin's pained expression morphed into mild amusement. "If that's why you've been chasing me all those years, you should've said. I wouldn't have run so much."

"No!" Vermen's hands curled into fists at his side and he jumped to his feet. "I'm not—"

"Interested?"

"Gay!"

"That's okay. Neither am I."

Seraphin Holt was mocking him. He sat there, holding his ankle, a superior smile etched on his lips. Years of hatred rushed back, making his head spin. Vermen stepped forward, his fist shaking. He would feel so much better if he hit him hard, taught him to shut up every now and then.

"What am I supposed to make of that answer?"

Seraphin's mirth vanished. His gaze followed Vermen's approach. "I don't know what to make of your kiss and you don't see me complaining. Calm down."

His demand had the opposite effect and Vermen let out a cry of rage. He had to get out before he smashed his only guide's head against a rock. He ought to find Maniel instead. She never made fun of him. He spun on his heels, ready to stalk down the river to their small caves. Huge boulders blocked his way, remains of the collapse. Only a tiny stream made it through the piles of rock and Vermen stared at the rubble. His anger vanished as dread hollowed his stomach. They were cut off from the others.

"Vermen..." Seraphin's voice was a lot quieter now. "Something squashed my ankle when I pushed you. I don't think I can walk on it. And I can't find my glasses."

The captain turned around and grimaced when he spotted the broken glasses on the ground. Great. Not only was he stuck with Seraphin, but the man was wounded and blind. This promised to be fantastic.

"Don't expect me to carry you around like a princess."

Seraphin leaned back with a ragged laugh. He'd spread his left leg across the ground, turning his foot outward, and while Vermen's retort amused him, the captain noted his controlled breathing. He was in pain, and trying to hide it.

"Not leaving me to die would suffice, I think."

He forced a smile on his lips and extended a hand. Vermen glared at it for a long time, trying to sort through his mess of feelings, and eventually caught Seraphin's pleading, almost apologetic look. He sighed, grabbed the offered hand, and helped the rebel leader to his feet. The Regarian leaned on him, one hand on his shoulder, and his amused smile returned. Vermen flushed, gritted his teeth together.

"If you say a single word about this I'm pushing you in a dank hole and never coming back."

A chuckle shook Seraphin's body, making Vermen keenly aware of his every movement. "A shame, but if you insist, Captain. Let's get moving. We need to go around, see if we can find Maniel quickly. Staying long in these caves without food does not seem like a brilliant plan to me."

On that, at least, they could agree. Vermen slipped under Seraphin's shoulder to better support him, snatched their lamp from the ground and started down their only available path.

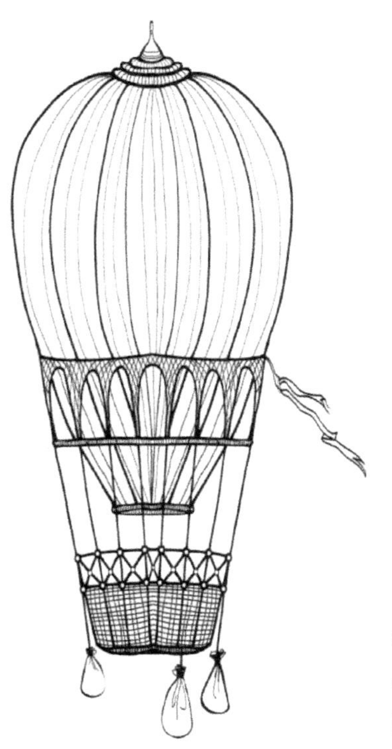

<h1 style="text-align:right">Chapter<br>Twenty-four</h1>

 the second salvo of bombs. Vermen had carried Seraphin through the snaking half-crumbled ways under Mount Kairn without stop, hoping to join with the rest of the group before their hunger grew too pressing. The explosions had shaken major structural foundations of the mountain's networks, creating new ravines and cave-ins and forcing them to make several detours. They'd made it to their original hideout and while it was intact, no one was left inside. After that, the captain had followed his companion's directions without questions and when they stopped in front of another pile of boulders and Seraphin swore, he understood they had reached their second destination. It hadn't survived.

"How far is the exit?" he'd asked.

Seraphin had shrugged. Who knew? Without something to eat they would not reach it. And where could one find food in these dead caverns?

They rested for a few fitful hours, searched the area for another way out. All they found was a long spool of rope and a broken lamp. Vermen picked up the rope, just in case, and they started off. Neither of them said a word but as the hours trickled by, Seraphin leaned more and more heavily on Vermen. His directions became disparate, irregular. Sometimes he dozed off, only to wake with a start when Vermen jolted his foot against a rock. The captain tried to shake him out of his daze. Without him he could not get out. He needed Seraphin awake and for that, he would need to feed him.

Then the voices drifted to him, distant. That was his chance—his only chance. He found a small alcove and propped Seraphin against the wall. The rebel leader opened his eyes. They could hear people talk, barely. Seraphin stared in their general direction.

"The others are there," he said.

"They could be soldiers. I'll check it out."

"It's dangerous."

Vermen's eyebrows shot up. Of course it was, but dying of hunger wasn't much better. "Worth it, though." He picked up the spool of rope and handed one end to Seraphin. He could use it as a guide for some distance, at least. "Stay here. I'll be back. And if I pull hard twice, I ran into trouble. Pull the rope back and leave."

Seraphin grunted his displeasure. He reached for something at his belt, behind his back, and offered him a switch blade. "Don't get killed, Hans."

Vermen snatched the weapon, grabbed the lamp, then hurried out, disturbed by the use of his first name. The rope slithered behind him as he moved through the tunnels, advancing toward the voices. Soon he ran out of rope and had to set it down. He continued, mindful of the turns he took. He hoped these were rebels, that he wouldn't need to try something dangerous, but he could not identify a single voice. When he managed to make out the first words of their conversation, he forgot about other rebels.

"No one's left here," a man said. "They got crushed by rocks or left. We're wasting our time."

Vermen shut his lamp, put it on the ground and stalked forward, cloaked in the darkness. His empty stomach churned in excitement and he glanced around a corner. Five soldiers advanced through a large cave with a bright lamp. One lit the way a few steps ahead while another trailed behind. The three in the center argued about the pointlessness of their mission.

"We ought to be up there in the sunlight with the others. These patrols are the worst."

Just as Vermen wondered why their officer tolerated their loud complaints, the older man in the center intervened. "Those are our orders and I don't give a damn whether or not they please you. Keep complaining and I'll stick you to dish duty for a month."

Vermen waited for them to pass his corridor before he emerged. He followed, careful not to scuff tiny rocks with his feet. All these men carried sacks, slung over their shoulders. The strap unclipped at three different spots, to free quickly should it get tangled during battle or retreat. The soldier trailing behind at the edge of the light listened to the argument, oblivious to his surroundings.

A perfect target.

Hans retrieved his knife, took a deep breath. Fear fought against excitement as he sprinted forward—a battle, however short, always caused this rush. He was in his element here, knew what to do and the risks involved. Nothing disturbing like kissing another man.

He grabbed the sack, pulled hard once. The soldier yelped, began to turn and bring his arms closer. Vermen slashed at him—keep him unbalanced, disorganized—then freed the package. He dashed off, prize in hand, as the four others turned around. Vermen sprinted toward his corridor, ducked as the first shots rang out. They clipped the wall behind him and he reached the entrance. Safe. At least for a few seconds. His heart pumping, Vermen picked up his lamp and returned it at minimum light. It wouldn't do to slam into a wall.

The soldiers followed close behind—too close for his taste. He had to lose them, but no sound covered the regular slap of his shoes on the stones or his breathing, steady but loud. His strength, spurred on by the rush of adrenaline, began to wane. Not enough food, nothing to fuel a long sprint. A mistake, this pursuit.

He wouldn't get away.

Vermen followed his path to the rope then skidded to a stop. He knelt, tied the sack and tugged hard, twice. At first nothing moved, then the bag snaked away, pulled by Seraphin.

At least one of them might get out of this mountain alive.

The soldiers' light grew nearer. Vermen waited, poised, until one turned the corner. Then he darted left, away from Holt.

"There!"

Perfect. He led them through winding tunnels, his strides growing shorter, his heart threatening to burst. Dark spots flashed before his eyes, obliterating what little light he had. Vermen pushed further, as far as he could from Seraphin. A gunshot rang, the bullet whizzed past his arm. A hair's breadth away. They wouldn't miss the next shot. He stumbled into a side corridor, dropped the lamp. Nothing here but a chute plunging into darkness. Too small for him.

Vermen spun on his heels as three soldiers burst into the tunnel's entrance. His hands shot up.

"I yield!"

His voice was raw, breathless. Bile rose in his throat and he felt himself sway. Despite the sweat covering his body, he shivered.

"Don't move!" the older soldier shouted. He made a sharp motion and the two others approached while he kept his gun trailed on Vermen. They brought his hands behind his back, pulling hard, and he grunted against the pain that shot up his arm.

Captured again. The ropes bit his wrists but he managed a half-smile. Don't get killed, Seraphin had said, but since when did he listen to the White Renegade anyway? At least he would die answering for his treason instead of starving like a rat.

The soldiers woke him with a sharp kick in the side. Vermen groaned and turned over. His arms throbbed, pulled back because of his tied wrists, and he had no strength left to sit up. The sprint had burnt his energy and he'd allowed the others to drag him, half-conscious, since his capture. He did not remember a pause, or collapsing to the ground.

"C'mon, get up."

They grabbed his arms and lifted him. Blood rushed to Vermen's head with the sudden movement. The world spun, black stains marred his view, bile rose in his throat. He struggled not to faint and the cavern floor slowly stabilized under him. Already he felt hot, feverish. Famished.

The men had set up camp in a smaller cavern. Beside their bright lamp was a fully-charged heater. They were opening cans of pasty meatballs in tomato sauce. The overpowering salty scent reached him and his belly retched. He might have vomited if there was any food for him to give back. He doubted his empty stomach would hold onto a heavy meal for long.

The older soldier leaned over him. Vermen had to focus on his visage and the cooking preparations behind blurred.

"Takes nerves to sleep at a time like this," he said. "Or utter idiocy. You even realize the mess you're in?"

Vermen sketched a smile and squirmed into a better position. The cavern wall was cool against his back. "Of course I do." His voice sounded distant, completely detached. He forced himself to concentrate. "Been in your shoes before, except my uniform had two stripes, not just the one."

The men behind froze and exchanged alarmed glances. Their leader, a corporal, clacked his tongue. "You're the one who vanished this fall. Now that'll disappoint Lieutenant Lungvist."

Lungvist. Vermen sucked his breath at the name and fought not to smile. If cautious, intelligent David was around, Hans might have a chance. Lungvist would always be on his side.

"He's in charge?"

"I'll ask questions, not you." The corporal spat at Vermen's feet. No point arguing further with him. "We never found our stolen pack. What did you do with it?"

"Threw it in the chute. Would've followed."

"So its disappearance has nothing to do with possible companions?" The soldier's mouth quirked. This one had brains.

"What companions?"

The blow came hard and fast. Vermen's head hit the wall behind and he lost track of time. When he came to, the other soldier waited, still towering over him. Had his mind slipped seconds or minutes?

"I'd answer, if you want to eat."

Vermen squeezed his eyes and held back a curse. He could take blows, but how long would they drag him around without food? Men had survived weeks without eating but they hadn't starved beforehand, walked through endless caverns, or been chased by union soldiers. He *needed* to eat, now, not in another four days.

"I'll talk to David, no one else. Lieutenant Lungvist."

They couldn't be far from the exit or the soldiers' heater would not have been charged. They needed sunlight for that, which was hard to come by in the bowels of Mount Kairn. David would feed him first, perhaps ask questions after.

The corporal laughed, snorted, turned to his companions. "Did you hear that, boys? Our traitor wants—"

A bullet ripped through his throat and silenced him. The old soldier toppled over Vermen and warm blood drenched the captain as gunshots rang through the small caves, to and from the union soldiers. He held still, half-protected by the dead man, while the others scrambled into a circle and drew their guns. Most managed to shoot once at the darkness surrounding them before they crumpled to the ground, dead or dying. The fight hadn't lasted a minute. Vermen took a deep, shuddering breath and squirmed out from under the corporal. There were meatballs just a few meters away, waiting for him.

A pale figure walked out of the darkness—emaciated, short blond hair stuck to his forehead, bones jutting at his elbows. The man was halfway across the cavern before Vermen recognized Stern. He smiled, relieved, almost laughed at the sweet irony there, then realized there was only fury in his eyes. Stern grabbed him, his fingers digging in like claws, and slammed him hard against the wall. It crushed Vermen's hands and sent another wave of vertigo.

"You'll *talk*, won't you? Let me guess. You killed Seraphin and now you'll sell all of us to buy your cursed life back, just like that."

Stern brought him closer, ready to shove him back into the stones. Outrage swirled inside Vermen and he smashed his forehead into the ex-soldier. They collapsed to the ground, both crying out in pain, and the fall knocked out what little energy Vermen had left. He felt Stern straddle him, groaned as the first punch connected with his jaw. With his tied hands he couldn't defend himself.

Other rebels rushed to his help and pulled them apart. Stern struggled while they lifted Vermen off the ground, but soon stopped. Jan and Joshua held him in place. Maniel had the captain's arm. Vermen's entire body shook, from anger and exhaustion. He wrested control of his breath and glared at the other.

"Sell all of you? I saved your asses when they bombed your mountain! I could've pushed Schmitt off a cliff and escaped. Or I could've ditched everyone after Andeal gave me the keys to my shackles. I didn't. You'd be dead, all dead, if I had."

Stern clenched his teeth. "You said—"

"David Lungvist had a twin brother, victim of the Threstle Plague, and he almost followed him to the grave. Nothing will shake his loyalty to the Union—nothing except perhaps the idea that Kurtmann and Clarin didn't *save* him, but rather killed his brother. Isn't that what you guys are all about?"

"How do you know that?"

"Schmitt told me." He took a deep breath, trying to settle his thoughts. David needed to know, and Hans trusted him to understand. They had always been close. "David would have listened, and while he did that he wouldn't ask about Seraphin, or anyone. I would *never* tell them anything that could harm him."

An uneasy silence followed and his cheeks flushed. He shouldn't have said that. Especially with that intensity. His head hurt and while they stood wordless, confused, the nearby supper cooled. Vermen turned to Maniel.

"I haven't eaten since the bombs. Untie me...please."

She didn't wait for anyone's approval and undid his bonds. Vermen scrambled to the opened can and grabbed a large spoon with trembling hands. Too bad if his stomach didn't keep it down. He shoved a first bite in his mouth and swallowed it.

As the warm tomato paste made its way down to his stomach, Maniel crouched in front of him.

"Hans...what happened to Seraphin?"

He didn't answer right away, finishing another spoonful first. "Crushed ankle. I dragged him until we couldn't walk anymore and..." Vermen frowned, glanced at the caverns. He'd lost track of his location while the soldiers dragged him. "We need to backtrack. He has food but no light."

Stern scowled, grabbed a lamp, and strode toward the tunnels with a sharp "let's move". Fear laced his voice, forcing Vermen to pause in his meal. For the first time he realized there were less than a dozen rebels with them. Had half of them been buried by the collapses? And those left looked half-dead. Broken. No wonder Stern was so tense. Vermen struggled to his feet and turned to Maniel.

"This isn't over. We'll find him."

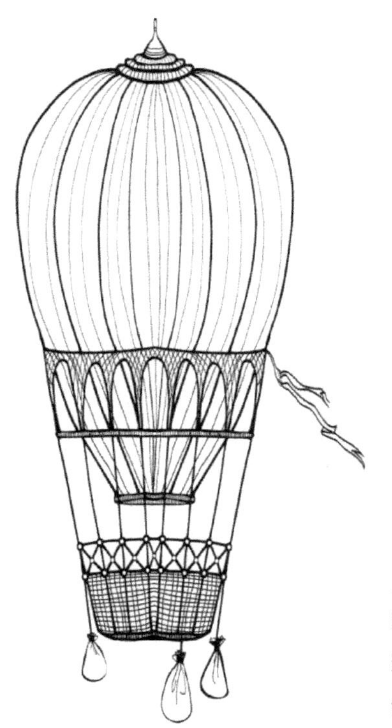

# CHAPTER
# TWENTY-FIVE

*Henry scanned the storeroom* full of radio transmitters and tried to fathom how he had ended up here in the middle of the night. How could their purpose for coming to Reverence transform from hiding to stealing government equipment and starting their own clandestine broadcast?

Treysh's fault, he decided. This was her idea.

She strolled between the large machines, her hands waving to the rhythm of the military music streaming out of speakers in the wall. Sometimes she even twirled or lifted her hat in a sweeping gesture. Completely disconnected. They were in the basement of the National Radio Tower, guards could walk in on them at any time, but she danced. Why had they listened to her plan to begin with? The more he got to know Treysh, the more she slid from 'eccentric' to 'dangerous lunatic' on his crazy scale.

Her initial reaction to the recording, however, had seemed so reasonable. She'd stared at the tiny disc, shook her head, and whispered,

"Everyone needs to hear this."

Andeal nodded. "We just don't know how."

"Easy. It's an audio track," she'd said. "Broadcast it."

Their gazes had met and excitement sparked in their eyes. Freshmen planning a bad trick. As they listed everything needed to start a clandestine radio show—what they could buy, what they had to steal, and where they'd steal it from—a terrified knot had formed in Henry's stomach. He swore this would not lead anywhere good, or safe. And indeed, one dangerous truth soon imposed itself: no one kept old radio parts but the National Radio Tower.

And here they were, thirty-six hours later, examining damaged transmitters.

"This one?" Henry asked, pointing at one of the smallest models. Most old transmitters were too heavy. They'd keep his balloon aground.

Andeal squatted in front of the device and examined it. He lifted loose cables to inspect them, played with the dials, and eventually carried the transmitter to the wall and plugged it in. Red and green lights turned on and as the engineer played with the switches, some turned off and others lit.

Andeal smiled and pulled the cord out.

"That one will do. It won't broadcast far so we'll need to travel a lot if we want to reach everyone, but most of it works. I can fix the rest."

Henry didn't bother to hide his relief. The faster they left the Radio Tower, the better he'd feel.

Treysh stopped her weird dance. "We have a winner?" she asked. "What time is it?"

"Seventeen to midnight."

"Guard'll be here any minute now. I say we hide behind the biggest machines and wait for him to go by."

They did and for the third time that night, Treysh's estimation of the security round proved accurate. Bored footsteps scuffled past as soon as they crouched behind the large transmitters. The guard didn't bother to check their room. He moved on, his sweeping torchlight visible under the door. Henry hurried to their chosen device and lifted it.

Time to get out.

"Say, I have an idea…"

Treysh's words, addressed to Andeal more than him, sent his heart plummeting. *Her* ideas could not be good. His arms wrapped around the heavy machine, Henry waited for the blow.

"Their broadcasting chambers are on the sixth floor. They don't do many rounds up there, mostly because they figure they'll catch intruders long before they get that far. If we're fast enough we could reach them before midnight and interrupt this dreadful music."

Henry bit back a remark about her previous waltz to the so-called dreadful music. There were more pressing matters to address—like this suicidal plan. "Why on earth would we broadcast our presence here?"

"To tell others." Andeal began pacing around the storeroom, pensive lines marring his forehead. "What's the point of a clandestine radio if nobody tunes in? People need to learn we exist. Then perhaps they'll listen, talk about us. And…they'll know we survived."

His voice softened toward the end and Henry realized the last 'they' referred to a very specific group. A very specific person.

"How do we know *they* did?"

"We don't. We have to try, though." He stopped moving in front of Henry. "There'll be no safe way to spread knowledge of your father's recording. The more attention we garner, the more dangerous it'll become. You can't escape this."

Henry's throat tightened. He'd known when he'd accepted to fly the rebels' balloon, but the enormity of their task only now began to sink in. How could they reach thousands of souls and make them believe their story while escaping an ever-growing search from the Union? Sooner or later, the Clarins' men would catch up to them and destroy what work they'd accomplished. Henry wondered what lies would cover the *Reverence Herald's* front page—what crimes they'd pin on them—to justify an execution.

"We won't have a chance if we're caught here," he said.

"We can outrun them. I've done it once, and I've got my secret weapons." Treysh patted the leather sack at her side with a confident grin. When they'd left her house, she'd called it her *infiltration pack* and refused to say more because 'it was a surprise and she'd hate to ruin it for them'. "Now let's go or we'll be late."

Andeal went ahead and peeked through the door. "All clear."

They crept into the empty corridor. Neons buzzed overhead, casting a bleak light over the dark gray floor. No paintings or photographs decorated the walls to alleviate the monotony—only the occasional black door. The military music had given way to weeping violins. No wonder their announcer had the energy of a zombie. The tower's grayness would drain the will to live from anyone.

Anyone but Treysh, Henry judged by the skip in her steps. Andeal's old friend seemed to find this whole escapade amusing.

Henry wished he had her confidence. He mistook every wild thump of his heart for incoming footsteps. When neons flickered he'd swear they'd been spotted and the power had been turned off. Every shadow became a guard slinking toward them. The transmitter's sides dug into Henry's arms, its weight shifting with every step. They couldn't be out of here fast enough.

As they arrived at the top of their first flight of stairs, returning to the ground floor, Henry demanded a stop. He breathed hard enough to cover his heartbeat and the climb's effort had turned him into a sweaty pile of nerves. He'd never climb to the sixth floor at this rate. He set the transmitter down.

"I'm not going up there," he said. "Not with that thing."

"Let's leave it in the employee's toilet by the exit," Treysh suggested. "The ladies' restroom ought to be empty."

"How do you even know they're there?"

"I've used them, of course." His questions seemed to confuse her, as if her deep knowledge of the Radio Tower's layout and security schedule was the most natural thing in the world. Treysh gave him a sweet, mysterious smile and added: "Both to hide and relieve myself."

He was dying to ask why she'd needed to sneak into the Radio Tower before. Chances were Treysh would tell him everything here and now, however, and he had no desire to stay longer than necessary. Whatever wild storytelling she was taunting him into would have to wait.

"Let's move."

They dropped the transmitter in the women's restroom and made their way back to the stairs. Andeal cast a nervous glance at his watch again.

"We'll be a bit late for midnight, but I doubt anyone will complain."

They hurried up, shunning the blessed elevator for the safer but more painful stairs. The violins playing out of speakers echoed down the stairwell, sometimes in synch with their steps. The hollowed sound gave Henry chills despite his physical effort.

The sixth floor turned out to be a whole new world. Large windows offered a splendid view of Reverence's skyscrapers and the lower green roofs crawling up the mountain slope. A lush red carpet muffled their steps and the smooth lamps replacing the harsh neons gave deep undertones to the creamy brown walls. The doors they encountered were made of rich wood instead of metal and sometimes flanked by large glass panes. Behind the protective blinds, he glimpsed posh meeting rooms. Although the Tower still had marks of a workplace—numbers on the doors, fire extinguishers in evidence, signs indicating the restrooms—it reminded Henry of a comfy house and erased a few knots at the bottom of his stomach.

Treysh ignored the luxurious decor, turned left, and rushed to the doors in the middle. Her trench and hat matched the rug's color, almost camouflaging her. She pulled on the handle and her eyebrows shot up when it refused to budge.

"That's new."

She knelt in front of the door and rummaged through her pack. Neither Andeal nor she seemed worried about this delay. Henry bit his lower lip and glanced back toward the stairs. What if the security rounds had also changed and were more frequent up here?

"Still good at lockpicking?" Andeal asked.

"Sure am. I changed technique, though."

That grin again. That large *I just had a terrible idea and I'm thrilled about it* smile Henry had learned to identify and fear. He should lock away, run, do something to remove himself from whatever dangerous plan she'd conceived to open locked doors. He couldn't. Threysh captivated him as few others had before. He watchedas she put leather gloves on and removed an airtight box and an enveloped butter knife from her bag. Her instrument at the ready, she unscrewed the container's lid, dipped her knife in a grayish paste, and snapped the box shut again. She wasted no time applying the paste to the small crack between door and wall, all around the lock. Then she removed a tiny flask from her pocket. Water? The liquid inside was transparent, but he wouldn't be surprised if Treysh carried potent acids with her.

"Step back, everyone."

Henry had already put two meters between himself and the door but he promptly added more. Andeal, a step behind his friend, leaned forward instead. Treysh opened her flask, poured it through the crack, and backpedalled. The paste sizzled on contact then exploded, flinging the door open and almost giving Henry a heart attack. White smoke rose from the half-melted lock and Treysh whistled.

"That was a bit stronger than expected."

"A bit?" Henry repeated, a hand over his heart.

Andeal laughed at his discomfiture. "Don't push it, Henry. We're lucky she didn't blow a hole in the wall."

He strode through the smoke and studied the electronic devices within. The recording room was split in two halves. The first contained transmitters, disc readers, and other sound devices Henry couldn't identify. The other half was behind a closed door and soundproof glass, with the microphone and a large desk. Only the six-disc reader and transmitter worked at the moment, spreading weepy violin music to households everywhere across Ferrys, Mikken, and Regaria. A clock on the wall ticked. Three minutes past midnight.

"Ready, everyone?" Andeal whispered. They nodded. No going back now. "When I signal, Treysh, pull that red cable and plug it there instead.

Henry, I need you to turn this machine on."

He motioned to a large, table-like apparatus with dozens of tiny levers, dials, and slides. Henry swallowed hard and wiped his palms. After a short examination, he found the power switch. He forced himself to take a deep breath, to focus on that simple task. To forget that the moment he pushed the button was the moment hundreds would learn of their presence here, including the security guards downstairs.

Andeal entered the second room. Though they saw him through the glass, they stopped hearing him as soon as the door closed behind him. The engineer adjusted the mic to his height, closed his eyes. His lips moved as he prepared his speech, then he raised his hand. His gaze met Henry's. He smiled and signaled.

They moved in sync, switching audio from the disc reader to the mic. Andeal set his palms on the desk.

"Good evening, ladies and gentlemen!"

His greeting burst from the speakers in their room and, without any doubt, from every radio receiver across the country.

Treysh let out a pleased exclamation and clapped her hands. It'd worked!

They were so dead.

"We interrupt your regular so-boring-it'll-kill-you program for a little announcement. My name is Andeal, member of the White Renegade's rebels, broadcasting from the National Radio Tower."

He glanced their way and Treysh gave him a thumbs up. Henry remained rooted to the spot, paralyzed by their brazenness. Only his stomach moved, lurching about and threatening to make him sick.

"I'm afraid I cannot keep you entertained for long. Should you wish to listen to another tune than the one dictated by the Clarin empire, however, keep your eyes and ears open for more of us. We'll soon broadcast our radio—*The Noodle Show*—on another wave of a higher frequency and wow, don't we have a lot of information some people would rather keep hidden. Time to change your news diet, folks. So spread the word, pass the signal, and until next time!"

Andeal pushed the mic away and hurried out of the room. Henry couldn't believe he'd just named the radio after him. He felt exposed. Honored but exposed. Treysh hug-attacked her engineer friend the moment he stepped out. "That was fantastic! Why the name?"

He pushed her away, breathless. "It's for Henry. I don't have time to explain. Let's run."

Run, yes. Before guards surrounded them, electric pistols and batons in hand. Henry snapped out of his daze and was the first to reach the busted door.

"You two go ahead," Treysh winked at Andeal. "I'll take a small detour."

Andeal thankfully didn't argue and joined Henry in the corridor. No point in trying to stop her. They sprinted toward the stairs, leaving the recording rooms wide open, while Treysh took the other direction. A loud alarm burst through the speakers as they reached the stairs. Henry covered his ears to block the shrill ring while Andeal pulled the handle.

"Shouldn't we wait for her?" Henry had to yell to be heard.

His question was answered as Treysh burst around a corner, a hand on her head to hold her hat in place.

"Go!" She called and, as she reached them, "They'll think we used the fire exit."

They took the stairs two at a time and Henry kept one hand on the railing to stop himself from falling. The loud clattering of feet against metal would wake the dead and covered even the horrible alarm. Treysh's latest trick wouldn't fool them for long. Henry's lungs burned and his throat was parched. How long did they have? They reached a level and he glanced at the wall. Third floor. Halfway there.

As he zipped past, the door flew open. Guards ordered them to stop, brandishing weapons. Was that a real gun? Panic gave new strength to Henry's legs and he sped downward, cursing with every step. He yelped as the first bang pierced his ears and he closed his eyes in a silent prayer. The bullet buried itself in the second floor sign. The two guards clambered down the spinning stairs after them.

"Almost there!" Treysh called.

They ducked three more gunshots, each of them drilling new fear in Henry's heart. He forgot his burning lungs, weary calves, cold sweat, and swimming vision. Nothing mattered but the wild run, the desperate escape. One foot in front of another, down the stairs as fast as he could carry himself. Out of bullet range.

Treysh reached the ground floor first and pushed its door open without slowing her strides. Their sudden appearance drew exclamations from another pair of guards. Which meant four potential guns fired at them. How many more before they reached the exit? As he hurried down the bleak corridor, he noticed Treysh held a tiny ball of metal in one hand and a book of matches in the other.

Andeal turned the last corner. Stopped in his tracks. Henry bumped into him, unable to stop his course, then he saw what had frozen his friend.

A fifth guard stood in front of the exit, weapon raised. Four others would be at their back in a minute. Henry's heart sank.

"We're dead."

Treysh ignored his statement and strode forward.

"Stay right there!" the guard called.

He aimed at her. Henry felt lightheaded and wondered if he'd faint. She raised her hands, showing both metal and matches, but took another step.

"I said stay—"

Before he finished, Treysh ducked to the left, shouldering her way into the ladies' room. A loud bang filled the corridor. Henry grabbed Andeal and plunged to his right. His friend cried out from sudden pain and held his leg as they fell. Henry didn't dare try to stand, or move, or twitch. They were done for. The fake fire alarm died, as if confirming their failure. Henry squeezed Andeal's forearm, giving him the reassurance he needed for himself.

Manic laughter rose from the restrooms. A shiver ran up Henry's spine but he found himself smiling. Another ruse? Treysh pushed the door open an inch and kicked her tiny ball of metal out. One end stretched out, on fire, and shone white.

"Magnesium, Andeal!" she called.

His friend's eyes widened, then snapped shut. "Don't look, Henry!"

Henry obeyed just in time. Even behind closed eyelids he saw the bright flash of light. The guard at the door and those following them cried out. Blinded. Andeal pulled on his arm and they scrambled to their feet, sprinting forward. Treysh's footsteps joined theirs. A volley of shots rang out and one ricocheted into something big and metallic right next to Henry. The others hit walls and neons, harmless. The trio barreled into the last guard, knocking him down, and crossed the exit.

Fresh air and cold wind whipped at Henry's face and he risked a glance. Both friends trailed behind: Treysh carried the transmitter, which had acquired a bullet hole in the front, and Andeal limped with every step. The engineer couldn't outrun the guards. Henry was about to stop and turn to help his friend when a loud explosion rocked the tower. Water splashed out the door, followed by white smoke. The latter came out of the restrooms' window, too. Treysh whooped and they dove into a side alley, out of sight.

They'd done it. Somehow, they'd snuck into the Radio Tower, stolen a transmitter, hijacked the national broadcast, and escaped in one piece.

Henry bent forward, panting. Andeal leaned on a stone wall with a pained expression. It seemed like the bullet had only grazed his leg but before Henry could ask, Treysh skidded to a stop next to them and set her burden down, a wild grin plastered on her face.

"That was *fantastic!*"

His definition of fantastic didn't include chases and gunshots, but a strange elation built from his unsettled stomach, the slow realization of how much they'd accomplished right under the Union's nose, and despite his crazed heart and exhausted limbs, Henry felt powerful. Unstoppable. And that *was* fantastic.

He smiled at her, nodded, and wiped sweat from his eyes.

"I can't wait to hear the news tomorrow." Henry picked up the transmitter. They still needed to move before the guards followed. "Let's head back. I feel like I deserve the biggest pot of noodles ever created."

Treysh's clear laughter echoed in the night. She kissed his cheek with a loud smack then half-walked, half-danced to Andeal and slid under his shoulder, providing support. Despite the still-present danger, Henry grinned like a fool as they made their way home.

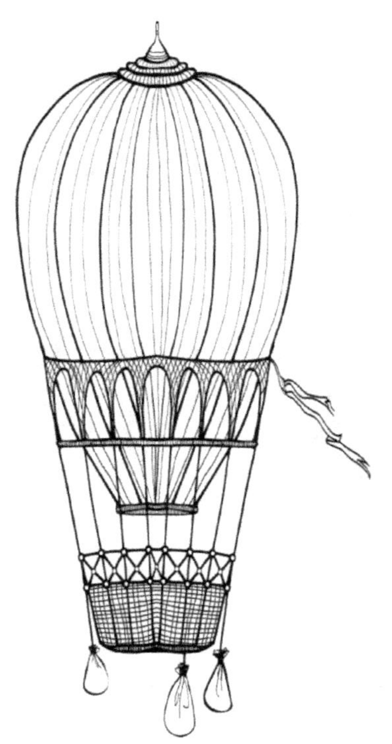

# CHAPTER TWENTY-SIX

*The bright sign hung above* a double glass door, its bold letters bringing attention to an otherwise unnoticeable grocery. Nestled between a fashion boutique and a hardware store, in a street on which shops succeeded one another, Kinsi's new business had a lot of competition. Henry had glimpsed his old friend through the windows twice, however, chatting with clients as he served them. Here he had a solid line of customers, at last, not a single patron too poor to buy more than handful of instant noodles.

He shouldn't have come. Ferrea was a ghost town, no longer part of his life. It mattered little how much he longed for a tranquil beer in Paul's pub. His daily lot consisted of scheming the downfall of the Clarin twins with a mad chemist and a blue engineer. Nothing ordinary there, and he was dying for a pause from all of this clandestine-broadcast and government-overturning nonsense. Seeking out Kinsi might be a mistake, but it was also an opportunity he couldn't resist.

Henry took a deep breath, crossed the busy street, and pushed through the door. The bell rang but with the constant stream of people going in and out, nobody looked his way. He slipped into the first row, out of the cashiers' view, and in his haste he bumped into a tall, gaunt man. As he apologized he noticed the pockmarked face. A Plague survivor. Henry wondered if the stranger had heard the broadcast, if he'd follow their radio one day, join them. The other man smiled and wished him a good day in a whispery voice. As he left, Henry allowed himself to slow down and appreciate his surroundings.

This grocery was twice the size of Kinsi's old one, with a high ceiling and an airy feel to it. Fruits were piled in large baskets, their bright colors dazzling him. No doubt they were fresher than anything Ferrea had offered in the last year. As heartwarming as the stall of glistening cucumbers, carrots, and lettuce was, however, Henry did not linger. He moved to the aisle with instant food and canned soups, where he knew he'd find his trademark meal. Buying anything else wouldn't feel right. He grabbed an armful and made for the tills. Nervousness had turned his hands into sweaty messes. What if Kinsi wanted nothing to do with him after their fight?

Customers kept Kinsi so busy he didn't look up until Henry dropped all the noodle packs in a heap on his counter. The grocer's jaw dropped but no words came out. A flush crept up Henry's cheeks. He forced a greeting out to break the bizarre tension.

"Hey."

"Henry!" Kinsi strode around the counter and gave him a tight embrace. Everyone else had their eyes on him now, including Kinsi's unknown coworkers. Not good. "I'm so glad to see you here, my boy! Tia's been worried to death since—"

"I know, I'm sorry!" Henry interrupted. The less the grocer spoke of his suspicious disappearance, the better. "Someone visited about my father."

The smile vanished from Kinsi's lips and he returned behind his counter without answering. His nose twitched, as it always did when he wrestled strong emotions under control. He grabbed the first pack of noodles and began Henry's bill.

"It's Wednesday," Henry said. "Perhaps I could tell you over a beer?"

"Ah! You've always been one for traditions. What will it be when you grow old and bitter?" He began sliding the noodles into a tote bag. "Whatever your old man did, it'd better be good because you sure gave your *other* family some sleepless nights. That'll be two-forty-eight."

Henry bit his lower lip and handed him the money. He'd disappeared into the night without a note of reassurance and hadn't spared a thought for Kinsi and Tia. Had he learned nothing from a decade of worrying about his father? Lenz had inflicted this treatment upon him and he'd hated it, but in the end he'd done the exact same thing.

"I'm sorry, Kinsi. Really am."

The grocer gave a non-committal shrug and handed him his change. "There's a good pub a block down the road. Be there at the usual time."

"I will," he promised.

He grabbed his bag and hurried out of the grocery, red-faced and unable to look back. Kinsi was angry at him, rightly so, but Henry needed someone to talk with now who *wasn't* a rebel. Andeal's dangerous universe had closed upon him and created a bubble he had to pop. Soon they'd fly out again, radio in tow, and he wouldn't speak to anyone innocent for months. Henry used to love solitude but his new responsibility weighed on him. Kinsi had always been there when he needed to vent. He would be again.

In fact, he was already inside the pub by the time Henry walked in that night.

The small establishment had none of Paul's ambiance. Garish red bench seats lined the walls in half-circles around black metal tables and took up most of the space. Courtball posters covered the walls and a blue-and-white shirt—probably Reverence's sport team's colors—hung behind the counter. A few men had clustered around a dartboard on the far end of the room. Two radios, one at each end of the room, played the national broadcast, but the announcer's drab voice was buried by cheering and the buzz of conversations.

Kinsi had selected an isolated table, far from the dart game. As Henry pushed through the packed crowd he noticed another familiar face. The pockmarked customer he'd bumped into earlier sat stretched on a bench seat, at his ease, with a huge tome propped against his knees. He smiled as their gazes met, then returned to his reading. Despite the city's ridiculous size, Reverence's neighborhoods acted much like a small village: if you hung around, you ran into the same folks over and over again.

As long as he didn't run into any of the Radio Tower's guards from that night, he should be fine. Henry kept his eyes to the ground as he hurried across the room and plopped down in front of Kinsi.

"Didn't know you were a courtball fan," he said.

"I'm not, but their ale is something to behold, the service is quick, and I don't mind the noise." The grocer hailed a waitress and ordered two more pints. Then he put a small bag on the table. "Cucumbers."

Henry didn't need to ask whose gift this was. He brought the bag close with a smile. "She had room for a garden?"

"She wouldn't buy a house that didn't. The tiny yard at my daughter's almost drove her mad. That's not something I ever want to see again." He stopped as the waitress came back with their drinks. Henry's eyebrows shot up—that'd been quicker than Paul, and they had dozens of others to see to. Kinsi grabbed the handle and drank deep, cleaning half of it in a single shot. "We aren't here for Tia's garden love, though."

"I guess not. It's a bit of a long story."

"I've got all night."

In truth, Henry would rather talk of Tia's garden craze. News from Kinsi's headstrong wife warmed his heart and made him forget the mess he'd stepped into, if only for a second. Everyday banter was what he'd come for but until he explained himself, he'd have none. He tried to drown the disappointment with fresh ale.

"Did you hear about the radio hijack? *The Noodle Show?*" he asked.

"Who didn't? It's on everyone's lips, any time there's no soldier around to hear." Something seemed to cross Kinsi's mind. He squinted at Henry. "Did you name it?"

Henry hesitated. Just how much could he entrust Kinsi with? The old grocer was no revolutionary and it wasn't fair to get him involved.

"These rebels...the guy who knew my father is one of them. He named the show. After me. Lenz had given him something for me before he died, a message they didn't understand. I left to help them decipher it. I needed to know."

Kinsi settled back in his seat and studied him with questioning eyes. Under the table, Henry tapped his foot. He tried to remain calm, but a doubtful expression surfaced on the grocer's face and he knew his story wasn't enough. Kinsi crossed his arms and spoke in a slow, deliberate manner.

"That does not explain the kicked-in door or the inquisitive Union soldiers that followed, looking for one of their own."

Henry's heart sped. The Union did not know a worse liar than him. How could he justify Vermen's disappearance? He cast a furtive glance about. No one seemed to pay them any heed. He wiped his sweaty forehead, though his arms were just as sticky from the heat. Before he tried to explain, however, Kinsi raised a hand and stopped him.

"Did they force you? Hurt you? Do you need help?"

"No."

"Is the captain alive?"

"I think so. We never hurt him but the bombs—"

"*We...*" Kinsi repeated. He leaned forward, more concerned than ever. "Boy, I can tell you stepped into a big fat mess. There's something healthier about you though, a drive that had died with the Races, so if you tell me you're in there willingly, I won't slip a word about it."

Henry didn't bother to hide his immense relief. His shoulders relaxed, he downed his ale in one hearty chug, then he bent forward and let his voice fall into a calm whisper. Now that they were talking about it, spilling the rest became easier.

"Father left because he had proof that mom's death wasn't natural."

"She died of the thresties."

"Exactly." He paused to let the information sink in. Kinsi rubbed his face but didn't comment yet. "He's right, Kinsi, and the rebels have tons of evidence pointing to the same conclusion. That's what the radio is for."

"So you're saying someone created the Threstle Plague."

"Clarin."

"He discovered the cure."

"Yes. Discovered."

Henry wasn't good with sarcasm, but Kinsi grunted as he caught the implied meaning. He kept his eyes half-closed, pondering.

"Will you listen to our radio?" Henry asked.

"Yes."

"Can you tell others to do the same?"

The grocer's mouth quirked at the question. "I might."

"You have to. We think Clarin could have another virus ready. He was testing—"

"Stop, please." Kinsi slid out of the bench and left a large bill on the table. Henry's stomach twisted as he understood what it meant. "Be careful out there."

"You're leaving?"

"Henry, I'm out of my depth here. I'll keep your secrets and follow your radio, but the soldiers have got your name and it seems to me that every minute in your company puts the rest of my family in danger. If you're ever out of options you can come and I'll help, but otherwise this business ain't mine, and I'd rather be kept out of it."

Words flitted through Henry's head as he searched for a way to convince Kinsi to stay and chat, but everything he came up with sounded false and self-serving to him and, in truth, it was. He'd sought only to fulfill his needs by coming here and hadn't even thought of the danger he put Kinsi in.

"I'm sorry," he said as his foster father turned to leave.

"Don't. At least we know you're alive...for now."

The grocer slipped into the crowd and disappeared from view. Henry slumped against his seat and tried to ignore the growing lump at the bottom of his stomach. He'd needed to escape the entrapping knowledge and fake, just this once, that he knew nothing of the Clarin brothers' evils. He couldn't. There would be no release—not until everyone knew.

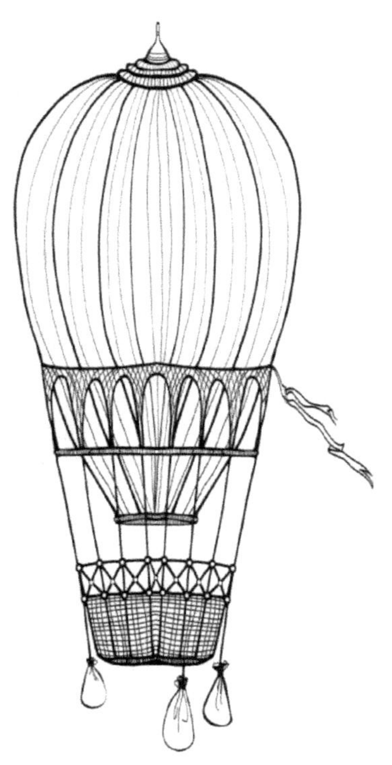

# CHAPTER TWENTY-SEVEN

*Elmsfield. An emerald glow* flanked by a thick forest and smooth farmlands. The first civilization he'd encountered since departing Ferrea, Seraphin's gun pointed at his back. As he sat in the tall grass and studied the tiny houses crowded together, their rooftops a cluster of green lights, Vermen contemplated how much his life had changed since he'd last walked into a village. He was once a proud captain, confident in his ability, full of unshakable certitudes. The rebels were naught but lowly criminals to be crushed, President Kurtmann was a man of honor, and nothing mattered more than his service in the Union army—except perhaps catching the White Renegade. He remembered driving down the slope to Schmitt's isolated shack, positive he'd at last accomplish his long-deserved revenge.

Now they approached a town similar to Ferrea, only livelier, and

Vermen had no idea where his steps led him. He walked among rebels instead of chasing them, wrestled with the idea Kurtmann and the Clarins had killed thousands to gain power, and had kissed his sworn enemy. He had more doubts than certainties and would rather stay behind to clear the mess in his mind.

The long grass rustled behind him as someone approached. Vermen kept his gaze on the bundle of homes in which honest folks slept. They'd sent somebody to fetch him. The time had come to sneak down there and wake the one person in this nowhere village who led a double life.

"Will you come with me?"

Vermen took a sharp breath when he recognized Seraphin's nasal voice. They had found him in the very tunnel Vermen had left him, crouched over canned meat with a heavy pointed rock, trying to smash it open with what little strength he had left. Still in a famished daze, Hans had moved to his side faster than anyone else. Too fast, judging from the curious look Maniel gave him as she followed. He stepped back to let her give Seraphin a quick examination and then, with Joshua's help, they carried him away, until they could find the caverns' exit.

Everyone had eaten since then and though the meager meals brought little satisfaction, they kept them on their feet. The Regarian strode up to him and sat in one graceful movement. The grass was so tall his hair mingled with its tip, both pale in the moonlight.

"I shouldn't," Vermen said. "I don't want to be identified as a rebel."

Seraphin turned to him with a frown. He seemed hurt. "You are one."

Vermen tore a blade of grass from the ground and played with it. "I feel like life misplaced me and forgot I belonged on the other side."

When he had saved Andeal, he'd buried the Union soldier inside him in favor of a friend. How had this morphed into preserving all rebels? Worse, how had it become kissing the White Renegade? His throat tightened and his palms turned sweaty whenever he thought about it. Even though he couldn't deny his attraction, he shouldn't have.

Seraphin wrapped his fingers around his pistol's cross. He traced the red string in a mindless, distracted manner. Vermen wondered if the Regarian even noticed when he touched his *skeptar*.

"Sometimes I think you were right and I deserve to die," he said. Vermen stopped folding and unfolding his bit of grass, stared at Seraphin as the rebel leader continued in a wistful tone. "What you did for us—the warning, despite your allegiance and your vows—I could've done for my family. I could have snuck from camp the night before they were killed and told them your brother had found their resistance cell's meeting place, that our platoon had orders to crash the next reunion. Instead I stood by and watched the tavern burn. What kind of man lets his family die without even trying?"

The same man that can meet another's gaze and blow his brains out. The words burned his lips, but Vermen held them inside. He cleared his throat but his voice remained hoarse.

"You avenged them. What kind of man helps his brother's killer and listens to his sob story instead of putting a bullet in his head?"

A tense silence followed his question. That hurt frown returned to Seraphin's expression. They both knew what had gone unsaid there, what Vermen had left out. He never wanted to talk about it again.

Seraphin, however, had a different plan.

"The kind of man who kisses him, too."

Vermen's temper flared and he grabbed a handful of grass to keep his hands from curling into fists. "Don't *ever* mention that again."

"No?"

Holt's lips curved into a mocking smile and he jumped to his feet, took a deep breath. He was getting ready to shout it! Vermen scrambled after Seraphin, grabbed his arm, and slapped a hand over his mouth.

"Don't."

Only then did he realize how close they were again, their faces only inches apart. He could feel Seraphin's hot breath in his palm, his warmth in the night. Vermen's head spun, his breath deepened. He gritted his teeth and tried to wrestle control over himself. Yet when Seraphin locked his gaze, he removed his hand but did not step back. A spark of amusement danced in his companion's eyes as he put a hand on Vermen's hip. The captain froze, blood rushing against his temple, torn between running away and the strong desire to just not move.

"Please," he whispered.

He didn't even know what he meant by that. Seraphin did, apparently.

He leaned forward and kissed him, the hand on his hip tightening its grip to keep him from backing away too fast, but Vermen didn't even try, too stunned. Too amazed. His lips parted and he let Seraphin in, shutting out his thoughts and the world. Reality would catch up soon enough. Just once, he wanted to believe he could kiss a man—*any* man—without consequences. When Seraphin pulled back, Hans almost held onto him. The Regarian smiled.

"See? It's just a kiss." His voice was soft and serious, devoid of the usual mocking undertone. "I've kissed men and women and people who are neither. It doesn't have to be a big deal. We leave for Elmsfield in ten minutes."

Seraphin turned around without another look and headed back toward the camp. Vermen watched his every step, hot, confused, half-certain he would wake up and discover this was a strange hunger-induced dream. He ran his thumb over his lower lip, took a deep breath when he felt it shake. Not a dream. No need to think too much of it, either.

With a smile of his own, Vermen followed Seraphin down the rise to their small camp.

They joined Maniel and Joshua, who flung an empty backpack his way. "Hurry up, Captain! They won't wait for us all night."

"Calm down, Joshua. They don't even know we're coming," Maniel remarked.

They started toward the small town anyway, Joshua skipping ahead and clearing a path in the tall grass, his hand drifting over the large blades as he hummed to himself. Someone else would be getting a kiss tonight.

"Will we be staying the night?" Joshua asked.

Seraphin snickered. "You'd love that, wouldn't you? But no, I don't want to risk prolonging our presence there. We go in and out under the cover of darkness."

Joshua fell silent after a quick disappointed grunt. They trekked through the field, the greenery rustling at their passage. The ground squished under Vermen's soles, wet from the morning rain, and a strong pungent odor filled his nostrils. He inhaled, glad to smell something other than dust and rocks. As they described a large arc around the village, Vermen allowed his eyes to stray toward the sky. The stars shone, the moon was full, the crickets chirped. A perfect summer night. Spring had come and gone while he was trapped underground.

They passed through the forest and he smiled as his boots crushed leaves and twigs. Every reminder of nature's presence gladdened his heart. They soon reached a large estate, isolated from Elmsfield by rows of old trees and a wooden fence. Joshua jumped it without hesitation. Vermen followed with more care and helped Maniel over. Seraphin tripped into it, however, as though he'd underestimated the height he needed to jump. He landed with a grunt and hurried to his feet. Since he had lost his glasses in Mount Kairn's bombing, the Regarian stumbled on a lot of small obstacles. Vermen had never realised how blind he was without them.

Hans waited for Seraphin to catch up, then they ran across the mown lawn and crouched under a long window. Joshua sprang up and knocked on the glass in a specific sequence. Minutes passed in silence. He glanced inside then repeated it. A knock, a pause, two knocks. Vermen's heart beat in sync as he mentally repeated the code. A light turned on inside, revealing a kitchen behind lace curtains. Seraphin's lips curled into a smile and he strode forward.

A man in his early sixties opened the window and leaned forward. He wore an old pink bathrobe with matching slippers and carried a thick tome. With a shaking hand, he set tiny glasses on his nose's end and squinted at the group. His wrinkled face split in a warm grin.

"Seraphin Holt, you young bugger! We'd begun thinking you were dead!"

"Dead, me? Stop this nonsense and open up."

The old man mumbled a curse, set his heavy book on the windowsill, and moved away. The nearby door's lock clicked and it opened with a plaintive creak. A white head peeked out.

"Come on in," he said. "And Joshua, Martin will need help with the tea."

"Yes sir. Right away, sir!"

He rushed inside under the amused gazes of his friends. Seraphin, Maniel, and Vermen followed at a calmer pace and the elder closed the door behind them, locking it fast. He led them to the living room where a selection of old sofas crowded around a low center table. A radio rested on it but it only gave background noise, ill-adjusted to the National Broadcast wave. A fire burned high, recently lit, and added a comforting warmth to the already enveloping atmosphere. Their dirty boots left clear mud marks on the floor. Now that he had a better light, the old man studied the group and his thin eyebrows shot up.

"You brought unusual friends," he said, then extended his hand to Maniel. "Maniel, I presume? It's a pleasure to finally meet you."

She smiled and shook the offered hand. "Same, Mayor."

Mayor Riley's smile vanished as he turned toward Vermen. He must know who he was already. Was the entire network aware he'd dogged Seraphin for years? Flushed, the captain strode forward and grabbed the elder's hand before it was even offered.

"Hans Vermen, at your service."

Seraphin tensed, but Riley chuckled and squeezed his hand with surprising strength. "You're one brash young man, to impose yourself like that despite your reputation."

Vermen struggled to find a proper answer, uncertain if the mayor had meant to compliment or insult him. He didn't want to start a fight, but he wasn't going to let this old man disrespect him.

Maniel came to the rescue. "He's the reason we're alive at all."

"He could've done a better job. You all look half-dead."

"We're starved," Seraphin said. "It's the main reason we came."

Riley frowned, but Joshua popped in from the kitchen. He held a tray with a teapot and empty cups. White steam swirled from it and a minty scent spread through the living room. The mayor leaned forward and grabbed Joshua's forearm.

"Boy, would you two cook some real dinner for everyone?" He paused, then added as an afterthought, "I'd understand if you'd rather stay to hear the news, but—"

"No, not at all, sir. I'm sure Seraph will tell me everything later."

This time, Vermen smiled with the others. Even about games of chance, Joshua had never shown so much eagerness. He suspected they could ask him to sit in complete silence for an hour and, if it was with Martin, Joshua might agree. Nothing like young love to make a man forget the most serious situations. Vermen risked a glance at Seraphin, now serving the tea, and forced his gaze away. This wasn't young love. It was a kiss. And they didn't have to make a big deal out of it. Riley tasted the tea before he turned to Seraphin.

"So you have no provisions. Is the entire group with you?"

"Yes. The nine of us left," Seraphin said in a hushed tone.

"Tell me what happened. I'm sure the Union left the juicy parts out of their account."

The Regarian leaned forward, put down his cup, and clasped his hands together. His voice quivered when he began the story. The cracking fire and clank of pots sometimes covered the words, but no other sound disturbed his tale. Mayor Riley remained motionless until Seraphin mentioned the first volley of explosions. His ice-blue gaze turned to Vermen, who felt the heat in his cheeks but refused to cast his eyes down.

Halfway through, Joshua arrived with their meal. He was followed by a man with silky brown hair, deeply tanned skin, and a shy smile. His bare feet made no sound as he distributed their plates. Vermen thanked him but received no reply, only a nod before Martin hurried onward. He didn't say a word, in fact, only kissed Joshua on the cheek as the Burgian sat with his dinner. He seemed about to flit out of the room but Joshua caught his forearm.

"Stay with us, please. You don't have to talk."

Martin hesitated. He pressed his lips together, nodded his thanks, and pushed Joshua over. The Burgian squirmed to give him enough room on his sofa with a laugh.

"Glad to have you with us, Martin," Seraphin said.

"Thank you."

He said the words slowly, with a singsong lilt, the second at a higher pitch. The rebel leader nodded, solemn, and picked up his tale where he'd left it while they ate. Vermen didn't pay him a lot of attention. He wolfed down the chicken pie, savoring every salted bite. When Seraphin mentioned traveling straight to Elmsfield after exiting the tunnel, Riley raised a hand to interrupt him.

"Are you saying I'm the first person you've talked to since the bombing?" He rose, agitated, and turned to Maniel. "Then you don't know about—" Before he could finish, the radio screeched and whirred. Riley sat back with a relieved smile and gestured toward it. "About this."

"Good evening, ladies and gentlemen, and welcome to *The Noodle Show's* third broadcast!"

Andeal's voice burst from the speakers, warm and healthy. Maniel gasped and her fingers tightened on Vermen's leg. He set his hand on hers and squeezed it, smiling. He couldn't remember such unbridled joy breaking her cool composure. Andeal was alive and had somehow gotten his hands on radio broadcasting equipment.

"It's a cold evening tonight but don't worry, we've got some flames to keep us warm. Now, I know I say this every night, but tonight is an important broadcast and I'll give you a few minutes to gather your friends and family and settle down with a drink. Here's some music to keep you busy. If I believe the inscription on the disc, it's some traditional jig from Regaria, but I make no guarantee."

He fumbled for a moment then the tune started up. Violins filled the air, their quick melody completed by an accordion. Martin picked up the tune right away, humming it to himself. Seraphin turned the volume down. His expression alternated between incredulity and amazement.

"How long has he done this?"

"He began about two weeks ago, though there was a week-long pause after the first night," Riley answered. "Started with quite a bang, too! They hijacked the National Radio broadcast to announce their own and slipped out of the guards' grasp."

Maniel shook her head, but she was smiling. "That stupid, lovely ass. If he doesn't get himself killed before I reach him, I'll do it myself."

They waited for the jig to finish, holding their breaths.

"Seems the writing on the disc didn't lie. You folks all ready? Because tonight we bust up a myth perpetrated by the Union these last two months." He paused. Everyone in the room perched on the edge of their seats. "You already know about the destruction of Mount Kairn, and I wager most of you have seen the terrible pictures of the defaced mountainside in newspapers. For weeks now, the Union has repeated that we planted hand-crafted bombs in tunnels to attack an icon of the Union's glory. I find that quite a curious statement. First, because I've lived in those very caverns for six years and I don't know a single sane person who'd blow up his home like that."

A strong wind blew across the microphone and Andeal interrupted his speech. He had a short background exchange with another voice, which they all immediately recognized. Joshua grinned and lifted his teacup in a false toast.

"Henry's with him! They both made it out."

The duo's whispered conversation ended quickly and Andeal cleared his throat. "Sorry about that. It seems I won't be broadcasting for long tonight. Where were we?" A slight pause. "Ah, yes, Mount Kairn, home of the Annual Races. Another tradition we should be blamed for destroying, according to them. And yet if you can find any of Ferrea's old residents— don't look in the town itself, they all left, unable to make a living—they'll tell you the Races had been canceled by the Union months before the attack. What I want to tell you is simple. They discovered our home and came in the night with a bomber blimp to rat us out. Union explosives defaced our beautiful mountain. You can blame us for living there, but they made the final decision to destroy it and you deserve to know as much."

There was a short silence. The fire crackled, its tall flames down to glowing embers. No one moved to put another log in.

"That's it for tonight! Don't forget we expect to see you on Union's Day in Reverence for our most important broadcast and a fireworks show to die for! The 22nd's celebrations will have never been so glorious."

The radio clicked and screeched, then returned to its initial static. Vermen stared at the small receiver through which their friend had suddenly come back to life. He had an educated guess about where Andeal broadcasted from. The sound of flame and strong wind suggested a location only the rebels would figure out. Henry and him hadn't wasted time since their first flight to further customize the already ridiculous balloon.

Maniel fell back into her sofa with a happy sigh, removing her hand from Vermen's thigh. "I can't believe he..." Her voice broke and she rubbed her eyes. He couldn't tell if she was about to cry or laugh.

"Mayor, would it be possible to take your radio with us?" Seraphin asked.

"I have a spare," Riley answered. "It's an old crumbling device, but it'll work. We'll add it to your supplies."

"Thank you." Seraphin closed his eyes and joined his hands, his index raised and touching his forehead while his thumbs rested near his lips. He remained in this deep thinking pose for a while, and none of them dared to speak. "I assume they have Henry's recording and will play it on Union's Day. Let's roll with Andeal's plan. We must convince as many people as possible to listen to him and travel in time for the Union's anniversary celebration. If they trust us enough to do that, they'll trust us enough to believe in the recording and act on it." He turned to the mayor. "What of your village? Could you get them on the road?"

"Half the residents have already tuned to the broadcast. We were hit hard by the Plague—almost every single family suffered a loss—and if your story's true, if you can convince the men and women here that the man who made the Threstle Plague might be preparing another pandemic, they'll travel as far north and east as you need them to." He pushed up his glasses and put on a solemn air. "I intend to lead them on the road, old bones notwithstanding, and demand justice for Susan."

Seraphin rose, his jaw set with determination, a hand on his *skeptar*. A strange light burned in his eyes, giving the pale blue an unnatural glow. He was in control now, confident. Gone were the doubts. Andeal had salvaged the rebels' purpose from the disaster at Mount Kairn and offered them a clear path to follow.

"This is it," Seraphin said. "We won't have the resources to start over, or a better occasion. If they don't listen now, they never will. Elmsfield won't be alone, though." He turned to Joshua and Maniel. "We'll split into two groups and cover as much land as we can, compelling others to answer this call and relay the signal. People are harder to deny than a disembodied voice. Joshua, you'll go with Stern and try to cover most of Ferrys' western regions, along with Mikken to the north. We'll travel east and into Regaria. Our story must spread faster than Galen's virus. By the time the first firework launches, I want Reverence's streets to be packed."

Vermen pictured the great city's snaking avenues invaded by a black moving mass and his heart sped. Would it work? Times were hard and the Union's army would control the solar-powered bus system. Civilians had never recovered individual means of transportation when Galen Clarin's oil-eating bacteria deprived their cars of proper fuel. Fast and safe travel had turned into a problem, isolating communities, making radio broadcasts and newspapers the main source of news.

The Threstle Plague had left scars of its own, however, and betrayal worked as a powerful motivator. What would happen when thousands learned someone had killed their family on purpose, lied to them about the Plague's origin and was prepared to repeat it all? He wondered if it'd be enough.

One thing was sure, however: he would be there, even if it meant walking beside Seraphin Holt.

Or, perhaps, especially if it meant walking beside him.

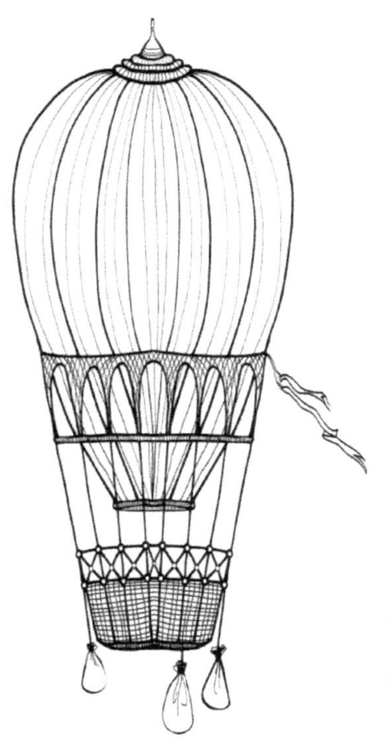

# CHAPTER TWENTY-EIGHT

*The chill night might've* killed Henry's good mood had he not flown thousands of feet above ground.

A month had passed between the moment he'd bade goodbye to the Lenz Balloon and the one he was allowed to launch it back into the skies. It had felt like years. After Kinsi had abandoned him in that tasteless courtball pub, time in Reverence seemed to stretch on, endless and unforgiving. He could not go out unless necessary and he spent most of his time in idle thumb twirling.

He used to waste entire days sitting around in Ferrea, staring at the ceiling and reminiscing about his father or the Races, but he could no longer bear it. He grew restless, paced through the numerous tiny rooms of Treysh's apartments, and sought a task to accomplish. Anything to busy himself and fill his mind. At first he tried to help Andeal repair the transmitter, but it ended with the engineer snapping at him, disgruntled and annoyed.

Treysh noticed, however, and invited him deeper into her dangerous world. Every day after breakfast, Treysh locked herself in a room and disappeared until dinner. They only knew she was alive by the occasional small explosion, the repeated curses and, once, by the foul-smelling fumes that'd slipped out the crack under her door. Henry had sworn never to go near that place. He preferred to remain in one piece.

She asked him if he wanted to see her projects one afternoon, after Andeal had suggested Henry glue himself to a chair and stop disturbing his work. The gleeful glint in her eyes as she offered to show him killed his resolve. He agreed, eager to see his painful boredom come to an end, but as a large grin spread on the chemist's face, he realized the full extent of his mistake. The last time she'd smiled like that, she'd blown up a door.

She led him into a full-blown laboratory, lit by a series of white neons. In the middle stood a huge wooden table where beakers and vials shared the space with alcohol burners and a dozen petri dishes. Each of the latter contained a different metallic powder, some dark gray while others had a brownish tint. An old sink lay against the left wall and a second, long table occupied the back of the room. Gift-wrapping paper had taken over its surface while long rockets and cone-shaped fuses rested beneath. Posters with weird symbols and equations plastered the right wall.

"This," Treysh said with a grand gesture at the room, "is my fireworks factory! Here, let me show you."

She hurried to the closest alcohol burner and lit it as Henry examined the crazy setup, slack-jawed. Wasn't such an installation illegal? Like that would ever stop Treysh.

"Come on, come closer. It won't explode, I promise."

"I bet you always say that."

He stepped forward anyway. Amusement danced in her eyes.

"Near enough. My favorite times are when I *don't* have to say it, though. Nothing like a good *boom* to pep up your day." She tapped the petri dishes with her fingers, her excitement barely contained, and selected the one marked with $Cu$. "You know what's marvelous about nature? How colorful it is. This is copper, you see, and it looks rather dull. But watch."

She picked up a curved metal spatula, dipped it in the copper powder, and brought it over the burner's flame. In an instant it turned from warm orange to emerald green. Henry let out a soft whistle.

"Is that how you dye your hair? Copper?"

Treysh's bright laughter filled the room and she extinguished her burner. "No. It's what I put in the fireworks, though. I'm afraid my hair's green color is nothing so fantastic. I buy it as is."

"Here I thought everything about you was extraordinary." He'd meant to tease, but the words escaped his lips with a serious and complimentary tone. She smiled at him and set her spatula down as heat rushed to Henry's cheeks. What was he thinking? And how had he ever found the courage to let *that* slip? He cursed himself for a blundering fool and cast himself upon the first *other* topic he could find. "How did you know so much about the Radio Tower?"

"I used to sneak inside all the time. I dated Kevin, their main announcer, and visited him when he worked late. At first I got caught but since he always defended me, I used the occasion to really explore." Her grin reappeared, and she added: "Getting in and out unseen was more fun than he ever was!"

Henry mumbled a smattering of words then stopped, too stunned to continue. *The* announcer? The man with a drawling voice who droned on for days, repeating the same insipid news without a trace of energy? Poor him. If he liked his life as tranquil as his tone, Treysh might've scared him out of relationships forever. She noticed his astonishment and waved it away.

"I know. I was silly at the time."

He tried not to laugh, but as he pictured his green-haired, explosive companion with the most dull, commonplace man he could imagine, a wild fit of laughter took over. Treysh joined in and soon they both held their pained ribs, one hand on the table so they wouldn't fall. He forgot about his worries—the recording, his disheartening reunion with Kinsi, his continuous boredom—and had, for the first time since landing in Reverence, a moment of true respite.

Once they recovered their seriousness, Treysh proceeded to explain what kind of fireworks each rocket held. He remembered little of it, had been more absorbed by her than her words, but even today, as a chill wind pierced his coat and pushed their balloon around, he snickered at the thought of Treysh dating the radio announcer.

A stronger gust forced Andeal to interrupt his current broadcast and brought Henry back to reality. He hated to waste fuel, but they couldn't remain at this altitude.

"Give me a sec," he told his friend as he pushed the gas levers and bright, warm flames burst into life.

Andeal sat cross-legged at the bottom of the balloon, microphone in hand. He turned and scolded him. "You ought to be quicker. You can't let wind interrupt me all the time."

Henry bit back a remark as they reached a higher altitude and the wind stopped. Andeal returned to his broadcast without another word. Henry waited, tapping the basket with his fingers in an attempt to contain his frustration. They'd left Treysh once the receiver was repaired. Ever since, his friend had been ill-tempered and prone to snapping. It had lasted long enough. Henry had no intention to endure his moods and, when Andeal hung up, he stepped forward.

"What's wrong with you?" he asked.

Andeal cast one piercing glance up then wrapped the microphone in its protective waxed paper. "What's wrong? What makes you think anything is wrong?"

Henry had to fight not to laugh. If *he* could see it, it meant something was obviously, terribly wrong.

"Since we've left, you've been in turn angry and brooding and...and mean!"

"Mean?" A smile reached Andeal's lips, but it curled into a sneer. He assembled his broadcast gear, put it back into their protective bags, and sprung to his feet.

"You heard me," Henry said.

His friend strode past him and knelt in front of the storage chest, shoving the sack inside. As his hands grabbed the lid's two corners, however, he stopped, closed his eyes and took a deep breath. Henry's stomach churned, uncertain this confrontation had been such a good idea after all.

"I want to be somewhere safe, with Maniel." He snapped the lid shut. "Instead I'm here, with..."

His voice trailed off, but Andeal didn't need to complete his sentence for Henry to understand. He clenched his fists and beat back the anger. As much as it hurt, he realized he could not replace Maniel. Henry stomped down his pride to try to lift his friend's spirit.

"Did I mention mean?" he asked in a weak, joking tone before crouching next to Andeal. "Listen, if I could make her magically appear in this balloon, I would. Since it's out of my very considerable power, however, you'll have to work your way around it. Sulking won't help. I spent a decade trying this technique and it never made my father reappear."

"Your father was dead."

Henry's mouth opened but he found no easy reply. He ought to think more before he spoke and implied horrible things.

"And Maniel isn't," he said. "Union's Day is but a few months away. You'll see her soon enough."

Andeal laid back at the bottom of their basket and stared at the extinguished burner and the envelope's inside. "If only I could know for sure..."

Henry mumbled an agreement then changed the subject. He had nothing to offer but platitudes now, and he had a feeling Andeal would bounce back to his usual self anyhow. He'd lived through two years of torture and built another life for himself. How could he not survive three months without his wife?

Or maybe he'd managed so well after the lab *because* Maniel was there.

Henry sighed. "You never explained why you called it *The Noodle Show*."

"The look you gave me was priceless," Andeal said. "That's not all, though. Galen's news are like your noodles. Easy to make, they fill you up but don't do much for your health—or mind, as far as the news are concerned."

Henry's mouth hung half-opened for a moment. He used to love the noodles. They'd always been there, cheap and easy to access. Reassuring.

"I can't believe you'd say that," he said with a pout.

Andeal chuckled, then shrugged and fell silent again. He wasn't out of his strange mood yet. Henry had no idea what to do about it, except wait.

With a sigh, he straightened and checked the balloon's altitude again. The helium contracted, its upward pull diminishing when the sun vanished, and this night's winds contributed to lowering its temperature. Since he had no desire to be awakened by the basket skimming treetops, he gave the burner's levers another push. Two beautiful flames shot up, sending a wave of pure warmth down on them and heating the balloon. The altimeter's needle inched upward. Henry waited until they had a few extra hundred feet then released the burners. His heart pinched when the flames vanished. He wished he had borrowed some of Treysh's copper, to throw into them. He missed her silliness. She would waste their fuel for the spectacle it offered, even if they needed it.

Henry hoped she was okay, back in Reverence, and that no one had linked her to their break-in at the National Radio Tower. They should have brought a radio receiver with them to keep an eye on the fabricated news.

"Henry?" Andeal had propped himself up on one elbow. A soft smile curled his lips, barely visible in their lamp's dim light. "Maybe I'm wrong about the noodles. I think I'll try it your way and munch on them until I feel better."

"Go ahead, take mine." He'd be glad if Andeal ate through his noodles. He was still attached to them, had brought the pile with him, but he hadn't had the heart to eat a single pack since his short evening with Kinsi. The crispy instant meal reminded him of a time now gone, and the memories knotted his stomach up every time. "You can have the whole stack, if you want."

He wasn't sure he'd ever be able to eat instant noodles again.

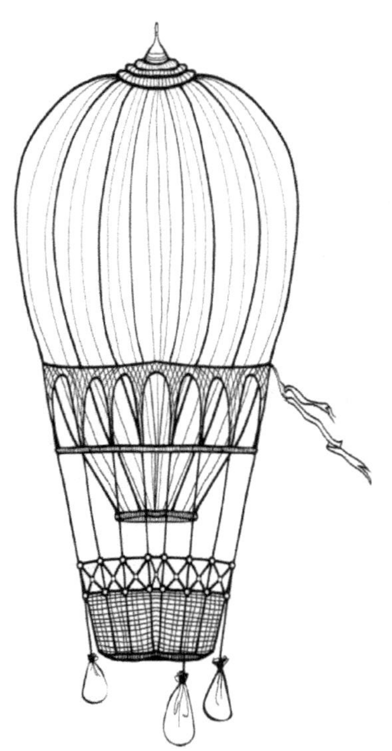

# CHAPTER TWENTY-NINE

*Vermen studied the endless* rows of small bottles, fascinated by the panoply of drugs with unfathomable chemical names laid out before him. He hadn't needed to enter a medical clinic in ages, instead referring to the army's docs for his occasional bouts of fever. Alfred Colton was one of Serenity's most reputable doctors and his business was an airy store with a pharmacy section that occupied almost every inch of the main room. Vitamins, creams, and pills were lined up on six different shelves, sometimes locked behind clear glass. The most dangerous were kept out of reach, on a counter only the pharmacist could access. The woman, a tall blonde with pinched lips, was engaged in a deep argument with a lady well into her seventies who seemed prone to taking twice her prescribed dose.

In the back of the store was the clinic proper. The pharmacy gave way to an intimate waiting room. Three sofas—one of them a two-seater—framed a round hazelnut table buried under magazines. Soft yellow lights lined the walls, spreading a warm light in that small area. A door at the back wall, next to the reception counter, led to the doctor's office. Seraphin had walked straight to the secretary, only to be informed by the zealous young man that Doctor Colton was in a consultation. He'd plopped down in a black sofa and tried to read a magazine. He bent further forward than necessary, concealing his white eyelashes and pale eyes. Every now and then, he reached up and ran a hand through his cut hair, a reflex that brought a smile to Vermen's lips. Discomfort. Seraphin didn't want to stay in Ferrys' second biggest city any longer than necessary. They had no choice, however: no one but this doctor could get Seraphin a new pair of glasses to help his major sight problems.

The office door clicked as it opened, announcing the consultation's end. Vermen tore his gaze from the white bottle he'd been examining, curious about this latest ally of the rebels. Everyone from their network seemed ready to spring into action and push their social circles to listen to the radio and travel to Reverence. Their intense conviction was as contagious as the Threstle Plague, and Hans became increasingly eager to talk another person into joining the movement.

Although some encounters were more mortifying than others. They'd met an agender tattoo artist by the name of Alex who clearly knew Seraphin was bisexual and joked about his relationship with Vermen and insisted on giving him "tips for the sexy times". They'd keep going until Vermen turned redder than Alex's bright coat, clearly drawing pleasure from his discomfort. Vermen took the jokes in stride, however—better them than the angry scowl his name had caused at first. Seraphin had needed to vouch for him twice, also growing redder each time, before Alex moved on. By the end of the short meeting, Seraphin had been more relaxed than ever before. He'd kissed Alex briefly before leaving.

In addition to Alex, they'd met a farmer, a policeman, and, of course, the mayor, but no one from the medical profession. When the two men walked out, however, Vermen spun back toward the shelf and feigned reading the labels once more. His heartbeat banged in his ears and he couldn't concentrate enough to make out a single word.

The good doctor was a short man in his late forties with a shock of burnt orange hair and a squarish visage, but Vermen's gaze didn't linger long enough to detail him more. The client walking one step behind him, however? Hans could describe him without even looking.

David Lungvist was all limbs, his skeletal frame stretching out in arms and legs of inhuman length. The Plague had sucked all fat out of him years ago and left behind lean muscles and a crescent moon constellation of pock-marks on his left arm, chest, and face. He hid most under his long-sleeved soldier's uniform, but the sickness' passage remained visible on his left cheek. He compensated for his physical weakness with ferocious devotion, excellent aim, and an incredible mind for observation and puzzles, and Vermen had enjoyed his company as a lieutenant for years.

The captain's throat tightened as Lungvist bade good day to the doctor in his particular soft, wheezing voice. Vermen fought his deep urge to walk over and greet him, to wrap his arms around David and tell him everything. Had his lieutenant ever let him down? He would understand, tell him it was okay, it hadn't been a mistake. Maybe even help them. Vermen swallowed hard, forced himself to stay put. Lungvist belonged to his old life. No amount of nostalgia justified endangering the doctor, every rebel in camp, and the broadcast as a whole. Vermen watched his friend walk out through the glass reflection, every one of his lanky strides sending needles through his heart.

Seraphin had already greeted Doctor Colton and was being scolded for losing his glasses by the time Vermen dared to approach them. He wiped his sweaty palms on his pants and tried to keep his cool. Holt threw him a questioning glance before he followed the doctor inside his office.

Everything in this room was strictly professional, from the papers on the desk to the filing cabinet, medical posters, diplomas, and honorific mentions that covered the walls. Once a new pair of glasses was promised for the following morning, Seraphin began explaining the reason for their coming—always the same speech about supporting the broadcast, gathering people in Reverence's plains and demanding justice for the Plague's victims. Vermen used the time to seek a trace of the doctor's personal life. No baubles gathered dust on the cabinets, and the desk's surface was clean of family pictures. He wondered if the plump doctor had removed them all on purpose. Sometimes it was easier to try to forget the past.

"I cannot do it." Doctor Colton's strict refusal surprised Vermen. Most others had been happy to recruit more travelers. "My patients give me their trust, Seraphin. They confide in me and listen to my advice. I will not abuse my position to push them on your dangerous quest."

"You're not pushing them, Alfred, you're opening a new possible worldview. How is that different than laying out all possible treatments, experimental ones included, and informing them of the risks so they can make an enlightened decision?"

"I'm paid to heal them, not to help an underground political movement."

Seraphin let out an exasperated sigh and slumped in the chair in front of the doctor's desk. He rested his elbows on the wooden surface and rubbed his face. "I need your help."

Doctor Colton shook his head. "I'll be happy to provide medical supplies and advice, as always."

"Aren't you also paid to keep your patients healthy?" Vermen interjected. "You've fought the Plague, you're old enough for that, and you saw what it could do. You believe us, or you wouldn't provide drugs. We're talking about a man capable of creating another such supervirus—a man already testing a new disease—and willing to spread it and kill thousands if it'll accomplish what he wants. I hardly think it a betrayal of their trust to do your utmost to ensure such an epidemic never spreads again."

The doctor's keen gaze settled on him with curiosity. "Who *are* you?" he asked. "Seraphin never visited with you before, yet you are arrogant enough to step in and tell me what to think."

Vermen smiled at the irate doctor. His logic wouldn't bother him so much if it didn't ring true. Before he could answer, however, three loud knocks interrupted them. Colton rolled his eyes and called out.

"What is it?"

"Mister Lungvist said he forgot to ask you some questions about his prescription," the secretary said through the door.

"Ask the good man to wait for a few minutes. I won't be long."

This time David's feeble voice answered. "I must insist, Doctor. Please let me in."

He *knew*. His tone had hardened with the last sentence, and barging in on someone else's consultation was unlike David. He would not do it unless he had another urgent reason.

"Do it," Vermen said. "It's too late now."

Colton hesitated but when Seraphin gestured for him to do as asked, he opened the door. The Regarian's gaze never left Vermen, however. The captain offered an awkward smile and straightened as David stepped in. He kept a brave face on but his insides had twisted one over the other. Despite his earlier desire, he wasn't ready for this clash.

His lieutenant wasted no time in masquerades and entered, chalked skin and lips pressed together, with his standard-issue gun raised. The doctor slammed the door shut behind him then backpedaled into a corner. Although Lungvist's hand did not shake, his entire body tensed with expectation and he made an obvious effort to keep his breathing slow. He looked at Vermen with the same expression he'd have when he was at a loss of what to do and sought orders.

The captain crossed the distance between them in a single stride and, his heart pumping, he set his palm over David's hand and lowered the firearm.

"You won't need this."

Vermen looked up and met his friend's gaze. After years of working with him, he'd learned to read when his second was confused and orders needed to be clarified. David's eyes held a single, simple question now: *are you with me?* When he received no answer, he stepped back and pointed his gun at Seraphin.

"I will. To arrest him."

The Regarian didn't seem to notice. His eyes bore holes in Vermen, asking the very same question David's had. Hans' stomach clenched as he understood the rebel leader didn't even trust him yet, not quite. He pushed the rising anger down. There were more important matters to deal with.

"No, Lungvist," Vermen said. "We need him."

"*We?*" he repeated. Panic crawled into David's tone, his soft voice rising into a high-pitched cry. "There is no *we* for you! You are a captain of this army, one of the best, and you are not one of them."

"Stop it. You understood the moment you walked past me in the pharmacy. You must have known when you recognized me." He advanced on Lungvist again and this time when he pushed the firearm down, he didn't let go. David let him with a crestfallen look.

"You always swore you'd never do this," he said in a whisper. "What of our brothers? Of your vows to protect? What of the Union and President Kurtmann?" His voice grew stronger, angrier. "When you disappeared I gathered your notes and tracked the rebels down. I understood the meaning of Galway's scuffle, drew the routes to Mount Kairn. Everyone told me to give up, to accept you'd be dead or a traitor, but I *knew* it wasn't true. It couldn't be, not you. So I kept going, and I've been dismantling this little band and their filthy lies better than you ever could, all because it might lead me to you. But here you are, and defending Holt! What happened to you?"

"What do you mean, 'dismantling this little band'?" Seraphin interrupted. Vermen cringed. He'd heard the anguish in David's voice, sensed the precarious position they were in. If they pushed Lungvist, they might not make it out alive.

"Don't you listen to the radio?" Lungvist retorted. "The *real* one, I mean." When no answer came but a tight-lipped silence, David leaned forward with a satisfied smile. "I had Ferrea's grocer tailed until Schmitt showed up, and the fool led me to his host in Reverence. We arrested her quite some time ago."

"Him," Seraphin corrected. His voice was tight and even Vermen saw through the bluff.

"Don't even try, your dismay is written all over your face. She's tall, green-haired, and has at least one loose screw. Talks all the time, too, although rarely about something that matters."

David had barely finished his sentence when the rebel leader sprang on him. Lungvist's arm jacked up and he shot but Vermen held it down, shifting his footing to come between the two men. The bullet lodged itself in the blue carpet at their feet while Seraphin crashed into the captain's back. They both fell to the ground as David scrambled back to avoid being caught in the tangle. Vermen's chin hit the floor hard, smashing his teeth together, and he struggled to keep his wits about him. Seraphin rolled off his back. Lungvist would be taking aim at him right now.

"Stop it!"

He pushed himself up, standing between them. David removed his finger from the trigger. All three men breathed hard. Seraphin's white face was twisted into an angry snarl, intense hatred running from one man to another. Vermen stepped closer to his faithful lieutenant, until the gun's barrel pressed against his chest and only Lungvist's long arm kept them apart.

"Seraphin isn't an enemy. He's..."

Vermen didn't know what he was anymore. As he struggled for a word to encompass his relationship with the rebel leader, he met David's dark gaze.

His lieutenant's eyes widened, went from him to Seraphin, then back to the captain. He took a step back, even paler than usual. As if Lungvist had understood, without even needing a word.

"I see."

An intense sadness filled his bitter whisper and it felt like a punch to Vermen. Lungvist's wheezing breath had acquired a new shaky quality and he seemed to fight an urge to pull the trigger.

"He's an ally. Nothing more." Vermen poured all the conviction he could into those words. All of a sudden, David's unrelenting commitment had taken a whole new meaning—not one he wanted to address now. Not at all. "We swore to protect all Union citizens, and as long as Galen Clarin is out there, free to create the microbial monster of his choice, no one is safe. The last pandemic wiped out entire families. It took away your twin. We cannot allow it to happen again."

David swallowed hard. "My brother's death was *natural*. The Threstle Plague was not man-made."

"We have proof. We think Galen was testing the next plague already, six years ago. David, you believed in me enough to get this far." Vermen put a hand on his forearm. The touch felt intrusive even to him. "Will you not trust me again?"

"Hans, I..."

David's eyes snapped shut, his brow knotted as he struggled with a decision. Every breath turned into a soft wheeze. Seraphin lurched forward to take advantage of his momentary distraction, but when Vermen raised a hand to interrupt, he had the decency to stop. In the corner behind Lungvist, Doctor Colton squirmed and wiped his sweaty brow. The poor man's fate might hang on the soldier's decision now.

David calmed his breathing and lowered his firearm. "Faith in you hasn't been very rewarding. I need more than that now. You say he is preparing another pandemic?"

"Yes."

"Do you have proof of *that*?" Vermen wished he could glance at Seraphin, but he was afraid it might trigger David's anger again. He shook his head. Lungvist slid his gun back into its holster. "I'll see what I can find."

As he strode toward the exit, Vermen called after him. "Be careful,

David. They'll kill you."

His lieutenant turned with a confident smile. "This is what I'm good at, Captain. This, it seems, is the only reason you kept me around for so long. I will get to the bottom of this. And if I find nothing...I'll be back." He set his hand on the doorknob, but a last thought seemed to cross his mind and he added: "In the meantime, Hans, enjoy yourself."

As the door closed behind David Lungvist, Vermen allowed himself to collapse into the closest chair. He couldn't tell if he'd escaped disaster or provoked it, but at least they were free and alive. He hoped the same would stay true of his lieutenant. Then Seraphin leaned over his shoulder, his expression set into an angry mask.

"If he does come back, I'll shoot him."

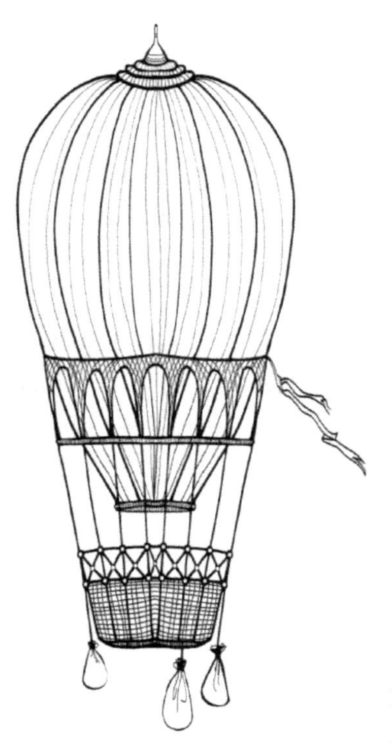

# CHAPTER THIRTY



*Andeal laid back on the* lake's beach and contemplated the perfect starry sky. No city lights marred the spectacle above. He'd yearned for the sight when trapped in Galen's labs, or as he lived under Mount Kairn. Sometimes he'd climb atop the peak and spend the night outside with Maniel, talking until sunlight muffled the stars' shine. He couldn't help but wonder if she was also out there, looking up at the same sky and thinking of him, or if she'd been buried under the rocks, never to see another star again.

He rolled over, frustrated not to find peace. Maniel haunted him, like a ghost already dead. Andeal stood, brushed the sand off his back, and stalked back to the balloon's basket, parked inside the forest's shadows. A bite might help him. It had, last time, if only for the amusement of reproducing Henry's coping mechanism. He'd just climbed in when the unmistakable sound of

286

Henry crashing through the underbrush reached him. His friend appeared between two trees, huffing and panting, with a backpack as tall as him strapped against his back.

"Very subtle," Andeal said. "How did it go?"

Henry set the pack on the ground with a relieved sigh and collapsed on the ground before he provided any answers. A film of sweat covered his forehead and his arms glistened in the moonlight. Andeal was glad he couldn't do those long treks into town. His gunshot wound had healed well enough but his leg was still rather stiff. Sitting all day in the balloon didn't help.

"Perfect!" Henry's voice had none of the enthusiasm such an answer should bring. "I strolled into an unknown village with an empty backpack, fumbled for words to draw reactions about our radio without being outright suspicious, trusted a complete stranger who caught up to the game and offered nutritious help, snuck into her house while her husband slept. Then I got lost on my way back, carrying a ton of food, so it took me a good four hours to reach this place. This expedition couldn't have been better. Give me water."

Andeal laughed as Henry extended his hand, then shook his head. "We've got none left. That's why you had to go, remember?"

"Oh yeah." He crawled to the pack, zipped the side pouch open and drew out a liter, which he promptly poured into his mouth. Once refreshed, Henry corked it and threw it in Andeal's direction. "Here, have at it. Best water I've ever had." He patted the backpack with a short smile. "At least with all this we won't need another trip for a while."

"Excellent."

Andeal climbed out of the balloon, grabbed the heavy pack, and brought it back on board. Henry had a point: his load weighted a ton. To think the poor man couldn't walk half the distance between Ferrea and Mount Kairn with a tiny pack before. He'd shaped up in the last months.

As his friend rested against a tree trunk, Andeal unpacked the new provisions. He stored what he could in their small chest, prioritizing anything that'd spoil if it got too humid. Most of the load was dry food—with a surprisingly small quantity of noodles—but Andeal eventually discovered a bag of fruits and vegetables. He couldn't help but squeal and shove an apple in his mouth. They hadn't eaten anything of the sort since leaving Reverence and he was dying for the freshness. Andeal paused, eyes closed, as he enjoyed the slight sugary taste. Perhaps they *should* do these expeditions again, just for the fruits.

"There's something else," Henry said, breaking his reverie. "Look in the side pouch, the one opposite the water."

Andeal obeyed and soon held the day's newspapers in hand. The headline read CHAOS IN ALTAER which, really, wasn't news at all. The students were always restless. Packing the Regarian city with universities— and as a result, young folks from across the continent—had always led to unrest. He had done his fair share of protests with Treysh, launching her homemade fireworks into the sky. Large protests didn't happen as often in the middle of summer, but something important must've triggered their passions. Could his broadcast have reached so far? If people had built their own transmitters as he'd asked, they might be able to pass the signal far enough to reach Regaria. That had been the idea.

Then the second title drew his attention. In the left bar listing other important news was a simple announcement: *Four suspects wanted for conspiracy.* His heart sped as he flipped the pages open until he found the article proper. The text was a brief tribute to Lieutenant Lungvist's investigative work following Mount Kairn's explosions, which now led to a large-scale manhunt for four individuals. And right under the summary, his picture stared back at him, along with Maniel's, Henry's, and Seraphin's.

The police forces had found recent pictures for the two latter. Henry might be three years younger than now and he faced the photograph with a large smile, waving the camera. They'd cropped the image close but Andeal could make out a crowd in the background. His friend didn't look the part of a dangerous criminal. Seraphin, on the other hand...The Regarian had his hair pulled into a long ponytail, wore a dark leather overcoat with the collar turned up. Tiny red veins shot through the blue of his eyes, giving him a mean, angry glare—an expression so far from Seraphin's mocking half-smile that Andeal stared, disturbed, for a long time.

The most interesting, however, was Maniel's and his pictures. They'd been taken out of their college albums, some eight years ago. He couldn't help but smile at his younger, fatter self. He'd always skipped exercise as much as possible during school, sometimes devising ridiculous apparatuses with Treysh to avoid moving around the house. For a year they'd had a special device that started the coffee maker on its own, with the right amount of water and coffee grain to make six cups. They activated it from their desks and only stood to pour themselves the much-needed caffeine—and only because multiple attempts at having the machine do that had resulted in failure and burns. Until the labs' experimentation sucked the fat away, Andeal had always been plump. He suspected he would be again as soon as he stopped starving—which he looked forward to. That was the strangest thing about these pictures: they predated their arrest and kidnapping, came from a time he was healthy. His skin was greasy, sure, but of a perfectly normal pink. Under the images, his appearance was detailed—height, weight, eye and hair color and, in his case, a short sentence mentioned that he *may have blue-colored skin.*

"I can't believe this," he said.

"Tough luck, isn't it? I don't think I can roam the villages in search of food again."

"No, no, that's not it." The newspaper rustled as Andeal held it, his hands shaking. "Henry, they are acknowledging we exist! Treysh said they told my parents I must've run away and refused to search for me. There is no paper trail of either Maniel or I at the police station we were taken to and certainly none after, at the labs. Yet according to this newspaper, we're not only out there, alive, but they admit I have blue skin. That kind of color doesn't just appear on runaways."

Andeal had given his name on impulse when they started broadcasting—a message to Galen that he'd survived, that his secrets weren't safe, and that he was coming after him. He'd never thought they'd dare to provide his description to the public. His heart hammered against his chest as he considered his next move. Henry studied him, looking a bit confused. Andeal smiled at him and snapped the newspaper shut.

"Launch the balloon. We have an important broadcast."

Henry groaned but lumbered back to his feet. "Here I hoped to sleep somewhere other than a cramped basket for once."

He offered no further complaints, however, and within an hour they'd joined the stars. Andeal deployed the antenna under them while Henry pumped gas out to give them altitude. The lake shimmered in the moonlight, outlined by black forest. He counted four nearby clumps of green roofs. Together they housed hundreds of honest citizens who'd receive his broadcast loud and clear tonight.

Andeal closed his eyes to calm his wild heart and gather his courage. Up until now, his radio had been all about the Clarin twins. He'd reminded them of Galen's role in the oil disaster—of how even as a young man, he'd managed to create an overpowered microbe, lost control over it, and tried to deflect the blame on others as the bacteria ate through the continent's oil—and he had expounded on Omar's less-than-stellar military record and on the Clarin family's long-lasting hunger for power. He'd read some of the papers Stern had stolen from Omar the night he left the army. Everything that could set up the twins as major actors in the Threstle Plague was on his program.

Now it became personal. *His* story, linked into the overall scheme.

Andeal cracked his knuckles, picked up his microphone, and flipped the transmitter on. The radio screeched for a moment, then stabilized. Henry gave him the thumbs-up.

"Good evening, listeners! We apologize for disturbing so late in the night again, but I'm afraid I can't choose my time for important news. Take a minute to gather your folks, we'll be waiting with some music."

He set the microphone down, checked the time, and wiped his hands on his pants. The ten minutes he allowed his audience to get comfortable stretched on, endless. His heart beat so loudly he wondered if they could hear it through the radio. Henry had turned the burner off and sat on their chest, listening in like all the others.

"All right, here we go," Andeal said. "I hope you guys followed my instructions on building homemade transmitters to pass the signal on, because tonight's broadcast is on a special subject and I would love to reach as many ears as possible. Tonight we'll be talking about me.

"If you've read the day's newspaper and followed our broadcast since the beginning, you realize my picture's in it. The blond college student who's a little on the fat side of life? That's me. Or, well, that was me eight years ago, when I attended classes in Altaer to become an electrical engineer. There's a strange note at the bottom of my photo that says if you were to meet me today, I might have blue skin—I do! And that's our program for tonight: *how* I acquired this particular skin color and all it implies. It's a long story, and not an easy one, but it is worth your time."

He glanced at the stars and thought of Maniel again. If she'd watched them earlier tonight, she would also be listening in now. He hoped she'd agree with his decision to disclose their tale, to talk about it openly on the air. And if she didn't, he prayed they'd have a chance to fight over it soon.

With a smile, Andeal brought the mic to his lips and launched into his narrative.

"And that, listeners, is how I came to be blue."

Andeal concluded his long monolog and paused. Seraphin's group of rebels—reduced to the Regarian, Maniel, Jan, and Vermen since Joshua and Stern had left with the others—sat around a small campfire some distance off the road. The captain lowered his gaze to his right hand, where minuscule scars still marked Andeal's bite. He remembered his friend's visceral terror, brutal enough to risk dying to get away. He'd guessed most of what had happened from that reaction and their short talk later, but hearing it laid out drove the reality home. Two years of ceaseless tests that would put some torturers to shame. How had they even pulled through with their minds intact? His short and, in retrospect, peaceful imprisonment among the rebels had nearly driven him mad.

"There is one last thing," Andeal continued, "a last experiment which I fear is relevant, even today, and must be detailed."

Vermen frowned and glanced at Maniel. She had stared at a specific tree branch throughout the broadcast, her lips pressed together, her back straight. There was a glaze over her eyes. She was listening, yes, but her mind had left the campfire and returned to their horrible cell. Young Jan sat beside her and put a hand on her shoulder, snapping her out of the daze. She turned to him with a brief smile but did not say a word as Andeal went on.

"Silver—which I received—is an antimicrobial agent. Maniel received specific antibiotics. Our third cellmate, Lenz Schmitt, was inoculated with the actual illness. He got sick."

There was a pained exclamation in the background, the microphone *thumped*—probably Andeal's hand over it—and a short, muffled exchange followed. Less than a minute later, Andeal continued his story.

"It started with headaches and coughing, but within two days Lenz had a fever and nausea and he complained about pain in his chest. That evening he spat blood and we all knew he didn't have long left. I started having headaches of my own..." Andeal paused. They could hear the tightness in his voice. Vermen wondered how Schmitt felt, listening to the gruesome details of his father's death. "We escaped the next morning and...and...I'm sorry, listeners, but this tale will have to wait. It's a better one, I promise. I'm just...I need a day."

The second pause lasted even longer and they all heard his ragged breathing. Maniel wiped her eyes and excused herself. Both Vermen and Seraphin watched her disappear between the trees. The captain wanted to follow, but if she sought comfort, she would've stayed. On the radio Andeal wished everyone a good night, then the familiar screech of a finished broadcast followed. Vermen gritted his teeth as it ripped through his ears. He'd never get used to that sound.

Seraphin hit the receiver's switch and turned it off.

"Well, I sure hope your lovesick lieutenant decided not to listen to *real* radio for once and heard all that."

Vermen's head shot up and he glared at the rebel leader. Since their encounter with Lungvist a few days ago, Seraphin had not missed an opportunity to ridicule the man. "Don't mock him. Lungvist is the most intelligent man the Union Army has in service. He found *your* base. He'll figure out where Galen's is."

"Oh really?" Seraphin stretched his legs with a half-smile. "I'll bet he wished you were half as perceptive as he is quite a few times, then. You never noticed how he looked at you? Can't have been easy."

"It wasn't obvious," Vermen replied, but there was no conviction in his tone. He wanted Seraphin to shut up because he knew he was right. He should have seen it, addressed it. Now that he looked back, he saw all the clues, the barely controlled impulses. Lungvist would've known, would have noticed his lingering gazes and heard what they used to say about him. He'd waited and hoped. "He doesn't deserve your derision."

"Then he should have left Treysh alone." Holt bent forward, clasping his hands together with a dangerous look. "This 'Reverence contact' he caught? She's Andeal's best friend. She knew him long before the labs and I'm sure seeing her for however long it lasted was an incredible relief. But now she's gone. We all know what they do with prisoners."

"He wouldn't—"

"He's not with her." Seraphin stood and glanced at the woods where

Maniel had gone. "Just like you weren't with any of the rebels you captured. Whether or not he knows, her arrest is a death penalty."

Vermen turned away, incapable of holding Seraphin's gaze. There would be no saving Andeal's friend. "What do we do?"

"We hope they take their sweet time executing her and go to Regaria, exactly as planned."

Seraphin strode into the forest, following Maniel and leaving Vermen to deal with his frustration. Running into Lungvist had exposed how detached he'd become from his old life. He wasn't that captain anymore, no longer held any of his prejudices or aspirations. Hans was ready to scrap it all—or almost all. David could be convinced to join. He'd been an incredible partner for years. Vermen hoped he wouldn't get killed looking for the truth, and that he would get a chance to sort things out before the end. Not any time soon, though. They had a long road ahead to get to Regaria.

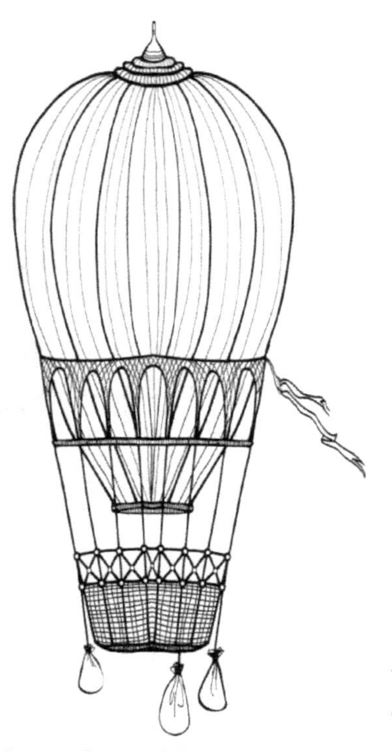

# CHAPTER THIRTY-ONE

*Hard rain beat against their* balloon's envelope, weighing it down. The horrible weather had held up for hours, forcing Henry to sacrifice his waxed coat to cover their chest and protect the radio materials within against water. Now his clothes stuck to his skin, drenched, and he could hear his shoes squish with every step despite the battering rain and howling winds. They had been in the sky for weeks now, but he couldn't remember flying in worse conditions. Henry had developed many tricks since launching off Mount Kairn and grown into an expert pilot, but none of them were any use in the rain. He hoped he'd never have to do this again.

A powerful gust rocked their basket and he clung to the slippery railing until the turbulence passed, cursing the rebels for removing the security holds inside while they redesigned it. Had nobody thought flying for weeks would lead to rain and wind? Those rope handles were built in for a reason!

He could think of several enhancements for the Lenz Balloon, but its engineer had crouched inside the basket, a hand over his mouth, half-sick. *He* hadn't expected such storms and wasn't built to deal with them, that much was obvious.

When his footing was secured again, Henry moved to the gas indicators on his current tank and wiped them off. He squinted, trying to read the arrow despite the water still blocking the way. Not much left. They'd burned through half a tank staying aloft today. He peered through the thick curtain of rain, desperate for a better view of their surroundings.

"Can you see the mountains?"

His question forced Andeal to pull himself up and study the sky ahead and under them. On his knees he was barely tall enough to see above the railing, but Henry knew if he stood, he'd fall back right away.

"Nothing. It's like we're flying in an endless shower."

Henry cursed, then cleaned the altimeter as best as he could. He'd kept the balloon high, terrified of an unavoidable mountain flank looming suddenly before them. Serenity's surroundings were known for their treacherous valleys and cliffs—not a good area to land in the best conditions, let alone today. With three weeks before Union's Day, passing over the large city before curving their path back toward Reverence had seemed a must, however.

He regretted that decision now. The weather showed no signs of letting up and the water dragged them down, forcing a difficult choice upon him. Would he waste more fuel by landing now and going through another consuming take-off, or by keeping their balloon in the sky until the rain diminished?

"What's that?"

Andeal pointed to an oblong shape at the edge of their vision, flying at their height. As Henry studied it, it grew closer and closer, and he soon realized the quandary had been taken away from him.

A Union warship was headed straight toward them.

"Zeppelin," he said, beginning to feel sick himself. "This day can't get any better."

Henry grabbed the control line of his parachute vent and pulled it open. The balloon dropped right away and Andeal flattened at the bottom of the gondola with a gasp.

"Sit on the chest, it'll keep my wax coat from flying off. And hold tight, will you? This will be rocky."

"They won't just fly by us, will they?"

"At this range they've tried to hail us through short-wave radio and we haven't answered. Not that we'd have a registered code name to respond with anyway. So right now we're an unidentified craft meant for pleasure— and who in their right mind would cruise the sky today for *fun*? No, I don't think they'll let us go."

"Can you land us?"

Henry gave a barking, stressed laugh. How could he know? He'd never flown before Andeal offered him the opportunity, let alone landed a modified balloon through heavy downpour before a war zeppelin shot them down.

"I'll try. Didn't think I could launch us by throwing the balloon off a cliff, so...why not?"

"Tell me...if you need anything."

From Andeal's grimace as the balloon lurched, losing more altitude, Henry doubted his friend would be any use. He'd have to get them to the ground alone.

He crossed the basket, grabbed the propeller's lever, and shifted it from under the balloon to one side before pulling on the left-side vent rope. The balloon shifted, placing the whirring blades between them and the zeppelin. The extra speed might not mean much in the end, but Henry intended to take all possible measures to save their asses.

He returned to the main ventilation system, giving the control line small and frequent pulls as he kept an anxious eye on the altimeter. Every tug opened the envelope's top a crack, letting hot air escape and killing their lift. Rain and wind whipped at his face, niggling at his concentration, but he kept their descent fast and steady. Trees appeared through the water curtain and clouds, waiting for them.

Trees.

Henry's stomach churned. He needed flat ground to slide across, not outstretched branches that'd rip through his envelope. Once they crashed through the treetops, there'd be no horizontal movement, no slowing their balloon until they could climb down, safe. And at the speed they plunged right now, there'd be no soft drift through the canopy. The impact might break the gondola.

"Andeal..."

He stopped and closed his eyes. His heart had raced into his throat, blocking all attempts at breathing. They might survive the landing. The Lenz Balloon would not.

"What?"

Andeal huddled on his wax coat, pale and worried. His hollowed cheeks and grim expression pained Henry. Every day without news of Maniel smothered his fire. This hot air balloon was his child—the only he could have right now—and Henry didn't have the heart to break the news to him.

"Hang on tight," he said. "It'll be a rough ride soon."

The zeppelin's great shape loomed over them now, stretching out in the sky. The airship's length surpassed even his balloon's height and put their cubic meter capacity to shame. The pliable solar panels along its edges glowed the same soft green as they would at night, unable to bring much energy to their ship. As Henry contemplated the monster closing in, squinting to see through the rain, he noticed small figures running around the gondola. Readying weapons.

He gave another desperate yank on his ventilation and leaned over the railway. How long before they peppered holes through the entire balloon? The ground rushed toward them, faster than Henry was comfortable with. Only Treysh would love this kind of speed. His altimeter dropped like crazy. Andeal had crouched over the chest and spread his arms to keep the wax coat from flying off and secure the radio apparatus. The Union soldiers turned their automatic cannons straight at them, ready to shoot at their all-too-large target. Henry slammed his eyes shut, switched to the thick red emergency rope, and pulled it. The balloon's top detached itself and their helium pouch flew off, hot air rushing out with it. The free fall gave them a last, sudden burst of speed.

And then, way too late, Henry remembered the antenna. It remained stretched under their gondola as they crashed through the treetop.

The impact threw him off his feet and sent him sprawling inside the basket, out of breath. Branches cracked as they crashed their way through the canopy. Some snagged in the envelope and gave a heartbreaking rip. Their fall barely slowed and they smashed into the rocky ground with all the speed of their rapid descent. Sparks flew before Henry's eyes as his breath followed the hot air, escaping into the skies. The wicker splintered with a resounding crack and the shock spread through his spine.

Then the basket flipped on its side and tumbled down the slope they'd hit. Half conscious, Henry reached for a hold. He found nothing but slippery wicker. He slid sideways, his feet touched the sides, then they clipped a tree and the wild ride spit him out.

He remained sprawled in the mud, unable to move, as the basket careened down a short way then got stuck between two trunks. Every cell in his body was in agony, the pain nailing him to the ground. He wondered if his spine hadn't shattered from the inside after all. Or perhaps the impact had turned his brain into a mushy mess. It would explain, at least, why the sky had gone from downpouring gray to large bands of gold and purple.

The envelope. Henry tried to focus his thoughts and shake out the thick mist sneaking into his mind. The sky wasn't golden, the envelope hung above him. And behind that, a killer zeppelin flew, ready to redecorate the forest with thousands of small holes. He couldn't stay on the ground and wait for death.

Henry rolled over and pushed himself to all fours. Nausea rushed through his system and he coughed his last meal out. A disgusting taste clung to his mouth as he wiped it clean, but the searing headache turned it into a minor concern. Henry reached for the back of his head. He'd knocked his skull hard when the basket hit the ground. Too hard, perhaps. His vision blurred until he couldn't distinguish one finger from another.

Strong arms lifted him off the ground and to his feet. Henry wavered and leaned against a hard trunk to avoid falling back. He focused his sight until he could make out Andeal's face. Blood had been smeared across his forehead and his cheeks were a deeper blue than usual, but his friend otherwise seemed fine.

"We've got to move, Henry. Take this."

He shoved their half-filled backpack at him then shuffled to a large, dark form in the mud. The transmitter, wrapped under Henry's wax coat.

He'd salvaged the radio equipment. Andeal's brains still worked, at least.

"Just a moment." Henry licked his lips, touched his head again, and took a deep breath.

"Are you okay?"

"Got myself a concussion, I think. Lovely headaches await me. I'll live."

Or so he hoped. For all he knew, he might be dying on the inside. He would die and never get to hear Treysh's lovely laugh and explosive plans. It was the last thing he'd expected to miss as they'd left Reverence, but he did. He hoped she thought of his grumpy complaining every now and then, and that she'd remember it if this head wound killed him.

His strength was coming back, though, the agony receding into a numb and persistent throb. He could walk. He shouldered the given backpack, took a successful step forward, then nodded at Andeal.

"Let's go. I'll rest once we've found a safe place."

They started uphill, slipping often on the uneven, wet ground. The sky returned to its depressing grayness as they left the envelope's protection and raindrops tapped against Henry's skull, each touch worsening his headache. Every step away from the balloon's wreckage demanded more out of him, as if invisible hands caught his ankles and grounded him. He endured in silence, unable to think much through the pain. A single thought managed to pierce the haze of his brain.

His flying days were over.

·

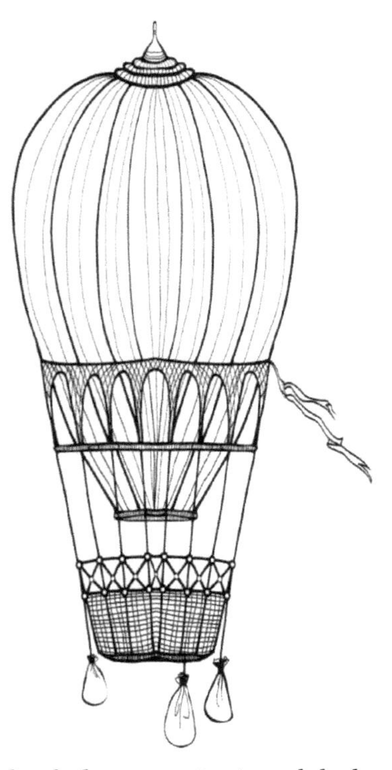

# Chapter Thirty-Two

*"Another one,"* Henry asked, waving at the waitress. The bar's loud, drunken crowd hammered at his headache, worsening it, and the heavy smoke stung his lungs. He'd rather be back in the mountains, breathing fresh air and nursing his growing cold, than here in this dump. Circumstances gave him little choice, though: if he did not bring back extra supplies and tools appropriate to fixing a transmitter, they'd never broadcast the recording.

Henry reached for the inside pocket in which he kept it safe, only to remember he'd given it to Andeal before he left. His muddied and torn clothes were no place to hide the all-important disc. They also condemned him to search for his benevolent soul in Serenity's rundown neighborhood instead of safer areas.

The waitress brought his pint and Henry settled in his chair, eyes closed. He tried to catch glimpses of the others' conversations but with the thumping in his head all he could hear was the National Radio. Their announcer babbled on about a great victory in Burgian territory. He managed to make this major military exploit—if half he said was even true—as meaningful as what he ate for breakfast. For the hundredth time, Henry pictured him in a romantic dinner with Treysh and grimaced.

The door flew open, breaking his daydream, and a tall soldier strode in, the distinctive stagger suggesting he'd had his share of alcohol already. Stains marred his beige uniform and he hadn't shaved in the last few days. The rough stubble couldn't hide the pockmarks on his cheeks, however. Henry studied the gaunt man with disproportionate arms and legs, convinced he'd seen him before.

Which, all things considered, could not be good news.

"Owner! A pint of your best and will you turn *that* off?" He pointed at the radio in one grand gesture. "Is there anyone with a lil' bit of judgment who still listens to this drivel?"

Henry's heart stopped as the man spat on the ceramic floor then, tipping dangerously to one side with every step, walked to his table and sprawled into a chair. The short scene had interrupted all conversations but as it became clear the drunken newcomer would say no more, the other patrons returned to their business. Henry gulped down his ale with difficulty. The soldier leaned forward.

"You're an easy man to track, you know that? Most predictable."

A cold sweat ran down Henry's spine. He ought to run, try to slip in the dark alleys, make a last-resort attempt at escaping, but he remained nailed to his seat, fingers clutching his pint. The man smirked at him, then slumped back into his chair and changed the subject.

"I wanted him to be wrong, you know." He tapped the table with his long index. "I wanted him to be wrong so I could go back and save Hans. Tell him he'd been fooled, lied to. Make him see his mistake."

The lanky man grabbed his pint of ale the moment it arrived and downed it. Henry tried to make sense of whatever the soldier rambled about. 'Hans' had to be Captain Vermen. Had they survived Mount Kairn, only to be captured? But then why would this man speak of saving Vermen? The drunk slammed his pint on the table.

"But I found it." A deep bitterness filled his wheezing voice. He ran a hand over his stubble, where the pockmarks were. "I found it all. Huge tanks of bacterial cultures lining the walls, dozens of rats in cages, schematics of the genomes. Tons and tons of notes, locked away. It was all there and I thought it had to be a nightmare but I still haven't woken up. It's still there and it's still so goddamn true. You need to come with me."

"What?"

He'd switched so fast from his slurred ramblings to serious business that Henry stared, his mouth half-open, dumbfounded.

"I thought you didn't matter. Just a poor bloke, I told myself, no one of importance, just ignore him. Big mistake. Biggest mistake I made in this hunt." He stared at his ale for so long Henry thought he'd forgotten about him. He was about to slide away when the soldier spoke again. "Your father, though...oh, he mattered."

Henry swallowed hard and focused all his energy on recognizing the man. He might feel less helpless if he had an inkling of what was going on. Then it struck him, and his confusion gave way to deep shame.

"I bumped into you at the grocery!" He'd thought himself so safe and subtle, talking with Kinsi. "Is he okay? He's not a part of this!"

"The grocer? Sure, I left him alone. He led me to you and you led me to…what's her name?" He stretched his fingers one by one and looked around as though the smoky ceiling would give him an answer. His previous anxious frown had been replaced by a smug smile.

"Treysh," Henry said, fighting the lump in his throat. "You're a monster."

"A monster? Don't be ridiculous. I needed to find my captain."

"Treysh never even met him! She has nothing to do with this. Leave her alone."

"Nothing?" A soft chuckle escaped his lips. "Don't waste your time. Holt all but told me she was one of his."

Hope pushed back Henry's fear for a moment. "Seraphin's alive too?"

He must have been with Vermen—and if these two had made it through, then perhaps so had Maniel and everyone else. He couldn't wait to tell Andeal! *If* he could make it out of here. The soldier clacked his tongue with distaste.

"Yes. Very much alive." He drank all that was left of his ale before setting it down. "And I let them go. Not you, though. It's funny how many things you understand when you start to listen, when you use what's in there to its full potential." He tapped the side of his forehead. "I figured the balloon out almost two months ago. All the elements were there: your slow movements through the countryside, the wind in the broadcast, the occasional flames behind. And when Andeal mentioned a Schmitt, I knew. Two Schmitts wasn't a coincidence. Leaving all the ballooning material in your basement and taking only the envelope wasn't exactly subtle, either."

Great. Now utter shame added itself to Henry's feeling of impending doom. They should have thought of cleaning up behind them. The other man continued in a pleasant tone, like he was talking to a friendly stranger.

"Is there a broadcast tonight?"

Henry pressed his lips together and gave him a defiant stare. He would not surrender more information if he could help it. No...as long as he could help it. He remembered too well what Seraphin had told him, after the incident in Galway, about what happened to the captured rebels. His heart clenched as he thought of Treysh. He didn't want to think about it.

"Not gonna talk?" the soldier asked. "There's no need. I know you crashed earlier. You must've come straight here because your clothes are still wet and covered in mud, which means you were in a hurry. There's two things I can think of that'd cause such a rush: food and radio equipment. It can't be food, however, because you'd never have wasted precious money on this hole's piss ale. So the radio must be broken."

Henry's mouth hung half-open from amazement. He searched for a way to counter the logic and deny the soldier's claim but found no flaws to attack.

"Who are you?" he blurted.

"I don't matter."

"Yes you do!" Henry's heart thundered, out of control. He tried to straighten his thoughts despite his pounding headache. "You're not *any* soldier. You knew Captain Vermen, met him again, allowed him to escape. You're here pushing my buttons and rambling and I can barely make any sense out of it, but you did say I wasn't going anywhere so yes, who you are kind of matters to me."

Henry gathered enough courage to meet the soldier's gaze and hold it. The other man tilted his head to the side and remained silent for a few seconds, as if he considered whether or not to answer.

"Lieutenant David Lungvist. I am—was—Hans' second-in-command." A bitter smile played on his lips and his voice fell to a whisper. "After I found the labs I reported to the only authority I could trust to be above Galen Clarin: President Jacob Kurtmann. He tasked me to find you—not any rebel, you specifically—before Galen. Congratulations, Mister Schmitt. You have a private meeting scheduled with our president."

"Th-the president?"

He had to have heard wrong. This made no sense. He was a nobody. Yet Lungvist confirmed it right away.

"Yes."

"Why?"

"Ask him yourself."

Henry swallowed hard and sank into his seat. What would President Kurtmann do with him? It couldn't be worse than prison, though, could it? Lungvist spoke of secret labs and of being faster than Galen. That had to be good. They didn't want the virus-wielding, power-hungry scientist to know about this. Henry wiped his sweaty palms on his pants. He hated to leave Andeal all night, hated that they might never let him go, but what choice did he have?

"All right, let's go."

He started sliding out of his chair but Lungvist grabbed his forearm. "I'm not done." His body tensed and the wheeze in his voice took on a rough edge. "I need to know what happened to Hans. The man I knew would never have—he wouldn't be with..." The lieutenant's voice tightened until he couldn't speak another word. He took a deep breath. "Tell me what happened at your house."

Henry recognized the deep pain in the wheezing tone. It reminded him of Treysh's uncertain fate, of how Henry's insides clenched when he thought of it. Lungvist's concern with Vermen wasn't a question of duty. He cared. Quite a lot. And Henry's silence killed what little patience the lieutenant's large alcohol consumption had left him.

"Tell me!"

His voice turned into a shrill whistle and he pressed his palms against the table. Henry withdrew but as he met Lungvist's intense gaze, as he glimpsed his desperate need to know, Henry understood he was not helpless here. His lack of self-restraint had put Treysh in prison. He hadn't *needed* to speak with Kinsi. What a ridiculous and risky idea it'd been. He had to try something, anything, to fix his mistake. Henry squared his shoulders.

"Perhaps I will. Everything. What happened at my house, what happened in the rebels' headquarters, what he did the last time I saw him. Everything." His voice was so calm, so in control, it might as well belong to a stranger. "But only if you do all you can to free Treysh."

Lungvist's eyes narrowed. "She's out of my hands now. I can't order her free."

"Try."

"Why would I even do it?"

"You love him, don't you?" Henry had never been a good judge of character, but this time he was certain of himself. Lungvist's pain was too relatable. Too similar to his fear for Treysh. "That's my condition. Promise to help Treysh and I'll share what I know."

Lungvist's jaw clenched and he withdrew his hands from the table, balling them into fists at his side. Henry couldn't deny his growing satisfaction as he watched the other man struggle for a decision. After a disappointed glance at his empty mug, the soldier gave a shrug.

"All right. Deal." He stood and dropped a few bills on the table. "There'll be ample time to talk on the way."

Henry scrambled to stand, bashing his knee on the table in his rush. He hissed and limped the first few steps, which drew a smile from Lungvist. The soldier pushed the door and led him outside. Though he wore his holster in the open, he did not bother drawing his gun. When Henry calculated his chances to outrun the long-limbed man in his current state, he understood why. Either way, escaping would ruin Treysh's unique, tiny chance. He owed it to her to stay, at least.

They traveled through the neighborhood's dark and broken streets. No lampposts lit the way and the day's heavy rain had toned down the roofs' glow to a weak green. Lungvist's earlier drunken stagger had vanished now and he took every stride with clear purpose. Henry almost jogged to keep up and he soon ran out of breath. He tried to start the story, hoping the soldier would slow if he had to pay attention, but Lungvist hushed him right away.

"Not here, not in the city."

"Not in the—we'll leave Serenity?"

"Yes."

He refused to say more until they'd left the confines of the city, slipping through the southern suburb and climbing up the mountain slope. Once they'd cleared the last house and started on a wide but deserted track, Lungvist demanded that Henry get on with his tale. Henry ignored the commanding tone, set his thoughts in order, and began.

Every word hammered a little guilt in his guts. This wasn't selling the rebels out, he repeated to himself. He had no idea where they were now and couldn't help Lungvist find them if he wanted. He was giving Treysh another chance, nothing more. Yet no matter how often he circled between these thoughts, he continued to feel sick. Not to mention Andeal would be waiting for him.

Time passed faster while he talked, however, and soon Serenity became little more than a sprawl of dimmed-out green lights wedged between mountains, a snaking dark line marking the river passing through. They climbed ever higher and as Henry reached his last encounter with Vermen, their trail went over a ridge. Lungvist put a hand on his chest.

"I want to hear the end before we move on."

His wheezing voice shook as he spoke and he wrung his bony fingers together. Henry hesitated, afraid the story might make him change his mind.

"You won't like it."

The soldier grabbed his shoulder. "I don't care!"

"We were outside, on a ledge, working. I talked about Galen's virus and our proof but he didn't seem very interested. Then all of a sudden he ordered me to shut up and listen. He'd heard the bomber blimp's engines above us, and we ran back to our balloon and he went on to tell the others. The point is, he warned the rebels about the attack. Without that we'd all be dead. Wiped out."

Lungvist squeezed his shoulder, burying his nails into it. Henry shook off the hold and took a careful step back. His companion's visage hovered between anger and anguish but neither emotion reassured Henry. He considered fleeing back to Serenity, discarded the thought as quickly as it'd come. Lungvist took a deep calming breath.

"That doesn't answer everything," he whispered.

"It's all I have. Andeal would've known more. I was a tad busy coming to terms with the idea the Plague that'd killed my mom was fabricated to pay a lot of attention."

Lungvist reached up to the pockmarks on his cheek, then withdrew his hand. He pressed his lips together and stared at Henry for what seemed like an eternity. After a moment Henry realized he wasn't looking, not really. Then Lungvist snapped out of it and headed along the way.

"Come," he said.

He went over the ridge and Henry followed him. A cold wind caught them as they crossed and he shivered under his humid clothes. Then his gaze followed the mountainside and what lay within the valley stole his breath.

The Great Whale. An airship thrice the length of regular zeppelins and twice the width, said to carry many times the weight in weapons its lesser cousins did. Its dark bulk lay nestled between the two mountains, on a plateau barely large enough to hold it. The landing must have demanded tremendous skill and coordination. Then again, you had to be competent towork aboard President Kurtmann's personal airship.

Henry's skull buzzed as he contemplated the huge zeppelin. He'd heard stories but none did justice to the monster awaiting below. The green lights flanking it blurred, strength escaped his legs, and he clutched at Lungvist's arm to avoid falling. The soldier shook him off with a disdainful cluck of his tongue.

"Let's go. President Kurtmann won't wait all night."

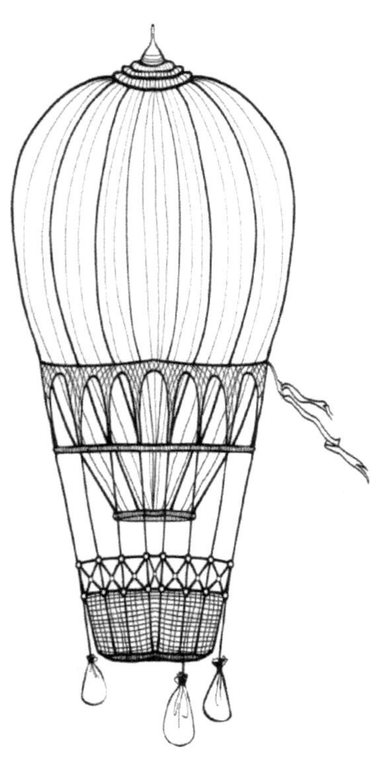

# CHAPTER THIRTY-THREE

*Perhaps if he threw the* transmitter hard enough at the wall, it'd repair itself. Nothing else seemed to work, anyway, and Andeal was ready to give up. The crash had destroyed the already used pieces and until Henry brought back the necessary tools and replacements, he could not fix their radio. Without it there'd be no more broadcasts, no build-up until they played Lenz's recording. There'd be no recording at all.

He plopped down on the cold ground of their cavern's floor and set his face in his palms. How did it always go south so quickly? He woke one morning with hope and determination, only to find himself despairing at the new odds by nightfall. First when they'd bombed Mount Kairn and tore Maniel away from him, then yesterday, when the zeppelin forced them to crash-land, crushed the antenna, and broke their transmitter. They'd abandoned the torn balloon, grabbing their rations and the essential radio parts before climbing into the mountain range surrounding Serenity. Tiny caves dotted their sides like thousands of ant holes and it hadn't been difficult to find one to hide in. The adventure had given them fresh bruises, tearing a gash in Andeal's leg right where the radio's guards had shot him, but neither complained: they'd both made it out alive.

Then they'd tried to broadcast and the transmitter refused to start.

Andeal had cracked it open but quickly realized he could not repair it with his hands and he'd sent Henry into the city to find tools. Afternoon turned into night while the engineer played with the cables inside the transmitter, trying to solve the problem, then dawn came again. His eyelids threatened to shut at any moment, his wounded leg throbbed, he had no news of his friend and he was beginning to think he'd never have any.

This is it, he thought. End of the line. Without the broadcasts only a smattering of foolhardy men would dare travel to Reverence, and their hard work would be for naught.

Andeal gathered the smallest pieces and screws of the transmitter and stored them in a tiny bag, which he placed in his pocket alongside Henry's recording. Then he gobbled down two of the painkillers he'd managed to salvage from their crash and settled against the wall. Perhaps he ought to sleep after all. He was no help if he couldn't concentrate on the repairs.

He'd rested his head for a minute when he heard the loud barks of dogs. Andeal startled and scrambled to their cave's exit. The sounds came from farther down the slope and he'd wager anything they were coming his way.

Union soldiers had tracked them from the crash site.

He couldn't have more than ten minutes before they fell upon him. He ran back inside and shoved their supplies into a backpack, starting with

Henry's noodle packs. Andeal might mock his companion's favorite food but the instant meals were light and small, good for travel. He added the recording and bag of screws to the lot, then threw a waxed coat above the transmitter and heaved it off the ground. Broken or not, he refused to leave it behind for the Union soldiers to find.

By the time he exited the cave, he could glimpse shadows moving through the trees below. He whispered a prayer to the Lady and hurried in the opposite direction. He'd need luck to get out of this alive.

The mountain track was narrow and treacherous, forcing Andeal to slow. He could not see his feet with the transmitter and took each step blindly. Whenever he could, he leaned against the stone walls flanking him to help his balance because if he slipped, his neck would join their ever-growing list of broken things.

Then his shoulder slipped into a crack. Andeal cried out as his body followed and he crashed to the ground, his heavy load crushing him. He'd fallen into a smallish cave, its opening barely large enough for him and the machine to pass through. As he lay on the ground, panting, Andeal thanked the Lady for listening. He could not outrun dogs while carrying the transmitter. This, however, was a perfect place to hide it. He left the device in the darkest corner and slipped back into the sunlight again, hoping the hounds would keep hot on his trail and never stop here.

This time he scrambled down the descent at full speed, half-jumping from one rock to another, his arms spread out. Every stride sent a shock into his knees and his teeth clattered together. As he reached the forest the slope lessened but branches slapped his face and forearms, leaving scratches and cuts. His lungs hurt with every breath, his wounded leg with every step. His heart pumped so loudly it rang in his ears, but the barks grew louder despite his efforts. He glanced behind and saw the men catching up to him.

As he turned back the trees gave way to an abrupt descent.

Andeal plunged with a surprised cry and tucked himself into a ball as he sped down the hill. He crashed through branches and bumped against rocks, rolling and rolling, every new bounce sending waves of pain through his body. A bough tore into his wound, ripped it open, and a trail of blood marked his path through the underbrush. He clung to his legs, eyes shut, one arm thrown over his head, when his shoulder clipped a dead trunk and he lost his grip. He stretched out and the twigs caught at his shirt and scratched his belly as he slid further down. He opened his eyes, trying to spot an end to his tumbling.

There was no flat ground ahead. Only a brusque vertical drop.

Panic swirled through Andeal and he grabbed at anything he could, tearing out ferns and lifting rocks. His course slowed, the gap grew closer. His feet went over the edge as his fingers closed around an anchored root, jerking him to a sudden stop. Andeal pulled himself back up and remained lying on the ground, panting. All his muscles ached, but his wounded leg throbbed harder than ever. He tried to stand but couldn't muster the strength.

Loud barks gave him new energy.

He lumbered to his feet, silencing his pained body through sheer will, and hurried to the closest tree. There he grabbed the lowest branch and heaved himself up. Heavy steps crushed the undergrowth as they approached, led by the growling dogs. Andeal had time to climb two more branches before they came into sight. If the Lady allowed, they'd think he'd rolled over the edge and leave him for dead.

Two soldiers stopped under his tree, out of breath and patience. One towered well over six and a half feet and had such pure white-blonde hair he could only hail from Mikken. The second had come out of the small and stocky mold, complete with close-shaven brown hair and a weasel face. They observed in silence as their dogs—two lean hounds—sniffed at his blood puddles. Andeal leaned forward and prayed hard they'd come to the wrong conclusion.

"What a shame," the weasel one said as he leaned over the edge. "I bet they'll send us searching that river for body pieces."

Below glittered the river that snaked through Serenity. It was narrower here than in the city and rushed through the mountains to eventually throw itself into the sea. Andeal couldn't help but smirk: even had he fallen down, he might've survived, depending on the water's depth. The jump surpassed the height of his frequent dives from the top of Mount Kairn with Maniel, but not by much.

"We should return to his cave and wait for the other. We can surprise him."

The giant had a thick northern accent, confirming Andeal's suspicions, but the knowledge brought him no comfort. They would wait for Henry and the poor man would have no chance to escape. The two dogs turned around his tree when the soldiers tugged on their leashes. One whined and kept pulling to stay. Andeal wanted to shoo him but remained motionless, holding his breath, staring at them.

A red drop of blood landed on the dog's muzzle.

"What was that?" the Mikken soldier asked.

Andeal's leg had bled throughout the men's inspection of this ridge, dripping on his branch, then on the leaves under him and finally through the foliage and onto the dog. The engineer slapped a hand over it but his heart sank when the giant strode closer.

"Blood," he said, then looked up. His eyes met Andeal's just as the engineer jumped down upon him.

He'd counted on surprise to win a frontal assault and scramble away, but the soldier's lips curled into a sneer. He dug his right foot in and crouched, then caught Andeal with both hands as he fell. The impact did not even stagger him, but it blew all breath out of the engineer's lungs. The world spun as he was held aloft by this giant, struggling against the iron grip even though he couldn't hope to match the man's strength.

"Nice catch, Magnus. Seems our fish is squirming."

"He's blue."

"Why yes. What a strange little rebel we've got here."

Andeal shut his eyes and fought against the panic constricting his throat as they discussed his peculiar appearance. He tuned out their conversation, desperate for an escape plan, but no matter how hard he tried, his thoughts scattered. To Maniel and Seraphin, Henry and Vermen, and all those he'd met in the last years. But mostly, they went to the labs. To the empty cell, devoid of sunlight and regular meals. To cold nights curled against Maniel. To secondary effects that went from itches to diarrhea, numbness, or hallucinations. To Lenz, bent over in a deep cough, feverish, dying. To the helplessness, the certainty of endless tests, the crying need to end it all. He couldn't do it again. Especially not alone. Better die than relive that hell.

Andeal's breath quickened and he fought, scratching and kicking with all he had. Tears ran down his cheeks and every new hit from his leg sent waves of pain up it, but he kept going, on and on. The giant pushed him against a tree and backhanded him. Sparks flew before Andeal's eyes. He fought harder. They hit him with another, stronger punch and knocked him out.

He came to a few minutes later, lying on the ground, the sun glaring. His stomach lurched and he rolled over, spilling his meager dinner at the two soldiers' feet. Andeal wiped his mouth as the giant grabbed his shirt and forced him to stand. His dizziness grew worse and for a moment he thought he'd faint again, but the shifting ground stabilized.

"You done being stupid?" the smaller soldier asked. "Three of you couldn't break out of Magnus' hold."

They tied plastic wraps around his wrists and set him against a trunk. Andeal let them handle him like a doll.

"We have questions," Magnus said. "Where is your companion?"

"Somewhere."

"Don't play with us."

"It's as good an answer as any."

When they rewarded him with a punch, Andeal folded forward. These two had no patience and were not to be played with. Or perhaps it was the other way around and they'd be funnier to provoke.

"Once again: where is he?"

Andeal leaned forward and his voice fell into a whisper. "Having tea with Galen Clarin."

Magnus grabbed his chin and slammed him back against the trunk. Pain wracked his spine yet he couldn't help but laugh. He was unlikely to have anything amusing happen for the remainder of his life and he intended to enjoy this pair's growing anger as much as he could. His mirth brought frowns to their faces.

"I don't think you understand the situation you're in," the smaller one said. "There's nothing funny about it."

"Oh, no, I think I understand a lot better than either of you." Their frowns deepened into scowls and a sudden thought crossed Andeal's mind. He held back another fit of laughter and lifted his head to meet Magnus' eyes. The giant's large hand still held his throat firm. "You're so proud to have caught me, but you'll be the first to pay for it. Especially you."

Magnus sneered. "Why?"

"This blue isn't natural. It's from another microbe Clarin created in his secret labs. It creeps into your skin cells, leeches off their resources, and produces the pigment as part of its life cycle. And it's contagious." Andeal looked down at Magnus' arm, raised his eyebrows. "You've been touching me *a lot.*"

The giant released his grip and stepped back, eyes wide in horror. Andeal dashed to the side. Thirty feet to the edge with a limping leg. Possible, if they didn't react fast.

A loud bang extinguished that hope. The bullet landed in the ground right in front of him, sending dirt flying and forcing him to skid to a stop. The second soldier had his weapon pointed straight at his heart. He took a victorious step forward.

"Nice try, but you're not going anywhere. You don't scare me with your lies."

"You just think you're safe because you haven't touched me. You're intelligent enough to realize I wasn't born with blue skin—in fact, you've probably seen the picture in the newspaper. You'll have noticed how much younger I am in it and must've wondered why. Strange, isn't it, that the one rebel without a recent picture is the one with blue skin? So maybe I don't scare you, but it's not because I'm lying. And you know it."

As he spoke he strode forward once. The soldier's gun didn't waver but doubt crept into his expression. Andeal smirked. Then spat in the man's face.

The soldier gave a shriek and reached up to wipe the saliva away.

Andeal wished he could enjoy the terror he'd provoked longer. Instead he spun on his heels and scrambled for the cliff. Magnus let out a deep, outraged cry that contrasted with his partner's shrill scream and cocked his gun.

The shot rang out as Andeal leapt into the gaping ravine. The bullet whizzed past him, inches away from his shoulder, then the rushing wind obliterated all other sounds. It snapped his loose shirt about, plunged into his leg wound and set it on fire, pushed at his muscles as he fought to stretch himself into a long diving position. The tied hands really didn't help. The water closed in as he gritted his teeth for impact.

He might die. It'd still be a hundred times better than returning to the labs.

The cold water enveloped his body from fingertips to toes, compressing his bones and threatening to rip him apart. The outside world vanished above the waves, leaving only a dull buzz as pressure tightened around his skull and obscured his vision.

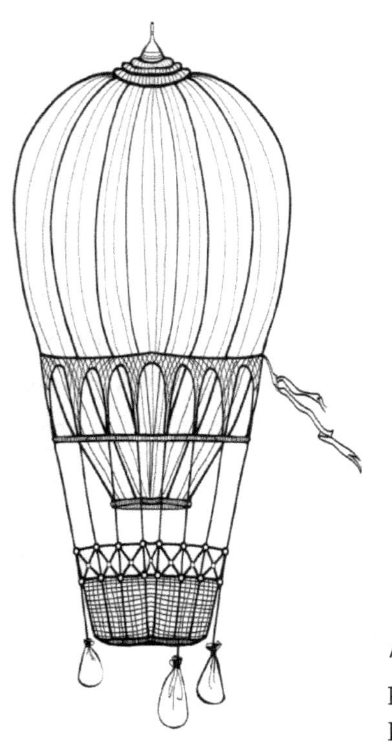

# CHAPTER THIRTY-FOUR

*Meeting the president came* pretty high on the long list of things Henry never expected from his life. Then again, almost everything that'd happened in the last months could figure on that extensive list, so perhaps this was the next logical step. As he entered the cozy living room inside the world's greatest zeppelin, Henry wondered what would be next, and if it would even surprise him. He waved the thought away, convinced that whatever he imagined—even a pool full of instant noodles—life would find a way to spring weirder things on him.

A tall figure sat in the darkest corner of the living room by a fireplace with a fake fire, leaning forward, broad hands set on his legs. Flickering shadows moved across his flat nose and squared chin, deepening the traits.

"Mister President?" Lungvist called. "This is Henry Schmitt. I'll guard the door."

He slipped out right away and the door clicked behind him. Henry gave it a wistful glance but instead took a step forward, deeper into the room. The seated man pushed himself off his large chair and approached with long, deliberate strides. His shoulders hunched forward from an invisible weight and a disturbing number of lines criss-crossed his face. President Kurtmann was in his early fifties but looked at least a decade older. He stopped a few feet away from Henry and smiled, stretching his arms out. The expression smoothed half his wrinkles.

"Your old man would be proud, I think."

An angry flush rushed to Henry's cheeks. Why would Lenz be proud? No matter how hard he tried, Henry made one wrong decision after another. First he'd been too afraid to accept the task, then he'd led Lungvist straight to Treysh and finally, he'd crashed their balloon and been caught before they could fix the radio. His current record of failures was nothing to be proud of. And besides, what did Kurtmann know about his father? Henry crossed his arms. He'd had enough of confusing banter for the night.

"You wanted to see me," he said. "What for?"

His straightforwardness seemed to surprise the president, but the wide-eyed expression vanished as fast as it'd appeared.

"I can help you. I want to."

"Help?" Their attacks might be focused on Galen, but they were also destroying Kurtmann's claim to power. With their version of events, it was easy to question how much he knew and whether he should be President at all.

"You should take a seat."

"I feel like standing." That was a big fat lie. Between the balloon crash, the concussion, and the long walk here, his entire body shivered at the thought of more effort.

"Don't be ridiculous." Kurtmann crossed the distance between them in a single stride, then grabbed Henry's bloodied shirt and pulled the sleeve up. Henry winced and avoided looking at the red line running up his forearm, surrounded by a sick bluish contusion. "I'm willing to bet you've got other such wounds, some perhaps more dangerous than others. Did you not crash into the forest? Sit."

He released Henry's arm and returned to his own chair, where he waited for his guest to take the other one. After a short struggle with his pride, Henry decided to obey. He dragged his feet to the second chair and collapsed into it. The cushion molded to his battered body and tempted him to close his eyes and sleep. He resisted the allure and straightened up. The president leaned forward and clasped his hands together, like a man about to tell a legend by the fireside.

"Your father was an old friend—the kind you always remember but don't see for years at a time. When I last saw him, however, it wasn't a happy reunion. He'd come to give me this." He searched the inside pocket of his tailor-made suit and drew out a small disc case. "I think it should be yours, now."

Henry frowned and reached for the disc, but Kurtmann withdrew it.

"There are conditions. The Clarins must never know how you came by it. And when you present it, you must linger on how they talk about me. This virus was not *my* idea. I never asked for it, or to be their puppet. I just..." He passed a hand over his face. "I'm getting ahead of myself. You ought to listen to it first."

He placed the disc in the reader on a side table. The name *Jacob* was written on top, with his father's handwriting. Same as Henry's recording.

Henry had never expected to find another disc like his. It made a lot of sense that his father would make several copies of such a precious recording, however. If the president really was an old friend...what else could this disc be?

"Don't bother. I know what's on it."

"You..." Kurtmann trailed off, his gaze fell and his shoulders slumped.

"Did you expect my father to give you the only disc in existence? What you hold is a copy. The entire radio show is a ploy to broadcast the original on Union's Day! We've had this information from the beginning, Mister President." Henry's anger built as the full ramifications of this settled in. He sprang to his feet, unable to remain seated and paced around the chair and away from the artificial fire. "There's one thing I do wonder about, however. If you've had the recording for so long, how come you never did anything about it? We sure haven't heard you denounce the Clarins in the last years."

"I wasn't inactive!" Kurtmann twisted in his chair to watch Henry pace. "I threatened Galen to reveal it if he didn't step down but he laughed, said I needed him and that if he went down, so did I. He was right, too: I couldn't have navigated through the Union's rough early years without the twins. I thought I'd learn to command him. I was the *President,* after all. I gave orders. But a man with a gun to his head never controls anything, and with the Threstle Plague, I was as good as dead if I said a word. You have to understand, Henry. He'd have me killed!"

"You mean like he killed my father? Like he would kill me, or Seraphin, or any other rebels if he put his hands on us? Like he will Treysh, because of that lieutenant you sent after me?"

Henry hadn't launched a hot air balloon through free fall, snuck in Reverence through the catacombs, stolen a transmitter from the National

Radio Tower, and dodged Union troops flying across Ferrys' territory to get 'they'd have me killed' as an answer. He could've died dozens of times since he'd accepted to go against the Clarin twins, and so had all the rebels. They'd taken the risks for perfect strangers to whom they owned nothing. But here was a man sworn to protect them, too scared of death to step up in their name.

Henry's pacing came to an abrupt stop. His hands balled into shaking fists and an angry flush rushed to his cheeks. He spun to face President Kurtmann and advanced on him, one deliberate step at a time.

"You are a coward," he said. "Your citizens believed in you. You appeared when they needed a hero and they gave you their absolute trust, and this is how you repay them?" He stopped beside the president's chair and leaned upon him. "Puppet or no, you deserve to go down."

Kurtmann stood, forcing Henry to back away, and straightened. He was a full head taller, with an imposing presence absent from the figure slumped in his chair.

"I did what I could and it is not your place to judge me. You cannot imagine how difficult the last years have been. I called you here to help your cause, not to be berated by a stranger, Lenz's son or not."

Henry stepped away. The desperate inflection underlying every sentence Kurtmann said gave him shivers. He'd always sounded strong and confident on the radio but tonight, in the privacy of his zeppelin living room, Henry heard a man hollowed out by his mistakes. How could someone so respected and revered turn out to be so pitiful? He fought not to grimace: they could gain something here. Kurtmann's voice mattered.

"Will you not speak up now?" Henry asked.

"It is too late for that."

"Never is."

"I said no."

Henry clenched his fists. Kurtmann had given up before he ever tried to fight. But he could still help them, even if he refused to act in public. "Then give me tools, a new antenna, and food supplies. Our radio transmitter is broken."

"I'll have Lungvist get them. Anything else?"

His stomach grumbled in response and the weight of today's events crashed on Henry's shoulders. He rubbed his temple and tried to think of something despite the pulsing headache and growing fatigue, but no idea surfaced through the mist in his mind.

"I...no. A meal, perhaps, and painkillers."

A concerned expression passed over Kurtmann's face. "How hard did you crash?"

"It's a miracle no one broke a limb. I smacked my head something bad."

The president moved forward, grabbed Henry's arm, and pulled him back to the large chair. A new energy animated him and he acted with the swiftness of a man who'd found his purpose. Henry sat, too surprised to protest, and Kurtmann—*Doctor* Kurtmann—crouched before him.

"Headaches?"

"Yes."

"Any nausea since you crashed?"

"Yes..."

The president clacked his tongue and straightened up, his worried frown deepening.

"You ought to sleep here. Chances are you have a concussion and whether or not your condition worsens remains to be seen. If something happens, I could help."

Henry felt fine, if he excluded exhaustion and headaches. He'd heard about people falling asleep and never waking up, however, and accepting meant a warm and soft bed for the night. Andeal would worry at the camp, but he'd probably agree staying was the best decision.

"All right. If you keep watch, I'll wait for tomorrow to return. Better late than dead, after all."

"Then I shall ask Lieutenant Lungvist to see to your comfort."

The president went to the door and pushed it open a crack. He had a quick, whispered discussion with the tall soldier, just loud enough for Henry to understand they were making arrangements for a meal and his rooms. He rubbed his stomach, absentminded, until Kurtmann gestured for him to leave. As he went past the president, the man touched his forearm.

"Your father never let anyone talk down to him or get in his way. It's good to see you've inherited that temper."

Henry quirked his eyebrows and studied Kurtmann's expression for a clue indicating he was joking. He found nothing but serious green eyes and lips sealed into a grim line. Here he stood, in the belly of the world's largest zeppelin after a rough and unpredictable day, and their jelly-spined president had just conveyed gladness at his *temper*. Henry couldn't remember hearing anything as ridiculous. Uncontrollable, shaking laughter took over his belly, and his companions stared, dumbstruck, until he wiped tears out of his eyes and asked, out of breath, to go to his rooms.

His wild fit of laughter left him lightheaded and relieved as he followed Lungvist down the Great Whale's corridors.

A loud metallic banging woke Henry with a start. He sat up, groaning as blades of pain stabbed through his skull, and glared at his door. Whoever smashed his fists against it had never learned manners.

"A moment, please!"

The previous evening he'd slipped out of his muddied clothes and into a hot shower, washing away weeks of dirt, sweat and weariness. His quarters consisted of a minuscule room with a bunk bed, a chair and a dresser, but the adjacent bathroom turned them into the best living space he'd enjoyed since Reverence. The president had arranged for a pair of clean pajama pants and another set of clothes to be readied for him, too, and he put on the clean shirt before trudging to the door. Every piece of clothing was two sizes larger than necessary and floated around Henry, making him feel goofy and inadequate. He fought against the shame, pulled the doorknob, and met his visitor's solemn gaze. The door-banging miscreant turned out to be Lungvist.

"No need to wake up the whole Great Whale!"

"No? Then why didn't you come when I knocked and called your name?"

"I—" Henry's cheeks burned and he stepped aside to let the soldier in. "Never mind."

Two long strides carried Lungvist to the middle of the room and he waited for the door to close before speaking again. He moved with precise movements and a grace unexpected from someone with such long legs.

"President Kurtmann said you'd have headaches for a week or two but no other complications, but I'd begun to believe you'd died in your sleep. I am pleased to see that is not the case."

"You've changed moods since yesterday."

Henry couldn't tell if Lungvist's sudden politeness relieved or disturbed him. The soldier had exchanged drunken bluster for a calm and calculating attitude. He seemed to pause and consider Henry's comment..

"Alcohol blurs my mind." He pinched the bridge of his nose, as if fighting a headache of his own. "I've had my fair share of rethinking to do, both this morning and in the past month. What you told me about Hans yesterday... it helped a lot. I only wish I could've talked with this Andeal."

Lungvist slipped his toes behind the chair's legs and turned it with his feet so it'd face the bed. He sat at ease and as his shoulders slumped, it seemed to Henry he'd lost an inch or two in height. Strange how one night had transformed Lungvist. The pensive pock-faced soldier sitting before him now seemed a lot more sympathetic than the arrogant drunk who'd bragged about capturing his friend.

"You *will* free Treysh, won't you?" Henry asked.

Despite his exhaustion, guilt had kept Henry awake through part of the night. His carelessness had shoved Treysh into a dark prison and he imagined the enclosed space—away from her chemicals and unable to concoct another devious plan—must be driving her mad. She'd be happily preparing a firework fest if not for Henry and the man stretching out on a chair in front of him.

"I already told you I would," Lungvist answered.

"Yes, but—"

"I'll do my best."

Henry forced a smile to his lips and nodded. When pitted against the rebels, Lungvist's best had brought great results. Perhaps he'd manage something for Treysh before it was too late.

"Then maybe I can do something about seeing Andeal? Escort me back to our camp. I could use the help. All the supplies ought to be heavy."

He remembered his last never-ending trek back to the hot air balloon, carrying a backpack as heavy as he was, and he had no desire to repeat the experience. If Lungvist came along, he'd be relieved from part of the weight and the soldier would receive more answers. A perfect solution. Except the lieutenant frowned and leaned forward, tense.

"That is…no longer possible," he said. "A report came this morning. Union soldiers tracked down your camp and pursued your friend. He jumped into a ravine. The drop is over a hundred feet. Even with the river at the end…"

Henry's head rang so loudly it drowned out the rest of what Lungvist told him. He half-sat, half-collapsed on the bed, staring straight ahead as he tried to absorb what he heard.

Gone.

Andeal was gone.

He'd chosen to dive into a canyon and crash into the riverbed rather than be captured. And with him was his father's recording, crushed to pieces or destroyed by water.

Henry took a sudden deep breath and shook his head. Perhaps he wasn't. Andeal had made such jumps before, with Maniel. She had told him so. But even if he lived, the recording was gone. All it'd taken was a single zeppelin and their current plan had crumbled like a castle of cards. Henry wasn't very good with back-up plans.

"He can't be dead. We need him."

"I'm sorry. The soldiers' report is flawless. It's him." Lungvist paused, giving Henry time to wrestle with his shock. "President Kurtmann insists that you should remain here, in the Great Whale, where you're safe. We will fly to Reverence."

"I don't have much choice, do I?"

Only Kurtmann's copy of the recording remained. He'd have to agree with the president's deal if he wanted to finish what they'd started. Without it, they had no proof against the Clarins and all they'd sacrificed until now would amount to nothing. Henry closed his eyes. His voice shook as he spoke.

"Tell President Kurtmann that I will stay and...and that I agree to his terms. He will, however, also need to find a functioning transmitter. Say those exact words. He'll understand."

Lungvist nodded, slunk from his chair and to the door. He turned to look at Henry before he left. "I'm sorry for your loss, Mister Schmitt. I'll do my best to reach your other friend in time, I promise. Keep your mind on the radio."

The door clicked behind the soldier and once his footsteps faded away, only the low rumbling of engines remained. Henry fought against his rising panic. This wasn't supposed to happen. First Maniel and Seraphin, then Treysh, and now Andeal...all his companions, taken away. He was alone to face Clarin. He tried to imagine an ally out of Lungvist's pockmarked face, but Vermen's second-in-command had shoved Treysh into a cell. His aid and the President's—however conditional—didn't bring him the warm support he needed.

Henry leaned back on the soft mattress, unable to tell if the concussion or grief caused his sudden nausea. He should have returned yesterday, his exertion be damned.

If Andeal lay at the bottom of a ravine, the rebels' success rested on his shoulders and he might one day need to tell Maniel she would never see her good-hearted husband again, or build a family with him.

The winds had shifted, pushing the drifting balloon of his life into yet another direction. He was heading straight into the raging storm and there was no one left to guide him.

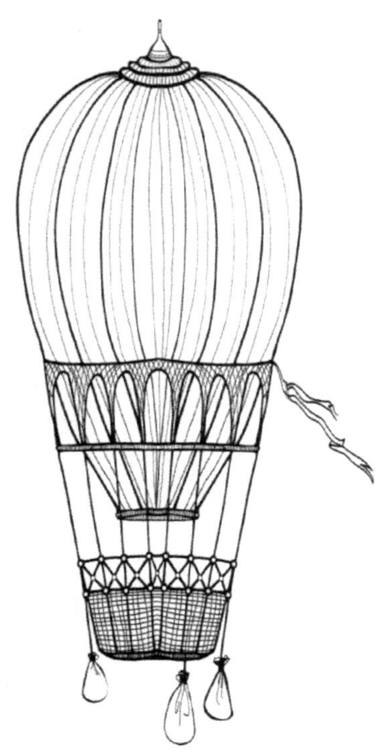

<h1 style="text-align:center">Chapter Thirty-Five</h1>


better about meeting Andeal's parents if they'd had news of his friend in the last two weeks. One day the almost-nightly broadcasts had stopped. No explanations, nothing but dull static to fill the silence. The first night they'd thought nothing of it. The second Maniel had wondered if they'd landed in a populated area and could not take the risk of another lift-off. When the radio silence stretched into an entire week, Jan made the first mistake. "I hope nothing happened to them," he'd said, only to receive a silencing glare from Maniel. "Nothing happened to them," she'd retorted. No one dared to bring up the topic again but they sat around the radio every night, all thinking the same thing, all refusing to voice the obvious.

Something *had* happened.

Perhaps it was just their equipment. They had to trust that was the problem, otherwise their work in the field would amount to nothing. It didn't matter how many gathered in Reverence if the promised radio show never happened, if the recording was never played. So they traveled on, never acknowledging the heavy silence from their receiver, until they reached the great city of Altaer.

Home to several universities and technical colleges all priding themselves on their uniqueness, Altaer was a cluster of varying architectures, mixing campuses and large green areas with skyscraper universities that towered over all other buildings. The overall design gave the impression of unruly chaos—which, when Vermen thought about it, described the city's residents quite well. Altaer's students were well known to put their studies on hold and flood the streets to protest any injustice.

Requesting their help in Reverence seemed a perfectly logical endeavor, so Vermen had expected Seraphin to organize a meeting with one of the student leaders.

When Jan came back to their shoddy hotel room and confirmed he'd managed to contact Andeal's parents at the university's courtball game, Vermen's stomach churned. If the broadcast's absence brought him a mounting sense of dread, how did they take it? The night promised not to be the happy reunion it ought to be.

They slunk through the backyard of a triplex, keeping to the shadows. Jan, the youngest and most anonymous of them, had been charged with hitting the most popular bars and pubs to gauge the city's mood about their broadcasts. He ought to mingle with the students his age easily enough and he would be spared this most awkward conversation. Unlike Maniel, who had grown increasingly nervous as the fateful moment approached. When Seraphin knocked on the back door's window, she took a deep breath. Her black leather boot tapped the cement, filling the silence with an unnerving rhythm until a tall man opened the door and welcomed them in.

Andeal's father—and who else could it be, with that exact same shade of straw-blond hair?—hurried the group inside and closed the door behind. He led them toward the kitchen and started talking right away.

"Sofia will be here in a moment. She may have broken the radio receiver throwing it against the wall yesterday, so she's in the basement, fixing it in her atelier. I'm Adrian."

Vermen's eyebrows shot up at the explanation. He slid into a chair without a word while Maniel tried to suppress an uneasy chuckle. Seraphin extended a hand to shake Adrian's.

"Seraphin Holt. This is Captain Hans Vermen and—"

"Just Hans Vermen, please. I'm not really a captain anymore."

He used to love the sound of the title before his name, but somehow when it came out of Seraphin's mouth it sounded all kinds of wrong. Vermen no longer belonged to the army. He could not claim to be one of them and despite a lifetime as a soldier, he did not want to anymore.

Seraphin studied him a brief moment, nodded. "And this is Maniel. She's..."

He didn't finish, instead turning to Maniel. She'd set her palms on the table and stared straight at Andeal's father with a proud and determined expression. "I'm his wife. We were both arrested in the same protest and met in Galen's labs."

Adrian studied her for what seemed the longest time, then his face split into an easy grin. The resemblance with Andeal's was striking: exact same smile, extra wrinkles. He strode to her and wrapped her in a tight hug. Maniel's eyes widened a moment. She laughed.

"I should've known Andeal's family would be big on displays of affection."

His father stepped back with a chuckle of his own. "That might be mostly me. Anyone want muffins? I've been baking. *A lot.*" He ran a hand through his hair, then grabbed a plate with several muffins and cookies and set it on the table. "Stress does that to me."

No one moved. They had traveled miles to get here, to speak with Andeal's parents, yet none of them expected the warm hospitality and Adrian's half-shy nervousness. It was too normal. As if Andeal was here with them, sitting in silent apprehension, waiting to see if the two chunks of his family could become one. Except he wasn't. Worse, his voice was not here either, drifting out of the receiver, a reminder that he still lived, somewhere. Vermen couldn't take a muffin. It would be a lie.

Andeal's father cleared his throat, dispelling the uneasy immobility. "Go ahead," he insisted, and Seraphin extended his hand with a guilty look, grabbing one of the small muffins. He'd started removing the paper cup when they heard running footsteps climbing a flight of stairs.

Sofia burst into the room with a repaired radio receiver in hand. A lot smaller than her husband, she had rich, tawny brown skin, Andeal's bright blue eyes, and a black braid so long it brushed against her ankles. She slammed the radio on the table, rattling the plate of muffins, and offered her hand to Maniel first, before she even looked at Seraphin.

"You have to be his wife."

Maniel frowned a little. "Have to?"

"Why, yes, it's the only thing that makes sense. Our son is part of a rebellion and its leader sits right there, about to eat one of my husband's prized muffins, yet Adrian keeps looking back at you instead of studying the

White Renegade's reaction to his food."

A light blush reddened Adrian's cheeks and he averted his gaze with a smile.

"I can eat one if it helps focus your attention on a single person."

Maniel picked up a muffin. She seemed so at ease, like she'd known them for years. They both laughed and while neither agreed to her proposal, Maniel started peeling her muffin cup. Sofia turned to Seraphin, her mirth vanishing. She squared her shoulders, an attitude Vermen had often seen in soldiers gathering the courage to begin a hard task.

"We are grateful you chose to visit us." She pressed her lips together and her tone hardened. "Although to be honest, we would have loved to receive news six years earlier."

Seraphin was about to eat a bite of muffin but stopped and set it down. "The risks—"

"I don't care about the risks." She leaned forward and set her palms on the table. "He's our son. He vanished. Those who say ignorance is bliss have never stood in my shoes."

"I cared about the risks. We took as few as possible to keep our headquarters secret."

"That sure worked out," Sofia mumbled.

Adrian put a hand on hers and squeezed. Vermen could see his own struggle to remain calm in the tensed shoulders and grim smile. Hans had fought with his stress in the last two weeks, anger and worry growing with every new day of static. How horrible would it be to endure this for so many years? And Andeal was a friend, not his son.

"Sofia..." Maniel's voice was subdued, devoid of her usual firmness. Vermen frowned and studied her expression. He did not remember such discreet vulnerability from her. "I have said nothing to my father, either. I am sure he and my siblings are worried to death, that hearing I lived for a time but might've died under Mount Kairn is killing them every day, but nothing—*nothing*—is worth the risk of returning to those labs. Andeal and I have talked about it and we both agreed: if we could not put Galen behind bars, if we could not ensure that we and those we love were safe, we would keep to ourselves." She rubbed the muffin's paper cup between her fingers but held Sofia's gaze, unflinching. "I wish he was here today."

"So do I." Sofia's hand went to the receiver. She licked her lips, shook her head. "Do you know what happened? Why he stopped?"

The three of them shook their heads at once. Seraphin leaned back in his chair. "We know little more than you do, in truth. We know how he travels and we know he is with Henry Schmitt, but that covers it. We don't know where he is or why there are no more broadcasts."

"His equipment might be broken," Vermen said.

Sofia scoffed at the thought. "Andeal could repair it in a snap." She did snap her fingers, close to his nose. "He learned from the best."

"Is that supposed to be you?" Adrian asked. "He never did take any of your classes."

"The best classes are not those with an official university stamp on them." Sofia set a hand on her hip and poked her husband's nose with her finger. "You know that, Mister Self-Taught Professional."

Before Adrian could come up with a retort, the radio gave a short screech, far lower in pitch than usual. They all turned to the table and stared at the tiny machine, breathless. Vermen's hands tightened on his armchair and he leaned forward. Someone cleared his throat on the other side, then they heard a hesitant "Hello?"

Henry Schmitt.

Vermen felt like a hot iron had been shoved through his stomach. He didn't want to hear Schmitt. Why would Henry be the one talking? Hans' gaze flitted to the others. Maniel had crushed the muffin in her hand and Seraphin managed to maintain a neutral expression, but Sofia didn't bother to hide her disappointment. She tapped on the table with her index finger as Adrian moved closer and wrapped an arm around her back.

"Good evening, and hum...welcome back to *The Noodle Show*."

He sounded so nervous and pathetic, barely audible above the immense amount of static this broadcast had. Vermen hoped he had an explanation for this, that he might tell them what had happened. He also feared Schmitt would do just that.

"First, well, I apologize for the literal radio silence. And I'm sorry we are changing radio hosts for the next month or so. Andeal was much better but, well, I'm afraid he can't anymore. So it'll be me."

"*Can't?*" Sofia repeated and as Henry started talking about the initial plan for Union's Day, she grabbed the radio. "Tell me why, damn it! I need to know what happened to him."

She slammed the receiver on the table and let out a cry of rage as Henry continued. Schmitt's voice didn't have the captivating rhythm Andeal had developed and he brought up nothing new, reminding them about Union's Day and how despite the host change, they should still be there. Vermen stopped listening. Henry's unwillingness to explain Andeal's absence was more alarming than anything he could've said. Did Schmitt even know? Perhaps they'd been separated.

"He won't tell or he can't tell," Vermen said. "Turn it off."

Sofia obeyed, in her own way. She shoved the radio off the table and the broadcast fizzled out as it crashed to the ground. An uneasy silence stretched on after her outburst, until she sighed and slumped into a chair.

"I apologize. The last two weeks have worn my patience down." She pulled her braid up and settled it on her legs to keep it off the floor, then turned to Seraphin. "Reverence is a long way from here, but we will be there. You should contact the local student leaders. They are already hard at work mobilizing everyone and will make essential allies if you intend to have an organized protest in the city."

"We've tried," Seraphin said. "No luck finding who to contact so far but trust me, I am not leaving Altaer without speaking to them. We'll need folks who know their business on the ground on Union's Day."

A large grin spread on Sofia's face. "Oh, I have names for you, my friend. Lots of them." She slid out of her chair, walked to the fridge and stretched up, barely reaching the notepad and pen on top of it. She scribbled the names without hesitation, tore the paper off, and handed it to the Regarian. "These are the usual suspects in Altaer's protests. They'll be thrilled to hear from you."

Seraphin gave the list a glance and answered with his unique, tight-lipped smile. He folded it, stored the paper in a pocket, and stood. "Thank you, madam. You're a lifesaver."

"If you could be the same to my son, that would be fantastic."

Maniel took a deep breath and straightened up, too. She walked around the table without a word, her dark fingers trailing on the pale wooden table, then stopped in front of Sofia and put a hand on the smaller woman's shoulder. "He'll be okay. He's never careful, but he always makes it out." She pulled Sofia into a tight embrace and they held each other for a long moment.

Vermen stood as Maniel stepped back. Something in Maniel's

determined refusal to accept his death made him crave human contact. His hand brushed against Seraphin's and he withdrew it right away, clenching his teeth. The rebel leader cast him a glance but did not comment, to Vermen's relief. He cleared his throat.

"We should go," he said. "Because we never found them does not mean there are no Union soldiers surveying this house. We shouldn't stay longer than necessary."

Adrian nodded but picked up a plate of muffins and shoved several in a small box. He handed it to Maniel with a proud smile. "A little help on your travel. We look forward to meeting you again."

Maniel accepted the gift and as they exchanged pleasantries, Vermen stalked to the back door. He glanced out and opened it in a deliberate push, half-convinced he would catch a glimpse of movement, hear a bang and feel a bullet bite his skin. Nothing happened. He took a deep breath, slipped out. He wished they'd had enough spare guns to give him one. Hans felt naked, useless. He searched the perimeter and when he returned to the door, the others were ready to leave.

"All clear," he said. "Let's see if Jan has heard of any of those names."

Vermen hoped he did. Having a mass of confused and directionless people concentrated in Reverence would cause nothing but useless chaos. With a few experienced leaders they could channel the righteous fury somewhere useful, even if it only meant a big show of popular anger. With Andeal gone, Vermen revised his hopes for Union's Day. He didn't trust Schmitt to see things through, not to the same extent.

The Noodle Man was all they had left, however. Hans Vermen hoped he would be up to the task.

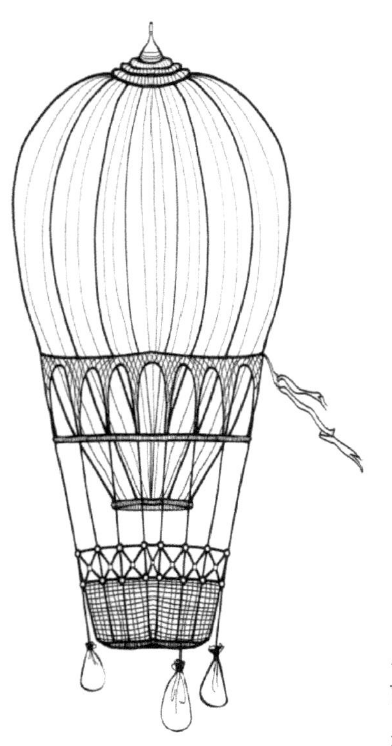

# CHAPTER THIRTY-SIX

*After a month, the constant* buzzing of the Great Whale's engines no longer bothered Henry. He'd grown used to the new flying experience: hanging thousands of feet above ground without ever seeing the sky or feeling the wind on your cheeks, trapped in a floating tin can. A huge, village-like one, but a tin can nonetheless. The president's zeppelin had its own bakery, general store, and tavern, all catering to the soldiers and engineers aboard. They could spend months without touching ground and be none the worse for it. Henry wished he was allowed to visit and take his mind off Andeal's absence, but a stranger would be spotted right away and might stir trouble. Instead he paced around his minuscule room and concentrated on the broadcasts.

He hated broadcasting. The voice they had come to trust was gone forever and all they had left was his pathetic attempts at reassurance. How did you convince thousands not to worry when your insides squirmed with fear? He knew he was bad, knew he was losing them with every passing evening, but what else could he do? He had to try to get them to Reverence on Union's Day or they had lost. Henry rubbed his temples and grabbed the microphone, ready to go again.

Two sharp knocks interrupted. He hurried to the door and pulled it open. Perhaps it'd be good news for once. Lungvist might've managed to free Treysh or Seraphin could've pulled off an epic, newsworthy scheme. But only President Kurtmann stood at the door, his shoulders hunched and his lips sealed in a grim line. He held a clean beige uniform and offered it to Henry.

"Put these on."

Henry's anger flared back to life. He was no dog you ordered about, and he refused to follow around blindly. He'd done enough of that for a lifetime.

"What's going on?"

His harsh tone caught the president by surprise. His eyes widened and he took a moment to compose himself. "There's a place I would like to show you," he said, "and I thought you'd appreciate the fresh air."

The mention of an excursion outside went a long way in convincing Henry to obey. The Great Whale reminded him of his time under Mount Kairn and being trapped inside was wearing down his nerves. He snapped the uniform down and imagined himself in it. What an awkward sight he would make. Nothing like the confident strength the same clothes had granted Vermen—although the door-kicking might've helped in making such a strong impression on him.

"Very well," he said. "Wait outside."

Henry changed quickly after the president left and joined him in the corridor. They walked in an awkward silence he had no intention of breaking. Let Kurtmann stew in his unease. It seemed a small irritant compared to those he and others had endured.

As they progressed the rumbling of engines diminished and they sometimes encountered other soldiers. Kurtmann nodded at them and Henry did his best to straighten his back and look like he belonged. He tried not to pull on the too-long sleeves or blush when someone's gaze lingered on him, but every little fault in his dress-up seemed a glaring mistake to him. No one questioned them, however, and fifteen minutes later they reached a small wooden door. The president pulled it open.

A strong gust blasted in, slamming into Henry, pushing him two steps back and stealing his soldier's beret. His heart soared and he hurried outside to receive the gale's full force. Dark clouds hung in the sky, heralding a storm, but no rain fell yet. Only the wind ruled the landscape below.

A familiar landscape, Henry realized as his gaze scanned the ground below. His heart sunk and he gripped their small platform's railing tight.

Mount Kairn lay at his feet, broken. The bombs had reduced the proud mountain to a hill half its original size and an entire section of its slope had been wrecked by the bombs. Enormous rocks had crashed into the forest below and toppled centuries-old trees. The ridge from which the waterfall jumped was no more and the water ran down the mountainside in three smaller rivers that disappeared among the trees without pooling together. The deep lake into which Andeal and Maniel had dived no longer existed, but an ugly hole remained behind.

Henry shivered and tore his gaze away. On a brighter day he could've seen Ferrea, behind Mount Kairn. He'd lived in this area his entire life, the mountain always towering over them, providing their livelihood. Not anymore. The Races' trail would be destroyed by rockslides, unusable. How could the event ever return now? Ferrea's last hope lay buried under the boulders.

Unless he traced a new path and cleared it. If he wanted a home to return to, Henry would have to rebuild it piece by piece. No more waiting for official communication from the government. Not anymore. He could do it himself and this time, they would be hearing from him.

Provided he survived to come back, of course.

The president waited by his side, studying the desolation below with evident sorrow. Henry wondered how much Mount Kairn meant to him. Jacob Kurtmann had won the Races three times in his youth. Nostalgia hunched his shoulders but the president stared at the demolished mountain, unflinching.

"Why show me this?" Henry asked.

"The racing trail took a sharp turn at the middle of a steep descent there." He pointed to a specific spot of the mountain flank, but Henry already knew which he was speaking of. The turn was legendary for its danger and racers had died in the past, slipping off it and tumbling down. "That is where I met Lenz Schmitt."

"My father always said running was senseless and dangerous."

"Did he now?" The thought seemed to amuse President Kurtmann. "Then we were both senseless young men. He's the one who broke my winning streak the third year."

"Broke?"

"He won, Henry."

"What?"

Impossible. If Lenz Schmitt had won the Annual Mount Kairn Races, he'd know. Die-hard fans had visited every year and bought figurines from his father's gift shop. One of them would've recognized the vendor, said something.

"Did he never tell you? History forgets I ran five times, not three. I ended second one year and never finished another. But it sounds better to say I won thrice, I guess, than to remind everyone of how fallible I am."

"That's what's on the figurine: triple champion. Tell me."

All these years, Henry thought of his father as a deserter with no history but his obsession for balloons. Andeal and Maniel had painted a different picture. Their Lenz Schmitt had a strong morale and the courage to act upon it—the kind of role model every kid should have. Nothing like the man broken by his wife's illness and barricaded in silence, the one Henry had known. And now it seemed Lenz Schmitt had competed in the Races he earned a living from and *won*.

"When he won the first time I hated him. I couldn't accept being beaten by an upstart nobody had heard about, not after two consecutive wins. He'd come out of nowhere and stolen my title and that didn't sit well with me. So when the next year came, I sprinted ahead and ran too fast. I exhausted myself to put as much distance between us as I could, but when I reached this turn...I stepped on a loose rock and fell. I snapped my leg at the bottom, couldn't move, and I was bleeding. Profusely. He stopped for me. He abandoned his first place to climb down the drop and help me. Neither of us won that year." The president leaned on the railing and shook his head. "I learned later that he'd paid his university tuition with his winning prize the first year. I had my family pay for the following years. We've always had more than enough money anyway, and I owed him."

Henry frowned. His father had never finished his major. Kinsi had told him he'd settled in Ferrea with his mom when they were very young and he was already on the way. Somehow, Lenz Schmitt had found the money to buy the decrepit tourist shop *and* a hot air balloon. Henry suspected he knew where from now. For an old friend of his, the president sure didn't know a lot about his father.

Kurtmann turned away from the mountain. The wind threw his short hair about, sometimes obscuring his intense green gaze.

"Money meant little to me. It was easy to give away. You were right the other day. When things became hard, I failed those who depended on me. I didn't have that courage, refused to risk anything for others. The time has come for me to pay my debt."

"Wh-what are you saying?"

Henry's knuckles whitened as his grip tightened on the railing. The president's eyes had a feverish gleam to them. He straightened and his lips curled into a determined smile. For the first time since he'd stepped on the zeppelin, Henry saw the confident and determined man who had subjugated so many. With the Great Whale's gray shape looming behind and the world stretching out at their feet, President Jacob Kurtmann seemed ready to conquer the world.

"On Union's Day," he said, "we will stride into the National Radio Tower and I will tell the world the whole ugly truth."

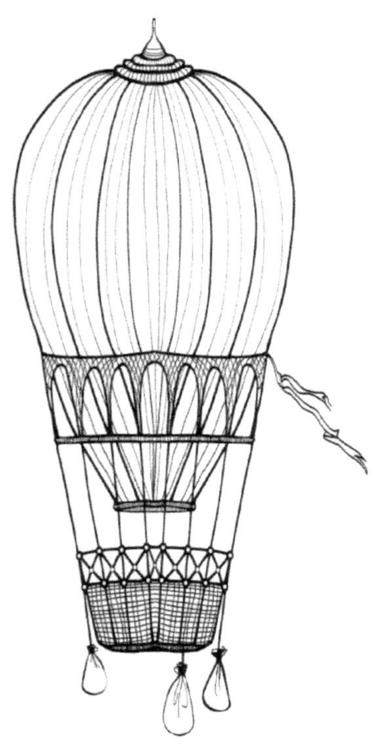

# CHAPTER THIRTY-SEVEN

*The long months of traveling* with Seraphin had taught Vermen to read the Regarian's moods better than anyone else. It was strange how well he knew the White Renegade now, how much he could read into a single grimace, a distant look or a smile. The knowledge had come by itself, from countless hours spent by his side, walking or sitting around a campfire, discussing the day's events or plans for the future. Seraphin's shoulders would tense before they met a new rebel, then ease as they were welcomed in. He would frown whenever his gaze fell upon the radio receiver, no doubts worried about Andeal. Hans would touch his shoulder, then, to draw him out of the dark thoughts. Seraphin would reward him with the strangest of smiles, sweet and ironic. Like there was a joke only the Regarian understood.

Perhaps the joke was the flutter in Hans' stomach and how at peace he felt around his sworn enemy. Vermen preferred not to think about it, not to ruin the delicate balance of their relationship.

Their productive meetings with Altaer's student leaders had put Seraphin in an excellent mood, yet in the last two weeks he'd grown more withdrawn, harder to decipher. Something other than the broadcasts was clogging his mind. When he'd awakened Hans at dawn and asked him to follow, Vermen hadn't hesitated. He could hear the hushed anticipation in his friend's voice and a strange, tentative stress.

Seraphin led him alongside a sandy road, to the top of a steep ridge. The slope plunged into a thick conifer forest and its tall trees almost hid the clump of roofs farther away, in an artificial clearing. A lot of Regaria's villages were like this: small settlements scattered across the countryside, deep in forests or nestled near protective cliffs, with almost no farming lands around. Seraphin stared at this particular town, his lips pressed together. Birds sang in the distance, the only sound filling the two men's silence.

Then Seraphin heaved a long sigh and broke it. "Do you know where we are?"

"No." Vermen had little knowledge of Regarian geography and all the forests they'd traversed had lost him. "Am I supposed to remember every backwater town in Regaria?"

"This is Iswood."

Iswood. Seraphin's hometown. The hamlet that had seen Hans' brother die. He tensed, scanned his surroundings as though he could find the splatter of blood and brain. He imagined a large tent, farther behind them in the field, with Seraphin in the entrance, pistol raised. In his mind the entire fabric was red, dripping with blood.

"Why am I here?"

His voice was rough. He didn't dare turn to Seraphin. Vermen wiped his hands on his pants. What kind of game was he playing? Did he find the reminder amusing?

"I'm not sure," Seraphin said. "I needed to come back. With you."

Vermen did look at him this time. There was a strange inflection in the 'you' that brought heat to his cheeks. He hated it. He thought he'd grown used to the rebel, that he could ignore the spinning in his head, the way his heart slammed, the conflicting thoughts about him. It had taken two words with just the right tone to bring it all back.

"With me?"

"Sometimes I wonder…If there wasn't so much bad blood between us, would you kiss me again?"

Hans froze. No, no, no. They didn't need to make a big deal out of it. Those were Seraphin's words. He'd convinced Hans to let it go, to both accept and ignore it at once. Why must he bring it back now? Vermen spun on his heels to face the White Renegade and stepped back. "Do you even listen to yourself? 'Hi Vermen, this is where I shot your brother, please kiss me again?' What am I supposed to say to that?"

"Yes?"

Seraphin's eyes widened even as he answered, as though he couldn't believe the word had just crossed his lips. Vermen stared. *He* sure couldn't. The cheeky bastard stood there, breathless, wide eyes studying his reaction. Scared. More terrified now than with a gun held to his forehead by a sworn enemy. Vermen's anger died before he retorted, whisked away by the realization Seraphin had never been more vulnerable. His throat tightened, his stomach lurched. Vermen raised a shaky hand, traced Seraphin's chin with his thumb. When had he stepped so close? He snapped his fingers away with a scowl.

"I can't." He turned back toward Iswood. What was he thinking? Kissing his brother's murderer? He had more honor than that. "This isn't right."

Seraphin cast his gaze down. "Maybe not."

"It's not. You killed him. It doesn't matter if he was a cruel man, if you had good reasons. He was my brother and you shot him. I can't do this to his memory." Vermen took a deep breath to calm the shake in his voice. "You of all people should understand."

Seraphin's white fingers wrapped around his *skeptar's* handle and he closed his eyes. "I do, in a strange way. I can't tell if this makes me wish I'd never shot him or if it makes me want to put a second bullet in his forehead." A bitter laugh escaped his lips. "I can't seem to make up my mind about anything. Join the Union Army to help it bring Regaria under the Union's fold, try to dismantle said Union later. Fight with my father, risk everything to avenge him. Shoot one brother, fall in love with the other."

Seraphin's voice trailed off. Vermen stared ahead, wishing he hadn't said that, wondering if he could pretend not to have heard. They weren't supposed to make a big deal out of it! Yet here they were.

"I can't," he repeated. "I can't be that for you."

"No, it's okay. I shouldn't have said anything. We have more important matters to think of."

The Regarian's shoulders slumped and, like Vermen, he set his gaze on the half-hidden town in the middle of the wood. It had all started here for them. It was strange to think that had Seraphin not put that bullet through his brother's skull, he would be chasing down rebels or participating in the skirmish along Burgia's borders, not doing his best to throw down an illegitimate government. He put his hand on Seraphin's shoulder and turned his way.

"I'm not going anywhere, though," he said. "We can see this through. I'll be by your side until the end."

Seraphin nodded in a small and repetitive movement and as he did his smile returned, determined. He was working himself into a better mood, but to Vermen it seemed forced.

"Perfect! After all, where would we be without the great Captain Hans Vermen?"

Dead, Vermen thought. He kept the comment to himself, however, and followed in silence as Seraphin headed down the slope toward Iswood. They were supposed to leave in an hour, but he suspected the Regarian wanted to pay respect to his family before they continued on the road.

Perhaps Vermen would, too, even if his brother hardly seemed deserving of the honor any longer.

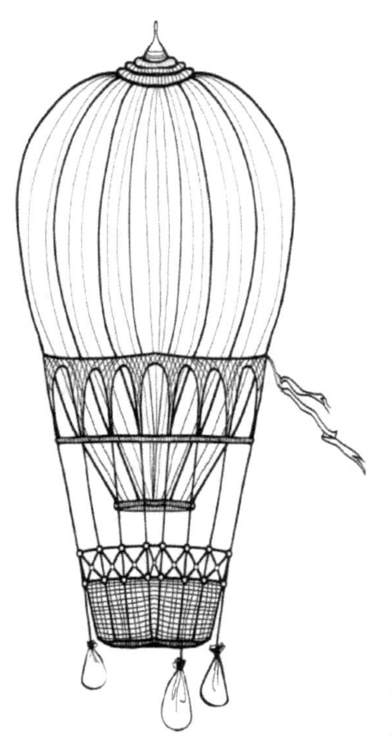

# Chapter Thirty-eight


thousands of campfires dancing on the plains surrounding Reverence, wondering if it would be enough to make a difference. He had never expected so many to travel the long road to the capital, could not imagine what they would look like in the morning, marching across the city. Perhaps their passage through Threstle should have tipped him off. The small village, a day's walk from the capital, was where Galen had started the virus. It used to be a bustling town on the highway from Reverence to Regaria, but the Plague had wiped out more than half its population. The place had a bad reputation now, condemned by superstitious and religious folks alike as being cursed. Not a lot of people lived there anymore. It had become more of a road stop on the way to Regaria than an actual city.

When they had arrived, however, the town wasn't just tranquil. It was deserted. Almost no one had remained in Threstle. They were all down there, among the campfires, ready to join the protest. No wonder. For the last decade they had thought their home cursed, the tragic start of a terrible plague. Now someone told them their troubles weren't due to fate. Galen Clarin had chosen their town to be the starting point of his terrible sickness. They had every right to be angry. Very few had decided to stay behind and it seemed the same could be said for many folks across the Union territory.

The radio screeched again and Vermen gave it a somewhat disgusted glance. Listening to Schmitt was painful and awkward. He missed Andeal's smooth voice, reassuring and dynamic. How many more fires would there be tonight, had his friend still be the show's host? But they still listened, just in case.

"Good evening, listeners, and welcome back!"

At least his greeting had gotten more confident. Henry had kept broadcasting on a regular basis. He had to know he wasn't good at it, but he'd tried. Hans had to give him that, at least.

"I won't be long tonight. First, well, I wanted to tell you to watch for another wavelength tomorrow. I'm done with this static, and we'll be switching things up for our special Union's Day broadcast."

Vermen wondered what he could mean by that. He could almost feel the field of small fires hold its breath for more information, but Henry changed topic.

"The big day's finally here. It's been, hum, great to have you with us on *The Noodle Show*. And I realized we'd never explained the name to you guys. Andeal named it, in truth. And part of it is a joke on me, but there's more than that. When I asked him, he told me Galen's news were a lot like my instant noodles. They're easy and cheap, and sometimes it's all you can afford. But there's not that much to them, you know? They're not a healthy diet. You don't know me, but I *love* my noodles. Spent eight years living on them. So when I say that Galen's news—his lies—they're like that, I mean it. They are not healthy for us. And tomorrow? Tomorrow it's time to change our diet."

Henry had said it with a surprising amount of conviction. He'd hit his stride all of a sudden, his voice firmer than it'd been before. Vermen turned to the radio with a curious expression.

"It's time. No more...no more noodling around! It's okay to have eaten it all up until now. I did too. We all did. Not anymore, though. I hope I'll see you all tomorrow in the streets, and don't forget to change your wavelength!"

Vermen had laughed at his noodle expression. There had been a hint of silly pride in Schmitt's voice he found amusing. As the characteristic screech of a finished broadcast emerged from his receiver, Vermen returned his attention to the large crowd.

A white figure gestured at him from down the slope and Hans smiled as he recognized Seraphin. He had gone to search for friendly faces in the crowd, saying that if he could find the largest gambling table, he could at least find Joshua. He'd wanted to discuss their plan for Union's Day.

"Any luck?" Vermen asked as Seraphin reached the top of the hill.

Seraphin shook his head. "We'll have to do without them. The crowd is too large."

The Regarian turned around to scan the assembled citizens and took a deep breath. He pressed his lips together, his shoulders tense. Worried, Vermen guessed. He ought to be more nervous too, but something about the constellation of fires below calmed Hans' nerves.

"How was the mood?" he asked.

"Grim. Expectant. Angry."

Vermen didn't know whether it meant good news or not. Anger meant they believed their story, but it could make such a massive gathering wild.

"You missed a broadcast from Henry," Vermen said.

"No, I heard. Everybody down there has a receiver. They must not have wanted to miss anything. What do you think he meant?"

"With his change in wavelengths?" He had thought about it for a while. It made no sense for him to change how he broadcasted unless he thought he wouldn't be heard otherwise. Although, Henry's voice *had* been more distant and he'd struggled with static throughout the last month. Whatever had happened when Andeal disappeared, Schmitt had been forced to change his radio equipment to something worse than their original setup. "I would say we should keep an ear out for the National Radio's wavelength."

Seraphin's concerned expression deepened into a frown. "He can't sneak in there in the middle of the day."

"I know, but...what else?" Vermen shrugged. "And if he planned on sneaking in, he wouldn't want to give advance warning."

They allowed for a silence to settle between them, both staring at the campfires. Vermen couldn't help but wonder what went through his companion's mind. What did he hope for? That by the end of the day the Clarin twins would be in prison? Dead? And what of the rebels? What would Seraphin Holt's ragtag band of idealist criminals become after Union's Day? If they succeeded they would have no purpose. Not unlike him.

"This is it, I guess," he said. "End of the line."

Seraphin's mocking laughter carried through the clear night. "Tomorrow isn't the end, Hans. It might even be another beginning. And remember, you promised to stay."

"That's not what I meant. I—"

"I know." Seraphin put his hand on Vermen's shoulder and smiled. "You leave whenever you want." The hand slid down his arm until Seraphin slid his fingers between Vermen's. "I just hope you'll stay around."

Hans didn't retract his hand. Perhaps he should, but it felt good to know they would be together on the morrow, that no matter what would happen, they would have each other's back. So instead he squeezed Seraphin's more delicate hand and let a peaceful silence stretch on. Laughter drifted from the gathered crowd below and the wind carried the prickling scent of smoke to them. Vermen eventually turned to his companion.

"What will you do? After."

Seraphin's eyes hardened. "Dismantle the Clarins' network of friends. They cannot have acted alone. We'll need someone wilful and incorruptible in charge to help clean the Union up. And then...I might return to Regaria. It was never meant to be part of this Union."

Hans couldn't help but smile. No vacations for Seraphin, no matter what. A man like Seraphin didn't sit still when he could see something in the world that needed to be fixed. And there would always be something wrong.

"I'll be there," Vermen said. "You can count on me."

"I know."

Seraphin leaned ever so slightly upon him. Hans smiled. He wasn't ready to kiss him again, not yet, but he knew he would be one day. Every time he thought of leaving Seraphin, of no longer spending days walking by his side, a pit formed at the bottom of his stomach. He no longer tried to fight it. He had spent six years chasing a man to honor his brother's memory. That was enough, he decided. He had his own life to pursue now. Starting in two days.

"It's strange to think that after all this time, our fate rests in the hands of Henry Schmitt," Seraphin said. "The poor man would barely look at me the first night."

Vermen tried to counter the words but his stomach clenched as he realized he couldn't. The Regarian was right. It all hinged on a single, noodle-obsessed man.

"We're doomed."

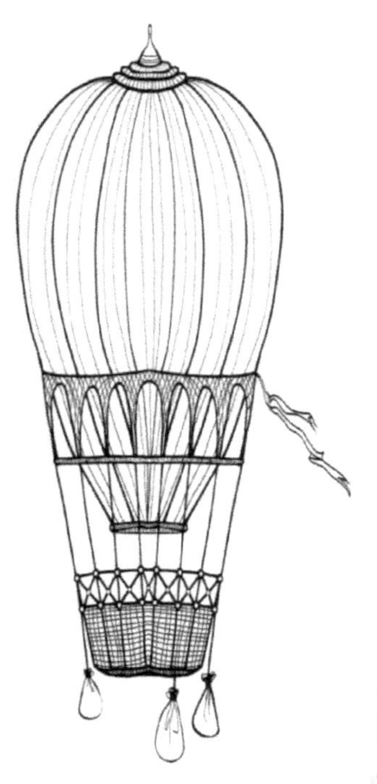

# CHAPTER THIRTY-NINE

*Hundreds of thousands streamed* into the city throughout the morning. The grim expectation from the previous evening had vanished. Strangers chatted with one another, sharing tales of their travels, trying to guess what the rebels had planned for this day. The lines of soldiers bordering the streets did not douse their good mood: they were so many, how could authorities dare do anything? Somewhere along the night, this had morphed from a chase after a handful of rebels to a mass protest.

Vermen, Seraphin, and Maniel had wormed their way into the great convoy. They'd thought to move unnoticed through the crowd but that illusion was soon crushed. Every now and then someone would spot Seraphin and come up to thank him, or wish him luck, or explain why they'd come or how they'd heard of him. Holt squirmed every time he heard his name. He answered in crisp, short sentences and forced himself to smile. His discomfort surprised Vermen. Hadn't he set himself up to be the figurehead of this movement? But when he thought about it, Seraphin had never been a crowd person. He worked with brilliant efficiency in the background. Vermen wished the others would stop coming. Not only did it make Seraphin uneasy, but it was dangerous. They did not want the entire squad of soldiers to know where to shoot first.

The soldiers lined up and stared in dour silence, a hand already on their batons. They'd equipped themselves with shields and protective helmets. Every tenth soldier carried a gun for gas bombs and sound grenades. Good. They'd prepared for crowd control, not mass shootings—or at least, the men they were allowed to see had. Vermen expected the fully-geared troops to lay in wait, ready to close the trap. The corridor defined by rows of soldiers might be leading them straight into it.

He hoped the students from Altaer knew what they were doing but doubted they'd dealt with anything of this scale. They'd brought megaphones, all wore bright green shirts, and they chatted with each other through tiny radios. Unlike the cheerful protesters, they often exchanged worried glances, convened for quick discussions in a low tone, or stared at the armed policemen on the sidewalks.

They must sense it too, Vermen thought. Despite its apparent good mood, tension ran high in the crowd—a fire waiting to be lit.

Chances were, Schmitt's next broadcasting would be the match.

Henry's soldier uniform burned his skin, a big lie waiting to be discovered. He could not believe no one had called his bluff, that apart from a single question by a guard outside the National Radio, no one had intercepted

President Kurtmann and him as they made their way to the top floor. The tower no longer scared Henry, despite being as empty on this holiday as during their nighttime visit. Perhaps it was the daylight filtering through the windows. Perhaps it was the president striding at his side with grim confidence.

Perhaps it was the spirit-lifting view from the great bay windows on the sixth floor, stealing Henry's breath and washing away his fear.

Thousands had invaded the city below, tiny ants crawling in an endless line. The procession snaked through Treysh's neighborhood, wrapped around the mountainside, and made its way toward the police headquarters. Its sheer length boggled his mind. Henry wondered if he knew anyone in there. Had Seraphin and Vermen made it in time? Were Maniel or Joshua or any other rebels still alive and marching with the protesters? Did Kinsi and Tia decide to take a more active role and step out of their home to join the fray?

As Henry thought of his foster father, of how he'd distanced himself from the broadcast months ago, his amazement at the protest crumbled. True, the line was long, but it was narrow and stretched. Thousands marched below. But tens of thousands—perhaps even hundreds of thousands—had gathered in the plains. He had seen the campfires from the Great Whale. This wasn't everyone. It was a fraction of those who'd traveled to Reverence. Henry's hope-spurred confidence turned to a bitter taste in his mouth.

"Where is everyone?"

"In the plains," Kurtmann said. "They came to witness, not participate. Come."

The president hurried down the corridor, but Henry watched the slow crawl a bit longer. They'd walked so far to be in Reverence on Union's Day.

Why would they stay away? Why would they *not* join the others in the protest? He didn't want them to take up arms and fight. Walking alongside everyone would be more than enough! Was that so much to ask? Henry tore himself from the infuriating view and joined Kurtmann in the main recording room. The president was examining the electronics with a frown.

"You're here. Good. Set this up so I can broadcast from inside?"

Henry stared at the jumble of wires going around the machinery. Military music was playing again, exactly like their first night. What had Andeal done to fix it? Henry licked his lips, wiped his forehead. He'd been so panicked, he hadn't paid any attention. He was too busy listening for footsteps or alarms while the competent members of his group had worked. But where were they now? Dead. Captured. Nowhere near to help.

"Well?" Kurtmann pressed him.

Henry lifted his hand, let it hover near a beige cable. Was that the one he'd moved? He hesitated, peered at the symbols on the machine for a clue, was sorely disappointed. Why did they make these things so complicated? Perhaps if his heart slowed, his mind wouldn't spin so fast and he could remember. He snapped his eyes shut, pictured that night. A clock had ticked, three minutes past midnight. Andeal had told them...

"Pull the red cable."

Andeal's voice was so clear, it might as well be real. No, wait. Henry frowned. The voice was just behind him, and it sounded like it was in pain. Nothing like the tense but excited tone Andeal had that first night. His breath caught in his throat. Henry spun on his heels, his heart hammering inside his chest, and he peeked through his eyelids, half afraid to have imagined it all.

His clearly-not-dead friend leaned on the doorway, holding his side with one hand and Lenz Schmitt's original recording in the other. A barely healed gash cut through his blond hair, above his left ear, and every breath seemed to pain him, but Andeal managed a crisp smile and shook the disc.

"Let's get this show going, shall we?"

The streets' enthusiastic atmosphere vanished when thousands of portable radios screeched in unison, the now-familiar-yet-still-painful sound announcing a final broadcast. Conversations died, breaths were held. They huddled around the nearest receiver, moist palms and speeding hearts. Vermen exchanged a long, worried look with Seraphin. Whatever Schmitt had in mind, it started now. Hans hoped the man would have more presence than in his previous broadcast.

"Good morning, ladies and gentlemen, and welcome to this special Union's Day broadcast!"

Andeal's cheerful tone sent a wave of shock through the crowd. They gasped and whispered, excited. Maniel bit down on her index finger, holding back a squeal or a sob, Vermen wasn't quite sure. He had an urge to laugh he could barely control. Andeal's deep voice brushed away so many of his doubts.

"Before we start, we have a request for you today. It's a bit of a full-loop thing for the listeners of our very first broadcast, you'll see. In order to have the greatest audience and the best quality broadcast we can, we're going to borrow the National Radio's wavelength again. So please, tune your receiver back there, and we'll see you in a tick!"

The radio's owner rushed to his homemade receiver and changed the wavelength. Maniel glanced about and wiped her eyes when she thought most weren't looking. As Vermen's surge of relief calmed down, however, he grew more uneasy. Something about Andeal's voice bothered him. It sounded weaker than usual. Judging from Seraphin's concerned frown, Hans wasn't the only one to have noticed. Whatever had kept their friend off the air this last month still affected him. The background noise on the radio died, killing the crowd's whispered conversations with it.

"Is everyone back?" Andeal asked. "Sure hope you are because our busy schedule isn't waiting for anyone. So, it's a special day. We had a special request. And now we have a very special guest. Someone at the heart of this story who'd like to share his...contribution to it, I guess."

Vermen caught Seraphin's gaze, but the Regarian looked just as confused as he was. Around them, suggestions began to fly, including many loud "It's gotta be the White Renegade!"

The noise drowned Andeal's next sentence and Seraphin soon snapped. "I'm right here, so shut it and listen, will you?"

Hans snickered as their blabber turned into gasps and apologies. Seraphin's glare killed the last of it and they fell into an awkward silence. Low voices argued in the radio's background but Vermen couldn't make out the words exchanged. Then someone cleared his throat:

"Listeners, please welcome President Jacob Kurtmann."

A deafening roar followed his announcement, shaking the streets under their feet and sending Vermen's heart racing. How much strength could thousands muster? Their outcry had felt like a small earthquake. What would happen if they unleashed their anger on the city? If those who'd stayed outside joined? Vermen glanced at the soldiers lining the streets, no longer confident in the adequacy of their weaponry. This crowd might not be the kind you could control. He hoped whatever Jacob Kurtmann had to say would not be the final spark.

"Citizens of the Union, this will be my last address as your president."

Kurtmann's voice was calmer than Andeal's, a tad more nasal. He paused, swallowed hard. Vermen held his breath. How had Andeal and Henry managed to get the president on the air for them?

"I want to start with the most important matter: the rebels' story is true. All of it. The Threstle Plague was never a natural virus. It was created by bioengineer genius Galen Clarin and spread on purpose. The vaccine and cure I used to fight this illness were also created long before the first cases appeared. Everything was planned. I did not know at the time."

President Kurtmann stopped once again, perhaps to let outraged reactions die, but he hadn't needed to. A heavy silence reigned in Reverence's streets. Everyone hung to the radio, too afraid to miss a word to move. Vermen licked his dried lips. His throat had turned raw and pasty.

"I discovered this truth two years after being elected from an old friend—not a powerful man by any account, only a husband who'd lost his love to this terrible curse. He came to me with a recording of the Clarin twins planning this operation. It was all there, in one conversation, their treachery laid out in no uncertain terms. That is where I failed you. I confronted Galen Clarin about this and he threatened to take me down with him. I chose to cling to power and never spoke of it again."

Angry shouts greeted his confession. Vermen's throat clutched as he evaluated the chances these men and women would turn into a violent mob in the next minutes. The tension gave him goosebumps. Would Altaer's students be able to channel all the energy into a determined march on the headquarters? And what would this crowd, already on the verge of bursting, do once they arrived? Vermen wished Kurtmann would stop now, before it was too late. The president didn't.

"I am undeserving of the love and trust you have granted me throughout the last decade. I am not a strong man, but I hope that in the end..." He stopped mid-sentence, took a deep breath. They could all hear the lump in his throat. His voice fell to a low whisper. "I hope you'll remember that in the end, I did the right thing."

Hans Vermen's stomach clenched as he caught the fatalist undertone. Two long seconds stretched. No one spoke. They waited, eager to hear or learn of this 'right thing'. Then Seraphin jumped to his feet with a soft swear.

The gunshot blasted through the low-quality receivers, distorted by static.

People screamed and gasped in horror, withdrawing from the radio, but all Vermen heard was the blood beating against his eardrums, Seraphin's repeated swear, louder this time, and the heavy silence from the radio.

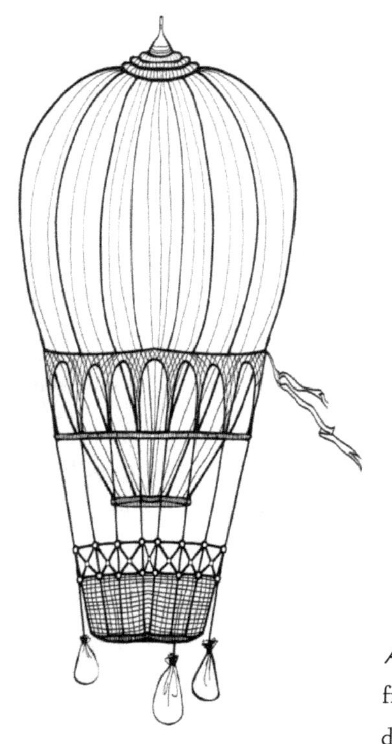

# CHAPTER FORTY



*A burning pain radiated* from Andeal's side. After his dangerous dive he'd been forced to half-crawl, half-march to Reverence. At first he had survived on berries from the forest, but as he grew nearer to the city, he encountered more and more people along the road, heading to the capital for Union's Day. They shared supplies, stories, and well wishes. None of them could heal or help his broken ribs and he doubted it'd ever heal properly now, but it didn't matter. He'd made his way into the National Radio Tower in time, recording in hand. Whatever happened after, he would have done his best. He just hoped Maniel still lived and that he would get to see her.

Henry touched his forearm, dragging him out of his daydreams.

"He's ready."

President Jacob Kurtmann stood inside the recording room, hands clasped behind his back, staring at him through the thick, soundproof glass. He seemed calm and solemn, but his thick line of tensed neck muscles betrayed him. Andeal redirected the sound to his microphone and gave the tall man a thumbs up. The president introduced himself in a deep voice and began his story.

"I don't know how you did it," Andeal said to his friend, "but this is the nail in their coffin."

"Mostly, I insulted him. I wasn't trying to convince him. I was terrified and angry to find out our president was even more of a coward than I was. Then they received reports saying you were dead..."

Andeal rubbed the back of his neck. Whenever he moved too fast, it sent a sharp pain through his nerves. "I jumped a hundred feet into a river barely deep enough. By all rights, I should be dead."

"I'm glad you're not. Being alone with the president is scary and I have nothing to eat with me."

Andeal burst out laughing—a series of painful hiccups—and held his side with one hand while he bent to ease the pain. Would anyone but Henry complain about a lack of instant noodles while the Union President admitted on a clandestine national broadcast that he'd protected the killer of thousands for his personal gain? Henry gave him an insulted, don't-mock-me glare, then turned away from him.

"Oh no. Oh no oh no oh no!"

His fright killed Andeal's mirth and he straightened as his friend dashed for the door connecting to the recording room. Inside, President Kurtmann had drawn a pistol as he spoke and shoved it under his chin. Andeal froze, clasped the control panel in front of him. The president's voice drifted through the speakers above him, thick with emotion.

"I hope you'll remember that in the end, I did the right thing."

Kurtmann met his gaze a brief moment, spun on his heels and pulled the trigger. Red chunks thumped against the window. Blood and brains. Slowly sliding down, right before him. Andeal ripped the sound cable out of its input, panting. Henry had flung the door open and rushed inside. He crouched next to the crumpled body, barely visible behind the screen of blood.

Everyone would've heard that. Every single person in this country. And now they had only silence left.

Andeal plugged the sound input into the disc reader. His hands were so shaky he couldn't aim right and had to try twice. Dazed, he put Lenz's recording in and pressed the play button. Galen's smooth voice floated through the room, filling the unbearable silence.

What now? Andeal tried to get his brain to function again, to find a way to segue out of this. What was he supposed to say when he next took the microphone? 'Hello listeners, sorry the president decided to shoot himself live! No need to panic, nothing's wrong here.' That'd work, for sure! Andeal rubbed his temples, desperate for a way out of this mess. And it was all going so well five seconds ago.

A loud crash covered the recording as the door behind him burst open.

"On the ground! On the ground!" a soldier shouted as Andeal spun around. He tried to step back, felt the machines against his back. Men rushed into the recording room, weapons raised. Hands grabbed him, turned him back around and slammed him face-first into the disc reader. The brusque movement sent intense pain into his side and neck, his knees gave in and he found himself on the ground, as ordered, held by soldiers. He never had time to say a word.

"Turn that shit off," said a calm voice—the exact same that was playing even now for the whole Union to hear.

Mounting dread clutched Andeal's throat as the recording stopped. He tried to twist, to glimpse and confirm, but the sharp pain kept him still. He didn't need the confirmation, though. He'd recognize Galen Clarin among hundreds of thousands. How often had he supervised an experiment, commenting on his state like you would on a broken toy? How many more times would he now?

Andeal struggled against the soldier's hold, fought through the pain to try to squirm out. Strong hands squeezed his arm and a knee pushed him back down to the ground, crushing his broken rib further. He gasped and tears rolled down his cheeks.

"Stop it, you're pathetic," Galen said.

Did it matter? If keeping his dignity landed him in Galen's clutches, he wanted none of it. He stretched his hand to reach the cables, hoping to pull himself. The soldier slapped it away, grabbed a handful of hair and smashed his head against the floor. Blood spurted out of Andeal's nose and large swaths of darkness obscured his sight. Every inch of his face throbbed. He lay still an instant, dazed, then the urge to escape returned. With his remaining strength, Andeal gathered his arms under him and pushed up hard.

A surprised cry from the soldier rewarded his effort. The man reacted by smashing his knee down hard into Andeal's back, slightly on the wounded side. Waves of nauseating pain spread out from his wound and he collapsed with a scream, shaking.

"Next time just knock him out," Galen ordered. "I wanted a little chat with my friend but if he keeps wailing while I make my public announcement, I'll be forced to go in that disgusting recording room."

Andeal froze. Henry hid in there. If Galen entered they'd find him. It'd be over, for both of them. But how much would Galen trade to know the source of all his problems was one door away? Henry didn't have a wife to return to. He hadn't suffered through this before. Wouldn't it be more fair for Andeal to walk away, instead of him? It didn't matter what price he had to pay. Andeal could not return to the labs.

"I can help you."

He regretted the words as soon as they escaped his lips. He couldn't trust Galen, could he? His voice was only a broken whisper, but the scientist heard. He must've given a silent order because the soldier removed his knee from Andeal's back and heaved him to his feet, turning him so he could face Galen. The man's pale brown hair had grayed in the last six years but his blue eyes hadn't lost any of their cold mockery. His classy dark blue waistcoat, white shirt and clean pants seemed bizarre to Andeal; he'd never seen him in anything but a lab coat.

"Was there some wisdom you wished to share?"

Andeal swallowed hard. He shouldn't have said anything. Too late now. "Will it save me from the labs?"

"Nothing will." Galen walked to him, his hands resting in his pockets. He leaned forward just enough to bring his lips to Andeal's ear. "You have no idea how much I'm looking forward to it."

A gaping pit opened in Andeal's stomach and swallowed what little fight he had left in him. He'd struggled so hard a minute ago but now the thought of raising a finger to defend himself pained him. There was no use. How could he have thought to sell Henry out for his freedom? Perhaps he deserved to go back there and die of some horrible experimental mishap. He turned his head away from Galen. There was one last thing for him to do:

keep Clarin out of the recording room.

"Move the red cable from the disc reader into the third hole from the left on the main control panel."

The scientist withdrew and glanced at the mess of cables, lights, and buttons behind him.

"Why tell me?"

"A man shot himself in front of my eyes and his brains are still displayed on the window behind you. Are you that surprised I want to get out of here?"

He couldn't care less about Jacob Kurtmann at this point, but he put as much conviction as he could into his answer. Galen considered his words for a moment then shrugged.

"You never did have much of a stomach for blood." He turned to another soldier and motioned for him to leave. "Get out and tell me if it works in the corridor."

He unplugged the red cable and placed it back where Andeal had indicated. His movements were relaxed, his shoulders at ease. Galen Clarin did not indicate he had any worries about today, or how it'd end. He tapped the microphone with his finger, waited for confirmation from his man, then yanked the cable out again. Andeal's heart thumped against his chest. Why didn't he just give his stupid message and be done with it?

The scientist made his deliberate way back to Andeal and put a hand on his shoulder. Andeal tried to squirm out of it, provoked another spasm of pain from his side. He reached for it, understood right away his reflex was a mistake. Galen took note, smiled, squeezed his wounded side. Stars burst in front of Andeal's eyes and he gasped as his knees buckled. The soldier held him up.

"Interesting." Galen picked up his chin. "I want you to stay and watch. If you make a single sound, however, I'll have your tongue cut out. You don't really need it. After all, tube-feeding you wouldn't be that much of a bother."

Still struggling to breathe, Andeal only managed a weak nod. He clung to the idea they would at least get away from Henry and give him a chance to escape. One of them would be safe. One of them would not have tubes forced down his throat, unknown substances injected into his veins, painful tests performed on him. Andeal choked on a sob as Galen gave him a satisfied pat on the head and returned to the mic. The scientist rolled up his sleeves, cleared his throat, and plugged the cable back in.

"Union citizens, ladies and gentlemen, this illegal broadcast is over. I am Galen Clarin and I have grave news. Today...today is a sad day for the Union. Settle down. Let me tell you what I know. I was awakened last night by my brother, Chief of Security, with very bad news. He told me the president had vanished. He was worried, almost panicked. Omar never is and it scared me in turn. We did our best to find him, put all our manpower on the operation, but...We were too late."

Galen took a dramatic pause, a devious smile creeping up his face. He winked at Andeal, then continued his lies.

"My good citizens, you all heard what followed. The White Renegade's rebels coerced our beloved president into a ludicrous confession and shot him down. Do you believe a word of it? Jacob Kurtmann is—was—the kindest and most courageous soul of this land. He would not have betrayed his people this way. Neither would I. Though I have erred before in my desire to help this country, the ruthless infection of tens of thousands as a bid of power is..." He stopped, groaned. "Even speaking of it makes me nauseated."

His tone turned sad, with a hint of anger. No one could see his smirk.

They would hear guilt, desolation, resolution. Not mockery and mirth. Was that it? Did they lose everything they'd built to one fell swoop from Galen Clarin? How could their story crumble so fast?

"I implore you, fellow citizens," Galen went on "do not let the rebels' tale poison your view of our nation. We have united diverging countries, drawing on the strengths of each to create a force to be reckoned with. We are beautiful. Never forget: in our greatest challenges, we stay united!"

Galen brought a hand to the mic to muffle sounds, leaned toward Andeal, and whispered.

"That's one speech for the history-makers, isn't it?"

Anger burned in Andeal's stomach. He repressed it before it pushed him to fight back. Galen wanted him to, but what would be the point? Nothing he could do would make a difference, in his life or others'. He wouldn't give the bastard the satisfaction of a reaction. Galen's smile vanished as he returned to his message.

"I am proud to announce we have captured the men responsible for this and charged them with treason, as we did their partner last week. Peace may soon return to our nation. To the men and women assembled in Reverence, marching in its streets: return home, to your loving families. You are now part of an illegal assembly. Farewell."

Galen yanked the cable out with a soft laugh and returned his attention to his prisoner. "Good show, don't you think? I do hope every one of these fools has the same horrified expression you do. It's delicious."

He pulled his sleeves back down and smoothened them before glancing to the blood in the window. The seriousness in his eyes betrayed his easy smile. Perhaps he hadn't worked out how to deal with the president's death or what to do next. Galen clasped his hands behind his back, made little thinking sounds, then shrugged.

"We're done here. Knock him out, soldier."

The order was barely finished when a pistol's cross smashed against Andeal's temple.

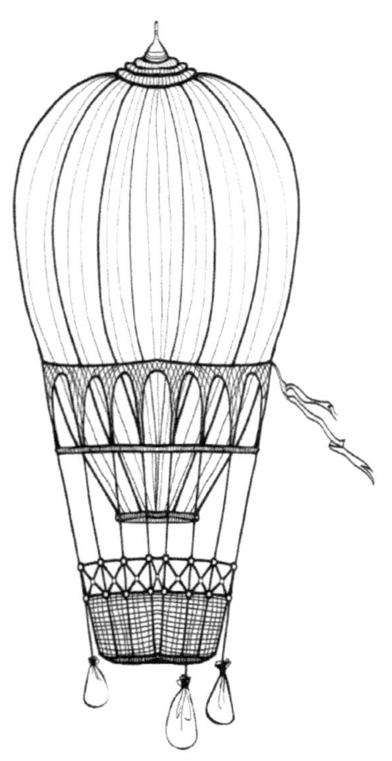

# CHAPTER FORTY-ONE

*Henry threw himself into* the recording room as Kurtmann pressed the pistol to his chin, slamming the soundproof door against the wall. He wanted to yell *don't you dare pull that trigger* but horror clenched his throat. He managed one stride before a loud bang pierced his ears. Warm specks covered his face and left a coppery taste in his mouth. Blood, his mind registered. The president's body crumpled as Henry stumbled to it, nauseous.

"You didn't have to do that, damn it!"

His shaky hands reached for the president's. He wanted to place them right, to give Jacob Kurtmann's corpse some dignity—as much as his blown skull allowed, anyway.

A powerful crack interrupted his movement and he spun about in time to see soldiers rushing into the booth, pointing weapons at Andeal. His room's soundproof door slid back in place and closed with a click, blocking all noises as suddenly as they'd appeared. Henry grabbed Kurtmann's gun and scrambled to the bloodied window, huddling against the wall and hiding out of sight.

He curled up, clutching the weapon to his heart. What was going on? He couldn't hear anything, could only feel the occasional vibration through the wall. Terror locked him down. Kurtmann's still-warm blood mixed with his cold sweat and drenched his shirt. They'd be coming for him. Any moment now they'd come through the door, find him, kill him.

His recording stopped playing—when had Andeal put that on anyway? What else had he missed? Henry wiped the blood off his face and forced himself to swallow. A part of him wanted to stand up and free his friend, but what could he do? He'd be shot down in a blink. Pushing guilt-ridden presidents to suicide was all he was good for.

The speakers gave a soft whirring noise, then someone cleared his throat.

"Union citizens, ladies and gentlemen, this illegal broadcast is over. I am Galen Clarin and I have grave news."

Henry barely breathed through the speech. Doubts began to gnaw at his determination. How could their mismatched story—assembled from a network of clues and conjectures, held together by a single recording and Kurtmann's confirmation, presented in bribes at irregular hours with a crappy transmission—how could it hope to compete with the benevolent and educated voice that had just explained it all away? Galen Clarin had pieced a defense together without batting an eye. How much easier was it to accept his version, to ignore these upstart rebels and believe that all was well? Henry had done so for years.

It couldn't end like this, not after all they'd done. Henry refused. If the smooth scientist's voice were the more credible of the two, then he'd let him do the talking. If only Henry could hear what was happening behind him! Galen's voice no longer drifted out of the speakers. How long had he cowered here, clinging to Kurtmann's bloodied firearm, while they held Andeal? Was his friend still alive? Henry hadn't heard gunshots. He would've, even through the glass. Andeal had to be okay.

Henry took a deep breath, tried to straighten his nerves. He had to move, do something. Act. He shifted to his knees, began a slow crawl toward Kurtmann. Blood seeped into his sleeves and pants. It dripped down as he reached into the president's pockets and withdrew the copy of the recording. Henry averted his eyes from the blown skull and retreated back to the window, sticking himself against the wall. Had they seen him? Were they still there? His trembling hands almost dropped the disc.

First step completed, he congratulated himself, clinging to the recording. He could finish this. He had to.

He raised his head slowly, to peek out the window. Thick blood obscured almost everything, but he spotted no human shapes. Henry wiped the screen with his already-dirty sleeve. No one. A weight lifted from his lungs and he took a deep breath. They'd left. He could move around.

Henry jumped to his feet and hurried out of the recording room, slamming the soundproof door behind him. No more blood everywhere. No more dead presidential body. He swallowed hard, tried to calm his heart. No use. Instead he moved in front of the console. The red cable just hung there, waiting. He could do this.

Before he lost his courage, he grabbed the cable and connected the microphone.

"People!" He'd said something! No turning back. "Hum...hello there. We're back." He had to gather his thoughts, do this quick. Galen Clarin would send someone after him. "This is Henry Schmitt talking, again. Son of Lenz Schmitt. My father is the old friend President Kurtmann mentioned. I'm going to play his recording again. That's what you heard earlier. The beginning of my father's recording. The start of the truth." This was getting easier. He'd never found a good rhythm in the last month, but since last night the words seemed to come on their own. "I hope it will have time to play to the end, but I make no guarantee. I'll do my best. Oh, and one last thing: Doctor Clarin, I'm coming for you."

He had no idea why he'd issued that threat, but it'd spilled right out of his mouth with surprising intensity. He almost sounded dangerous! Almost. Henry switched the cables about, put his disc in the reader, and started the audio once again. Broken pieces of the other copy lay at his feet. How fast would the soldiers get here and inflict the same fate to this one? Then they'd come after him...

Time to move. He strode through the broken door, glanced to each side, then started down the corridor. He kept looking over his shoulder, unable to shake his fear they'd appear behind him. His eyes caught something weird in the rug. Did it seem...wet? Henry squinted until he saw his own bloodied footprints, going from the recording room to him. Great. He left a blood trail on the floor. Henry bit his lower lip and hurried into the first door on his right. He found a classy office with a huge desk and an important-looking leather chair, with diplomas and prestigious certificates lining the wall. Whoever worked here mattered. Henry removed his shoes and threw them on the chair, where they'd be hidden from the doorway. The men would come here looking for him, following his tracks. He might be able to slip away.

Henry crept toward the stairs when he heard voices coming up from it. And if he used the elevator, they would see the lit number indicating the floor he was on.

He was trapped upstairs.

His heart pumping, Henry headed into a tiny conference room in front of the office, leaving the door opened a crack. A dozen chairs circled a smooth wooden table and a white board was nailed to the wall on one end. A large window connected the room to the corridor but dull white curtains blocked most of the view. Henry moved closer to them. He could take the soldiers by surprise while they checked the other room. His grip tightened on Kurtmann's pistol. He could still hear the recording from the corridor's speakers.

Two men stepped out of the staircase near the elevator, guns raised, their movements coordinated. Elite guards, no doubt. Sweat trickled down Henry's neck. These were no bumbling fools. They had been handpicked by Galen Clarin to protect him. Did he really think he could outwit them? He watched with increasing dread as they checked the small lobby then moved into the corridor, opening every door in a thorough search. His fake blood trail was pointless. He would not escape.

Henry swallowed hard, clung to his weapon. As he considered his nonexistent chances of winning a shoot-out, an electric crackle ran through the ceiling and all the lights winked out. His recording stopped mid-sentence and red emergency dots appeared on each side of the rug. The sunlight filtering through the windows sufficed to navigate the floor, but now his bloody footsteps were invisible. He wouldn't even have that distraction to help him. He needed a new plan.

His gaze fell on the fire extinguisher across from him. Compressed gas. Hadn't Treysh been building some kind of explosive device with compressed gas? How had that worked? He hit his head a few times with the heel of his palm in an attempt to jog his memory. He hadn't been paying attention to the science, really. He'd tried, but Treysh always lost him and he didn't want to stop her. She would have thought he was stupid. Worse, he would've broken her passionate momentum. He should have. Now he had to take a guess, shoot the thing, and hope it'd blow up. He had one single chance. If Treysh and him made it out alive, he promised himself to interrupt as often as he needed to understand.

The two men neared the fire extinguisher. Henry dropped to his belly and crawled to the door. The opening he'd left gave him a good angle. He aimed, imagined the bullet's trajectory. He could do this. They moved in a tight formation and he'd get them both. It would work. It had to.

The first soldier stepped into view. Henry counted to two. His arm shook despite his best efforts to stabilize it against the floor. He took a deep breath, closed his eyes, pulled the trigger. Again and again.

A roaring explosion shook the floor as the three bullets pierced the metal can, releasing the gas inside in one powerful blast. The soldiers crashed into the wall with surprised and pained screams. Henry scrambled to his feet and sprinted down the corridor. As he passed over them, one lifted a dazed hand, reached for his weapon. His movement forced Henry to stop his flight. He couldn't leave them here.

"I'm sorry, I really am," he said, before clubbing the stunned soldier with the butt end of his pistol.

Henry knelt next to the second and checked his breathing. Shallow but regular. Neither were dead. Good. He dragged their bodies into the posh office, picked up his shoes, then used the conference chairs to barricade the door. Now they couldn't come after him. He cast a nervous glance to the elevator and stairs, half-expecting a dozen other soldiers to appear and shoot him down. No one. All he could hear was his heavy panting and the soft buzz of the emergency lights.

Henry collected his thoughts, wiped his shoes clean on the rug, and put them on. He ought to turn the power back on, allow his recording to continue. They'd gone past that room, the first time, in the basement. Treysh had sang and danced. It seemed so long ago now. He wondered if Lungvist had managed to get her out. He wished he could apologize for landing her in prison. He wished he could tell her how alive she made him feel, how unique she was. He would, as soon as he could. Not now, though. Now was the time to get this broadcast back on the air.

Again.

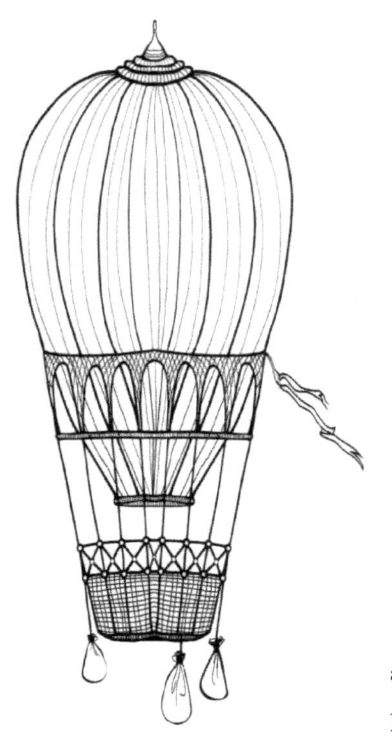

# CHAPTER FORTY-TWO

*Galen Clarin's speech cast* a heavy silence on the gathered protesters. Angry glares were thrown at the Radio Tower, worried hand-squeezing occurred between friends and family. Maniel paled and whispered to herself, her hands and voice shaking. Praying, Vermen realized. Hans recalled Andeal's terror when he'd threatened to bring him back to the army, how desperate he had been to escape. He'd been caught, in the end. He was back in Galen's hands.

The crowd turned toward Seraphin. Just a few at first, but one by one they stared at the rebel leader with one silent question: what now? The Regarian raised a hurt and angry gaze, shook his head with frustration. His fingers shook ever so slightly and there was a wild despair in his pale eyes, a cry of rage he could barely contain. All these people shoved their terror on him, demanding reassurance. He had no answer for them.

The police did.

A sound grenade exploded over their heads, punching holes through Vermen's ears and sending his heart into a frenzied beat. Panic spread through the crowd as they ran from the bang, hands raised over their heads. A tear gas can spun at their feet, releasing its chemical components with a hiss. Seraphin dashed out of the yellow cloud. Calls to run and disperse erupted all around, only to be buried under the rhythmic bang of batons against riot shields.

*Clang. Clang. Clang.*

A striking sound. Meant to intimidate, instill fear, warn of impeding violence. Like the old drums of war. Vermen gritted his teeth, drew on his trained discipline to keep his calm in the growing chaos. He could not stay alone. They needed to stick together.

"Seraphin!"

Gas plunged into Vermen's throat, scorching it. He scanned around but the smoke thickened with each sound grenade and tears marred his limited sight. The policemen closed in.

A smaller hand grabbed his forearm and pulled him away. A brown woman's hand, with Maniel's wedding ring. Vermen followed, relieved Maniel had found him, at least. He tried to wipe his gas-induced tears, but his eyes and throat burned and he knew it wouldn't go away. People screamed around them, panicked, scattering through the street, away from the advancing policemen.

"Everybody calm down!"

Vermen recognized Alex's voice. They had jumped upon a bench, a scarf covering the lower half of their face and wore protective lab glasses keeping their eyes safe. Vermen's heart lifted. As awkward as their first had been, he was glad to find another familiar face.

"Do not sprint!" they called. "Do not scatter. Grab the person next to you and walk fast, all in one direction. Do not run."

They pointed north—toward the police headquarters—and repeated their advice. Their voice turned raspy but Alex drank from a water bottle and kept going. The protesters obeyed without questions, linked arms with perfect strangers, hurried on. The police line emerged from the cloud, fully armored and gas masks on. One of them, a step behind his colleagues, shot another grenade over their heads.

It burst next to Alex's head and the shock sent them stumbling off their bench with a cry. The policemen sped the tempo of their batons then charged as they fell, and Alex's reassuring advice vanished from everyone's minds. They bolted—a disorganized crowd running into one another. Vermen and Maniel rushed to Alex's aid and gave them a hand up. They stared at them with a dazed look, their knees and elbows scraped and bleeding. When the police threw a tear gas can their way, Maniel kicked it back with an angry grunt.

"Where's Seraphin?" Alex asked.

"Let's go," she said. "We'll find him again, but later."

The line had reached them. Policemen screamed for everyone to move. They pressed behind, never more than a stride away. Insults flew as they herded the mass of confused protesters, yelling for everyone to go faster. Anger tightened Vermen's throat. *Faster?* When his body pressed against that of strangers, when every step he took almost crushed someone else's foot, when the crowd was so compact that weaving through others would be impossible? How were they supposed to go faster? He clung to Maniel and Alex, afraid to lose them to the current, aware that if he did he would not find either again.

Just as, despite his best attempts, he couldn't find Seraphin's white head through the crowd.

The houses flanking them on either side gave way to an intersection a little farther ahead. They could use the space. To breathe, but also to sneak deeper into the crowd—to position themselves *not* one step ahead of the police.

Vermen's hope was short-lived. A second shield-wielding line of policemen emerged from the intersection, from the left. Sound grenades exploded overhead from both groups, causing protesters to sprint away or crouch down with surprised screams. When the rhythmic banging picked up pace again, someone panicked behind Vermen and shoved him. Hans' foot caught another's and he tumbled to the ground.

He fought to get back on his feet but was hit by random knees, feet, and forelegs, forcing him back down. Someone stepped on his hand as he pushed himself up. He screamed and withdrew it, flattening against the ground and smashing his chin. Then the crowd thinned; he'd reached the police line. Vermen's heart skipped a beat. He scrambled up as fast as he could, but it didn't suffice.

"Move, asshole!"

A baton smashed against his hind leg, another on his forearm. He stumbled, almost crashed again, but this time he caught himself.

"Vermen!"

Hans lifted his head and spotted Maniel ahead, fighting against the current. He dashed, felt the swoosh of air as another baton missed him, and sprinted until he reached the relative safety of the crowd line. She linked her arm in his, but they had no time for relief. The second row of policemen crashed into their group, from the left.

The terrified crowd split in half under the assault, some going north, others running east.

"No! All to the north!"

Seraphin's voice rose from the crowd, commanding. The fleeing crowd slowed despite the incoming police and some stopped as they reached the east and north streets, at the edge of the dangerous intersection. He stood in the middle, half-hidden by swirling smoke, as white as the gas that spiraled around him. One hand rested at his hip, his *skeptar* in plain view. Vermen's breath caught in his raw throat. There was an aura of power about Seraphin that was ridiculously attractive.

"Keep going!" the Regarian called. "North, everyone together. Don't linger, go!"

Some moved but most stared at him even longer. They whispered to one another. *The White Renegade*, they said. *It's him.* The riot squad stopped. Seraphin stayed put. Alone. Such an easy target. Vermen noted sergeants speaking into a radio, just behind their police line. And here he was, doing nothing, like a teenage idiot drooling over his crush.

"Seraphin!"

The rebel leader turned at the sound of his voice and a thrilled grin split his face. "Hans, I'm so glad to—"

"Get down!"

The sergeants had gestured to their men and three gas cans hit the ground at Seraphin's feet, in perfect unison. The Regarian stepped back, bringing an arm up to protect his throat. Vermen broke into a sprint as a sound grenade blasted to his friend's left. A wracking cough emerged from the cloud just as Hans heard a clear order from the enemy line.

"*Fire!*"

Three consecutive gunshots rang out. Not regular ones. Hans noticed the air-release from crowd-control rubber bullet guns. Two fleshy *thumps* followed, the first drawing a surprised cry of pain, the second ending it abruptly.

Vermen's heart stopped, too.

Shot.

No, he had to get a grip. They were rubber bullets. Seraphin was out cold, not dead.

Maniel had already dived into the tear gas. Vermen plunged in too, just as the protesters moved again—northward, in one scared group. Batons hit shields, their fast pace in sync with Hans' heartbeat. The burning in his throat returned and his eyes watered, so he used his feet to sweep the ground. Glass broke as he stepped on a pair of glasses, the sound squeezing his insides. They had another trip to Serenity planned, now.

A wracking cough stopped Vermen's search but he heard his companion let out a soft exclamation.

"Here! I have him."

The coordinated slap of boots on pavement warned them of the approaching police. Vermen hurried to her side and crouched. He patted around the ground until he touched a shoulder.

"Take his head and I'll grab his legs."

As he tried to find a hold, his fingers touched something warm. Blood, running down Seraphin's cheeks and neck. Hans swallowed hard and tightened his grip on the Regarian's head. They could not stay to examine his wounds.

"Go," Maniel said. "Follow the crowd."

They moved out, carrying the Regarian as fast as they could. Hans refused to look at Seraphin's face when they left the smoke but every gasp their passage drew crushed his heart. Those rubber bullets weren't meant to kill, he told himself, but they weren't meant to be shot at close range into someone's face either.

Maniel swore and called out to the crowd, to no one in particular and everyone at once. Desperation laced her voice. "I need to put him down and see to his wounds!"

Her first answer was another sound grenade. Everyone around ducked but Vermen clung to Seraphin's head. The riot squad accelerated their shield-bang warning and charged. Most protesters ran but a courageous few linked arms into a protective line between them and the police. Vermen struggled to keep up. With each of his long backward strides, Seraphin's weight strained him and the baton hits he'd received earlier flared in pain. They couldn't keep this up forever.

"Vermen...Vermen, what's that ahead?"

At Maniel's question he twisted around to see. People were disappearing down a small flight of stairs, on their left, but this was no intersection.

"An open door?"

His heart raced. This was their chance! They had to get inside before this benevolent soul slammed the door shut.

"We have a wounded man," he yelled. "Let us through!"

A handful of protesters stepped aside but most ignored Vermen. He sped his pace anyway, pushing through. Although her voice was drowned in the ambient chaos, Maniel kept demanding for room to be made. Her voice was hoarse, broken. If she didn't look after Seraphin soon, he would die.

"Let them pass. Nobody's in my house until they are!"

The man's voice covered the screams, the faraway sound grenades, the stomping of the incoming riot squad. Relief flooded through Vermen as he rushed inside, past the bald dark-skinned man. His wife greeted them, ushering them through a crowded living room and into a backyard garden. They set Seraphin down between rows of cucumber and tomato plants. Panting, Vermen thanked her as Maniel pulled her hair into a ponytail and crouched down.

Seraphin's pale skin had taken on a sick yellowish hue. Sweaty clothes clung to him and blood clotted his white hair and stained his collar. His skull seemed sunken in under all that red. Vermen swallowed hard, knelt, and brushed strands of Seraphin's hair aside, clearing his forehead. Explosions, yells, and gunshots still rang outside but they'd found a safe place.

"It's okay now," Hans whispered. "I'm sorry about your glasses."

His words seemed to shake their hostess out of a daze. She cleared her throat. "I'll get hot water, compresses, and my sewing kit."

"Don't." Maniel withdrew the two fingers she'd put at Seraphin's neck. "There's no use."

Her gaze found Vermen's and she shook her head. Too late. She let herself fall into a sitting position and took a shuddering breath.

"No." Vermen reached over Seraphin's body and grabbed her shoulder. "Reanimate him. Do *something*."

Maniel slapped his hand away. "I know my job! He's dead, Hans. Gone."

Tears ran down her cheeks despite her angry scowl. Vermen didn't push the matter. He knew she was right, even though he didn't want to hear it. His hand grabbed Seraphin's inert fingers and squeezed. He wanted the terribly pale blue eyes to open again, to tell him not to make a big deal out of things. This wasn't fair. He had been ready to do just that, to turn their first kiss into a big deal and leave his brother's ghost behind. But he needed Seraphin for that. He had spent six years trying to be the one to put that bullet in his head, rubber or not. And when he hadn't been able to, he'd found himself wishing someone else would.

Someone else had.

They had known. They had aimed for his head at short range. Someone had given this specific order. Vermen's hands drifted down, to the pistol at Seraphin's hip.

"Can we ask you a few questions?"

Hans snapped his hand back when their hosts interrupted. The Burgian man had joined them in the garden. He stood a step behind his wife, his arms crossed, his expression hovering between concerned confusion and an angry frown. Vermen was not in the mood to indulge strangers with long explanations, but they had sheltered them. Too late.

"Only if you really want the answers."

The man paused to consider for a moment, then nodded. "That's the White Renegade, isn't it?"

"Yes."

"So you two, you're his companions or something?"

"We are." Maniel pulled herself up and wiped her bloodied hands on her pants. "I've been with him since day one."

"Okay, okay."

The Burgian looked at his wife for support, nervous now. Neither of them must've expected to shelter the Union's most wanted criminals when they opened that door. If these two weren't in the streets to begin with, they probably didn't want anything to do with this mess.

"So what's the plan?" the husband blurted out, proving Vermen wrong. "Is anyone going to the Radio Tower to help Henry? You're the ones who put all these ideas of rebellions and heroics in his head, you know. You can't let him face soldiers alone!"

"You know Henry?"

Maniel's surprised question echoed Vermen's own. Something else bothered him, though, something more urgent.

"What do you mean, 'face soldiers alone'?"

"We raised him when Lenz vanished," the woman answered. "A few minutes ago our boy got on the radio and told the whole world his name and how he had that recording to play, but he didn't expect to get to the end of it—and he was right. It cut without warning and we don't have a clue about how he's faring. So tell us, because I think we deserve to know: what was the plan?"

Vermen reconsidered his early assessment of these two. They weren't random citizens living in Reverence, unable to watch peaceful protesters get assaulted by policemen. Hadn't Lungvist mentioned tailing a grocer from Ferrea to Reverence? Maniel provided their names just as he reached his conclusion.

"You're Kinsi and Tia," she said with a soft smile. "Henry missed you so much."

What was he supposed to tell Henry's foster parents? Vermen gritted his teeth. If he didn't have time for *his* grief and fear he sure as hell wasn't going to deal with theirs. The truth would have do to.

"There was no plan," Vermen replied. "Henry was with Andeal when they bombed Mount Kairn. We've had no direct contact with them since.

We're no better off than any of you."

Protesters had begun to gather around them as Hans clarified how little they knew. The White Renegade was dead. His rebels had no plans. They all sported stunned expressions of incomprehension, but added to those worried looks was determination and anger. Alex pushed through the crowd, bright red coat torn and fingers bloodied. Sweat covered their dark skin and their curly hair had entirely escaped their ponytail. Hurt shone in their eyes, which strayed to Seraphin's body over and over. "I can't believe they got him. We...we can't leave it at that. If we all stay hidden in here, we're no better than those who stayed out in the plains."

"We won't hide." Maniel's brow furrowed into her characteristic stubborn frown. "My husband is in the National Radio Tower and last I heard, he was in need of some serious rescuing. We didn't have a plan? Here's one. We grab everything that can be used as a shield—trash can lids, cardboard, planks, things like that—as well as sticks and poles to defend ourselves against the soldiers' charges. We find scarves and other clothes to cover our mouths against the gas and we try to get our hands on as many glasses or protective eye-gear as we can, in case they start to pepper spray us too. We dodge the riot squads whenever we can, fight if we must. Once in the tower we barricade ourselves in."

"Won't they already be at the tower?" someone asked.

If they weren't when the day had started, they would've blockaded every entrance with Andeal's first words. Their main hope was to be numerous enough and to use the policemen's reluctance to kill civilians. How long would the last one hold, however? If Galen was on the radio, General Omar Clarin must be in charge of today's operation. He had enough at stake to authorize deadly force.

Odds couldn't be helped, though. Maniel and Alex began to organize the expedition. She distributed scarves brought by their hostess, formed subgroups in which people had to watch for one another, designed an ideal route with help from the locals. Her confident pragmatism seemed to boost the morale of everyone around, and Alex had obviously seen several protests before. They had strong leaders again and they would take the Radio Tower.

It wouldn't be enough. Not while Omar Clarin lived to give the order to open fire upon them. Seraphin had known that. That's why he'd led others toward the headquarters—toward the chain of command and their captured rebel. Toward the man whose orders had gotten him killed.

Vermen crouched next to Seraphin's body again. Holt had a plan, he always did, but what? He wondered if he had meant to do what he had six years ago: walk up to a ruthless general, raise the flint-and-lock pistol, blow his brains out. Deal with the consequences after. It'd worked the first time, hadn't it?

And it'd brought them together.

Hans ignored the twisting pain in his stomach—he couldn't think of that, not now—and reached for the *skeptar* at Seraphin's belt. He wrapped his fingers around it and the red string felt warm against his palm. As though the rebel's spirit lived in it, beckoned to him. Had Holt joined his family inside? Seraphin had used this pistol to kill Vermen's brother and avenge them. The *skeptar's* task was not over. The red string chafed Vermen's skin as he held it, a reminder of the task ahead.

He was not going to the Radio Tower.

Vermen retrieved the holster and tied it to his belt. This weapon had turned his life upside down. He might die carrying it today.

"What are you doing?" Alex asked. "It should be buried with him."

Hans raised his chin and met their gaze. They had a radio tower to reclaim. He intended to walk into the enemy's headquarters and take down their general, giving Maniel a chance to succeed.

"I need a weapon. You need me to have a weapon. There's no point in taking the tower if you can't keep it. And you won't. Not against Omar Clarin's troops. His soldiers are loyal. If he tells them to wipe out the unruly mob at the door, they will, no questions asked. We can't give him the opportunity to give that order because he won't hesitate to do so." Vermen's grip tightened. His voice, too. He glanced at Seraphin's body and for a moment it seemed like the soil under his feet had vanished. Hans shook his head and grounded himself. Not now. He was a soldier. He could work through this pain the same way he'd ignore any other wound. He had to. "They *aimed* for his head. We should get theirs."

"Hans..." Maniel whispered his name, must have understood how slim his chances were of making it out alive. Perhaps the *skeptar's* luck would follow him. Seraphin had escaped a camp full of soldiers, after all. It could be his turn.

"I'll bring it back, to be buried with him. Focus on Andeal, Maniel. He needs you."

A bitter laugh escaped her lips. "He often does. Good luck, Hans."

Vermen returned the courtesy with a smile. He slipped out of the house and into the deserted street. The policemen's lines had moved elsewhere, but he could hear the distant smash of batons against shields. He still had no idea how he'd get into the headquarters. One step at a time, though. First he had to get there.

Seraphin's *skeptar* at his hip, Hans Vermen dove into the snaking streets of Reverence.

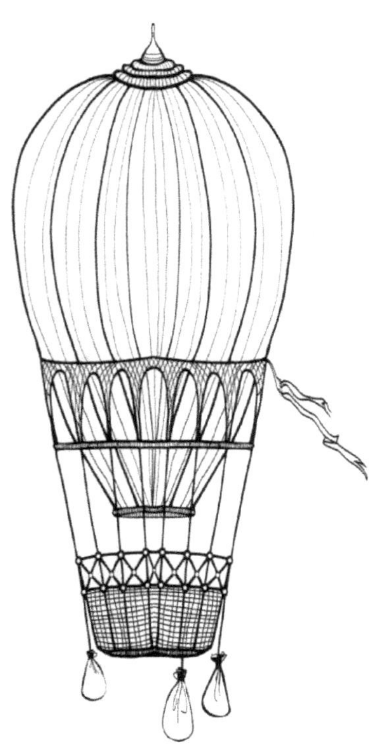

# CHAPTER FORTY-THREE

*Sneaking through the city* reminded Vermen of his first night forest battle. He could hear gunshots, screams, sharp orders and feet slapping the ground as folks ran around, but he could not see any of it. Houses and shops obstructed his view from explosions and whirls of smoke kept him guessing about what was happening a block away. Chaos seemed everywhere, waiting for him. His heart pumped with every corner he turned, every intersection he traversed. He stalked through Reverence's winding paths with the certainty that sooner or later, he'd end up face-to-face with a riot squad.

He was wrong.

Vermen made it all the way to the headquarters' neighborhood, sneaking past the last riot squad by climbing up an emergency staircase and heaving himself onto the roof. The baton hits from his earlier fall throbbed and he rested on his back, trying to catch his breath and calm the pain. The day's constant sprints, leaps, and climbs were starting to take their toll.

Or maybe that was just what he preferred to blame. It was easier to deal with physical exhaustion than to let his thoughts linger on why he was on this roof, Seraphin's pistol at his hip. Alone. Hans had almost never left the Regarian's side in the last months, but Seraphin had been ripped away from him. He would no longer wake to the sly smile, or watch Seraphin protect his sensitive eyes from the sun's glare. He wouldn't get to hear his short laughter, or share stories around a campfire, or touch the Regarian's shoulder to reassure him.

Hans would never get to pull him close and run a hand through his pure white hair, to look into the pale blue gaze and smile and kiss him again—*really* kiss him this time.

He had waited too long, had let the past drag him down. And now it was too late.

Vermen ran a hand over his face and realized he'd been crying. He swore, pushed Seraphin's memory away, and pulled himself together. He couldn't afford to break down now. Maniel depended on him, and Andeal and Henry. Hans took a deep breath, then crawled around the solar panels set on the rooftop. They gave no light during the day, only absorbed the sunrays and became almost burning to the touch. Vermen avoided them as he moved to peek over the ledge.

The headquarters' octagonal structure could be spotted three blocks away, higher than the surrounding buildings. The top floor had large yellow-tinted windows—a recent invention that combined glass and solar technology. He'd heard it would be tested in some buildings, that they planned to use it in high apartment towers if it worked. After months dwelling in caves and crawling through forests, such a living area seemed alien. His journey with the rebels had disconnected him from the real world. Perhaps it was time to get in touch with his old soldier self again.

Vermen surveyed the roads below him. He'd heard the quick whirring of electric motors half a dozen times during his trek through the city. Lone soldiers rode motorcycles out of the headquarters, speeding toward the city's hot spots. Couriers, carrying messages and orders too important to risk saying out loud on the short waves.

These men went back and forth so often, no one questioned them about it.

Vermen's lips curled into a pleased smile as he clambered down the ladder. It was his turn to hunt. He stalked down the street, strode across an intersection, then reached a narrow road many couriers sped through. He'd have to knock the man unconscious and off his bike without damaging either too much. Gunshots would bloody the uniform, while caltrops would destroy the tires and make him suspicious. The antique houses on each side sported staircases that led to the second and third floors' balconies, putting him almost right on top of the biker's path. A jump from above was the best he could think of. He had no time for anything more elaborate.

As he started toward the street, his gaze fell upon an old, bright orange rope at the top of a nearby trash bin. He hurried to it, tested its strength; thin, but sturdy enough. Perhaps he did have time for something more elaborate, if frankly more ridiculous. He grabbed one end of the long rope, tied it tight to a metal staircase—with a few extra knots for safety—then ran across the street. If anyone showed up now, as he repeated the operation on the other side, he was well and truly screwed. Ousted before he could complete his cartoon-worthy trap.

Vermen finished the last knot, then checked what rope he had left. The spool was still long enough for a second line, as he'd hoped. He sprinted back to the start, his palms sweaty from stress and exertion. A new messenger could be there anytime now. They should, judging by their average frequency.

A soft motor whirring confirmed his suspicion. Vermen hurried with his last knots but as his heart pumped faster, his fingers began to slip. He swore, steadied himself with a deep breath, and finished. Then he dashed into the nearest alley, crouched, and prayed the two tight lines would suffice.

The courier hit the accelerator as he reached the long stretch of road. He sped up as he came nearer to Vermen, bent over his bike, without a helmet. His gaze remained glued to the road and at the very last moment, his eyes widened: he'd spotted the rope barring his way. Hans could imagine the silent swear as the courier straightened up, hit the brakes. Too late. The motorcycle screeched, its tires smoked, but the taut line caught the messenger at shoulder height and flung him off his vehicle.

Vermen sprinted out as the man hit the ground with a scream, arms over his head to protect himself. A bloodied trail marked his passage on the cracked asphalt. The courier rolled over and pushed himself to his knees, then reached for his gun despite his dazed look. He would shoot before Hans could knock him out. Vermen prepared to duck but unless the crash had messed up this soldier's aim, he was dead.

Another gunshot rang to his left, far from the courier. The soldier gasped and reached for his neck as blood welled between his fingers. Vermen closed the distance, his heart hammering against his chest, and kicked the courier out cold before he recovered from the distraction. Panting, he whirled around and searched for his unexpected ally. Stern strode out of a nearby alley with a familiar, victorious sneer.

"That was the worst ambush in existence," he said. "How did you ever become captain?"

Irritation mixed with Vermen's relief. Couldn't it have been Joshua instead? Or any other rebel, for that matter? Stern hadn't changed since their split in Elmsfield, except for a new scar along his chin. He held his arm close to himself, though, in a strange position. Vermen ignored him and used his sleeve to staunch the blood from the courier's neck wound. Splatters of red already marked the man's clothes.

"You bloodied his uniform."

"Not a lot. I can bluff that away." Stern stopped right behind him. Vermen frowned as he heard a strange tightness in his voice but before he could do anything, he felt a cold barrel against his neck. He froze, holding back a curse. Stern cocked his gun. "You need to explain what you're doing here with Seraphin's *skeptar*."

Vermen stared at the ground, his hands clenching into fists. "They shot him, Stern."

"So you figured that was a perfect time to get a trophy and run while Maniel tried to save him, is that it?"

Run. Did it look like he was running? Vermen took a deep breath. He didn't have time for Stern's ridiculous theories. He pushed himself to his feet, ignoring the firearm pressed against his neck. "You misunderstand. He's dead." His voice was hoarser than he'd have wanted. He could hear the broken parts of him in it, showing through. Stern whispered a soft denial and Vermen turned around to face him. "The *skeptar* is him now, and we're going into those headquarters to get the man behind that order."

It seemed to take Stern an eternity to recover. The rebel stared at

Vermen, silent, and Hans recognized the strange mix of anger and sadness in his eyes. Then Stern's shoulders slumped in defeat. He removed his gun and withdrew a knife.

"I tried to warn him about you when we split." He started cutting the ambush's ropes, struggling not to use his left arm, talking more to himself than to Vermen. His voice shook. "I told him not to trust you with his life. You know what he said to that? He said 'it's okay, Stern, he's already saved my life more often than you have. Besides, I kinda like him.' And he laughed. You know the one. The dismissive, you-worry-too-much laugh."

Stern hacked at the lines but without holding them with his second arm, they didn't cut. Hans suspected he didn't care. He ignored the other rebel and pulled the scratched bike and body out of the narrow street before another courier came through. Stern's words clung to his mind, however. *I kinda like him.* In Elmsfield? Vermen recalled a long kiss on the top of a hill. He remembered being told *not to make a big deal out of it.* Would Hans have been faster, had Seraphin not said that? Could they have been together, even for a little while? His head fuzzy and light, Hans pushed the questions away and started unbuttoning the soldier's uniform. Stern joined him as he removed the shirt. He threw the spool of orange rope at his feet.

"You're not going in. I am."

Vermen's eyebrows shot up. No way. He straightened to face Stern again. "No."

"I'm one of his oldest friend."

There was an unsettling plea in Stern's voice. His scowl displayed Vermen's own grief and hurt and thirst for revenge plainly, and Hans had to look away. They both knew what *he* was to Seraphin, or could've been. Vermen let the matter slide. There were more practical—and less awkward—

concerns. "You have a broken arm."

"It's my left, I'm fine. I can do it."

Vermen's temper flared and he grabbed the front of Stern's shirt. Wanting to avenge Seraphin himself was one thing. Lying about his well being and risking its success was another, far more stupid one.

"Do you actually think I never noticed you were left-handed? You punched me several times with that left arm, under Mount Kairn." Vermen let go before he turned violent. His urge to destroy something had grown steadily since Seraphin's last pained scream. "You can't shoot straight, they would remember a courier with a broken arm, and General Clarin's entourage knows you. I am not endangering this mission to sate your desire for vengeance."

"Yours though, that's fine."

Vermen shrugged and started putting on the uniform. "I'm not going to fail."

Stern tensed but did not answer for the longest time, turning away as Vermen removed his pants to change into the courier's. Hans almost laughed at his reaction. How many naked men had he seen in the showers, only to be bothered by the thought of him in his underwear? Vermen kept the comment to himself, however. Angering Stern any further would not be productive.

"All right," the other rebel said at length. "You go. But remember...When you shoot down Omar Clarin, you are not only doing it for Seraphin. You are doing it for every rebel you put in prison. For all of us."

Vermen lifted his head and met Stern's gaze. The specific wording was an intentional reminder of his part in their deaths. He remembered what Andeal had told him, about rebels being like a second family.

"I understand." His answer was met with a doubtful frown. Hans ignored it and pulled his boots on. "Maniel and Alex are trying to take the Radio Tower. Go help them."

Stern accepted the order with a reluctant nod. He detailed Hans from top to bottom until his mocking sneer returned. "Fits you like a glove. Good luck, Captain."

The rebel strode away before Vermen could return the courtesy. Hans gritted his teeth. Something about the rank jarred him. He hadn't been a Union captain in a long time, yet when he looked at his reflection in a window, his heart tightened. Instead of a downtrodden outlaw crawling through caves and countryside, he faced a proud soldier, ready to do his duty. His thumb ran over the red string, still warm.

They had a rendezvous with Omar Clarin.

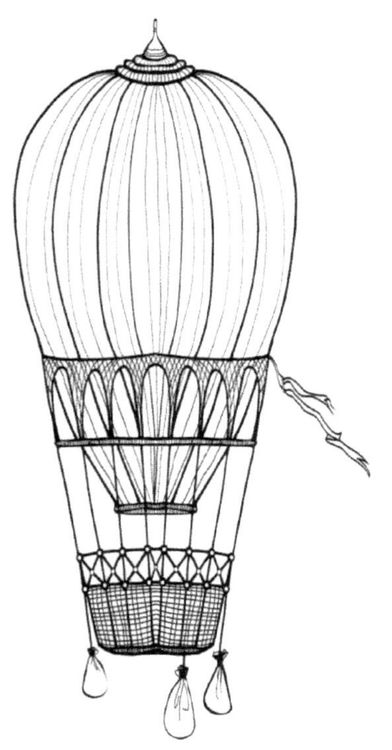

# CHAPTER FORTY-FOUR

*Before he could find General* Clarin, Vermen wound up in front of a holding cell, in which a green-haired prisoner waited tied to a chair. She had to be Seraphin's captured rebel. She matched the description Lungvist had given of her, was the only civilian he'd seen since entering the headquarters, and her face and neck were covered in bruises. Those were not from David. Omar Clarin had probably interrogated her.

He ought to leave her there. Freeing Treysh was not his objective and an escape attempt would alert the soldiers to an intruder in their midst. He should get to Clarin, shoot him and then—if he still lived—come back for her. On the other hand, no one had questioned him since he'd entered. He'd blended into the crowd with surprising ease. His quick answers and sharp demeanor screamed old-time soldier. Added to the courier outfit, it'd granted him a free pass around the headquarters. If they searched for an intruder, he might not be their first target.

And there was only one guard at the door, a young man from the local police with a set of square glasses. The missing partner was an anomaly too odd not to investigate a little.

"She's the rebel?" he asked as he looked through the window.

"Yes sir. I hear she's as crazy as they come. Guess you've got to be, to join their little band."

"Indeed." Vermen moved out of the window and closer to the guard. "Shouldn't there be two of you? They did trick thousands of people into marching toward this building. I suspect they'll try to free her."

"They already did. A man came here disguised as a lieutenant. He had false papers from the president requesting a transfer. My guess is those pieces of trash forced Kurtmann to sign them before they got him to broadcast. My partner's guarding the traitor and waiting for General Clarin to arrive before returning here."

Vermen tried to make sense of the story. They hadn't sent anyone with false transfer information, so who had? Perhaps Treysh had a couple of unknown friends who'd mounted the operation. Or Andeal and Henry had found rebel sympathizers to help. They'd die for her. Alongside her, even. Omar Clarin would see to that. Vermen kept his expression neutral and indifferent to the rebels' fate.

"Where can I find the general? I have a message for him but compared to my backwater outpost, these headquarters are a maze."

"He ought to have reached the fake lieutenant by now. Just go down the corridor, up the stairs, then turn left. It should be the second room on your right."

Vermen nodded as he memorized the instruction. He glanced at the door, then back at the lone guard. "Thank you."

He ought to leave. Go kill the general. She wasn't his priority. She wasn't even his problem. Vermen started away, just one step. Stopped. How many rebels had he thrown in prison and allowed to die? And this one was Andeal's university friend. Could he risk avenging Seraphin to save her? Would shooting Omar mean anything if he let another rebel die? Vermen swallowed hard, looked back at her constellation of bruises. He spun on his heels to face the guard.

"One last thing, soldier…" Hans closed the distance between them, drew Seraphin's pistol, and smashed its hilt against the man's temple. The poor sod had just enough time to raise his arms in defense before he was struck. He crumpled to the ground without even a scream, his glasses skittering across the floor. "I still can't believe your partner ditched you. Bad decision, that."

Vermen bent over his body, withdrew the key, and unlocked the cell's door. He pulled the unconscious soldier inside, closing the door behind them. His heart hammered as he straightened up. He'd have to be fast. The longer he stayed here, the more likely it was that they'd be discovered. Treysh raised her head, flicked her hair back. From up close, Hans noticed a thin film of sweat on her forehead. He wondered if she was always so pale. Judging from her wide grin, though, she wasn't too hurt.

"Now that's a rescue if I ever saw one!" She squirmed in her chair and gestured to indicate she wanted her hands free. "I've got to admit, I expected a familiar face, though."

Vermen moved to her and slid the key into her manacles. The moment she was free, she jumped to her feet, shook her hands with small huffing sounds, then waved her arms up and down in a wide, relaxed gesture. He felt like he'd unleashed an energy bomb. With every passing second, David's assessment of her seemed more accurate.

"I'm Hans Vermen," he said. "Former captain."

"Oh! You're *that* guy!" She clapped her hands, delighted by the idea. Then she bent over in a sudden coughing spell. Vermen waited it out with a slight frown, but she continued on like it never happened. "We have a friend in common. You know...tall guy, wheezy voice, put me in prison?"

"Lieutenant David Lungvist."

"Yeah! He had so many questions about you. Poor guy, if I didn't know better I'd say he's smitten."

Vermen pressed his lips together. Had everyone seen it but him? His head felt hot and he wondered how red his cheeks had just turned. Treysh didn't comment, though. She stretched her legs, then her back and neck.

"So what's the plan?"

A part of him already regretted saving her. She seemed unable to keep it shut for more than a few seconds and would alert the entire headquarters before long. He needed to get to Clarin as fast as he could.

"You're on your own." He opened the door a crack and checked the corridor. No one in sight. "I have a general to shoot."

Vermen expected Treysh to protest, to ask for an escort out. Instead she laughed and crouched next to the unconscious policeman. "Sure thing. Don't get killed."

"Not before I'm done."

His answer drew a giggle from Treysh, which turned into another cough. Vermen stared at her as she recovered from it, then she began unbuttoning the guard's uniform. One loose screw, Lungvist had said. He never did have much patience for eccentrics. Neither did Hans, in truth, and he had no plans to stick around.

"Enjoy your freedom."

Vermen left the cell to the sound of her delighted laughter and a quick, confident "Oh, I will."

He hoped she'd make it to the exit without being caught and even more importantly, without raising the alarm. If the headquarters learned they'd been infiltrated, he would never reach Omar Clarin.

No one forgot Clarin's deep bass voice. It reached inside and resonated through Vermen's bones, shaking his confidence and making him feel small, unimportant. Hans paused, struggling with his doubts. Would he be up to this? Could anyone really waltz in and put an end to such a great man? He leaned upon the wall and wrapped his fingers around Seraphin's pistol, touching the warm string. Holt's *skeptar* renewed his courage. Seraphin had done it before. He was with him now. Hans could not turn back.

Then another voice reached him, familiar and quite alive, prompting him to hurry.

"These papers were signed by President Kurtmann himself. I'm sorry to interfere with normal chain of command, General, but his order does precede yours."

Lungvist's speech was Omar Clarin's opposite in every way: wheezy and unimposing, it rebuilt Vermen's spirit as fast as it'd been taken down. Hans inched closer, his grip tight against the pistol. David must've found Galen's secret labs. As predicted. Hans wished he could underscore how right he was to Seraphin, and delight in his defeated pout. Vermen could always count on his lieutenant. And while he had no idea how his discovery had led Lungvist to the headquarters, trying to free the very rebel he'd put behind bars, it sounded like his friend needed to count on him now.

"Haven't you heard, Lieutenant?" Omar asked. "Your precious president is dead, shot live on today's broadcast. So these papers..."

The ripping sound that followed chilled Vermen. He swallowed hard and covered the distance between him and the door. His heart hammered in his chest. A gun clicked inside and Hans resisted the urge to peek. He could not risk it. At least Omar was still talking.

"We expected an escape attempt but I must say, you disappoint me. We trusted you to uphold the Vermen brothers' legacy. I hope you're at peace with your treason."

Heat rushed to Vermen's head and clogged his mind. That was a death sentence, all right. And on his behalf? Had the Clarins been feeding lies to Lungvist before he'd seen him in Serenity? Not that it mattered. Now was an excellent time to interrupt. With a soft prayer to the entire Holt ancestry, he burst into the room.

"General Clarin, sir, urgent message!"

Despite being no taller than five foot six—quite a bit shorter than Lungvist—Omar Clarin dominated the room. His mere presence imposed upon others, in a way not unlike his voice. A third soldier—a woman, probably the guard's missing partner—waited at the back, at attention. Clarin held David at gunpoint, his arm angled upwards to compensate for his height. That was bad. The shock from a bullet might make him press the trigger. No choice, though. Clarin's and Lungvist's eyes were already widening in recognition. David began to crouch as Vermen raised the *skeptar*.

"It's from the White Renegade."

Hans Vermen pulled the trigger. Before he thought too much about the risks for Lungvist and formulated second thoughts. Before the general could spin around completely and shoot him. It really was that easy. You just walked in, aimed, shot. The blast deafened Vermen and the old weapon recoiled with surprising strength. A dazed satisfaction swirled in his stomach as the bullet sank into Clarin's heart. The general twitched as he reached for the wound, his fingers clenched. He licked his lips, tried to utter a word but blood welled out of his lips. Omar Clarin collapsed. Vermen never saw him hit the ground.

Two successive gunshots rang out and pain exploded in his knee and hip.

The soldier, Hans thought as he fell. Good training. Good discipline. Never kill if you can question later.

His elbow smashed against the floor and he hissed to vent the pain without screaming. He clutched his knee as darkness obscured his sight. Vermen forced his breathing to slow despite the crippling agony. The bullets felt like white-hot iron through his bones. He clung to consciousness long enough for the throbbing in his ears to subside and his vision to clear. Panting, Hans struggled into a sitting position. Blood already soaked his courier uniform.

Lungvist had knocked the firearm out of the other soldier's grasp and shoved her against the wall. She struggled but he was stronger, taller, and better trained. He had enough control to turn to Vermen.

"Brilliant, Hans! How do you plan on escaping now?"

Vermen gritted his teeth. Talking. Now that would require focus. "I just saved your life, you ingrate."

"You compromised yours, and since I'm not leaving without you, I think it's safe to say you only bought me time."

A thin and satisfied smile stretched on his lips. David's typical I'm-right-and-you-know-it expression. Lungvist loved having the last word. Even now, with soldiers on their way to capture them, he enjoyed winning this argument. Vermen wiped his brow, smearing blood all over it. When he answered, he had to punctuate every sentence with a painful gasp.

"I'm okay with that. I came for Clarin. You're just...just an unnecessary extra."

His friend faked hurt then laughed, a familiar soft wheeze that comforted Vermen. Hans stretched his hands to grab the *skeptar* and bring it back, close to him. It seemed he wouldn't be able to return it to Seraphin's body after all. At least he'd managed to take Omar out.

"That's..." Lungvist didn't finish his sentence. "Where are the others?"

"Dead, dying, fighting. Winning, maybe, if the police and army can't reorganize fast enough."

Vermen expected reinforcements to arrive any time now, so he straightened up, determined to meet them with what dignity he could muster.

A policeman did enter the room, but not the type he expected. This one had dark green hair stuffed under her beret, her old guard's square glasses perched on her nose, and an excited grin. Seraphin's rebel girl hadn't escaped when she could, it seemed. Hans didn't know if he was more relieved or annoyed.

"Why are you two idiots standing there?" she exclaimed. "It's like you actually want them to catch you!"

Vermen wanted to point out 'standing' was not an option for him but before he could reply, Treysh strode to the held soldier and smashed her firearm's hilt against her temple. Like Vermen had for *her* guard. The woman slumped in David's arms and he slid her to the ground.

"What are you doing here?" Vermen asked. "You should've left when you could."

"Did you really think I was leaving?" She checked the unconscious soldier's pulse as she waited for an answer. When he didn't give one, she burst into a cheerful laugh. "Oh boy. You don't know me at all. I'm saving your asses, that's what I'm doing."

She pranced to Omar and crouched over the dead general, reaching for a short-wave radio at his belt without the slightest hesitation. Vermen didn't like the eager grin on her face, like she was about to pull off the best of pranks. Treysh pushed a button and let out a questioning "Hello?"

Two seconds later a furious voice answered. Hans recognized the same smooth man who had interrupted the recording and declared the protest illegal. Had she called Galen Clarin directly? Why would she warn him? He held Andeal hostage and surprise might be the only way to save him. He called for her to stop but Treysh brought the radio to her lips anyway, her words lost under his exclamation and the dull thump in his skull.

Then, before she could keep going, Treysh bent over and protected her mouth with her arm. The deep cough that followed sounded almost as painful as Vermen's knee. Lungvist withdrew from her, all the way to the opposite wall, his eyes wide with horror. "When did you get sick?"

Treysh straightened with a groan and rubbed her face. "Sick? I'm not. I..." She stopped, reached for the wall behind her, as if dizzy. "They gave me something this morning?"

David's panicked swear acted like a powerful hand squeezing Vermen's heart. Perhaps he shouldn't have been so dismissive of Treysh's coughs when he'd freed her. Something was up, and it terrified his lieutenant.

"Stay away," David ordered. "Don't approach me. Don't touch Hans."

"We need to get out," she answered.

"No! You'll infect everyone." Lungvist reached for the pockmarks on his face. "It's started. You're only the first. I should shoot you now." His hands rested on his empty holster. He shook his head. "You're lucky I promised Schmitt I would save you. We'll figure something out. Try not to breathe on anybody."

"Fantastic!" Treysh lifted her arms but her grin hadn't vanished. Almost like she didn't care. "But hey, I am a crafter of explosive miracles, I should be able to live without breathing, no probs. Soldiers are coming. Allow me to save you all before my contagious cough becomes the harbinger of death."

David's terrified expression morphed into an angry scowl. "Be serious. Galen—"

"Hush!" Vermen glared at them until neither talked back. He could hear the soldiers coming. How had he managed to be more reasonable than both of them combined, despite the buzzing in his head and unstable floor beneath him? "Argue when we're out. Treysh, follow your plan."

"Yes, Captain!"

She gave him a salute—one so lax he'd have soldiers punished for it— and ran out of the room, her wide smile replaced by a credible grim frown. Hans hoped the plan was a good one.

"Here!" she called to the incoming soldiers. "That rebel trash escaped. She killed General Clarin and shot a courier. We need an ambulance, ASAP!"

Lungvist and Vermen cringed. 'An ambulance' wasn't the call they used in the military. She wore a local policeman's uniform, though, so they might let it past. Vermen hoped they did. He couldn't maintain a complex bluff. Thick sweat drenched his clothes, his vision blurred again. One hand slipped from his hip wound, drained of the strength to hold it. He tried to tighten his grip on the *skeptar*. David crouched at his side and applied pressure for him before taking his hand.

"Hold on, Hans. It's just a bit of blood."

Vermen stifled a chuckle and squeezed his lieutenant's fingers as hard as he could—which mustn't have been all that much. Soldiers crowded the room, orders were shouted, but everything appeared distant to him, part of another world. Even the pain in his knee receded, along with the floor's reassuring cool. He had no idea how much time passed, if he'd lost consciousness and come back. Lungvist hadn't moved.

"David." Vermen swallowed hard, gathered his thoughts. His head was hot and he couldn't focus. He wouldn't be any more help to Maniel and the others. But Lungvist...Every word escaped his lips in whispers. "I need you." David's eyes widened and he clung tighter. Hans shifted a little and gasped as sharp pain erupted in his knee. "I need you to get me out. Alive. Finish this and protect..."

He pushed Seraphin's pistol toward Lungvist. The lieutenant stared at it for a second, then slipped it in his holster.

"You can count on me."

The wheezy voice seeped into his mind, enveloped it. A soft smile drifted to Vermen's lips.

"I always can."

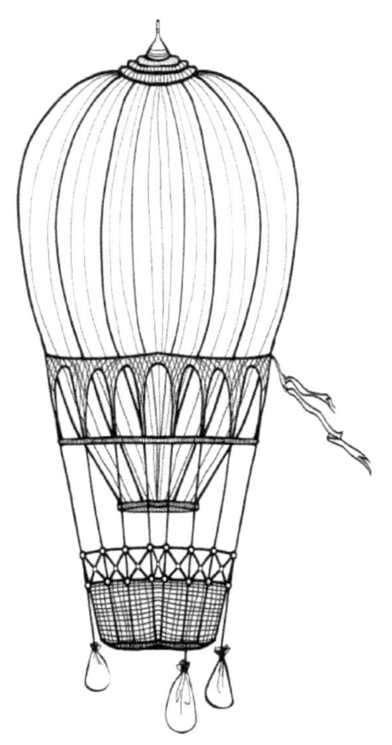

# CHAPTER FORTY-FIVE

*Fingers pinched Andeal's* nose and woke him. He shook his head to get rid of them and took a deep breath when he was released. Andeal's instinctual panic calmed and he tried to get his bearings despite his powerful headache. They'd stopped in a small room with unfinished walls and an open cupboard full of janitorial tools. Andeal was manacled to a pipe, sitting on the concrete floor, his side still radiating dull pain. The area around had been cleared of anything he could use as a weapon. An emergency solar lamp provided the only light. They must be in the basement. Galen Clarin welcomed him back with a crisp smirk.

"As you can see, we are not out of the tower yet. We had a little...inconvenience."

Andeal pulled himself to an upright position and massaged his stiff neck with his free hand.

"What inconvenience?"

He feared the answer but if this was why Galen had bothered to wake him, he'd hear it whether he wanted to or not.

"You're not a fool, don't act like one. He hid in the recording room the whole time, didn't he?" Galen clacked his tongue and crouched next to Andeal. "You became so helpful when it meant keeping me from entering it."

Andeal clenched his teeth and avoided Galen's gaze. What had Henry done? He should have escaped while he could. Saved himself.

Fake pleasantness had vanished from the scientist's tone—a rare occurrence, never a good sign. Galen grabbed the back of Andeal's head and forced him to meet his eyes.

"My men will hunt him down and bring back his body riddled with holes. Just like his father's. I'm done with the Schmitts."

Mention of Henry's father brought angry bile to Andeal's throat. How much had Lenz given to free Andeal, and Maniel, and unravel the truth about the Clarin twins? First his son, then his freedom, and finally his life. All for nothing. They had failed him. They'd failed everyone, really. He was surprised Henry still fought at all. He'd always been rather stubborn.

"You'd be surprised what Henry can do."

Galen replied with a scoff. "I've read a detailed report that qualified him as clueless and incapable. It was wrong about his role in your little joke but I am confident in this evaluation of his skills."

"It's those you don't expect who are the most dangerous."

"We'll see." After a dismissive shrug, Galen straightened up, pulling Andeal by his hair in the same movement. The engineer moaned from the sudden pain, like a bolt of lightning through his neck. 'You lied to me. That's a bad habit to have."

The meager defiance Andeal had summoned to defend Henry vanished. He cowered against the wall, a lump of solid fear in his throat. He knew that soft, angry tone, like a father with a disobeying child. It starts now, he thought, and it never ends. His breathing turned into a hiss. Galen patted his cheek.

"Let's be honest, here. I haven't done any human testing in the last, oh, three years? I was rather busy chasing your group." Galen lifted Andeal's left hand, placed it over a section of wall devoid of pipes, then spread his fingers, one by one. "What we'll be doing together is torture, plain and simple. We'll still call it science, though. It looks good on paper and I find it amusing. Do hold still."

Andeal obeyed, too confused about Galen's intention to rebel. It had *always* been torture to him, but the scientist's cool admission added a layer of horror to it. What could he have planned that even Galen refused to consider science? Andeal fought his growing nausea. He had to pay attention. Every mistake would worsen his case. The scientist stepped back twice before he seemed satisfied with Andeal's position. He remained still for a few seconds, studying his prisoner. Andeal's heart sped as he waited for his sentence.

Galen's hand flew to his pistol without warning and he shot. Andeal withdrew his hand with a surprised yelp and the bullet hit the wall. Tiny shards of plaster stung his skin as he brought the hand close and held it against his torso. Andeal panted, eyes wide, stunned. Galen lowered his firearm with a slow shake of his head. Now even his smile had vanished. Moving was a mistake. He should have let the scientist shoot his fingers.

"I told you to hold still," Galen scolded. "I'm a bit rusty and if your Henry is as dangerous as you say, I need to practice." He gave a dramatic sigh and moved to a table buried under construction tools. His hand drifted over them before landing on an electric drill. "Now I'll have to screw it on."

Andeal choked on a sob. He tugged on his manacled hand several times, pulling as hard as he could, the metal chafing his skin. What was he thinking? Never defy an order from Galen. The payoff wasn't worth it. Andeal's gaze landed on the drill and tears ran down his cheeks.

"Please..."

"You should've thought about it," Galen snapped back. "Now stop fighting or I'll end up nailing every part of your body to the concrete."

Galen Clarin approached with his drill, grabbed Andeal's hand, and slammed it against the wall, over the bullet hole. Uncontrollable shudders ran through Andeal's body and he feared Galen would mistake them for a fight. The tears blurred his sight but he gasped as a cold tip touched the middle of his palm. The screw. Andeal blinked the tears away, tried to slow his breathing and steel himself. Galen powered the drill mid-air—a terrifying, warning whir before the screw's pressure in his palm increased. Andeal shut his eyes tight. The cold metal jerked when Galen settled the drill in place.

Then he pressed the button.

Metal dug into Andeal's palm and sent waves of crippling agony through his body. He screamed. At least he thought he screamed. The drill's noise tore through his ears and pain flared all his senses. Andeal's legs kicked out despite his efforts to keep still while his stomach climbed all the way back to his throat, threatening to eject itself. It lasted a few eternal seconds, then stopped as abruptly as it'd started.

Andeal slumped and hung, his legs devoid of strength. Gasping sobs interrupted his panting and he couldn't stop either. He flexed his fingers, moaned at the flashing pain in his palm. He felt both numbed and strangely conscious of every part of his body—the blood running down his sleeve, the bitter aftertaste in his mouth, the throbbing in his heels after too many hits against the wall. It was all there, close to his mind but paling compared to the cold sensation of solid metal through his palm. He let out a long, shaky breath while Galen set his tool back on the table and admired his handiwork. He picked up his pistol again and Andeal closed his eyes. He didn't need to watch Galen take aim a second time.

Galen's short-wave radio emitted a loud burst of static, then an enthusiastic "Hello?" came through. Andeal looked up as he recognized Treysh's voice and a warm feeling spread through his belly. The scientist snatched the small radio from the table.

"What are you doing with that?"

The cold fury in his tone extinguished Andeal's meager hope. Whatever she said, whatever she did, he would be the one to pay for it.

"Remember me, Galen?" she asked. The heavy static could not erase her cheerful tone. "Your twin's dead, my friend, and I am coming to cough all over you. Over and out!"

They heard part of her laugh before the communication was cut. Galen's hold tightened over his radio until his knuckles turned white. He stared at a point on the wall, his mouth twisting into a snarl, little by little. Then he slammed it down on the table with a cry of rage.

"No." He snatched the drill, set the tip into the screw once more. "Dead? They think that's a good thing, don't they? They think they can just kill Omar and get away with it?"

Andeal whimpered as Galen powered the drill again. Except this time, he unscrewed him. The metal twisted in his palm, through flesh and muscles at a slow, excruciating pace. The lights turned back on then, all at once, and

Galen's younger, smooth voiced filtered through the radio station's speakers once more. Andeal mumbled Henry's name, shook his head. He received a powerful slap from Galen.

"You and I have places to go. One in particular." He sped the drill and removed the screw altogether. Andeal fell to the ground with a moan, only to be picked up by Galen. "Did you know Omar liked to be loved? He was always the one pushing to 'do this right'. He wanted to be remembered as a savior. A hero." He scoffed. "I don't really care. And since you are so determined not to give our family the love it so rightly deserves, we'll at least make sure you peasants learn to fear our name."

Andeal tried to ignore Galen's rant, bringing his hand closer to him, but the tone and increasing pace terrified him. This *one place* could only be his new labs. The scientist slid a finger under Andeal's chin and forced him to look up. "You already shake at the mere thought of it, my blue friend. Surely we can teach everyone else."

Galen Clarin pulled Andeal back to his feet, holding him in a slumped, standing position by the armpits. Andeal clung to consciousness, on principle more than anything, dizzy and nauseated. The scientist grinned at him and there was a renewed excitement in his expression. Not unlike his smile as he lied on the radio but darker, wilder. A cold shudder shook Andeal's body as his captor undid his manacles.

"Let's head home and prepare them a gift, shall we?"

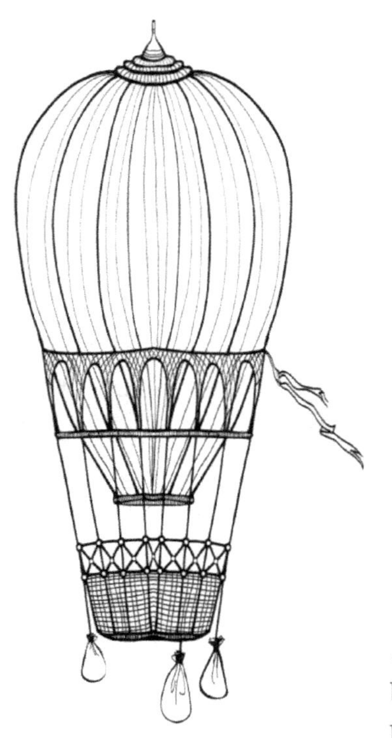

# CHAPTER FORTY-SIX

*Henry climbed the stairs* between floors two and three, satisfied by the neon lights brightening his path once more and Galen's smooth voice coming out of the speakers. That was good, no? The radio was running again. He had no idea for how long, just like he had no idea what to do now. His father's recording played in the background. He'd accomplished what he meant to, and now he was alone in the Radio Tower. Since he lacked better options, Henry opted to be ready to continue the broadcast once the recording had played.

Then a door somewhere below swung open, the push-bar smashing against the heavy metal. Henry's heart rushed into his throat and he froze mid-step. Galen's voice reached his ears—not from the speakers, but right here in the staircase with him. They hadn't left.

"Hold him for me, will you?" the scientist said. "He's smearing blood all over my clothes."

Blood all over. Andeal was with him. He had to be. Henry took a deep breath and gripped his pistol with a trembling hand. Could he save him? He had taken out two elite guards at once. Maybe he could do it again.

A soft moan bounced off the staircase walls from below as bodies shuffled around. Andeal.

He *had* to do it again.

A strange determination calmed his frenzied heartbeat. Henry thought of his first visit to the tower, of how they'd accomplished the impossible so far. He remembered the exhilaration pumping through his veins as he'd sprinted out of the National Radio, transmitter in hand, lightheaded at the risks taken and overcome. He clung to the memory of Treysh's peck on his cheek, too. For a moment he had felt invincible.

That's what he'd need now. Invincibility. Even without it, though, he was going to try.

He padded toward the stairs and took a first step down, settling his foot on the metallic step as gently as possible. He peeked down the staircase well and glimpsed four heads. Blood smeared Andeal's blond shock of hair. Henry took another determined step down. They began climbing up. There were four of them and they were more noisy, but he was convinced every time he moved, the little scuffle of his feet on the ground would reverberate straight into their ears and they would look up.

They didn't.

Not until he was half a floor above them. Henry lined up his pistol, cursing silently at his constant shake. Blood pumped against his temples and he leaned forward, aimed. The pistol tip touched the railing. Just a small tap, a split second. Enough for a crystalline *ting* to echo through the stairwell.

One guard looked up. Henry shut his eyes and pulled the trigger.

The gun's kickback surprised him, a tremor going through his arm and shoulder, and his shot went wide. He'd set his elbow firmly in the ground earlier and hadn't realized how big a difference it made. He heard his shot thunk into the wall, then a bullet whizzed past his head and Henry threw himself to the ground with a yelp. He covered his head, despite the shots coming from below. Breathe, Henry. What a ridiculous idea this was.

"Henry?"

Gunshots almost buried Andeal's hesitant question. Henry raised his head and crawled to the edge of the stairs. He glanced over, for a fraction of a second, before another volley forced him back.

"Yeah!" he called out.

His first answer was a soft, mocking laughter from Galen Clarin. Henry clenched the gun's hilt tighter. He hated the sound. He'd never heard it before and he already abhorred Galen's laugh. Once again, he leaned over the edge, risking the guards' carefully aimed shots.

"Next time I might get your head!"

This provoked another derisive chuckle from the scientist—and from the sound of it, he was moving away. Henry's heart tightened. He had to do something now or they would escape But they had him pinned there, huddled on the metal steps and reduced to ridiculous empty threats. He stared at his bloodied pants, as though they would give him an answer.

It came from Andeal instead.

"Henry, Omar is dead! Galen is taking me to the labs, he—"

A resounding slap interrupted him. Andeal's cry of pain ripped through Henry's insides. He jumped to his feet and tried to aim at the guards, shooting twice in a row. They grabbed Galen and Andeal and pulled them out of sight. A bullet hit the railing right in front of Herry and he scrambled back. As silence fell again, Galen's voice rose.

"We have to be off, Mister Schmitt." The level of scorn the scientist put into his name impressed Henry. He couldn't help but feel a little proud about it. "Enjoy your silly radio show while it lasts."

The ground floor's door opened. Henry could hear Andeal's brief struggle and muffled protests as they forced him through. He wanted to follow, to run after them, but the certainty of a bullet to his head kept him glued in place. What good would it do? All he could do was stay here. Stuck in the tower, pinned by the relentless shots of Galen's guards until they were all out of reach. Then he would be free to enjoy his radio show, while this horrible self-congratulating scientist would take his best friend back to the torture chambers. "Laboratories".

Henry flung the pistol at the wall before him with a frustrated yell. All he was good for was blowing hot air into a balloon's envelope and eating his damn noodles. He was so useless Galen didn't even bother to go after him. He'd left him alone. With the radio.

*With the radio.*

If he couldn't stop Galen Clarin, others would. They had killed Omar, hadn't they? They were out there, in the protesting crowd—Maniel and Vermen and Seraphin. Stern and Joshua, too. Even Lungvist. They were all out there, ready to help. He had the means to contact them.

Henry jumped to his feet, the knot in his throat unwinding under the effect of renewed hope. He sprinted all the way up the stairs and shoved the sixth floor's door open. As he emerged in the lobby, with its great window, he caught sight of the billows of smoke over Reverence. He edged closer, to get a better view. Gas and smoke obscured half the panorama his vantage point offered. He spotted burning trash cans and barricades built from fences, dumpsters, and everything else at hand—was that pink from a lawn flamingo? Protesters huddled behind their meager protections to hurl flaming projectiles at unyielding lines of riot police. Other squads pursued pockets of rioters, chasing them through the smaller streets.

But the battle was the most intense at his very feet. The area around the National Radio Tower was thick with scarfed protesters, armed with makeshift shields and the wooden sticks of broken signs. Hundreds of them faced not only riot police but Union soldiers—a handful of them, who had retreated against the radio's main doors. Henry's eyes widened as he noticed the army's men raise their firearms and line them up at a group of protesters. Their officer lowered his arm in one sharp movement. The screams and gunfire came muffled through the window, the civilians fell like dolls, and it all seemed from another world.

It wasn't. He had allies right outside his door, and they were dying.

Then another group of protesters threw several projectiles at the soldiers—rocks, flaming bottles, a trash can lid—and charged. They plunged through the ranks, clubbing their enemies with improvised weapons before any more shots could be fired. Henry didn't stay to watch the ending. He prayed they had a few radio receivers down there and ran to the broadcast booth.

The screen of blood in the window made him squirm but Henry grabbed the red cable and switched from the disc reader—his recording had finished while he stared at the fight anyway—to the microphone. He wasted no time with introductions.

"Guys!"

The sound of his own voice in the speakers startled him. He took a deep breath to calm his nerves. If he didn't sound dignified they might not listen to him.

"To the people fighting outside the radio...Galen Clarin is about to escape. He has Andeal with him. I think he has a car, maybe? He's trying to go to his secret labs. Something about Omar Clarin being dead and maybe he wants to avenge him? You have to stop him."

He was dying to run to the window and check if his words had provoked any reaction. What if they didn't hear? What if they didn't care? He had to believe they would. They were fighting to get inside the Radio Tower. To him. To Andeal, too. Henry had to trust they were capable of accomplishing what he'd failed to do. The radio was all he had left but with it, he might still stop Galen Clarin.

"He killed your families. He will do it again. Please. You traveled all the way to Reverence. You refused to stay in the field and came with us in the streets. This is the last thing we ask of you: stop that car. Stop Galen Clarin and save Andeal." Henry ran a hand through his hair, grimaced at the dried blood in it. Kurtmann's, he knew. "It's your turn now, people. I'm counting on you."

Henry put the recording back on. He didn't know what else to say and refused to let silence take over every receiver in the Union's territory—not today. While Galen Clarin once more explained the progress of his plans with Omar, Henry returned to the window. He pressed his nose on the glass and watched as disciplined soldiers retreated from the mass of protesters, their leaders screaming into short-wave radios just behind them. Although he could hear none of what was said below, there was an aura of careful confusion about the troops' movements, like they didn't know if they were supposed to back down or charge.

Henry wished he could see Galen's car. It had to be out back but the suspense was killing him. He tried to read either discouragement or a cheer from the rebels as they progressed and reached the Radio Tower's door.

Someone would be up, sooner or later. He kept staring through the window, letting the minutes pass by. He heard running footsteps coming up the staircase. That was his answer. He hoped it would be the one he wanted.

Stern pushed the door open and called his name.

"There you are," he said.

His tall friend held one arm close to his chest while the other held a blood-splattered pistol. Pain shortened his breathing and his grim expression twisted Henry's insides. Stern had never smiled much but now the snarl of his lips, tensed shoulders, and forceful tone denoted a deep anger. They hadn't stopped the car. He didn't even need to ask. Henry rested his forehead on the cold glass.

"I tried. I really tried."

"So did we. He ran over Joshua." Stern moved closer to the window. "Maniel is down there too, trying to save him. You said Omar was dead?"

"Andeal yelled it to me."

Stern took a deep breath and his gaze went north. Henry wondered what he could be staring at so intently, but he never had the chance to ask. The other rebel sighed.

"Now he's off to those secret labs no one ever found."

His words sunk into Henry like one powerful fist. Not of dread and powerlessness, though. As Stern brooded over their failure to stop Galen Clarin, Henry realized this wasn't over. Someone *had* found the laboratory compound. Someone could lead them straight to Andeal. How had he not thought of it sooner?

"I'm an idiot."

Henry Schmitt did not explain his declaration. He spun on his heels and ran back to the microphone.

Arguing voices—one of them muffled—tugged at Vermen's mind, bringing him back to consciousness. A thick haze slowed his mind but he forced his brain to concentrate on the words he could not decipher. Meaning was assigned to them as he emerged from his torpor, until Hans realized they were arguing about...fireworks? He opened his eyes with a frown and tilted his head to the side. Lungvist was sitting on one side of his stretcher while Treysh was in a corner of the ambulance, a mask over her mouth. Whiter than before, too, which made her bruises even more obvious. David held his hand, squeezing it whenever the rebel girl irked him—quite often, in short. They were going on about whether any illegal fireworks were left in her home. Treysh seemed to think the idea Lungvist could've found them all ridiculous.

"Do you two ever stop?" Vermen asked.

They did. Both fell silent the moment he spoke up. David let go of his hand, pressing his lips together and forcing a smile on them. After two blessed seconds of silence, Treysh broke the peace.

"It's not my fault your lieutenant is such a pretentious know-it-all."

"He's *your* lieutenant, soldier. Watch what you say of ranking officers." She must really get on David's nerves, if he couldn't stay calm enough to stop her from breaking their cover. This was not the kind of mistake he made. "How's my leg?"

The wracking pain had morphed into a persistent throb since he'd lost consciousness, but he suspected that was the painkillers, not actual healing. Neither Treysh nor David dared an answer, confirming his doubts. The paramedic in the back with them leaned forward. "We'll get you on an operation table and remove the bullets soon. It should manage. We arrived in time."

The intense wave of relief made Vermen dizzy. *It should manage.* He had seen soldiers broken by the loss of a leg and he did not want to be one of them. His leg should be fine. *They had arrived in time.* Not only had he avenged Seraphin, he would live to tell the tale with barely more than a scratch. How strange, that both of them could take down a general in his base and survive it. It should not have been.

Hans thanked the paramedic, then touched David's wrist. "The pistol?" he whispered.

His lieutenant nodded. He did not need to say more. Vermen gave him a slight smile.

Then a familiar voice burst out of the radio on the ambulance's dash, covering the machines' regular beep with a desperate warning. As they listened to Henry plead for the protesters to stop Galen's car, Vermen thought of Maniel. She had to be in that group, a scarf covering her mouth, cardboard shield in hand. Ready to rescue her husband. Could they block the vehicle in time? He exchanged a worried look with David and Treysh but none of them commented. The paramedic gave a disapproving grunt, then called to the driver. "As long as they don't try to stop our ambulance."

"Let them try."

Treysh interrupted their discussion with a long and deep cough. It sounded wetter to Vermen, like the insides of her lungs were coming off, hundreds of thousands of bloody cells she was trying to spit out. Or perhaps his painkillers were messing with his brain. He took a deep breath. The occasional bump in the ambulance's speedy flight through the street reverberated in his wounded knee and reminded him his current ease was artificial. He could feel himself slipping back into darkness as the silence stretched on. Then Henry's voice returned, even more urgent and strong than before.

"David, we need you here. We need you now."

With a slight frown, Hans glanced at Lungvist. Had he been in contact with Henry? Even his cobwebbed mind could see how that linked the president and Schmitt together, how it made perfect sense. And really, who else could this 'David' be? Lungvist had tensed, teeth gritted together. He seemed to hesitate. His dark gaze went to Hans' leg and Vermen understood.

He would need a vehicle. To get there fast, to go after Galen if he'd escaped. But if the ambulance never reached the hospital, Treysh and him might pay the highest price. Vermen swallowed hard. He brought to his mind the absolute terror the thought of returning to the labs had provoked in Andeal, ages ago when Hans had tried to escape, and he drew all the courage he could from it.

"This guy sure doesn't need a courier," he said. "That's a clear message if I ever heard one."

Then he gave David a meaningful look. Lungvist took a deep breath and wheezed out, "It sure is."

They both turned to Treysh, who answered with an excited giggle. David set his hand on the pistol hilt at his side and Vermen recognized the bone handle and red string. The paramedic caught on just as his lieutenant sprang into action. He had time for a "wait a minute..." before Treysh jumped him and smacked her own firearm against his temple. David moved behind the passenger seat and pointed Seraphin's *skeptar* at the driver. Vermen wondered if he realized it had no more bullets inside.

"My apologies, but we *are* trying to stop the ambulance. Do it and leave."

Hans couldn't see his lieutenant but he heard the man's smirk in his tone. So did the medic, judging from the strength with which he hit the driver's wheel.

"Your buddy's legs will—"

"I'm aware," interrupted Vermen. "Stop the ambulance."

The vehicle finally slowed, until it came to a full stop. Treysh dragged the second paramedic out and offered them both a cheerful apology and her thanks before she climbed back up. Lungvist flipped the emergency sirens on as she slammed the doors behind her. The ambulance lurched forward as David hit the pedal, the electric motor's whirring loud as they gained speed. Hans Vermen closed his eyes and tried to ignore the nagging throb in his knee. It was nothing. They were going to save Andeal.

Perhaps he wouldn't escape killing Omar without a scratch after all.

When an ambulance came to a screeching halt next to Joshua's broken and bleeding body, a deep knot unwound in Henry's stomach. His friend's luck hadn't abandoned him yet. Someone had called the emergencies and the paramedics would help Maniel. She still bandaged the wounds she could with ripped clothes, blood spatters on her sleeves.

Then Lieutenant David Lungvist sprang down from the driver's seat and Henry realized that *someone* was him. He stared at the pock-faced soldier, his mouth wide open. Maniel jumped to her feet and reached for her weapon.

"No, no, he's with us," Henry said. "This is David Lungvist. He knows where the labs are."

Her gaze flickered between the two men and she relaxed. "Tell me you have morphine back there."

"No idea." An amused smile played on the lieutenant's lips. "I have a captain with his knee busted and a pestulance-ridden green-haired girl but as far as medical supplies are concerned, you'll have to take a look yourself."

Henry's heart leapt into this throat. A green-haired girl! He'd done it. Lungvist had gotten Treysh out of prison and saved her. He sprinted toward the back of the ambulance and grabbed the handle, pulling the doors open with great enthusiasm. The second part of Lungvist's description sunk in as Henry's gaze fell upon Treysh's sweaty white face, her obvious wounds and the mask held to her mouth. Pestulance-ridden? He didn't climb inside. What did he mean, pest-ridden? What had they done?

"Oh, hey Henry!" Treysh exclaimed, with just as much energy as she'd always had. "We heard you on the radio. Need a lift? Hop in."

"I...yeah. Are you okay? I'm so sorry!"

He pulled himself into the ambulance, wondering if she knew all of this was his fault. Had Lungvist told her how he'd discovered her involvement with the rebels? Would she forever hate him?

"Apologies accepted. I can't believe you'd send this jerk after me not once, but *twice*? He is the worst at rescues, I tell you."

Before she could say another word, a terrible cough forced Treysh to bend over. Henry listened to the deep, wet sound with growing horror. How had Andeal described Lenz's illness? He took a step forward and reached for her, hoping to give her a measure of comfort. Treysh waved his hand away.

"You should stay back. Wheeze-man thinks I'm super contagious."

It felt like a stab to the heart. Henry stopped breathing for a moment, blood drained from his face, and the world's noises seemed so distant. They had given it to her. For the second time in his life, a woman who mattered to him—no, a woman he loved—was dying from one of Galen Clarin's plagues.

"I don't want to stay back."

He did anyway. Despite his petulant tone, he remained rooted to the spot. Treysh's bright gaze met his. She wasn't scared in the slightest. She clapped her hands together and he was certain she was grinning under that mask.

"I'm glad you're here with me. Now let's go save Andeal, shove all the drugs in the world into my body, and then launch the most beautiful firework show the Union has ever seen!"

Lungvist climbed into the ambulance before Henry could answer. He let out an exasperated sigh, then put his hand on Henry's shoulder.

"Go sit up front and make room. We'll get your Burgian on a stretcher beside Hans. That way he can join our club of potential carriers of Galen's most recent gift. It'll be fantastic."

Henry couldn't help but note that despite his sarcasm, he had already risked having Vermen near Treysh for a long period. The captain didn't seem conscious at the moment but all his vitals beeped normally. A glance at his bloodied knee and hip was enough to tell Henry he couldn't be called healthy either. He jumped out of the ambulance and ran to the front seat, sitting down as Lungvist and Stern helped Maniel heave Joshua in. A third person— Alex, they introduced themselves—stayed with Stern to protect the

Tower.Although Henry's head still buzzed from the strange shock, he couldn't help but smile when Treysh exclaimed "You have to be Maniel!"

Despite the two wounded men next to them and Maniel's frantic work on Joshua, despite Lungvist's dangerous driving through Reverence's streets as they made for the secret labs, emergency sirens on, Maniel and Treysh picked up a conversation long overdue in the back of the ambulance, talking like two old friends who had a lot of time to catch up on.

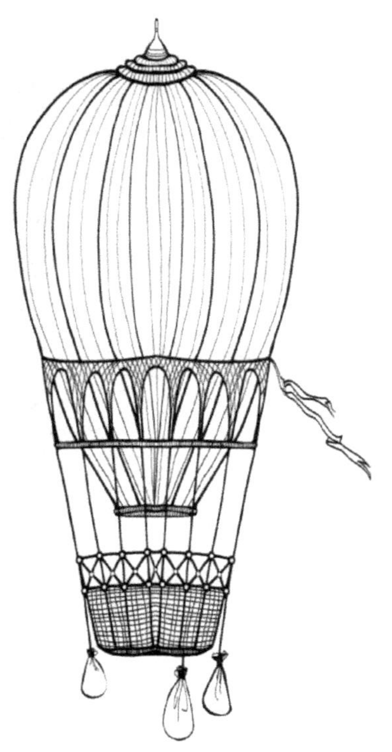

# CHAPTER FORTY-SEVEN

*Andeal's first hint of* consciousness was the stinging pain in his abdomen. He fought against it, knowing on instinct he didn't want to return, didn't want to step back into this world, to no avail. Cold stone against his back drew him further out of the darkness, and all the hurts across his body soon followed. He shifted with a moan. His left hand slipped from his lap to the ground and sharp agony flared from his palm. Andeal straightened with a gasp, panting, then swallowed hard.

They'd left him alone in a posh office, on the ground behind a large black desk, propped against a wall. They'd manacled his feet but left his hands free. Two bookshelves stretched on either side of him. The walls were white and empty, there were no windows, and the only door was as dark as the desk. The latter had a stylized lamp but a powerful neon illuminated the room at the moment. For a long time, Andeal remained put, his gaze drifting across the numerous titles. All science handbooks on genetic manipulations, different techniques, or treatise on virology and microbiology. Sometimes a binder broke the monotony of wide, colorful spines with overly serious titles. Andeal stretched his hand to slide one out, curious. Judging from the ton of papers inside, it was either articles or correspondences with other scientists. Andeal pushed it back where it belonged.

This had to be Galen's office. Perhaps he should smear blood all over Galen's precious books, just to annoy him. Andeal's heart tightened into a painful ball at the thought. No matter how small the slight, Galen would give it back tenfold. All he needed as a reminder was a glance at the shredded flesh in the middle of his left hand. He tried to flex his fingers and the influx of pain made him choke. They only twitched. All but his pinkie, which folded, and the ring finger, which moved a little.

Andeal's gaze caught on the remarkable absence on his finger and a powerful wave of nausea climbed into his throat. The simple leather band he'd exchanged with Maniel was gone. Galen had taken his only memento of her. Andeal brought his legs closer and stifled a shaky moan. He leaned his forehead on his knees, fighting against the tears and anger. He must have taken it after they knocked him out in the car.

Henry's attempt to save him in the staircase had given him a new surge of hope. He remembered discovering the mass of protesters outside, armed, advancing on the car with the clear intent to stop it. A rock had hit the side and made Galen swear softly. They'd shoved him into the backseat, alone with the scientist. With the two guards in the front, he'd thought maybe this was his chance. Maybe he'd given up too early, maybe it wasn't over yet. He'd smashed his elbow against Galen's nose, drawing a much louder curse out of him, then reached for the lock. His hands shook so badly he'd fumbled on it, unable to flip the switch, then the cold barrel of a gun had pressed against the bottom of his head. He'd hesitated, considered fleeing anyway. Better dead than in the lab.

Then he'd spotted two beloved figures outside. Joshua came running out of the intersection first, his shorn red mane regrown into natural brown hair. Andeal's gaze didn't linger. Right behind him followed Maniel, her ponytail trapped under the scarf tied over her mouth, holding a chunk of wooden fence as a shield, angry determination painted on her face. She was beautiful and alive. Beautifully alive. He'd gasped, whispering her name, and flattened his hand against the window, breathless, like he'd never seen her before and was falling in love all over again. Like they were alone in the world.

"Run them over."

Galen's cold voice shattered his illusions. The car's electric engine roared to life. The surge of hope their proximity had brought morphed into voiceless horror. Andeal read the surprised swear on Joshua's lips, watched Maniel scramble back while he remained rooted to the spot. The dull thunk of a body had crushed Andeal's insides as surely as it did Joshua's bones. He bent over in his seat, nauseated. A hand grabbed his shoulder and turned him around.

"You look like you could use some sleep," Galen said.

He'd smashed his temple before Andeal could react and until he woke in the office, it was the last he knew.

She was alive. The leather band might be gone, but she wasn't. Andeal remembered how she'd laughed when he had offered the ring. He had presented it like it was the most beautiful thing in the world, like they hadn't just moved into a damp cave and dared to call it home. *You always do that,* she'd said. *No matter how dark our situation is, you never let it get to you.* He had never told her she gave him the strength to carry on like that. He should have.

Now he would have to get out to do so.

Andeal struggled to his feet, wincing at the sharp pain in his ribs. He never should have given up. What was the point of waiting for torture? Better to die trying to get away. But he had been too terrified to see it. Months aboard the hot air balloon had dimmed the memory of his strong-headed, brilliant wife. And the last few weeks crawling through the countryside, pained and famished...after a time he'd thought of the Union's Day's broadcast as the end of everything. Galen might not have convinced the rioting protesters it was over, but he had convinced Andeal.

Not anymore, though. A glimpse of Maniel had breathed new courage into him. It didn't matter how often he failed or what kind of reprisal Galen Clarin inflicted on him: he had to escape. Andeal scanned the room for a plan, any idea, no matter how desperate. He clutched the bookshelf for balance, his legs weak. He couldn't run with his feet manacled, but he should be able to move about the room. He tried the door and found it locked. No surprise there. It was unlike Galen to leave him alone at all and Andeal suspected Omar's death was affecting him more than he let on. Not to the point of leaving him in an unlocked room, though.

He had, however, forgotten his short-wave radio atop his desk. Andeal's heart sped and he shuffled closer, then reached for the transmitter through which Treysh's voice had interrupted his first torture session. He had to set his wounded palm flat on the desk to maintain his balance and gritted his teeth against the pain. He could suffer a little for a chance to talk to Treysh—

to talk to *anyone*, really. Andeal inspected the device for an instant then pressed the communication button and brought the mic to his lips.

"Treysh? Treysh, it's Andeal."

His voice was broken and raw. Too much screaming, not enough talking. Andeal held his breath as he waited for an answer. His hands shook and no matter how hard he tried, he could not calm them. Then there was a quick static and his friend's blessed voice came through.

"Andeal? We're coming. We're on our way, buddy, don't you worry."

He choked down a sob and collapsed into Galen's tall leather chair. He didn't want to know how they could be on their way. It was enough to know they were. The radio gave another slight burst of static. Another voice followed.

"Stay safe, love."

"Maniel!"

He'd grabbed the radio and jumped to his feet, only to lose his balance and fall against the desk, dropping the transmitter. Andeal scrambled for the short-wave, for the chance to say more than her name, when he heard the door unlock. He froze, laying flat on the cold floor, one hand outstretched. The paralyzing fear crept back in him as Galen entered the room. Maniel called his name through the radio. Dead giveaway, even if his latest act of rebellion was not already plain.

"Lovesick?" Galen asked as he strode into the room and snatched the radio from the ground. He hit the speaking button with a wide smirk. "I'm sorry, my dear, he's a bit busy at the moment. If you want to join him, however, I would be pleased to have you both back. I forgive easily."

Andeal closed his eyes as long seconds went by without an answer.

When Maniel replied, her voice had turned cold and tight. "I don't."

Galen laughed and snapped the radio to his belt. He crouched next to Andeal and pulled him up by his shirt. He should fight but had no strength, as if Galen's mocking tone had drained all his fleeting courage.

"She's lovely."

Andeal met his gaze. Perhaps he did have a little bit left. He spat in Galen's face, causing the scientist to drop him and backpedal with a disgusted exclamation.

"You aren't," Galen added.

A soft laugh escaped Andeal's lips. He didn't fight as Clarin lifted his shoulders off the ground and dragged him out of the office. He would pay for this. Galen did not forgive—that was a lie and everyone knew it. He would make Andeal pay for using the short-wave radio and spitting, but also for Henry's interruption in the stairwell, for the elbow in the car.

Most of all, however, Andeal would pay for Omar Clarin's death.

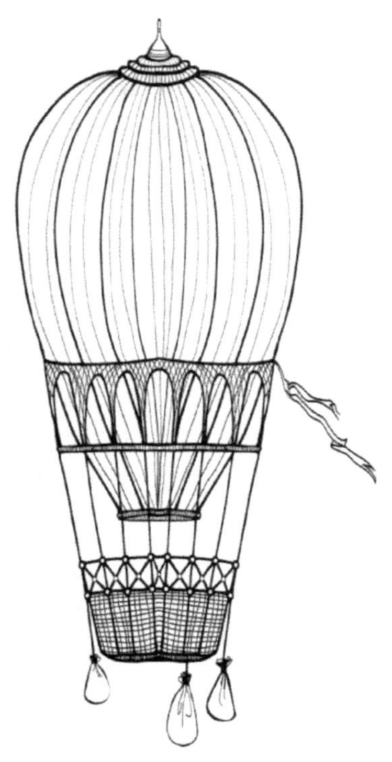

# CHAPTER FORTY-EIGHT

*In Henry's mind they would* all enter the secret labs. Even Joshua and Vermen would rise from unconsciousness and stand beside him, ready to kick down the main doors and assault the facility. When he found himself alone with David Lungvist, creeping toward a side door with a loaded pistol in hand, he was a little dumbfounded. It made sense, though. Maniel was the only one who could keep a professional eye on Vermen and Joshua, while Treysh's coughing fits had gotten so bad that despite her assurance all was well, everybody knew she was dying. Dying fast, unlike his mother, who'd endured long bedridden weeks. Henry wondered which was worse. Which would be harder for him, too.

But the question was void. Treysh wasn't going to die. David Lungvist would get her drugs while he tried to find Andeal. His stomach still clenched at the thought of sneaking through the compound alone. When had everybody decided he could accomplish anything with a measure of success? What kind of ridiculous idea was that? But Henry didn't have a choice, so he clung to his rare accomplishments. He'd shot that fire extinguisher, after all, and he'd played the recording three times and no one had been there to help with those things.

He was not a hero. He had told Joshua that, once, and hadn't understood what his friend had meant, saying it didn't matter and that none of them were heroes. But he understood now. They hadn't needed heroes. They had needed regular folks flooding the streets of Reverence instead of staying in the fields. They needed people to act, to try what little they could.

That's what he was doing. He was trying.

If he could succeed, too, that would be fantastic.

At least the facilities weren't the scary glum building he'd expected. No electrified fences surrounded the white-brick building and its roof was the same flat style as all the others, most likely also covered in solar panels. It looked like a small industry's disrepaired warehouse, not an ultra-secret laboratory containing microbes capable of wiping out the entire capital. At first even the corridors inside were cracked old cement and dull beige wall, mold running up and down like they owned the place. Perhaps Lungvist had the wrong location?

Then the floor turned to brand new tiles and a fresh gray paint covered the walls. Instead of the dusty, rank odour, the place smelled of strong alcohol, blended with several chemicals he didn't care to identify and a faint sulfur scent. Henry would've thought he'd stepped into a hospital, if Lungvist hadn't led him into a larger, warehouse-like room.

Except no crates were stored here. Four large tanks filled with a yellow, nasty liquid lined the walls on each side. Unknown pipes sprouted from the steel tops and disappeared into the ceiling. The containers had to be taller than seven feet, more than enough to enclose a man. Fans and other machinery gave a soft hum that reminded him of the Great Whale's belly. Henry approached and squinted at the liquid. Billions of tiny particles gave it an almost opaque look. Not particles, he realized. He set his palm against the glass and his stomach twisted when it felt a little warm. Body temperature warm.

"Are these..."

He couldn't complete the thought. Did Galen really have so much bacteria ready?

"Yes." Lungvist's voice was tight. Stressed. He brought his arm over his mouth and gave a single, deep cough.

Henry scowled. "You caught it, didn't you?"

The lieutenant met his gaze and answered with a deliberate nod. "Your girlfriend has been coughing all over me."

"She's not—"

"Don't care." He cleared his throat and squeezed his eyelids, as if in pain. "My lungs never recovered from Clarin's first plague. I'm not surprised. If he hasn't moved them, though, the antibiotics aren't far. I'll be fine."

"All right. Okay. Is this where we split?"

He didn't want to. Sick, annoying Lungvist was better than no one at all. The lieutenant nodded, however, and gestured at a door on their left. "I go through there. You go that way." He indicated the two larger swinging doors at the other end of the area. Henry wished he'd pointed to something less intimidating. He gritted his teeth as David continued. "This isn't a big place. You should be able to find—"

A loud scream interrupted David. It'd come from upstairs, above their heads, and Henry's breath caught in his throat. That was Andeal. He swallowed hard and his hand fell to the small radio transmitter at his side—the one Treysh had stolen from Omar. They'd taken it in case Andeal managed to send another message, but now Henry was dying to yell at Galen and tell him to back off. His grip tightened on the short-wave receiver.

"I don't think I can wait for you," Henry said.

"The stairs will be on your left. Take your chance if he's alone."

"I'm a terrible shot." Henry couldn't help but argue, even knowing there was no point. David had to get those meds as fast as possible. If they did not contain the Plague, thousands would die. With Andeal's scream still echoing in the back of his mind, however, all those nameless citizens didn't seem to matter as much.

"I'll be as fast as I can," Lungvist said, coughing again. "Good luck."

He spun on his heels and stalked off, his lanky legs stretching into long strides. Henry watched the strange gait for a moment, reminding himself that the potential victims weren't all nameless. A second, jerky yell from Andeal called him into order and he sprinted off. He didn't have a second to waste, not if he wanted to put an end to the agonized screams tearing through the building. He pushed through the swinging door, his heart pumping so hard he could feel the blood pulsing at the very tips of his fingers. Henry hurried into the staircase, taking the steps two-by-two until he reached the top. Only then did he slow. He didn't want to alert Clarin he was there.

As he edged out of the staircase and into an aseptic corridor much like those below, Andeal's moaning plea drifted down the passage. The dull thud of a hit followed, drawing another yelp. Henry prayed Maniel could not hear him, that no open windows allowed the heartbreaking sounds to carry out into the city. Staying behind had enraged her. He could not imagine how she'd feel, being forced to listen to her husband's screams while she was stuck in the ambulance, unable to help.

Galen Clarin's mind must have followed a similar path because at that moment, the short-wave receiver at his belt gave a quick burst of static. Henry scrambled to turn it off with a low swear but he had no idea what buttons to press. The scientist's educated voice filled the corridor, both from his radio and an open door farther down.

"Since you enjoy communication so much," he said, "let's make sure we keep it open for your friends to hear."

"No, no, don't—"

Andeal didn't finish his plea. Henry thought he'd heard the crackle of electricity but Andeal's scream covered it immediately. He heard it like a strange echo: one clear and loud, less than a hundred feet away, while the other, full of static, seemed to come from a distant land. It didn't last. Galen stopped his torture as fast as he'd started it.

"We have company," he said. When he spoke again, his voice was louder, steeped in amusement. "Come out."

Henry froze. He wanted to swear and throw the receiver at a wall, to curse himself for carrying it and curse Galen for using it at this very moment. He wished he could disappear or go back in time and try again. He was so close to them and yet he'd failed, in the most pathetic of ways.

Sometimes trying wasn't enough.

A gun clicked through the radio. "Don't be childish and make me count. You have three seconds to step through the doorway and surrender or your little blue friend will meet my brother's fate. I'd love a chance to reproduce President Kurtmann's masterpiece with his brains."

Despite the horrible joke, Galen's mirth had vanished with his warning. His voice became terrifying when it lost that fake but pleasant, well-meaning undertone. Henry swallowed and hurried to the door, hanging just outside its frame. If he dropped his weapon they would shoot him down on sight. He was stupid, but not *that* much. When he stepped into view, he had his gun leveled at Galen Clarin.

Henry's stomach lurched as he took the scene in. Andeal hung next to an incubation tank—smaller than those below—his right hand manacled to a thick pipe coming off the top. He held the left one close to his chest and through all the blood Henry could see a dark hole in his palm. Beads of sweat ran down his friend's forehead, into the almost purple streaks of tears. Galen pressed a gun to his chin, but it didn't seem to bother Andeal. Instead his friend stared at Henry with a feverish, pleading gaze. *Don't surrender*, it said. Henry clenched his fingers around his pistol's handle.

"Free him."

"Really?" Galen chuckled and shook his head. "No one gives away their favorite toy. Now drop your weapon."

Henry shook his head. Bitter anger swirled in the pit of his stomach. He refused to surrender, not to such a monster, not now. But with Andeal's life in the balance, he couldn't bring himself to shoot either.

"Henry..." Their gazes met. All Henry could read in Andeal's was resignation. "It's okay. Really. I'm okay with it."

Irritation flashed through Galen's expression and he dug his barrel deeper into Andeal's chin. To Henry, however, he gave a wide smirk. "Come, now, you're not that kind of man. You would sacrifice a friend? I know you, Henry. I've watched you. You don't have the guts for it."

Henry's hands shook so much he doubted he could even aim. He tried to calm himself with reminders of all Galen had done. This was the man who'd sacrificed thousands in a bid for power, killed his parents, poisoned Treysh. And now he was torturing Andeal. Everything they'd done was meant to take him down. He had a chance to finish it—but it'd cost Andeal his life. What would he tell Maniel? His throat tightened and he could barely breathe. He avoided his friend's gaze and gave a slight shake of his head.

"You're right. I can't," he told Galen.

He lowered his weapon ever so slightly. With a triumphant grin, Galen removed his gun from Andeal's chin—or started to. Henry squeezed the trigger, shooting the scientist's foot, and blood splattered on the ground. He heard the man's yell and gunshot reply as he fell but dared not glance at Andeal. Instead Henry shot again at the falling body, hitting his torso this time. Not quite where he'd aimed for but Henry would take what he got. Good thing he was so close to Galen or he'd have missed. The scientist crashed to the ground and his weapon slipped from his hand.

Henry thought his heart would explode. Blood trickled down Andeal's neck but it seemed superficial. A new bullet hole had appeared in the ceiling rather than in his head. Relieved, Henry advanced on the fallen scientist. It was over. Somehow, Henry had done it. He wasn't a complete failure.

With an enraged grunt, Galen grabbed his gun.

Time slowed for Henry as the scientist took aim. The barrel moved through the air as though it was thick gelatin, stopping as it lined up with his heart. Not good, Henry thought. His head buzzed. He froze, wondered how much it would hurt. Andeal yelled something at him but the words were a garble. His friend swung from his hanging hand, kicked out as far as possible. His foot reached the gun and tipped it as Galen pulled the trigger.

The detonation preceded a flaring pain in his shoulder by a split second. Henry stumbled forward with a gasp, reached for the wound. His fingers came back bloodied. Galen's gun had flown to the left, out of the man's reach. The scientist struggled to push himself up but collapsed with a moan. Blood soaked the front of his shirt and his smug grin had turned into a grimace.

Henry ignored his agonizing shoulder and stripped off his leather belt. He tied Galen's hands behind his back, then to another solid-looking pipe. The scientist fought, wheezing, but his strength was trickling out of his wounds and he never managed to overpower Henry.

Only once Galen was immobilized did Henry turn to Andeal.

"I'm so sorry about this," he said.

"Sorry?" He broke into a soft, mirthless laughter. "You just saved me!"

"He could've shot you."

Andeal's unsettling chuckles stopped. "Better dead than with him."

Henry could only stare at his friend, short on words. He had nothing comforting to say, wasn't sure any words would make it past the lump in his throat anyway. He managed a weak nod, then glanced at the manacles. Galen must have the key. Henry searched for it, checking the scientist's pockets while ignoring his glare. Every movement was painful, but it kept him busy, which saved him from finding an appropriate answer. As it turned out, Galen did not have the key. Henry straightened up, clacked his tongue.

He didn't want to leave Andeal alone but he'd need to find something to snap the manacles open.

"Maniel's waiting for you outside, you know," he told his friend. "I'll get these things open and you'll be in her arms in no time."

Galen Clarin scoffed at his reassuring words and the derisive sound broke Henry's tentative calm. Too many friends were wounded or sick or tortured and here was Galen Clarin, genetic engineer genius, mocking him. He had lost and he was still laughing at them.

Henry squared his shoulders and glared at him. "Why don't you shut it and bleed to death? It'll do all of us a lot of good."

Galen shrugged, still smirking, and closed his eyes. Henry clenched his fists and returned his attention to Andeal. His friend did not smile. Henry hated the serious and broken expression on Andeal's visage. He wanted the smiling, joyful Andeal back, but he knew it wouldn't be that easy. It would take time. Henry squeezed his friend's shoulder.

Andeal barely reacted, just tilted his head to the side a little. "Give me his gun and go, Henry."

Something in his tone was off. Henry's throat tightened, but he nodded and obeyed. He couldn't leave Andeal defenseless, after all. It already pained him to abandon his friend like this, hanging from a pipe, only the tips of his toes touching the ground. Someone needed to get the keys, though.

"I'll be quick," he promised.

For Andeal's sake, but also his own. He couldn't wait to have some strong painkillers shut down the horrible throb in his shoulder.Henry threw another hateful glare at Galen Clarin and hurried out.

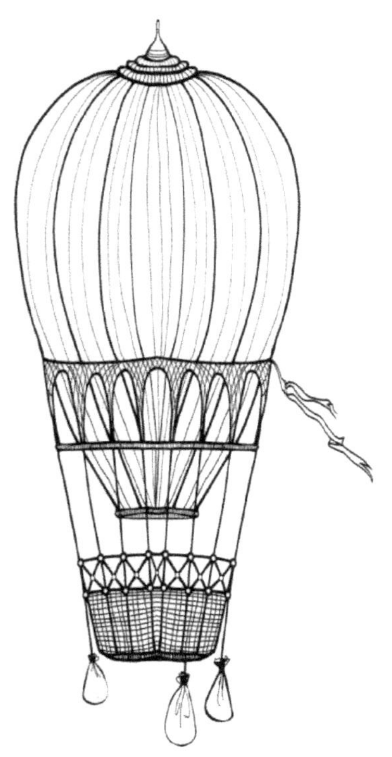

# CHAPTER FORTY-NINE

*Andeal closed his eyes and* tried to lean on the incubation tank behind him. The manacles bit into his wrist and his feet were stiff from trying to reach the ground, but the two sensations paled compared to the flaring agony Galen had inflicted on him. The electric cables he'd used to zap him lay on the table a few feet away, next to the short-wave receiver that had betrayed Henry. Andeal scanned the room in a dazed, unbelieving state. He hadn't slept in days and every little bit of pain from the last hours—every moment of despair—was combining itself into one crushing exhaustion that numbed the hurt in his entire body. He had no strength left but he didn't need it anymore.

Henry Schmitt had saved him. Like father, like son. Thankfully the latter didn't have to give up his life in the process. It was amazing how far away the reluctant man tied down in his little town was now. He wondered if

Henry realized it, if he'd intended to use that projection of a weak, scared man to trick Galen. Perhaps it had all been impulse. Even Andeal had trouble telling how much control Henry had over his fears now. *Enough*, to be sure.

"I warned you about Henry," Andeal said.

All this time, he'd avoided looking at Galen. He knew what had to be done but was scared that the sight of the scientist would paralyze him. He forced himself to turn. He wanted to be able to look at Galen without fear, without the despairing certitude that his presence meant Andeal's doom. The scientist leaned against the tank's base, his classy outfit stained with blood and stuck to his skin from sweat. Without his well-groomed smugness, he no longer gave the impression of being in control.

"You did," Galen said. Then he chuckled. "You think you've won, don't you?"

The sneering undertone sent a chill down Andeal's spine. They *had* won, yet Galen managed to instill doubts with a handful of words and the proper inflection. Andeal's fingers tightened on the gun's handle. He let the scientist go on. Something about his easy certainty fascinated Andeal and kept him from putting an end to this.

"If I haven't given you this marvelous new plague yet, it isn't because I want to keep you alive as long as possible. Though that certainly is an added bonus. It's because it's already out." Galen squirmed and straightened into a more dignified position. His lips parted into a predatory smile. "Your old college friend—Treysh, was it?—she shouldn't live much longer. It doesn't matter how things unfold now. At least she'll pay for shooting Omar. And she'll transfer my gift to everyone around her. I wish I could see your face when you hear Maniel's first cough."

Andeal shook his head. It wouldn't be like that. They already knew where to look for a cure this time, and they would find it.

Three gunshots echoed through the labs, cutting through Galen's monolog. Andeal's heart sank as the scientist laughed. What now?

"That must be my guards. I guess your Henry Schmitt wasn't all that miraculous."

Andeal snapped his eyes shut. No, no, no. There would be another explanation. Henry hadn't seemed nervous at all about searching for the keys, and he was *Henry*. If there was the slightest chance of him being in danger, it would've been written all over his face. Galen was trying to manipulate him, to make him believe it was over. And it was, but not for Andeal.

"Congratulations on making this Union's Day very disagreeable," the scientist went on. "But I'll heal. I might even be able to put the blame of this strange new epidemic on your little group and prove my goodwill by working out a treatment. This is how it goes, you know. If I get out of here alive, I write history. The Clarins' name will be marked down alongside those of other great names, as it should be."

For a moment, all Andeal could do was stare at the scientist. Galen Clarin was tied by a belt, slowly bleeding out on the floor of his labs, unarmed and defeated. Yet he spoke of glory and victory like they were right within his reach, like he just had to stretch his fingers to achieve them.

It wasn't terrifying anymore.

It was ridiculous. Disconnected.

Andeal laughed, and though his voice was rough and broken, though there was no real joy to it, he was mocking the man who'd haunted him for the last six years, and that felt great.

"You're wrong," Andeal said. "I might have no idea what'll happen to any of us if Henry is dead. We might die—blood loss, contamination, executions. But even then, we've won. We have brought together thousands of people, more than you ever killed, and they all know the truth about you. It is nestled in their hearts and guts. Things started changing the very first night I gave my name on the National Radio's broadcast. They will continue to do so whether or not any of the White Renegade's rebels survive the day. But that's not even the best!"

Galen sneered. "What would that be?"

Andeal shifted his grip on his firearm, setting the ring finger over the trigger. One working digit was more than enough. He felt lightheaded, a step removed from the world. Part of him wanted to laugh again. Galen had killed Lenz Schmitt, tortured Maniel and him, even made Treysh his patient zero. He had exterminated thousands years ago, was trying to do the same again. Yet he couldn't imagine what would be 'the best' for Andeal, here and now.

"You'll be dead."

Galen's eyes widened as Andeal raised the pistol and squeezed the trigger. The bullet pierced the scientist's chest and Andeal shot two more. Just to be sure. Galen thrashed at the first hit, twitched at the second, stopped moving at the third. Blood pooled under him, dark and oozy.

Andeal dropped the gun and leaned his forehead on the tank, eyes shut. He should be angry and relieved and worried and lots of other things right now, but all he had was this cold emptiness. Was that how Seraphin had felt when he'd taken out Vermen's brother? He shivered, fought against the rising nausea. Warm tears flowed down his cheeks, uncontrollable. He had no idea what was wrong with him, why he cried. Galen was dead. He'd shot him. At last. The thought spun in his mind and he wished Henry would come back.

No, he wished Maniel was here, with him, that she'd hold him close. Safe in her arms he could cry until the tears dried, then fall asleep from exhaustion. But only with her.

Henry found Andeal pressed against the tank, crying. He stopped in the doorway, cutters in hand, and watched as silent sobs shook his friend's shoulders. Every sniffle tore a shred of his heart. Andeal had gone through so much, the release must've been too much for him. The faster Henry got him to Maniel, the better. As he stepped into the room proper, he noticed Galen's weird position, the extra bullet holes in him, and the pool of blood. The pistol he'd given Andeal was on the floor at his friend's feet, covered in red smudges. Guilt pressed against Henry's lungs. Why had he left them alone? He should have known Andeal was in no state to handle Galen alone.

He hurried to Andeal's side and stretched to set the cutters against the shackles. Andeal's sobs subsided when he approached and he turned his head to Henry.

"I couldn't let him..." Andeal glanced at Galen's body and started crying again. He wiped the tears away but couldn't stop the flow.

"It doesn't matter."

He snapped the manacles open and Andeal collapsed into his arms with a moan, his legs unable to carry his weight. Henry caught him and held him tight, running a hand through his hair as he would a child. After a moment Andeal's breathing calmed. He pushed himself away and straightened up, but Henry refused to let go of his arm. He didn't seem strong enough for that.

"The gunshots?" Andeal's voice was strangled and raw.

"Must have been Lungvist." He read the passing confusion on Andeal's expression. "Vermen's lieutenant. He led us here. We can explain all that once we're out."

Henry slid under Andeal's shoulder and led him out of this horrible room. Andeal's feet scuffed against the floor as they moved and soon he began crying again, but this time Henry remained silent. He suspected his friend would weep a lot in the next few days—or weeks or months—and there was nothing he could do about it but be there.

They would all be there for him.

Even Treysh, he hoped.

When Vermen came to this time, no one was arguing above him. They were no longer moving, either. He opened his eyes and found Joshua's unconscious body next to his. Bad contusions covered the side of his face and part of his torso. Fresh bandages were wrapped around his belly and Maniel was working on his leg. From what he could tell at this angle, the skin had been sheared off by a long slide. It didn't look good. He wondered if it was as painful as the growing flare in his knees.

Vermen groaned but refused to look down at his own leg. He did not want to see. It no longer mattered. Not if they brought Andeal back. Hans took a deep breath. He hoped they still had more painkillers.

"I did it," he said, still staring at the ambulance's roof. "I shot Omar."

"Treysh told me," Maniel answered, "and it allowed us to get into the Radio Tower. You were great, Hans."

He managed a crisp smile. *Great* would not save his leg or bring Seraphin back. Vermen shuffled on his stretcher, trying despite all to put his leg in a more comfortable position. He was hot, and cold, and while the world seemed so distant, every sensation was intense. He reached for his burning forehead, closed his eyes. He'd need a hospital soon.

"Sitrep?"

Maniel wasn't one of his soldiers—he wasn't even a captain anymore—but asking for a situation report as a commanding officer would gave him a sense of stability. Like he still had control over what would happen. She put a cool hand on his before she answered.

"David came back with some powerful drugs. They knocked Treysh right out, but I have no idea if it'll be enough. She was pretty far out when he returned."

"Gives us some well-deserved silence," Vermen muttered.

Maniel chuckled and let go of his hand. She started checking his knee wound. He could feel her fingers and the occasional jolt of pain, but the entire area was numb beyond that.

"You've been sleeping off the pain and fever," she said.

"Perhaps. What about Andeal?" A pause. All he needed to draw some basic conclusions. "He'll be fine."

"Your lieutenant said he'd heard screams, then two separate salvos of gunshots. He had no idea what it might mean, if it was Henry's gun or another. He went back."

"Andeal will be fine," Vermen said again, because what else could he tell her? That it had all been for nothing? He refused to believe it. And for all his mocking of Henry Schmitt, the Noodle Man tried really hard. He even succeeded at times. Without him, they wouldn't be at the labs.

Then he heard Maniel's loud gasp and she let go of his knee. Vermen frowned and propped himself on an elbow when he heard her jump out of the ambulance. She had thrown herself into the arms of a thin, blue-skinned man, his blond shock of hair matted with blood and his face streaked with tears. Henry and David stood two steps behind, silent. The former had the largest of grins as Andeal held his wife tight. Andeal kept one bloodied palm outstretched. They parted after several minutes, and the engineer wiped his eyes.

"Fine isn't how I'd define myself. But I'm here."

Maniel grabbed his chin and kissed him. Poor Andeal seemed to have trouble standing and she wrapped an arm under his shoulder to help. Hans' gaze met his lieutenant's and David smiled before climbing into the ambulance besides him. His mirth vanished after a glance at the leg.

"That bad?" Vermen asked.

A slight nod. David turned back to Andeal and Maniel. "Forget your leg," he said in a soft, wheezy voice. "Look at them."

Hans did, for another few seconds. As heartwarming as it was, however, it didn't wash away the pain in his knee, and it reminded him of another pain, one that went far deeper. Vermen set his hand on David's. "Think you can get them to do it in the ambulance? I'd still very much like to get to a hospital."

Lungvist squeezed his hand with a soft chuckle. "Yes sir."

He held onto his hand just a moment longer, long enough for Vermen to regret him letting go a moment later, then slid back out of the vehicle. A few minutes later they'd all hopped inside, squeezed upon each other. Maniel kept Andeal close to her, bandaging his pierced palm. For the longest time he only looked at her, as if entranced, but eventually his gaze met

Vermen's.

"You look like shit," he said.

Vermen laughed—a sharp, pained bark. "So do you."

They would have time to get better now, though. As the ambulance jaunted to a place where they could finally heal, all sirens blazing, Vermen thought of the one person who'd never get that chance. Seraphin was gone. He would never see Andeal again, hadn't even lived long enough to know he was safe. Despite the seven of them crammed in this ambulance, it felt empty, like the Regarian's absence occupied more room than anyone's presence.

Hans Vermen stretched his fingers to touch the *skeptar* and closed his eyes. He had already lost something far more important than his leg.

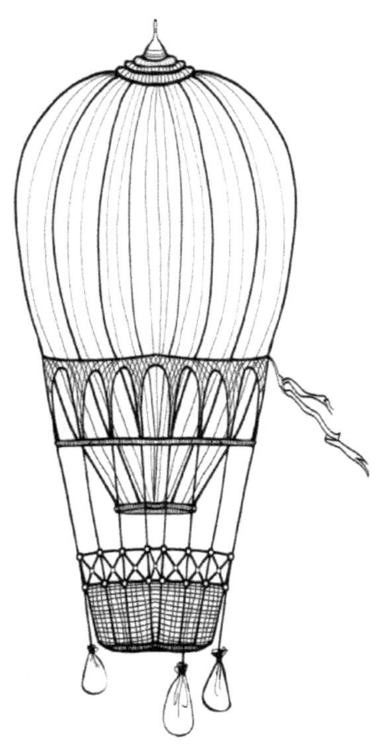

# CHAPTER FIFTY

*Henry wished he could stop* time and *not* have to live through the sad part of this day. It had all started so well! He'd gotten up early and picked up Treysh at the hospital, where she had finally received her leave from the Rebels' Quarantine—that's what they called it on the radio. It wasn't the only sealed zone in Reverence, all aimed at containing the handful of outbursts of Galen's Plague, but it was the one they'd all been housed in, and it seemed to have gained a certain level of fame.

Henry could barely contain his excitement. Since they'd thrown him out of the quarantine two weeks ago, he'd visited every day. Sometimes they allowed him to put on a biohazard suit and sit by her bed, but most of the time he had to watch and wave from afar. Everyone but her had made it out of the hospital by now—Vermen just three days ago, Andeal a week before that. The latter had his parents waiting at the exit.

Sofia had hugged him so tight Henry had almost expected to hear bones crack. "Nice radio work," she'd said.

Andeal had laughed, but he'd seemed on the verge of crying. His father couldn't help himself and was doing just that, two steps behind.

"Of course that's the first thing you'd tell me," Andeal said. "It was nothing. I just took the best of each of you."

"Liar," his mother answered. "I bet you still don't cook at all."

That was true enough, Henry knew, though he had no idea why she'd bring it up. Probably a reference to Adrian. He'd ask later. At that point he hadn't wanted to leave Treysh's side at all.

She'd spent several days hovering close to death, plugged into an artificial breather while they saturated her blood with drugs he couldn't name. The doctors said her lungs were shot. She shouldn't do anything involving smoke or dust or fumes and avoid strenuous exercises. Henry had nodded along with the recommendations. He knew she would follow none of them. She'd already muttered to him that no doctor would stop her from crafting more fireworks.

Her stay had lasted long enough that the natural roots of her hair had regrown, a deep black. Henry had hunted down green dye for her. They'd spent the day redoing her color and eating a bunch of noodles and he'd finally gathered enough courage to ask her out, at which point she'd laughed and given him far more than a peck on the cheek, and the dizzying feeling had carried him through the day. The kiss had sent his head spinning. He hadn't believed anything could be better than flying a hot air balloon. He had been wrong.

Henry's euphoria vanished as he stood on the side of the road, watching

Andeal and Maniel load the electric truck borrowed from Kinsi. They had provisions for a long voyage to Regaria. Vermen had tried to help, only to be promptly shooed away by Andeal's mother. Hans hadn't protested. They all knew his prosthetic leg still hurt by the end of the day. He sat on a large rock and tried to readjust it. Lungvist, checklist in hand to make sure they didn't forget anything, kept throwing worried glances his way. Others joined them as they completed the preparations. Joshua hobbled on his crutches under the attentive gaze of Martin, his boyfriend, while Alex chatted with Adrian. Stern carried a fair-sized box with a grim expression.

Seraphin's ashes.

When he'd learned almost all the rebels were trapped in quarantine, Kinsi had made arrangements to cremate the Regarian's body and kept the ashes safe. It was long past time to bury him with his ancestors. They had waited for Hans and then, learning she ought to be out soon, waited for Treysh. Both were here, now.

Which meant that soon enough, Andeal, Maniel, Alex and Vermen would be gone.

Henry didn't want to see them leave. He knew he wouldn't be in Reverence forever, either—he was working on permits to rebuild the Annual Mount Kairn's Race path and would one day return to Ferrea and breathe new life into it—but he clung to the little bubble of peace they had. Like life had forgotten about them at last and everyone was allowed to take a deep breath and recover.

Their departure popped that bubble. Not unlike Seraphin's arrival had, that very first day. Henry guessed it was proper. It didn't make it any easier.

When they were all done and Andeal approached, Henry threw himself into his arms and hugged him, drawing a surprised exclamation from him and amused chuckles from his family.

"Promise you'll visit," Henry said.

Andeal smiled. Large bags decorated his eyes and he was exhausted most of the time—Maniel said he barely slept because of nightmares—but he seemed more content than ever before to Henry. He had his family now, would find a place to live, just like he wanted. Galen had left him a lot more scars than partial paralysis in his right hand, most of them invisible, but there was something peaceful about the way he teased his parents or held Maniel's hand, like he knew he could work through it.

"Of course, Henry. When I finally get my degree, I won't miss my chance to celebrate with Treysh and you."

"You'd better not!" she said. "We haven't drunk to mine yet, either."

"Make sure you don't kill your lungs before I'm done, then." He gave a friendly tap on her hat as she protested, then turned to Henry. "You should come instead. Dad's a great cook."

"I will."

Andeal knew he couldn't refuse good food. Well, food of any kind, really. His friend chuckled and stepped back, glancing at Vermen. His eyes widened ever so slightly and they all followed his gaze. Hans was standing very close to his lieutenant, on the tip of his toes, whispering in his ear. Judging from the way he held David's thigh, the light blush on the lanky man's cheeks, and their general proximity, Henry doubted there was anything platonic about that whisper. And if he, of all people, could see it...

Treysh whistled loudly at them and burst out laughing as David pulled back, turning a deep red. He glared at her and struggled for a retort, which only amused her further.

"Don't be ashamed," she said. "I'm lucky my man isn't going on a month-long trip to bury his first love."

Audible groans welcomed her comment. Vermen shook his head, his expression stuck somewhere between anger and amazement. "Sometimes I think I should've left you in that cell."

She answered with a proud, wide grin, at which point Hans chose to ignore her and direct his attention to Stern. They stared at each other for a long time, neither saying anything, then Seraphin's old friend handed Vermen the ashes.

"Take care."

"You know I will."

"And tell him I'll visit as soon as I can."

Stern had somehow inherited the 'official' command of the White Renegade's rebels—like there was really anything like that left—and spent his days answering questions and requests from government agents, lawyers, and media alike. He'd had help from Mayor Riley and, as soon as he got out of the hospital, from Joshua, but he couldn't just leave for a whole month. Not so soon.

"Let's go," Vermen said.

He climbed into the back of the truck with a final wave to David. Andeal, Maniel and Alex followed, exchanging their goodbyes, and every time someone disappeared into the car Henry's heart shriveled a little more. He grabbed Treysh's hand and squeezed it, tightening his grip as the car drove away. She turned to him and whispered, "You know I brought a small firework in my pack, right?"

"Really?" Why did he ask? Of course she had. "Quick, before they're out of sight!"

It was silly and illegal and he didn't care in the least. They planted the long blue rocket in the ground with childish giggles, ignored Lungvist's protests, and scratched the matches in one big dramatic movement. Henry's hand stayed over Treysh's as they brought it to the fuse.

"Remember when we hijacked the radio the first time?" Henry asked. "I thought you were wild."

"You were right."

"Well, don't ever stop."

The rocket launched before they scrambled back, singeing their eyebrows and drawing excited laughter from Treysh. It burst high into the sky, showering bright green particles all around and drawing an appreciative 'ooh' from Joshua. Henry remained sitting, his fingers brushing against the grass and his neck bent backward as he appreciated the explosive send-off. Stars were beginning to shine and the sky to the west was ablaze, reminding Henry of the many sunsets he'd shared, flying with Andeal.

One day, he promised himself, he would also return to the skies.

# Acknowledgments

Well, here we are. I published my first book, and there are so many people that encouraged me through this project, it's hard to know whom to thank first.

Truth is, there probably isn't enough thanks in the world for Brenda. She gave this book not only her undying love, but also her considerable editing talent. You are amazing, and without your help this story wouldn't be the same.

Many thanks to Sommer, Caitlin, Tricia, Robin and Sheila, for the writerly advice and encouragements, and to Matt for believing in this project and helping me bring it to the world.

And now, because it wouldn't feel right to do this in English...

Milles merci aussi à Marianne, Eric, Audrey et Jonathan, pour avoir suivi avec autant d'attention les développements de mes histoires, et s'exciter avec moi sur la moindre nouvelle idée. Vous êtes à bien des égards responsables de la profondeur de ces personnages et de ma persévérance.

Dans la même veine, un grand merci à la communauté NaNoWriMo de Québec, pour leur énergie et leur humour. Votre jus créatif sera toujours impressionnant. Vous êtes trop nombreux pour tous être nommés, mais une mention toute spéciale à Alexandra, avec qui le tout premier germe de cette histoire est né, un soir d'Octobre à déconner.

Merci également à ma famille, pour son support constant et varié—à ma mère qui insiste continuellement pour lire mes histoires, à Gabrielle pour la fabuleuse couverture, à Catherine pour les séances d'écriture.

Finalement, merci à Eric (encore) pour son amour et son endurance—pour avoir su faire de la place dans sa vie non seulement pour moi, mais pour le nombre incalculable de personnages qui vivent tous les jours dans ma tête et dans nos discussions.

# WANT MORE?

If you enjoyed this read, please be sure to leave a review wherever you bought or downloaded it. Every review makes a world of difference, in addition to keeping the writer thrilled and happy.

Follow Claudie's works and new releases by signing up for her newsletter! Find more at claudiearseneault.com

Looking for great reads featuring ace spectrum characters
and dystopian governments?
Turn the page for three you don't want to miss!

# CHAMELEON MOON *by RoAnna Sylver*

The city of Parole is burning. Like Venice slips into the sea, Parole crumbles into fire. The entire population inside has been quarantined, cut off from the rest of the world, and left to die—directly over the open flame. Eye in the Sky, a deadly and merciless police force ensures no one escapes. Ever. All that's keeping Parole alive is faith in the midst of horrors and death, trust in the face of desperation... and their fantastic, terrifying, and beautiful superhuman abilities.

Regan, silent, scaly stealth expert, is haunted by ten years of anxiety, trauma and terror, and he's finally reached his limit. His ability to disappear into thin air isn't enough: he needs an escape, and he'll do anything for a chance. Unluckily for him, Hans, a ghostly boy with a chilling smile, knows just the thing to get one. It starts with a little murder.

But instead of ending a man's life, Regan starts a new one of his own. He turns away from that twisted path, and runs into Evelyn, fearless force on stage and sonic-superheroic revolutionary on the streets. Now Regan has a choice—and a chance to not only escape from Parole, but unravel the mystery deep in its burning heart. And most of all, discover the truth about their own entwining pasts.

Separately they'd never survive, much less uncover the secret of Parole's eternally-burning fire. Together, they have a chance. Parole's a rough place to live. But they're not dead yet. If they can survive the imminent disaster, then everything will be okay.

# FOURTH WORLD *by Lyssa Chiavari*

IAMOS, S.C.D. 8378 – Nadin's planet is dying. As its atmosphere drains away, her people are forced to live huddled in domed cities for protection. With only enough resources to support the population for one more year, time is running out. Nadin thinks she's found a way to save Iamos, but it will mean defying the planet's rulers, the *geroi*—and betraying the *geroi* could cost her everything.

When a strange boy from another world appears out of nowhere outside the citidome's glass walls, Nadin knows for sure that her plan will work. But to build the device that can save her people, Nadin must first find the legendary city of Elytherios. And to do that, she'll need the help of the mysterious alien boy named Isaak.

MARS, 2073 C.E. - All Isaak wanted was to get through his senior year at the Academy in one piece. Everything would have been fine if he hadn't found that ancient coin among his missing father's possessions. The coin seems to have a strange connection not only to Isaak's family, but to Mars' ancient past. But how is that possible, on a planet that was supposed to be dead until just forty years ago?

Now Isaak's got agents of the Earth's government on his tail and a deranged factory worker stalking his every move. Everyone is desperate to get their hands on something called the Key. And the only way to escape is to unlock an even bigger secret, one that could change his life—and the fate of Mars—forever.

# DAYBREAK RISING *by Kiran Oliver*

Celosia Brennan was supposed to be a hero. After a spectacular failure that cost her people their freedom, she is offered a once-in-a-lifetime chance at redemption. Together with a gifted team of rebels, she not only sets her sights on freedom, but defeating her personal demons along the way.

Now branded a failure, Celosia desperately volunteers for the next mission: taking down the corrupt Council with a team of her fellow elementally gifted mages. Leading the Ember Operative gives Celosia her last hope at redemption. They seek to overthrow the Council once and for all, this time bringing the fight to Valeria, the largest city under the Council's iron grip. But Celosia's new teammates don't trust her—except for Ianthe, a powerful Ice Elementalist who happens to believe in second chances.

With Council spies, uncontrolled magic, and the distraction of unexpected love, Celosia will have to win the trust of her teammates and push her abilities to the breaking point to complete the Ember Operative. Except if she falters this time, there won't be any Elementalists left to stop the Council from taking over not just the country, but their entire world.